The Home Grown

Elite Hockey Book Four

Alys J. Clarke

THE HOME GROWN

Copyright © 2025 by Alys J. Clarke

Cover Art by Tom Drake
Additional Art by Caroline Taylor
Editing by Anthony G. Muller MBE
Proofreading by Open Eye Editing

Paperback ISBN: 978-1-7384632-5-1
Independently Published First Edition: August 2025

Dedication

To my sister Laura, for being nothing like Kathryn.

Trigger & Content Warning

False accusations / online slander
Abortion: brief mention
Emotional manipulation
Grief / death of a sibling: brief mention
Family tension / toxic sibling dynamics
Adult Content
Alcohol use
Brief mention of blood
Cheating (not main characters)

Definitions

Home Grown:

The definition of a "homegrown" player is a player, who, irrespective of their nationality or age, has been registered with either:

1. Their current club (who is a member of the EIHL); and/or

2. A club and/or any other Ice Hockey club affiliated with Ice Hockey UK ("IHUK"), English Ice Hockey Association ("EIHA") or Scottish Ice Hockey ("SIH") for a period, continuous or non-continuous, of two seasons or 24 months prior to his 18th birthday (or the end of the season during which they turn 18).

Import:

A non-homegrown player is usually classified as an import. A team is allowed a maximum number of imports as decided by the league.

The roster spots for imports to consume are known as 'import slots'.

(stylised as 'Home Grown')

Tape Job (or, T.J.):

Act of applying tape to a hockey stick to:
a) Protect the stick from wear and tear
b) Change the way the stick feels

Alternate Captain:

Each team must appoint a captain and not more than three alternate captains from among the skaters listed on the game line up. When the captain is off the ice or unavailable for the game, any alternate captain on the ice is responsible for fulfilling the captain's official role as liaison to the referees.

Chapter 1

Ellie

He still hasn't texted me.

I check my phone for the sixth time in twenty minutes, convinced I felt it vibrate, but surprise, surprise—it didn't. There's nothing. Not even a notification for the weather to fall back on.

I stare at the screen, briefly wondering if I can manifest him into texting. I mean, he said he would so he will, right? It's only been, what, twelve hours?

I unlock the screen just to double check I haven't missed anything, when Kathryn clears her throat.

"You'll go insane if you keep checking it," she says.

She watches me for a moment before dipping her head, continuing to rummage through the open cardboard box on the bed—the contents of our parents' loft, the remnants of our childhoods reduced to old bits of paper.

I lock the screen of my phone and throw it, face down, onto the bed with an air of contempt. No pocket. No phantom vibrations. Problem solved.

"No news is good news, yeah?" she says. "They still had three slots left last time I checked. Just because you haven't heard anything yet doesn't mean you won't."

I shoot her a puzzled look.

"Wait—what? Who?"

Kathryn sighs. "The magazine."

Ah, so we're not talking about the same thing. That clears things up. Kathryn thinks I'm checking my emails about the bridal stylist magazine feature I applied for three weeks ago, but honestly, I've pushed it to the back of my mind since I've already resigned myself to failure. And since I'm embarrassed about the real reason for checking my phone, I don't correct her. I nod instead, keeping my eyes on the box I'm working through.

Only a second passes before I feel her watching me again.

"What's going on?"

"Nothing," I say.

But she doesn't buy it. I can feel her gaze burning into me like she's trying to read my mind.

"Right. Are you going to tell me what's wrong? Because you've been in a grump all day—more so than usual," she says.

I keep my focus on the box, paying an unnecessary amount of attention to a bundle of old receipts.

"Ellie?" Kathryn prompts, her voice sharp.

And that's all it takes. The authority in her voice, causing me to snap like a split end.

I pause, clutching at the receipts for moral support as I raise my head to meet her eyes.

"Okay," I say, taking a deep breath. "I'm not waiting to hear from the magazine."

She raises an eyebrow, folding her arms over her chest as she waits for me to continue.

"I met a guy last night. I don't want to go into it, but he said he'd text, and he hasn't," I say.

And there it is.

A smile.

A smile that creeps across her face in such a way, my stomach tightens.

Here we go.

"Which guy?" she asks.

"It doesn't matter. I probably won't hear from him," I say, layering in the self-doubt before I can stop myself.

I can't help it. I don't remember the last time someone asked for my number. And someone who looked as good as he did? Probably never. This sort of thing doesn't happen to me.

"Come on," Kathryn says. "You can tell me." She pauses, then widens her eyes. "I guess it was one of Greg's friends, I suppose ... and I reckon it's someone he doesn't see all that often, because you've met most of his friends before."

Kathryn did all the invites for her and Greg's engagement party; she'll know every single guy who was there last night.

She tilts her head as if a visual parade of Greg's friends rolls through her mind. She's probably trying to deduce who, if any, would ask me out. But, aside from him, there's no one else I would have given my number to.

Crap.

"Forget it," I say.

"Why are you so reluctant to tell me?" she asks.

"I just—" I cut my words off, not wanting to admit that I'm scared of her judgement. Her ridicule. Because I've heard it before...

But Kathryn narrows her eyes in a lightbulb moment. "Is it someone you've met before and were interested in but haven't told me?"

I exhale.

"We're not doing this," I say. "Quit it."

I reach for a pillow from the head of the bed and fling it toward her, but she bats it away.

"El—"

"Shush," I say. "No more questions."

Kathryn purses her lips.

"Fine. But I'll ask Greg later," Kathryn says. "See if anyone's said anything to him."

I turn away from the bedroom, grabbing one of the boxes stacked on the landing labelled 'Eleanor', before returning to the spare room and setting it down on the bed.

I'm half-expecting Kathryn to launch back into the fifty questions, but she's busy again, her nose buried in the book she's validating and I've never been so relieved.

"Will I need my year nine maths homework?" she asks, flicking through a workbook before tossing it back into the box.

"Why did you keep any of that stuff?"

She shrugs and tosses the book toward the recycling pile. "I honestly have no idea. I probably thought I'd need to reflect on linear equations while I fix someone's broken nail."

"If you've got no immediate or future need for it—bin," I say.

Kathryn grimaces. "Savage."

"All I'm saying is there's a good reason all this stuff has been untouched in the loft for years. Don't you think we'd have noticed by now if there was something we needed ... or something we'd misplaced?"

"True," she says, pulling out odd bits of paper from the bottom of her box. She flicks through the pages before scrunching her nose. "Ugh. Year Ten science."

She tosses it toward the recycling too, before dipping out to grab another box from her stack.

I can't help myself. Once I'm sure she's gone, I reach for my phone, checking the screen on the off-chance he's texted.

Still nothing.

And it's frustrating as hell. This is why I hate the dating scene. It's full of hope and wonder and desperation and—

I throw my phone like it's burnt me when Kathryn slips back into the room, but, lucky for me, I don't think she notices. She's busy wrestling with an overfilled 'Bag for Life', repurposed as document storage.

"Mam said this is a bag of random bits," she says, dumping it on the bed. "Looks like old phone bills and stuff."

She roots through the bag as I gather another pile of papers from my box and discard them.

"Yep. Old bills and ... oh, this is yours."

She hands me a red plastic document wallet and I peek at the top sheet of paper—a travel insurance plan from a trip I took to Germany when I was eighteen.

What started off as a girls' holiday somewhere hot and sandy ended up with us booking a trip to northern Germany, all because my friend Jessica was sort-of seeing a guy who was spending his summer at a youth hockey camp or something.

It feels like a lifetime ago. A version of myself I can barely remember.

"Anything exciting?" Kathryn asks.

"Uh, no—just junk."

Kathryn resumes her rummaging, and I flick through the contents of the wallet.

Aside from the travel insurance documents, the wallet is full of odd bits of paper—tourism leaflets, hotel bar receipts. Nothing worth keeping. I'm close to chucking it all in the bin when something half-folded catches my eye, crammed between two other sheets.

I pull it free and peel open the paper, skimming over the text—trying to figure out what it is.

It looks familiar but also doesn't ... all at the same time.

Despite its age, the paper is crisp and clean; the ink legible, albeit slightly faded. I take a second to process what I'm looking at—and another second to realise why it looks so familiar.

Then it hits me. My breath catches in my throat, involuntary and loud enough for Kathryn to hear.

"What?" she says.

I blink several times, my eyes scanning the document.

"El?"

My stomach tightens.

"I—nothing," I say, stuffing the paper away.

Kathryn glances up. "Is everything okay?"

My heart thuds, panic moving through my veins.

"It's, uh—" I swallow. "It's an old parking ticket I didn't pay," I lie. "I'm going to Google it, see if there's anything I need to worry about."

"Greg can help with any legal stuff," she says.

"Yeah, maybe," I say, my voice a shaky mess, because I'm sure this is not something I want to run past Kathryn's fiancé.

I grab my phone along with the document wallet and disappear into the bathroom, clicking the door shut behind me before sliding the lock into place. Then I check the door, pulling the handle to make sure I'm safely locked in. Alone. Uninterruptible.

I root through the pages again, scrambling for the paper almost clumsily.

Deep breath.

Deep breath.

My fingers brush the document, and a pang of nausea washes over me. I count to three, gearing myself up, trying to push away the knot of dread sitting heavy in my stomach.

Then I unfold it. Returning my attention to the text again—properly reading it this time.

Except I can't.

Because it's in Danish.

Danish.

It's written in Danish.

The whole thing is in Danish ... well, everything bar—

I piece it together, my eyes roaming over the words as they dance across the paper—unreadable and cryptic. Maybe if I—

But there's a knock on the bathroom door, jump-starting me and I scramble to shove it away. To hide the evidence.

"El?" Kathryn says through the door. "Greg's back with the takeaway."

I glance back down at the paper, nestled between two tourist leaflets, then back to the door.

"Uh, I'm not hungry," I say.

There's a pause before Kathryn speaks again.

"Are you sure?" she says.

"Yes," I squeak. "My stomach—I feel a bit … queasy. It's probably the wine from last night."

"You didn't drink that much," she says.

I force a laugh. "Yeah, but … you know me. I can't handle my wine."

There's a silence before Kathryn replies. "Okay, if you say so."

Her steps retreat on the landing, and I sink down onto the edge of the bath, clutching the document wallet with a shaky hand.

Bettsy

I KNOW THERE'S SOMETHING going on as soon as I pick my phone up.

Messages. Missed calls. Notifications.

At first, I figure it's about my best mate screwing around with my sister—big news, sure. But not this big. Not this kind of mess.

"Rochelle," I say, clenching my jaw. "Fucking—"

She's typically all bark and no bite. Except, while I skim over a forum post several people have sent me, I'm lost for words. I can't believe what I'm reading. I actually can't. To double-check, I close the browser and click on the link that was forwarded to me again, antsy as I wait for the page to load.

Yep. There it is. Plain as day.

This has got to be a wind-up, right?

I pace the floor of the dressing room, my face getting hotter as I read it again.

This is far worse than I could have imagined.

The door swings open, and there's a flurry of movement from the tunnel as the rest of the guys filter in—post game sweat dripping from their brows. Danny, one of the second line wingers, slips through, but instead of heading for his cubby, he changes direction and stops in front of me.

"You okay, mate?" he says, pulling off his helmet.

I don't answer him straight away, opting to skim through the post one more time instead, letting myself get angrier by the second. Because this is not cool. This is so not cool, and I don't know what the hell to do to fix it.

I'm supposed to be riding on the high of not only advancing to the Challenge Cup finals, but also getting a shot at Team GB.

Instead, I'm seeing shit posted online by my ex. Pure slander.

And I'm livid.

"Here," I say, holding my phone out to Danny, "read this."

He's gloveless already but wipes his palms against his jersey before taking it.

I sit down at my cubby and begin to remove my gear at speed.

My instinct is to drive over to Rochelle's place, demand answers, maybe throw a few choice words in her direction too … but deep down, I know that would do more damage than good.

"When did she post this?" Danny asks, running his finger along the screen as he scrolls. "Because—"

I wave him off, already in defensive mode.

"I didn't. You know I didn't, right?"

Danny passes my phone back, then walks across the dressing room to start his own de-kitting routine.

"I know you didn't mate," he says, sitting. "But I hope it doesn't cause any dramas for you with the roster."

Shit.

Fuck.

And another shit.

Danny's another Team GB hopeful, getting named on the preliminary roster like me. But preliminary is the key word here. We're still only potentials. It's not over until we've done training camp and the coaching staff make their picks.

What if this blast on the fan forum is enough to make the general manager of the national team change his mind about me? Because I know I'm not the only eligible defenceman in the league.

"Fuck. Honestly, if this … I'll kill her." I tug my jersey over my head, rolling it into a ball and throwing it so hard at the laundry bin, it wobbles on impact.

"Who are you killing?" Johnny says, striding in from the open door. He stops at his cubby, the one directly next to mine and slumps down in his seat.

"Look at this," I say, reaching for my phone and shoving it into Johnny's still-gloved hand.

He tucks his left glove under his arm and switches hands, eyes locked on the screen as he reads.

I watch him carefully—though I'm shit at reading his expression. Always have been. He's one of these 'heart-on-my-sleeve-in-a-locked-wardrobe' guys.

Johnny frowns, scoffs, then makes a choking sound that has me edging closer to him.

"You're kidding, right?" he says finally. "When was this posted?"

"I wish I was. It went up last night and one of the boys I played with in juniors sent me the link … along with about five others. People are fucking commenting on it too, Cap. What the hell do I do?"

The thing about British Hockey is, it's a tiny world. And all us Brits know each other. Either from junior hockey or playing on the same team at some point or from a party. And when Greer, from my junior team, sent me the link … and I'm not so naive to think he only forwarded it to me. It's likely sitting on every single group chat of every single team in the league by now.

Johnny glares at me. For a second, I expect him to say something about me calling him 'Cap' since technically, he's not our captain at the moment—even if everyone's still treating him like he is—but he doesn't. He just frowns and hands me back my phone.

"I'll speak with Vicky. See if she can get it taken down."

I worry my lip, trying not to throw up.

Vicky, Johnny's sister, occasionally helps with public relations alongside her social media and photography gig. If anyone can help, it's her—not to mention she's got a fiery personality that I wouldn't want to be on the wrong side of.

But not even Vicky can undo the damage this has already done.

The internet never forgets, does it?

"Nah, if you take it down—people might think there's truth in it," Danny says, causing my stomach to fall out of my ass.

He reaches for his phone and frowns at the screen before tossing it back onto his shelf.

Case in point.

"What the hell do I do?" I'm frantic. Actually raging. Because there's no truth in it, but people don't think like that—they assume the worst. They leap to conclusions. And I'm hardly the type of person who thinks before he acts. I'm spontaneous. Reckless. And now it's biting me in the ass—hard.

And we all know that people love to gossip.

"I'll speak with Vicky," Johnny says. "And probably Kirsty from HR to see how we can approach this."

Great. PR and HR. Which only means a fucking mess. And this is all my fault.

"But you know it's not true, right, Cap?" I plead with Johnny.

He nods and pats me on the back. "Of course, bud. Try not to worry about it."

There's a flash of something in his eyes, but I can't place it. Does he believe me? Because I couldn't handle Johnny thinking of me as a liar—he's the only one with any sense in this place. Probably why I wasn't all that pissed off to learn he's seeing my sister.

He's the one guy I fully trust.

I sit down in my cubby and spiral into a rabbit hole of self-pity.

How did I get myself in this mess? How did I—

Then it comes to me.

Sex. It all comes down to sex.

All of this is a result of my desperation for sex.

But there's no way I'm letting this happen again. Not if I can help it.

"That's it. I'm never having sex again," I announce to the room. "It only leads to a world of pain."

That's when the laughing starts. I look around, and despite everyone being half-dressed, I win the attention of the room.

"You're joking, right?" Hutch, my roommate, says.

"No. I am not. My dick is staying firmly in my pants for the foreseeable—except for when I need to take a piss. Actually, I'm not even wanking anymore. Because you never know—"

"Stop. We'll fix it," Johnny says, a voice of reassurance.

But I mean it. I'm off sex. What's the point anyway?

"C'mon, mate. Try to forget about it for now," Danny says. "We're supposed to be celebrating tonight."

"I guess if the end is nigh, I may as well go out with a bang … but without an actual bang."

Danny rolls his eyes. "You're being ridiculous."

"Am I? Because I disagree."

"Danny's right," Johnny says. "You are being dramatic. Vicky will figure out a way to fix this. Until then—" He looks around the room at the guys, "No one is to talk about this. It's gossip. And I don't stand for gossip in my dressing room." The good thing is, no one argues with Johnny. "We're all going out for drinks to celebrate, not one, but two of our guys making the prelim roster. That's the focus this evening."

There's a roar of cheers and I'm forced to join in.

But despite the smile I have plastered all over my face, I don't feel even slightly happy. I feel powerless and angry beyond anything I've felt before. But I do what I always do to lighten the mood—crack on and pretend like everything is okay.

Nevertheless, I have a feeling things are about to get a lot worse.

Chapter 2

Ellie

KATHRYN FLOPS DOWN NEXT to me on the bed of our parents' spare room.

"Are you still waiting for your mystery man to text?"

It's been forty-eight hours since my sister's engagement party and Mark still hasn't texted me.

Usually, I'd be obsessing over every word we said, picking it apart. But right now, all I can think about is the red document wallet on the bedside table shouting for attention.

"I'm trying to catch up on admin," I say.

It's not a lie. I am trying. I even have the spreadsheet open—though I've been on the same cell for the past half-hour.

Kathryn props a pillow behind her back.

"I'm so grateful for you, El. If you need any extra help, I'll ask Greg."

I roll my eyes.

My sister owns a beauty salon and even though my official job title is 'beautician and stylist', my services extend to the role of 'lead skivvy' which involves a ridiculous amount of admin.

She waits until I've busied myself by moving to a new worksheet before talking again.

"So ... this guy," she says.

"What about him? He hasn't texted me. I'm not bothered and—"

"I think I know who it is," she says, cutting me off. "I mean, if I guess right, you'll tell me, yeah?"

I scowl at her.

"Is it Mark?"

My cheeks could out heat a curling wand, but even with my eyes on cell B43, I can feel my sister's smugness radiating.

"I didn't think you'd go for him," she says, tilting her head to the side as she gazes upward. She looks back at me, pursing her lips before saying, "don't you think he's a bit out of your league?"

I divert my attention to flash her a glare of contempt. "He asked for my number. Not the other way around."

"I'm only saying," she says. "You set your heights too high. You set yourself up for failure."

"Can we let it go?" I snap.

The embarrassment sets in because—thinking about it now—he probably is out of my league. But at the time I didn't think so. I thought he was interested as much as I was.

More fool me, I guess.

"I'm only saying, you—" she snaps her mouth shut, running a long nail across her jaw. "Do you remember that boy who lived next door? Not the one who died, his younger brother. That was a similar thing. I don't know why you let yourself get so—"

"Thanks, Kathryn. Thanks for the reminder," I say.

She can be so crude. But I know exactly *who* and *what* she's referring to, and so does my nervous system. I peek a glance towards the red document wallet, unable to stop myself.

"What was his name again?" she says, acting like she doesn't remember. There's a pensive look on her face while she pretends to think. Then another moment passes before she blurts it out, "that's right—Michael Betts. Didn't everyone call him Bettsy or something?" She scoffs in a mock-laugh. "Ridiculous, if you ask me."

I clench my jaw, putting my attention back on my laptop.

"Let me check something for a moment. Gimme." She whips the computer from my lap, my hands still suspended mid-air like I'm about to type.

"Hey—"

"Just a moment," she says.

I'm relieved to see she at least minimises the spreadsheet before pulling up a web-browser, tapping her inch-long nails against the keyboard as she enters 'Michael Betts' into the search engine.

"See? Total escape from catastrophe."

My stomach does an involuntary lurch as his picture fills the screen.

There he is. The same Michael Betts who did indeed live next door.

Except—he's different. Older, obviously, and he's bulked out, grown into himself and—I bite my lip, trying to force the queasy feeling away as Kathryn drops the laptop back onto my thighs.

I know I should close the page, but I don't.

My eyes fix on the screen and I skim the text, reading his basic information and hockey stats. It's all stuff I don't understand, but I read it anyway.

"Wait—Rick plays hockey?" I say, frowning at the screen. "Looks like he and Mike played junior hockey together and..." I keep reading. "They're both listed on the preliminary roster for the Men's Team GB Ice Hockey team—apparently, they're holding trials or something. Wow."

"Huh," Kathryn says, flashing a look at the screen before becoming overly invested in her cuticles. "I guess so."

Rick, or Patrick, is Greg's best man, and according to Kathryn, they are far too 'bromancy' for her liking. She's been trying to get Greg to change his mind for months, but he's refusing—much to Kathryn's dismay.

"Anyway, are you wanting to eat here before you head home?" she says, climbing off the bed.

"Yeah, thanks," I say, keeping my eyes fixed on the screen as my sister slips out of the room, pushing the door closed behind her.

This should definitely be my cue to return to my admin, but I can't stop myself. Curiosity gets the better of me and I fall down a rabbit hole of nosiness, digging deeper into the hockey history of Mike Betts.

In fact, I only drag my eyes away from the screen when my phone vibrates on the duvet next to me.

A contact I don't have saved.

My heart flutters and I extend my hand to reach for it when something catches my eye: a thumbnail photo of Mike Betts, tagged in another article.

A queasiness fills my stomach when the page loads.

The article mentions a fan forum, and a new post pertaining to the social life of Mike Betts outside of hockey.

I know I should probably leave things alone, but I click through to the forum, scanning the page before navigating to the post.

"I just wanted 2 come on here 2 let people know that Michael Betts (who wears no. 6!!!) is a complete and utter dickhead. Not only did he get me pregnant, he lied to me about his intentions and made me leave my previous bf for him. And... (this is the rly bad part) he forced me 2 get rid. Literally dragged me to the hospital. He also paid me 2 do it so he wouldn't have 2 tell anyone he's a complete asshole. But MIKE. If ur reading this ... I hate you. And you weren't even that good in bed. And your dick is tiny. I don't even know how you got me pregnant in the first place.

But women all over ... STAY AWAY!!! I wouldn't be surprised if he's got an STI or something."

I'm stunned into silence, and it's only a little bit to do with the way it's written.

When Kathryn sticks her head around the door to ask me another question a moment later, all she gets is a view of my face, frozen in shock.

"Are you okay?"

"Come and read this," I say, angling the laptop towards her as she approaches the bed.

I wait for her to read the post, the laptop screen reflecting off her glasses as her eyes move in quick formation left and right. She frowns, then widens her eyes, then scoffs loudly before scrunching up her nose.

"Do you think any of this is true?" I say, shifting the screen back towards me.

"Well, he sounds busy, that's for sure ... but this is what I'm getting at. Rick's the same, which is why I don't want him getting involved with Greg ... or, I guess, having Greg involved with him."

"I'm not sure I believe it. I mean..." I skim over the words again, trying to work out if the post is someone's poor attempt at humour. "I'm sorry, but who trusts someone named *'IlovetoPuck29'*?"

"Yeah, but look at the replies," Kathryn says, tapping the screen with a glossy nail.

PrestonsBiggestFan19:

I knew he would be the type.

Johnny4Life923:

Typical of him. The club should fire him, or worse, trade him!!

"People believe anything they read online," I say.

"Well, I guess but anyway, it's nothing to do with us. Pasta or rice?"

"I don't mind," I say, willing myself to close the lid of my laptop.

But I don't. I can't.

Bettsy

BY MY FIFTH BEER, I have decided the whole 'no-sex' rule needs breaking. It didn't last long, but I can't help it—bars and women? I'm programmed to flirt. Flirt and be flirted with—or at least I hope for the latter.

"I think I was being harsh on myself," I tell Danny. "I think I may ... I don't know, see who catches my eye tonight."

He takes a sip from his beer, a grin forming on his lips. "I wondered how long it'd take you."

"Yeah, well..."

"Has this got anything to do with this forum stuff? Because I don't think you need to worry about it. The GM hasn't called you in yet. That's got to be a good sign."

I tighten my jaw. "That's a problem, mate. It's only a matter of time."

"Really? I guess I thought he'd want to see you pretty much straight away," Danny says. "And since he didn't..."

"It's coming. Trust me."

I take a sip of my own beer as I peer around the bar for a distraction.

It's one of Johnny's favourite places because it doesn't get loud or overly busy. That, combined with it being a Sunday—a rare weekend evening off—means it's pretty chilled in here, but there's still several potentials scattered around the room.

My attention falls to the right side of the bar, and I nudge Danny's arm.

"What about her?" I point towards a tall brunette making her way through the sea of tables towards us.

"Nah, she's too pretty for you," Danny says, taking another swig of beer.

While I should take offense, he's right. I'm a five at best with my teeth in and, on a good day, I can bag a seven—all thanks to my winning personality.

"What about her then?" This time, my attention is on a cute blonde with six-inch heels.

Danny does his best 'casual glance' before facing me, shaking his head.

"Nah, again … too pretty. I think you need to invest in some glasses, Betts." He surveys the bar, taking his time to sip at his drink. "She's decent." He gestures to another blonde about twelve feet away. "Still too pretty for you, but you could consider it a challenge."

Short hair—maybe a little too short for my liking, and a face full of makeup that looks slightly over-the-top. Rochelle-type style...

"Nah, I think I need to switch it up. Because we both know what happened the last time I thought with my dick."

Danny raises his eyebrows as he takes another swig. "If you say so."

But we observe the steady flow of guys trickling past the table she's sharing with some friends. I'm keeping tabs of who she dances with, how many guys seem interested in her … which fuels my competitive side—and the challenge Danny mentioned? Even if I don't take her home, I can still talk to her, right?

"Let's say hi," I tell Danny. "Wingman?"

He grins, draining the rest of his beer, and I do the same—standard practice as it gives us the opportunity to ask the girls if they want a drink.

I flash her a grin, grateful that I put my teeth in, and she gets the message that I'm seeking her out by smiling back.

I stop next to the table—which is about the same time I realise she's got really pretty eyes. Not so much like Rochelle, after all.

She looks to my right at Danny, checking him out maybe, I can't tell, but since I'm funnier than he is, I stand a good chance.

"D-Eight?" I say, leaning down to talk into her ear.

The music is louder here, and I bend funny to get into the right position to speak with her since I'm easily half a foot taller than she is.

She sips her drink, sucking gently through the straw resting in a half-full tumbler of a something-and-coke before swallowing—it's as if she's trying to draw attention to her mouth.

"Is this the vending machine chat up line?" she says, raising an eyebrow.

"Nah," I say. "I was referring to a chess board—I'm trying to make a move on my queen." I cringe inside but break out a smile.

"That's terrible," she says.

"Give me a chance ... I'm just getting started," I say, trying to keep my confidence up.

"Go on then, give me your worst." She sets her glass down before leaning back against the table, folding her arms over her chest.

I will my eyes to take even the smallest of glances downward to her boobs. Her dress is cut low and even though I'm definitely an ass-man, I typically can't say no to tits either.

But the way she tightens her expression makes me forget how pretty her eyes are, and instead, forces me to think about Rochelle.

Rochelle and the absolute hell she put me through.

I know she's waiting for me to say something, but my voice has frozen inside my throat.

Is this woman likely to do the same as Rochelle in several months' time after she's exhausted my generosity? Because that's all I am. A good-time guy who's dumb enough to be taken for a ride. Again and again.

But I'm realising my tank has run out of fuel.

"Are you okay, mate?" Danny nudges me, speaking into my ear.

"I think I need another drink," I say, and instead of asking blondie if she wants one too, I turn on my heel and head back to the bar on my own where I order a fresh beer.

Danny joins me a moment later.

"What happened? I thought she was into it," he says, nudging me.

What am I supposed to say to that? I let my ex get in my head? Nah—I can't be admitting that to Danny.

"I'm thinking I want more of a challenge," I say, trying to inject some confidence into my voice. "Maybe I'll save my energy for camp ... you know, I hear they have an 'ice team'—those cheerleaders who scrape the ice."

Danny scoffs. "Not a bad idea, actually."

The bartender taps me on the shoulder, placing my beer down on the bar and I take my wallet out to pay, as there's a chorus of cheers from the corner of the bar, loud enough to get the attention of everyone in a five-mile radius.

The rest of the team are crammed into that corner of the bar, one booth and several extra tables pulled up to accommodate the numbers—and I can see from a glance that Johnny and my sister are missing, but I decide I don't want to know where they've gone.

"Shit—what's going on there?" Danny says. "Let's find out."

"I'll be over in a sec," I say.

He disappears into a small crowd of people.

I take the alone time as an opportunity to throw back some shots, letting the liquor burn the back of my throat as it slides down, then I get my phone out of my pocket, wondering if I should call Rochelle and tell her what a piece of shit she is, but before I can make any rash decisions, Danny's hand slaps me on the back.

"You'll never guess what?" he says.

I shove my phone away in time to see Liam and Ryan Preston sliding into the space between Danny and me.

"Don't tell him," Danny says, flashing a look at the guys. "You'll break his heart, Lee."

"Vicky and I got engaged, that's all. We weren't making a big deal of it but—" Liam says.

"What do you mean you weren't making a big deal of it? This is great news," I say, forcing a smile.

I'm happy for them. I am. But I'm also jealous—not because I'll have to stop the harmless flirting with Vicky, but because I don't think I'll ever find what Liam has with her.

"Shots?" I say, since I've already got the flavour.

I signal to the bartender before anyone can protest.

"Shouldn't you be laying off a bit—with camp coming up?" Liam asks, though he's the first one reaching for the tray of shot glasses when they're deposited in front of us.

"Yeah, but a few shots won't hurt," I say.

And it's true.

Shots don't hurt at all. Heartache on the other hand...

Chapter 3

Ellie

SEVEN DAYS. THAT'S HOW long I avoided it.

If I ignore something long enough, it'll go away, right?

Wrong. Because the red document wallet from last week is still there on Sunday afternoon. Still there. Still begging for attention.

And I know, deep down, I can't leave it any longer.

I reach for my laptop and stare at the lid for longer than necessary before I pry it open, trying to think of any reason not to do this. But I can't. This is the only way.

I wait for the login screen, tapping my fingers against the table, then I pull up a fresh browser, tapping his name into the search engine with shaky hands.

My search returns almost instantly. His hockey profile. A bunch of news articles. That forum post ... then I find what I'm looking for.

His social media.

Page after page of 'Michael Betts' but there's only one that's actually his and I spot him straight away. A profile picture of him wearing a pair of novelty sunglasses. His grin shining through the screen and a pang of nausea ripples through me.

Oh, God. There's no way this is a good idea—this is a complete nightmare.

But before I can talk myself out of it, I slide right into the DMs of Mike Betts.

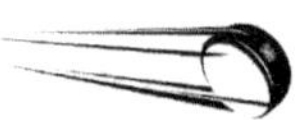

He still hasn't read it by the next morning.

After the worst night of sleep I've ever had, there's no way I can go on like this—half-guessing, overthinking, waiting.

I need answers, and I need him to check his inbox.

By ten o'clock, I've done a full set of nails and a spray tan, and when I check again ... there's still no reply. My message just sits there, unread.

I tell myself if there's nothing by eleven o'clock, then I've got no choice but to seek expert help from Greg, Kathryn's fiancé.

Another full set of nails later, I'm nipping into the stockroom under the guise of checking the quantity of waxing strips.

Once I'm sure that Kathryn is busy with a client, I pull out my phone and scroll to our sparse message thread—odd comments about Kathryn, a birthday gift for Dad.

Which is probably why he texts back straight away when I ask him if I can come and see him at lunch.

Greg

Everything okay?

A danish. Ironic and painfully so.

I slip my phone away and check the wax strip stock, in case Kathryn asks, then head back into the salon and bide my time. Watching the clock. Waiting...

As soon as Kathryn's back from her break, I duck out onto the street and head straight for the bakery.

Two coffees and one pastry later, I check that the pavement is clear and slip into Greg's legal firm two doors down.

"Come in and take a seat," he says, pointing towards a plush tub chair in the middle of his office.

"Why can't I tell Kathryn about the danish?" I say, handing him the paper bag before sinking down into the chair.

"Probably the same reason I can't tell her about your visit." He peers inside, his tongue poking out a little as he reaches for the pastry. "She's got me on a diet. For the wedding, you know."

"Right. But she's not watching you at lunch, is she?"

"No, but she'd know if I bought one. At least I can say a client got me one and I couldn't say no—I take it you're not here to talk about your duty as the maid of honour? Has Rick texted you yet? He asked for your number and—"

"Yeah, he did. I think he's trying to work out a few plans ... but—" I clear my throat.

Greg takes a bite and leans all the way back, like he's lounging on a deckchair.

"So ... I appreciate you sparing me some time. I know you're busy and with—"

"What's going on, Ellie? Is this about the parking ticket?" He comically pops his seat up so he's facing me, a rogue flake of pastry dangling off his beard. I stare at it for a moment before answering.

"There wasn't a parking ticket ... which is why you can't tell Kathryn."

He shrugs, eyeing the danish. "We've already established that this is a confidential meeting."

"You've got a little something ... anyway. Let me ..." I slide my handbag off my shoulder and open the clasp, all while Greg watches me, his brows furrowing together as he waits. The red plastic document wallet makes an appearance, and I undo the popper with a shaky hand before reaching inside.

"Just wanted to get your take on this."

I hand the offending scrap of paper to him, trying my hardest to keep my hand steady. He sets the rest of his pastry down on the paper bag, wiping his fingers on the leg of his trousers before taking it from me.

"Wha—" His eyes flick between me and the paper for a moment before studying the document.

"It's in German," he says.

"It's in Danish," I correct.

He turns it over in his hands before settling on the upper side, musing over it for several seconds before pulling his phone from the top drawer of his desk.

I watch in nervous anticipation as Greg follows the same process I did last week, almost step by step. He taps something into his phone and waits for the results to return, his face changing in expression several times before he settles on a sombre, professional bearing before meeting my eyes.

Then he flicks them back down to the paper.

Then back to meet my eyes again.

"Uh—" He shifts in his seat. "El, you know I'm a conveyancer, right?"

"Well, yeah, but law is law, right?"

"Well, yeah, but no. This isn't my bag."

"But you know someone who can help?" My tone rises a few levels as desperation sets in.

"Sure but—" He runs his hands through his hair and reaches for his coffee, taking a gulp before loosening his tie. "Where did you get this?"

"It turned up in the bags of old papers. I wouldn't have thought anything of it, but then I saw a video while doomscrolling and ... look."

I pull my phone out of my bag and work my way through the process of pulling up the video I'm referring to before handing it to Greg; waiting for the longest time as he watches.

He frowns several times before clearing his throat.

"Are you sure this is legit?" he asks.

"Honestly, no ... which is why I'm here, but I don't have the best luck with this sort of thing."

He studies the paper again, rubbing his beard.

"I'll need to make a few calls. Are you okay leaving this with me?" He holds up the paper and I nod.

"How long do you think you'll need?"

"I'm not sure, but I'll try not to drag it out."

I nod again, shoving the folder back in my bag and getting to my feet.

"Thanks, Greg."

I'm halfway to the door when his voice stops me in my tracks. "El?"

"Yeah?"

"If I were you, I'd find this Michael Betts fella."

My stomach drops. "I was afraid you'd say that."

"Well, yeah, but ... do you know where he's living now?"

"Not really," I say.

"I suggest you ask around," he says.

I dip my head. "Right."

"And remember—Mum's the word." He taps the side of his nose as I exit.

MY AGE IS CATCHING up with me because two-day hangovers are now a thing, apparently. I've got the mother of all headaches—and to make things worse, Johnny has summoned both Danny and I to his apartment to make a plan.

I'm stretched out on his sofa, shoes off and the hood of my team jumper pulled up over my head to shield my eyes from the light.

The only good thing about this is Johnny being far too wrapped up in his notebook to care that I've got my feet up on the sofa. Shoes or no shoes, he lets none of us do this—not even when you're hanging out of your ass like I am.

"Now this is where the hard work begins," Johnny says. There's a fumbling before I hear his laptop being thudded down on the coffee table. "Getting selected is the straightforward part. We need to figure out who you guys are up against."

"What's there to plan?" I ask. "Surely we turn up to camp and show them what we've got." I prop myself up on my elbows to peer at Danny, sitting opposite me in the single armchair.

He nods, reassuring me that it's not a crazy idea.

From what Coach Adams, our league coach said, we've got a week to prove ourselves—to keep in the running to be named on the official roster. And considering Team GB is already quite an established team, there's only two or three slots available.

"Absolutely not," Johnny says. "If I was up for Team Canada … I'd already know who my competition was—and I wouldn't be hungover." He glowers at me, judging me for another post-game drinking session.

He picks up his notebook and flicks through the pages, stopping on a fresh sheet near the back, opposite a list he's already compiled.

I peer out from under my hood at his scribbles, blinking several times to make sure my eyes are working correctly.

"Please tell me that's not Patrick Langdon's name at the top?" I groan.

Rick Langdon is a complete ass-hat and I hold him personally responsible for losing around three grand of earnings last summer.

I had plans to work with Danny at his old-man's construction site to save up some cash for a rainy day, but Langer had other plans for me.

Due to his inability to perform a clean hit, I was on concussion protocol. My parents forced me to stay at their place for the off-season while my mother engaged in 'cotton-wool deployment'—as my sister put it; ever since we lost my older brother, no injury or mild-headache goes untreated when Judith Betts is concerned.

"Yep—he's had a similar output to you this season, so I think it's only fair to assume he'll be at camp too."

"Fuck's sake." I let out an exasperated breath before grabbing one of Johnny's sofa cushions and shoving it over my head. I may as well end it all now. Because it'd be a damn sight more enjoyable than being up against Langer.

Another cushion comes flying at me from Danny's direction, and I abandon the attempt on my life.

"One defence spot, by the look of it," Johnny says. "And two wingers."

"How did you figure that out?" Danny asks.

"Well, we know who retired last year, and we know where they were on the roster," Johnny says. "And Buttons has an injury. There's a spot right there. Honestly, you guys don't pay any attention."

I pause, half debating grabbing the cushion again, because that will mean that Langer will literally be the one to beat. Johnny's right—I'm unprepared and I don't know if I stand a chance.

What if I got selected to make up the numbers because the pool of British defenceman available is slim pickings?

Johnny reels off names of wingers and Danny looks like he's thinking along the same lines as me.

"Got any of the good coffee, Cap?" Danny says. "I think we could all do with a cup."

"In the cupboard—right, Betts ... defencemen ... Patrick Langdon and Sean Knowles. That's my guess."

I consider this for a moment. Knowlsey's a good guy but I think my presence is more effective in the PK ... but Langer—he's a piece of work and the more I think about him, the more my head hurts.

"Please, can you bring some paracetamol with the coffee, Dan? And a banana."

"On it," he calls back from the kitchen.

"Betts—you know this needs to stop, right?" Johnny says. "I'm starting to sound like a record stuck on repeat, but the partying and late nights need to be done with."

"I agree—but we were celebrating. Again."

Johnny sighs.

But in all seriousness, the news of being up against Langer is forcing me to re-consider my actions. Starting tomorrow ... no booze and no junk food, along with my vow of no sex.

A banana comes flying at me a second before Danny places a mug down on the coffee table, alongside a blister pack of pain killers.

I force myself into a sitting position and pop two tablets into my mouth, swigging them down with a bottle of water I had on the floor next to me. Then I get started with the banana.

Instant relief.

I'm about to reach for my coffee when my phone buzzes in my pocket.

Hutch's name is flashing up on the screen and since he's a texter, not a talker, I answer it straight away.

"There's some girl buzzing on the intercom for you," he says. "And before you ask—it's not Rochelle."

"Who is it then?" I ask.

"Not sure."

Hutch and I share an apartment on the fifth floor; with Johnny being on the eighth floor, it means I can be home in a matter of seconds. However, since I'm not expecting anyone, and I'm busy, whoever it is can wait.

"Tell her I'm unavailable," I say.

Hutch hangs up, and I tune back into Johnny.

He's got a spreadsheet open now, adding stats and various bits of information he deems necessary, but since he's got it in hand, I make myself comfortable so I can drink my coffee.

He's explaining the importance of 'off-ice' performance when his intercom buzzes. All of us swivel our heads towards the phone on the wall and, a few moments later, he rises to his feet to saunter over to the receiver.

"Hello?" he says.

And the voice on the other side of the line is faintly audible from where Danny and I are sitting.

"I'm looking for Mike Betts—Bettsy. I'm looking for Bettsy," says the voice. And the first thing I notice is that she's got the same accent as me. Do I know her?

I peer over to Johnny who's eyeing me with question—and I shake my head. Despite being curious who it could be, I leap to the possibility of it being an ex from back home who I definitely don't want to see.

Johnny mouths something I can't understand, then hits the button on the intercom to talk back. "Umm, he's just stepped out, but who shall I say is asking?"

Okay, I can live with that. But what I don't expect is the reply we get from the voice on the other side of the intercom.

"Can you tell him it's Ellie—Ellie Kitchener," she says, pausing before adding, "Kitch."

The sound of her nickname sends a rush of excitement flow through my body, right before the anxiety kicks in.

Chapter 4

Ellie

Twenty Minutes Before

I can't believe it's come to this. It's threatening to rain, and I'm standing outside what I think might be Mike's apartment building, wearing a coat that's more fashionable than functional.

All I've got to go on is a dodgy forum post from some anonymous fan who thinks sharing the local hockey team's address is a public service. Not cool—but then again, neither is being ghosted after eight years and left with more questions than answers.

I should go home, forget the red folder, forget Mike Betts ever existed. But here I am.

As I look over the intercom system, I realise I don't have a plan. I should probably write this whole thing off and go home.

Except, I can't.

I'm rooted to the spot, wondering what I'm going to say to him.

What if he doesn't remember me? What if he—

I bite my lip, wondering why I didn't think this through properly, when the sound of an engine revs behind me.

I swivel my head and spot a car covered in decals, progressing up the street. It slows to almost a stop before turning towards the entrance to a car park, stopping at the barrier briefly to swipe something before driving in.

I recognise those decals.

My heart beats a little faster at the idea this may not be a wasted journey after all. All I need to do is wait for the driver to park up and hopefully ... hopefully, he'll make his way around to the front of the building where I'm standing, and I can ask him if he knows Mike.

Simple.

But of course, it's at this moment the rain starts. Cold February rain—and it's not even a gradual spitting, it's a full-on downpour that catches me out.

I dump my bag on to the floor under the canopy sheltering the entrance of the apartment block so I can rummage inside for my umbrella, pulling several items out before my fingers brush the handle at the very bottom of my bag.

I don't realise the lobby door has opened until it slams shut again.

Crap.

My umbrella opens in a wrangled mess of aluminium as Mike's teammate disappears behind the door marked 'stairwell'.

I toss it into a nearby bin and pull the hood of my coat up, sticking as close as I can to the wall of the building.

The lobby is empty as I gaze through the window trying to come up with a plan 'B'. But since it looks like the only way in is to use a door access fob, or likely, someone buzzing you in via the intercom, I'm faced with two options: wait until someone comes or leaves and ask them, or press every single button on the calling system. Here's hoping someone will give me some information, or—best-case scenario—I buzz Mike's apartment on the first try.

I wait it out, but after ten minutes of no one either leaving or returning home, I'm forced to push aside my pride and start ringing some apartments, because the longer I stand here, the more damp and uncomfortable I become.

There's a metal panel on the left-hand side of the main door, two rows of buttons, each with a number etched above. I study the panel, wishing for another idea to float into my head but nothing comes.

Nothing.

I brace myself for the awkward conversation before pressing the button for '101'.

Several seconds pass as it rings out, and likewise, 102. I move on to 201 and someone does eventually answer, but they hang up almost instantly when I mention Mike's name, which doesn't give me a good feeling.

I'm wondering if this really is the right building or if that teammate of his was simply visiting a friend, but apartment 301 gives me the reassurance I need.

"He may or may not live in this building," the voice says. "Who's asking?"

"Ellie," I say.

"Are you sure?" the voice says back.

"Yes..."

There's a beat of silence before the voice carries on, a sceptical tone coming through the speaker.

"Right. So, this definitely isn't Rochelle? Or Leah? Or..."

God—my sister was right. He is the type.

"No ... my name is Ellie. I'm—" I can't bring myself to say I'm an old friend. Friend is too strong a word. "—and I'm wondering if you know how I can get a hold of him?"

"Has he blocked your number? Because that's a telltale sign he ain't interested," the voice says.

"No, no—it's a long story. I've not seen him in a long time."

"Probably a good reason for that—look, I've got to go."

The intercom cuts, and I exhale in frustration.

My first instinct is to call them back, trying to explain myself but my embarrassment forces me to move on, so I press the call button for the next apartment, gearing myself up for more difficult conversation.

Someone picks up after only a couple of rings out.

"Hello?"

"Hi, I'm looking for—I'm looking for Mike."

"Who?"

"Michael Betts. Do you—"

"Ah, yeah, Bettsy. Fifth floor."

There's a click as Mr 302 hangs up, and I celebrate the tiny win of not needing to call anyone on the fourth floor but allowing myself a second to breathe.

I try 501. It rings and rings, eventually cutting off, so I move on. 502 sounds like it's going to be the same, until a second before I'm about to give up, the line turns fuzzy as someone answers.

"Yeah?"

The voice is curt, like I'm keeping someone from doing something important, so instead of dragging out an introduction, I dive straight in.

"I'm looking for Bettsy," I say.

"He's not around—wait ... is this Rochelle?"

I blow out a breath. "No. But do you know where I can find him? It's urgent."

The guy sounds exasperated. "Give me a minute."

The intercom cuts off and I stare at the little speaker in desperation. Should I call him back? Can he pick up the internal handset and connect to me? I'm rolling it over in my mind when the line crackles to my relief.

"You still there?" the voice says.

"Yeah—honestly, I don't even want to see him. If you could pass a message on for me—maybe give him my number and tell him to text me or something."

The guy sighs. "Right ... but look, I'm sort of busy and—"

"Please, can you pass on my number?"

He clears his throat. "If you tried an apartment on the eighth floor, you may find that he's there—though I didn't tell you that."

He hangs up, and despite my frustration, I don't waste anymore time. I hit the button for apartment 801 and wait.

There're approximately three rings before someone picks up. "Hello?"

"I'm looking for Mike Betts—Bettsy. I'm looking for Bettsy," I say, almost robotically.

There's a pause before the guy responds. "Umm, he's just stepped out, but who shall I say is calling?"

I freeze, like a rabbit caught in headlights, completely dumfounded that I found him. It takes my brain a second to catch up, realising that the guy on the other side of the intercom is waiting for me to reply.

"Uh ... can you tell him it's Ellie—Ellie Kitchener," I say, then I add, "Kitch," because he made that a thing, for some reason. Maybe it'll prompt a memory, or something.

I'm about to ask the guy on the line if he can take my number to pass on when he speaks again.

"He said he'll be right down."

Ah, crap.

My pulse thuds in my ears because I haven't seen Mike in around eight years, and I have no idea what to expect. Will I recognise him? Will he recognise me?

I take a deep breath, telling myself that all I need to do is hand him Greg's business card and get the heck out of here. But there's a noise from inside that has me almost shaking with anticipation ...

I think he's coming.

The door to the stairwell opens, and a figure fills the doorway. He's wearing a tracksuit, like one of those team issue ones, with the hood of his top pulled up over his head. And a sickly feeling of loathing fills my stomach.

His amber eyes meet mine and there's a tinge of a smile on his lips.

And he's got the audacity to have aged well.

As if.

He presses a button on the inside of the lobby and there's a mechanical clunk as the door unlatches; and a moment later, I come face to face with Michael Betts.

Bettsy

I BLINK SEVERAL TIMES to check my eyes aren't playing tricks on me.

Ellie Kitchener.

Yep. It's definitely her and fuck me, she looks good.

Big brown eyes and pouty lips ... not to mention she's filled out with a fantastic rack and curves that have me wanting to sneak a peek at her ass, just to see—but I don't. I maintain some level of decorum.

"I—" She clamps her mouth shut.

"Hey, you," I say.

I can't stop myself from grinning, but when she doesn't beam back, my smile drops.

I get the feeling she's pissed at me. Her shiny lips are in a straight line and she pulls her eyebrows together, like she's trying to hold in some anger.

"Is everything okay? What are you doing here? Not that I'm not pleased to see you or anything but—"

"Here." She swallows hard before holding out a business card. "I've been in touch with a solicitor, and he said I should contact you. To figure things out."

I frown and take the card from her, my brow pulling tight. "Figure what out?"

I glance down at the text.

Greg Jamison. Conveyancer.

"I'm sure if you wanted me to consider him for my future house purchases, you could have called me."

She scoffs. "Ignore the conveyancer bit—besides, I don't have your number, and you apparently don't check your messages. I've lost a full day of earnings coming to find you."

"You say that like you've been trying to track me down or something."

"I have. I had no choice but to trawl the internet. By the way, your address is online. You may want to fix that."

"What the—" I dip my hand into my pocket to pull out my phone but I can feel her glaring at me, so I decide that's a problem for later.

I have no idea what's going on. I haven't seen this girl in, what, seven or eight years and she turns up out of the blue and hands me a card for a solicitor—one who specialises in property—and has a pop at me for loss of earnings.

It makes zero sense.

"I'm really fucking confused," I say.

"I thought you'd say that." She folds her arms over her chest and looks down at the pavement.

"Well, maybe if you told me why you want to—"

"That wedding experience?" she says. "Ring any bells?"

Wedding experience?

I let my mind wander back to the last time I saw Ellie.

Ellie and some friends of hers came to visit when me and my old hockey buddy Sam were in Germany on a training camp.

Everyone sort of paired off and Ellie and I were left alone.

I remember taking a ferry over to a Danish Island—'Ærø' or something like that. We'd only planned to go to the beach, but we ended up making a day of it. What started out as a guided tour led to a few drinks ... and—

It clicks.

That wedding experience.

"I—"

"I think it was real," she says.

"What?"

"I think it was real, Mike. I think ... we're actually married. And the only logical conclusion I can come up with is that you must have known. Don't tell me you didn't because—"

I actually feel my jaw drop.

She's flushed red, her arms drop to her sides as she clenches her fists, like she's gearing up to punch me.

I hold my hands up in surrender.

"I honestly don't know what you're talking about."

"That bit of paper they gave us ... oh, I bet you found it hilarious. A 'right laugh'." She does the air quotes. "I've had that document for eight years, Mike. Eight years. Thought nothing of it. But what did I see online a few weeks ago? Someone showing the world that exact same piece of paper which they too, thought was part of an experience..."

I can't stop myself. I burst into laughter, because the thought alone sounds completely ridiculous. But the redder Ellie gets, the more I'm inclined to conclude that she's taking this very fucking seriously indeed.

I give a nervous chuckle.

"No way, that was a pretend thing. People do shit like that all the time. Me and a mate got fake 'Vegas' married in a nightclub once ... it's not real." I laugh again, but Ellie's face stays sombre.

I try to elaborate.

"Just like our 'experience' wasn't real. We queued up and played along with getting married. There were like ... " I think for a moment, "... two other couples doing the same thing."

"Two other couples who are also married without knowing about it," she says. "I've been googling it."

My heart picks up speed. And without hesitating, I pull my phone from my pocket and start typing in search terms.

Weddings Ærø

Can you accidentally get married?

How do you know if a wedding certificate is real?

I skim read as quick as I can before jabbering.

"Nah, it's impossible. It says here that you need to apply to the Danish Agency of something or other ... and we'd have had to pay them." I flash my phone screen at Ellie. "See—it says they take up to five days to approve things, and we didn't give them

ID or whatever. I don't think you can get married without ID. Or banns being read or something like that."

I skip back to the search results page before spotting a video posted to a social media site.

Ellie says something, but I'm not listening. I'm focused on this damn video. The woman talking is basically describing the same experience we had. Word for word. The same date and everything.

I chuckle again.

"Nah, stuff like this doesn't happen in real life. It's like ... something out of a film or whatever. She probably put the video up for views. Click bait, you know."

But when I catch her expression, a pang of something hits me in the chest.

Fuck.

"You knew all along, didn't you?" she says. "Did you submit a request or something? Did you—"

"No. How could I? I don't even—"

"Then why the hell did you ghost me the very next day? You disappeared, and you weren't anywhere to be seen—right up until I had to fly home. You knew, and you were probably laughing at my expense."

"I had camp. I was in an intensive training schedule with the kids. I texted you when I got home, and you never texted me back."

I can't even fathom this. Because I definitely did not know, and why would I do such a thing? Why would I lure someone into marriage?

Yeah, I was massively into this girl, but there's an enormous difference between wanting to sleep with someone and forcing them to marry you without their knowledge.

But Ellie's reeling.

"Then you were going out with Julie Goldsworthy. You got back from Germany, and you were hooking up with her..." she says.

Julie Goldsworthy? I don't even remember a Julie Goldsworthy.

"Honestly, I wish I never—" She stops. Instead of finishing her sentence, she sniffs loudly and wipes her hand over her eyes as she steps backwards.

Shit. Is she crying?

"I thought you ghosted me," I say, but she's not listening anymore.

"Contact Greg. He's expecting you to reach out," she says before backing away.

And for the first time in my entire life, I'm genuinely lost for words.

Chapter 5

"DID YOUR FRIEND FIND you?" Hutch asks.

He pops up from the sofa when I enter our apartment. He's in exactly the same place he was when I left him this morning, sprawled out, and sinking into a box set marathon. Today is a non-practice day, which means Hutch has morphed into lazy mode, apart from a run he likely has planned for later this evening, because he's weird like that.

I head straight for the dining table, grabbing my laptop before striding into the kitchen, where I set it down on the breakfast bar.

"I need a drink," I say. "Do you need a drink?"

Hutch stares at me, then watches on as I grab a whisky glass from the kitchen cupboard before rooting for a bottle of whatever I can find. I have a feeling there's a rogue half of a bottle of something at the back of the cupboard from Christmas.

"Shit, what's going on?" he says.

I find a bottle of whisky, dust off the cap and the liquor hits the glass and then my throat in less than five seconds. I slam the tumbler down on the worktop then I flip open the lid of my computer—pouring myself another drink while I wait for it to boot up.

"What's going on?" Hutch says again, getting to his feet. "Did something happen?" He walks over to the counter and leans against it, trying to make eye contact with me.

I do everything in my power to avoid him, taking a seat at the breakfast bar and focusing on my laptop instead.

"Shit—she didn't tell you that you've fathered a child, did she?" Hutch says.

I huff in disbelief. "For fuck's sake. Why does everyone think I'm going around getting people pregnant? No."

"What then? Who was she? Because you've never headed straight for the bottle before ... except when—shit. It was Rochelle faking an accent, wasn't it? Oh, mate. I'm sorry."

"No, no. It wasn't Rochelle," I say, genuinely relieved it wasn't.

Whatever shit Ellie brought to my door is nothing compared to the crap from Rochelle in the past.

Hutch continues to watch me as I log onto to my computer, and as I pull up a browser, his glare intensifies.

I let my fingers hover over the keyboard, but I type nothing. I don't even know where to begin. This morning, I was going about my business, worrying about the next couple of weeks with Team GB and now, I'm sitting here wondering if I'm married or not.

Fucking married. I mean ... I'm not sure I actually believe it.

Maybe this is all one big joke to add to the shit storm I'm already in. Things happen that way, don't they? Everything in threes. Which means there's something else about to rear its ugly head.

I look at Hutch, still gaping at me, I quickly decide this is not something I want to get into right now. Not until I know it's legit—and even then, I'll have to consider if I want anyone finding out.

I can hear the guys now… *'Bettsy the fuck up'… 'Bettsy's done something crazy again'… 'Typical, Bettsy'.*

Hutch dips his head. "You don't look good, mate. In fact, you look—"

I force my best fake smile as I cut him off. "Nah. Everything's fine."

"Who was the girl then?"

"Just an old friend. She was just passing and wanted to say hi."

"So why the…" He looks at the clock on the oven, "… early drink?"

I'm already primed with a reply. "Hair of the Dog. Keen to get rid of the hangover and this fucking headache. Hey … speaking of headaches, guess who Johnny has marked for the other defensive slot?"

I mentally pat myself on the back for diverting the conversation.

"Go on…" Hutch says.

"Langer." I fix my eyes on the screen of the laptop and dance over the keyboard with my fingers, typing his name in.

Hutch winces. "Patrick Langdon? I guess that answers my next question…" He flicks a glance towards my laptop. "So, I guess you need to make sure you're in a good place for prelims?"

"Yeah … he reckons Sean Knowles is in too, but let's face it…"

Hutch scoffs, breaking my flow, before launching into a speech about keeping your enemies close, and I'm grateful for the distraction actually.

Before I left Johnny's apartment earlier, Cap was adamant that I spend some time reviewing footage of Langer with an aim to understand his weaknesses, and now with Hutch watching me, I'm forced to do just that. I guess if Johnny asks, Hutch can vouch for me.

I pull up a clip from his most recent game and hit play, forcing myself to stare at the screen, hoping I can distract myself completely with the playback.

Focus on Langer, Betts. Focus.

"God, I didn't realise how much of a goon he is," Hutch says, peering at my screen.

Focus, Bettsy.

I observe the way he plays the puck, how he always plays further forward than his pairing, his blue-line presence on the forecheck, and how he …

"I think we're married, Mike. And you knew about it…"

I study the way he works the corner—not overly a strong point for him, that's for sure, and how he looks slow to pivot…

"I've had that document for eight years, Mike. Eight years…"

"—and that's all you can do." Hutch taps the screen, and I shake my head, trying to push Ellie's voice away.

"Huh?"

"Have you been listening to anything I've been saying?" he says.

"I, uh … I think I need to take a lay down," I say, snapping my laptop shut.

Hutch stares at me before nodding. "Look, mate. I know it's stressful, but you'll be great—you know you're better than him, right?"

"I—thanks. It's just a bit … I don't know. I feel a bit stressed and overwhelmed, I guess. Maybe I need to take some time to myself, you know, clear my head a bit."

"That sounds like a great idea. You get your head down and I can help you prep when you're feeling up to it," he says.

I stand up and grab my laptop, tucking it under my arm before retreating to the safety of my bedroom. And if Hutch's got any sense, he'll assume I'm going for a tug and not bother me for a while.

After I settle myself down on my bed and pull up my social media accounts, quickly checking my message requests.

I skim through all the crap before finding Ellie on the list—at least I assume it's her because despite her name being her name, the profile picture isn't the one I remember from the last time I went snooping.

Instead of a photo of a silhouetted figure on the beach, it's a logo for some sort of beauty salon back in my hometown.

I click on the profile and have a peek, taking my time to dig through her life—what's available to the public eye, anyway.

I definitely didn't get the correct profile last time. Not only are there photos of Ellie in the depths of a shared album that I would have noticed if I'd looked at the correct profile. The other one said she was engaged—this one says 'single', and I scoff at the irony.

Navigating back to my cluttered inbox, I click into her message and tap the 'accept' button.

Ellie

> Hey, Mike. I know this is random, but please, could you text me? It's urgent.

She's dropped her number underneath, and I stare at it for a moment, wondering if I should call her, try to reason with her. But instead, I save it in my contacts and open a fresh browser.

Married.

The word floats in my head—almost in big neon lights, highlighted by my monumental cock-up.

I'm restless and I can't figure out where to start, so I launch into procrastination mode, pulling up some porn to distract myself, only to close it a second later.

I'm not in the mood. I'm not in the mood for anything. I feel like I'm stuck in a state of limbo where the path forward is muddy and uncertain.

No matter how hard I try, my conversation with Ellie creeps back in, determined to not let me forget.

"Then why the hell did you ghost me?"

But I didn't. My phone didn't work properly while I was out in Germany, and when I got back, I texted her several times.

I texted her. I know I did. And if I remember rightly, I called her too, only to be told to 'never call this number again'.

It was that phone call which put me off knocking on her door, and since we didn't have school together anymore ...

I sigh. Tossing my laptop aside and lay back on my bed, running over the conversation again.

JUST WHEN I THOUGHT things couldn't get any worse, I load up Friday morning's calendar on the salon computer to find a change in my schedule.

"This can't be right," I say to Kathryn, who's busy opening the blinds.

"What can't be?" she says.

"My appointments look ... different," I say. "My nine-thirty was supposed to be—" The salon door creaks open and in walks none other than Judith Betts. "—Mrs Smith."

Mike's mother stands in front of me at the counter, beaming at me with a perfect set of teeth. Her hair, an auburn poker straight bob, shines in the light from the window.

"Oh, yeah, I had to move some things around. Something came up. Judy's after a full set of gels which you're more than capable of," Kathryn says, moving towards the counter to stand next to me.

I feel sick.

A heavy knot of anxiety sits heavy in my stomach because, not only has Kathryn arranged for me to treat Mike's mother, she's also cancelled one of my regulars.

I wish I could say this is the first time, but Kathryn has pulled this trick before with no consideration for me.

"Right," I say, trying to keep my smile from waning.

All I can think about is that she knows, and that's why she's here.

She knows, and she's come to confront me—ask why I lured her son into such a fate ... but when she talks, she sounds positively happy to be here.

That's not the reaction of someone who knows.

At least, I don't think it is, anyway.

"Oh, my goodness. I didn't realise this was your salon, girls," she beams.

Damn. I forgot how nice she is. And now I'm definitely of the opinion she doesn't know. Even though I feel a flicker of warmth toward Mike's mother, bitterness toward him knots in my chest—and his face clings to my thoughts like a balloon snagged on a branch, refusing to drift away.

"Yeah, well, it's mine, but Ellie helps me out," Kathryn says.

"Well, that's lovely. How are your mam and dad? I bet they're thrilled you're doing so well here."

Kathryn reels off a reply while I stand here, completely flabbergasted that this is even happening. Why, out of all the salons she could have picked, did Mrs Betts choose to come here?

I catch a peek at her nails—they look good. Like she keeps on top of her nail care. Which means she's probably been going to another salon or something ... okay, so maybe she knows after all. She knows, and he's sent her here to talk to me.

"Ellie?" Kathryn says, nudging me in the ribs. "Are you okay to take Judy's coat?"

I blink, pulling myself back into the room.

"I—uh, yeah. Of course."

Mrs Betts smiles expectantly and I take several seconds to spring into customer service mode, taking her coat and hanging it on one of the pegs at the front of the salon.

I show her to the nail station and then offer to get her a drink, using it as an excuse to follow Kathryn into the back room, where she's just slipped out of sight.

"What the hell are you playing at?" I whisper shout, coming to a stop behind her while she rummages through her handbag.

"What?" she says, turning around.

"Why did you cancel Mrs Smith and replace the slot with a nail appointment?"

"I have plans. Judy booked in with me and I figured Mrs Smith can reschedule. She's one of your usual clients, El. You've already got her on board ... now Judy, on the other hand is a new client. It's an opportunity to gain a repeating appointment."

I gape at my sister. "You had no right."

"Uh, yes I do. This is my salon, so I'll do whatever I need to do. Now if you'll excuse me ... I need to get on with something."

Kathryn grabs her coat from the arm of the small sofa we have crammed in the backroom, slipping her arms into it before slinging her bag over her forearm.

She waltzes past me back into the main salon without a backwards glance.

I grab a glass of water and make my way back to Mrs Betts.

"Shall we get started?" I ask, forcing a smile.

"Is everything okay?" she counters.

"Yeah, all good. Sorry I took so long." I push down the unease. "Anyway—what are we after?" I take her hands and rest them on the towel.

"How long has it been since I saw you?" Mrs Betts says halfway through the appointment. I'm usually all over the chit-chat, but for reasons very much known to me, I'm pre-occupied with my thoughts instead.

"Oh, I was probably eighteen or nineteen, I guess?"

She nods. "Yes, I think it was shortly after that time Michael went to Germany. Just before Tony and I sold the house."

And there he is. Dropped into the conversation— and that memory of Germany, too. My two least favourite things biting me in the ass at work.

"Yeah, I think that's right." I grit my teeth, forcing myself to ask the next question purely out of politeness more than anything else. "How are the rest of the family?"

I try to keep it vague, not wanting to single out Mike, and I figure this will give Mrs Betts the go-ahead to launch into a ramble, leaving me to listen and get on with my job.

It's days like these I wish I never let Kathryn influence me. Thanks to her persuasion, I not only do hair, but I also do nails, spray tanning and waxing. Courses booked and paid for by me with the ultimatum of *'if you're not multi-skilled, you can't work in my salon'.*

"All good, thanks. Stacey's married now ... and Kelly's got a boyfriend ... and she's doing well with her music—and Michael..." My heart sort of lurches unexpectedly in my chest. "He's got a trial this week for the Team GB men's hockey team."

She swells with pride while I dig deep for enthusiasm.

"Please pass on my congratulations," I say.

I mull it over—all their lives turning out great and perfect and successful—as Mrs Betts keeps talking.

I nod and smile and pretend like I'm doing just as okay as they all are, right up until she asks me if I'm seeing anyone.

"Sorry, what?" I say, averting my eyes away from her hands to meet hers, amber and warm, just like—

"Are you seeing anyone? I saw an engagement ring on Kathryn's hand, so just wondered if—"

"Oh, yes. Yes, I am," I say, snapping my mouth shut as soon as I realise exactly what I've done.

It's a simple subject. I've answered this question hundreds of times before, but this situation has caught me in a lie.

"Oh, that's exciting."

"Well..." I say, putting my attention back on her nails.

"I've seen that look before," she says. "But I won't pry."

I offer her a shy smile. "Anyway ... do you have plans for the weekend?" I'm scraping the conversational barrel now. We both know it, but I'm at the point where I'm soon to be reaching for the cuticle oil ... I've almost made it.

Or so I think.

Judy's phone chirps in her bag and instead of ignoring it, she cranes her neck to glimpse inside before assembling a huge smile.

"Ellie, love. Can you just grab that? Would you mind?" She nods towards her open bag, her phone peeking out.

I glance at it, trying to decide if it's appropriate before hesitating. "I'm not sure I—"

"It's fine, love. It's right on top. Just grab it for me, will you?"

I feel conflicted, but since I can't think of a reasonable excuse not to, I face no choice but to reach for her phone.

I bite the inside of my cheek when I spot the caller ID. Bold and offensive, just like the caller: *Michael.*

Well, if this isn't already awkward enough, I set the handset down on the space to my left and without hesitating, Judy uses the pad of her index finger to swipe up, answering the call, before tapping the speakerphone button.

And as soon as his voice rings out, that sickly feeling of loathing washes over me.

"Mam—just a quick one," he says. "I'm just going through my schedule and—"

"You're on speakerphone, love," she interrupts, filling with pride as she lowers her voice to fill me in. "The Team GB hockey trial is being run from here. He'll be close to home for a short time, so I'll get to see him a bit more than usual."

"Who're you talking to, Mam?" Mike says.

And my heart, already sunk to the bottom of my stomach, descends lower.

"You remember, Ellie? From next door? I'm having my nails done at her salon."

Kathryn would revel in correcting her, but I don't. I sit in the awkward silence that stretches over the telephone line for a beat longer than anyone would expect. Perhaps he's thinking of a snide remark, or he's gearing himself up for a confrontation ... or does he think I told his Mam?

Mike's voice trickles through again, quiet and uneasy. "Uh, yeah. I remember. I thought Stacey's friend did your nails?"

"She moved away," Judy says.

There's a muffled scramble before he speaks again.

"Actually Mam, I've gotta go. Got something on that I need to ..."

I feel the blood drain from my face. I'm not sure what I was expecting, but that wasn't it.

"I'll pass your number on, shall I? Maybe you can catch up when you're back. Though—she is seeing someone..." Mrs Betts flashes me a smile.

Kill. Me. Now.

"Maybe, yeah. I've gotta go, Mam. Talk soon."

The line goes dead, and I reach for the cuticle oil with a shaky hand, fumbling to open the lid.

"I wish he'd meet someone decent, Ellie," she says sadly as I finish up. "He puts himself out there and gets his heart broken. I don't like to speak ill of anyone but the girl he was seeing last ... nasty piece of work. You know, he had to change his number. She was harassing him and putting all this stuff online ... anyway, I'm thrilled," she says, holding her hands out to admire her nails.

We make our way to the counter, and she grabs a business card after she pays, slipping it into the back of her purse.

"Oh, and I almost forgot..." she pulls out her phone and jots Mike's number down on the back of a scrap of paper before thrusting it into my hands. "Here. I'm sure he'll be pleased to hear from you."

Judy departs, leaving me with Mike's number. And because I'm still pissed at him, I scrunch it up and toss it into the wastepaper bin with enough force to make it wobble.

Chapter 6

Ellie

A PHONE CALL ROUSES me from the snooze I'd been enjoying since it's my late-start this Saturday. The plan is supposed to involve Kathryn and me alternating weekends, giving us both the chance of a lay-in. Though, I genuinely don't remember the last time she didn't coerce me into swapping, so my initial thought is that it's her, desperately waiting on the other end of the line for me to pick up ... guilting me into going in as soon as I can.

I yank the charging cable free from my phone before picking it up, but once my eyes fall into focus, and I read the incoming call on the screen, I realise it's not her.

No caller ID.

My stomach tightens with nerves as my mind begins to spiral, leaping to the conclusion that it's Mike on the end of the phone. But what could he want? Maybe he's spoken with Greg ... maybe—

I deliberate for too long; my thumb hovering over the Accept icon just as the call rings off, replaced by a 'missed call' notification, and a few moments later, by an alert of a new voicemail.

I swallow hard.

A voicemail.

Nothing good ever comes from a voicemail left by a withheld number. Everyone knows that. And since I've already convinced myself it's Mike, my insides—already pulling and tugging with nerves—kick up a few notches, forcing me to sit up in bed so I can hug my knees.

Five minutes crawl by. I watch the digits on the clock change, minute by minute, as I will myself to tap the play button—telling myself I have until the twenty-five-past marker. But it's not until the clock hits the half-hour mark, that I finally cave. I pull the covers over my shoulders as I tap to play the message, waiting for Mike's voice to fill my ear ... his deep, maddening velvet-smooth rumble.

Except ... the voice is nasal and bouncy—like someone trying to be polite when they really can't be bothered.

...I wanted to touch base about your application for our bridal stylist feature.

Listen, your work is solid, but to be honest, your social media just isn't where it needs to be for our audience. We're really looking for stylists who are already engaging online and have that buzz around their brand.

The words swim in my brain.

I'd suggest focusing on building a stronger online presence—show off more of your work, connect with your audience, that sort of thing. Maybe down the line we can revisit.

We appreciate you reaching out, and best of luck.

Disappointment hits me in the chest—almost knocking the air out of my lungs.

I wasn't mentally prepared for this. I wasn't ready.

A tight pressure contracts around my stomach, like I'm about to throw up ... but I don't. I drop my phone on the stretch of empty bed next to me and cry instead. Silent, hot tears trickle down my cheek as I hug my duvet.

The magazine. The rejection I sort of knew was coming but I wasn't ready to give up that tiny slither of hope I'd been clinging on to. I guess I should be relieved to finally know ... accepting that it wasn't meant to be, but the sting thrums through my bones, reminding me I'm not quite good enough.

Not yet, anyway.

I give myself another ten minutes of wallowing before prying myself out of bed and heading to the shower, turning the water on with an air of someone keen to wash away the pity, because that's not going to get me anywhere. What I need to do now is dust myself off and figure out how I can move forward—how I can be better.

Half an hour later, I make it out to my car and head towards the salon, taking a quick detour via the corner shop to grab a copy of their latest magazine, keen to find out who I'm up against.

I flick through the pages of glossy photos before stopping on a feature and honing in on the name of the stylist and her social media handle, pulling my phone out of my bag to have a look.

A photo gallery of visual bliss presents straight away. Uniform, organised, aesthetically pleasing to the eye.

Everything mine isn't.

I flush with embarrassment; grateful I'm in the refuge of my car. What was I thinking?

I don't have a website; I don't have reels or short videos showing clients what a day in my life looks like, or what sets me apart. And honestly? I don't think I have the energy for it. It looks exhausting—like something built for people with time, money, and confidence.

Money.

If only I still had my share of what Grandad left me.

But I don't. I loaned it to Kathryn to help her open the salon. Long gone now, no doubt.

And suddenly, the burst of desire for betterment fizzles out as I shove the magazine, and my ambition, into the glove box before pulling away, driving towards my sister's dream instead.

***

I don't tell Kathryn about the magazine. A tactical decision because I'm not in the mood for her false disappointment, nor her inability to show genuine empathy.

In fact, I try my best to avoid her chit-chat for most of the day, opting to keep myself busy around my appointment times by cleaning and sorting through old paperwork—though that probably wasn't my best idea considering the crap it dredged up last time.

I make it right through to closing without too much stress—unless you count Rick's message pestering me for hen-party updates ... but as I close the blinds, Greg walks in through the door, his typical move for a Saturday, collecting his beloved from work.

He closes the door behind him, guiding the latch into place silently as he looks around the salon.

"Where's Kathryn?" he asks, keeping his voice low.

"Just finishing something upstairs," I say, making my way back to the counter.

"In case you're wondering, I still haven't heard from him," he says in a half whisper, leaning his hip against the desk.

"Oh, I haven't thought about it," I lie.

"Well ... your husband ..." A smirk slips across his face, but he drops it when my expression remains stoney. "Sorry, I mean ... I spoke with my buddy, James, and he said the certificate isn't the full version, so we need to see if we can get hold of that before we can proceed."

I freeze midway through replying to an email, fingers halting mid-strike on the keyboard.

I adjust my head slightly to glare at Greg.

"You're kidding, right?" I say. "So, you're telling me it's definitely real, then?"

Greg straightens up.

"Well, it's still up for debate, but he's worked in family law for years. He's seen this sort of thing before. He said there's typically a formal document or something—in addition to what you've provided me. Do you remember there being anything else?"

"Like what? I thought I gave you the—" I lower my voice to less than a whisper, mouthing the words 'wedding certificate'.

"No, what you've got is a partial marriage registration—"

"Shh," I hiss, checking the threshold to the stairs. "So, until we get the full version, we don't really know? It could be a false alarm?" I ask.

"It could be," he says. "But we need to get James on board officially."

The word 'officially' has my stomach swimming. Because that means money ... money I don't really have.

"Right."

"Just let me know how you want to proceed," he says. "If this is legit, we can sort it without him—but financially, it'd be way easier if he cooperated. I'm not sure what kind of person he is but, he could rock up in the future and demand half of your house and whatever. I mean—the likelihood of it being a success would be low, but it's still a thing. And a stress you don't need."

I blink at him, unsure what to think, let alone say.

My head reels with the possibilities, and I mentally kick myself for letting myself get into such a ridiculous circumstance.

All I know is, I cannot be married to Mike Betts.

First, he's stolen my dream wedding—ripped away the perfect day I'd imagined since I was a kid. The fairytale. Fall in love, get engaged, have a story worth telling. All of it... ruined.

Second, he's a dick.

"Okay," I say, blinking back the tears.

I put all my concentration back on the email, keeping my eyes away from Greg.

Greg and his perfect proposal.

"Maybe he has a copy of the original certificate? Did you get his number? I could call him on your behalf."

I cast a look toward the wastepaper bin—now empty—before shaking my head.

Greg shrugs.

"Well, hopefully he'll reach out soon."

The staircase creaks—Kathryn's footsteps killing the conversation like a guillotine blade.

Bettsy

I'VE HATED NO ONE as much as I do right now.

Hate's a strong word, but right now it's running so deeply, my blood burns through my veins.

All I can see is Rick Langdon's ugly face out of the corner of my eye through the glass dividing the home and away benches. He's grimacing at me as if he's ready to rip my head off—which only adds to my fury because if anyone's doing any ripping, it's me.

"Do you think I could take him?" I ask Hutch.

I move closer to him so I can gesture towards Langer without making a big deal of it. But Hutch likely knew who I was talking about anyway, since all I've done for the past year is plot revenge on a dirty hit Langdon forced upon me last season.

It just so happens that I've been doing a tremendous job of maintaining a little self-control, but tonight, I'm feeling in the mood for a fight.

Hutch studies me for a second before leaning forward to get a better look at Langer. He flicks his eyes between us several times, sizing us both up before giving me his answer.

"Yeah, I think so," he says. "He's about the same size as you—or actually, maybe he's a little bigger. I can't tell with the pads ... so maybe not."

"Nah, you got it right the first time. We're about the same size, only difference is, I have better aim." My voice is full of confidence, but I'm pretty sure Hutch is right—Langdon is carrying more bulk than me.

Hutch shrugs, shifting his attention back to the game I should be watching too, but I'm busy stewing on the animosity I have for Langdon, the reason threefold.

Not only did he ruin my summer, but he also plays for my least favourite team in the league—my old junior team. But this is me being a sore loser, because when I reached my time to progress upward to pro, they didn't want to sign me because I wasn't good enough.

That shit stings like a motherfucker.

I haven't been able to say their team name ever since, nor bring myself to wear anything that resembles their team colours.

Finally, there's one spot for a defenceman on Team GB and both Langer and I want it.

"Fuck, did you see that?" Hutch says, jabbing me in the ribs. But I'm still fixed on the home bench, seething over the fact that Langdon has more teeth than I do, something I can probably rectify if I aim high enough. "Betts?"

"Sorry, I'm just—"

Wham.

The glass directly opposite shakes as Danny takes a second hit.

He skates away a second later with the puck, unphased.

"We need to pull back that goal," Hutch says, casting his eyes to the jumbotron.

He's right.

We're down a goal and we need these two points a win will give us.

Two points.

These two points will put us in a position above them and with only a handful of games left in the season, we need all we can get. They're last year's league winners too, which makes the hate burn just that much stronger.

The truth is, I've been simmering on a high heat ever since Ellie showed up at my place last week, and now I'm looking for any excuse to let off a little steam.

Not only have I spent all my free time desperately trying to piece together the events of that day, but I've been trawling the internet looking for anything relating to weddings in Denmark.

And I'm not sure if Ellie knows, but that video she showed me wasn't the only one. There're several. And I've watched every single one of them multiple times, even debating whether to reach out to the authors and ask more questions.

I didn't. I can't.

I guess I'm still living in denial of my own stupidity.

"I think I can take him," I say, quickly concluding that Langer's face would be an ideal target for my pent-up anger.

But Hutch isn't listening. He's busy watching our defensive zone, just as the home crowd roars as another goal sails in for them.

"You know what? Maybe we need the energy." Hutch tightens his jaw as he looks up at the scoreboard. "Just pick your moment."

I shift in my spot, leaning forward to focus on the game as the play resets. I need to forget about Ellie for now, because there's no way I'm going to keep my focus if I let myself wallow.

Johnny's shift is over, and I track his movement across the ice, keen for him to get back so I can take advantage of the minute we'll have to chat while our third defensive pair play a shift.

The door swings open, and he steps off the ice. Hutch disappears and I shuffle up so Johnny can sit himself on the very end of the bench, making it his turn to exchange glances with my favourite person.

"That wasn't my best effort," he says. "We need to connect our passes—this could go sour pretty quickly if we don't take control. But we need to think about the next goal. That's all."

Typical Johnny.

I study him for a moment before deciding now is the right moment to test the waters, so to speak.

"Do we need to up the energy?" I ask, letting my focus slip to Rick Langdon for a second.

Johnny notices straight away, angling himself so he blocks off my view of the opposing bench.

"Please don't get any ideas ... Kel—"

"I know, I know," I say, my jaw tightening.

My sister, Kelly, is here tonight—not for me, but for Johnny.

Since they're trying to make a proper go of things, she's been coming to games to show her support for his dreams or whatever, but the catch is, Kelly hates fighting, and Johnny knows it all too well. So, if she thinks he's encouraged me to get into a brawl, she'll give us both hell—which means I'll end up getting crap from them both.

I'm not sure I want the hassle.

"We need to focus on our next goal," Johnny says again. "Because it's—"

The sound of rubber hitting metal sails through the air, paired with a collective groan from the crowd as one of the twins sends a shot a little too high.

"Of all the teams we play against … you know I don't enjoy losing to these." My tone is sharp. Every single iota of rage I have for them shining through.

I lean forward to get another look at Langdon, but Johnny follows my movement and blocks my view. He frowns, reaches for a bottle and squirts a stream of water into his mouth.

"I know you're holding a grudge, but please just let it go," he says.

"He cost me my summer job," I snap. "And he's one of *them* … I'd say he owes me a few grand. But I'd settle for teeth in this instance … and maybe just a little blood."

Johnny stares at me indignantly. "For the love of …"

Luckily for me, the left D-man from our third pair rolls home and I take my cue, standing up and taking a seat on the shelf briefly.

"I mean it, Betts. Play safe, because fighting aside, you don't need any more penalty minutes. Think of your prospects and consider who you're up against."

He's referring to my opportunity to make the Team GB roster and the fact that training camp starts on Monday. Or at least I hope it does. I'm still waiting for the GM to 'have a word with me', which, according to Vicky, will be when he decides he wants to—something I knew was coming sooner rather than later.

Instead of throwing Johnny a flippant comment in return, I take in his words because I know he's right.

I hop onto the ice and break out into a burst of power towards my position on the blueline. I come to a halt, receiving a pass from one of the twins—I can't tell which—before sailing it across to my right pair, Yatesy, just as a shoulder nudges my own, pushing me right into the boards.

I know who it is without seeing his offensive jersey.

Fucking Langdon.

"What the hell do you want?" I murmur.

He grins at me for a second before skating away and because the play moves over to the opposite side of the ice, I follow his lead, hot on his trail as I mark him, poking at the toe of his stick as the puck shifts into his possession briefly.

It frees enough to give me an opportunity, sailing it over to the forward waiting in front of the net who fires it towards Greer, the opposing netminder, but he makes an easy save, causing the stripes to whistle up and reset the play.

Greer is decent. Another Brit who joined their roster last season after his stint on the national team upped his skill-set and made him a strong contender against the import goalies most teams go for—our team included. And Greer may be my soon-to-be teammate, but today, he's the enemy and I'm focusing in on his position so I can play the puck appropriately.

I skate towards my position behind the face-off when the ref calls Danny in for a quick chat.

That's when I spot Langer skating towards me. He makes out like he's going to sail right past, but he bumps my shoulder hard, almost shoving me over.

"Feeling nervous?" I taunt. "Because we both know we're teasing you by giving you a lead."

Langdon smirks.

"Nervous? You're kidding, right? You couldn't score on an empty net … and just because you have Jedward on your team … it means shit."

He's referring to the Preston twins—our ex-NHL contingent. Even they know hockey is a team sport, and they alone can't win us any silverware.

Langdon, though—I've got to give it to him—forces a genuine laugh from me, but I keep it back, determined not to let him have the last word.

"You're a liability. All talk and no action … how many shots have you blocked with your face this season, Langer? Wait … I don't think…"

There's a whistle from the ref in the distance, but I tune it out since Langdon is in my ear, chuckling softly—taunting me.

Jani, our first line centre, moves in to take the face-off.

I ignore the calls for me to get into position as I shove Langer hard with my shoulder, causing him to twist on the spot.

He pushes me so violently into the boards with the shaft of his stick, it snaps in half, causing the crowd to erupt into cheers.

"C'mon Betts, let's see who's better then? Or is this about the prelim roster? Because we both know there's only one defensive spot," he spits, making it really fucking hard for me to say no.

But there's nothing stopping me from drawing a penalty.

I have every confidence that I can force a bigger reaction from Langer by not reacting at all. I know how these types of guys work because I'm one of them.

It takes another ten seconds of me smirking back at him for him to throw a punch, right into my cheek. But the pain that shoots through my face is a small price to pay for Langer getting two minutes in the box for instigating.

And I'm so fucking proud of myself for not punching him back.

"I'll see you on Monday," I call as he's carted to the penalty box.

And given my upcoming chat with the GM, I hope to Christ I'm right.

Chapter 7

Bettsy

THE LAST THING I expect to see when I get out of the shower is a message from Vicky telling me the GM is making a special trip to see me.

Tonight.

In approximately fifteen minutes, to be exact.

And what's more unsettling? She's taken it upon herself to have a suit dropped off.

"A fucking suit," I whisper under my breath, watching whilst Johnny and the rest of the guys pull on their tracksuits for a comfy coach-ride home.

I fasten the buttons of my shirt and grab my tie.

Honestly, knowing he's made a special trip to see me has me in a cold sweat of panic, which isn't ideal considering my tie feels tight—almost suffocating. I keep it locked in place as I wait, figuring if he tells me I'm fired, I'll at least look half-decent.

I pace over a small area in the dressing room.

"You'll be fine," Johnny says, patting me on the shoulder. He keeps his voice low as he talks. "You played a good game tonight, kept a level head, and we won. He'll be in a good mood."

But when he doesn't make eye-contact, I can tell he's feeling as nervous as I am.

"What if this is it, Cap?" I ask, picking at the skin around the nails of my right hand. "Because one forum post is just gossip, but several—"

I've been trying not to think about the increase in posts, which became apparent on the coach ride earlier.

"Nah, it's not, bud. Trust me. There's absolutely no truth in any of them. They are all gossip, and the GM knows it. He's not dumb—he knows that some people have no problem bad-mouthing others. Trust me."

The door to the away dressing room creaks open and my heart lurches, but I exhale when I spot one of our equipment guys.

He grabs the last bag of gear before announcing that the coach is ready to board—but as instructed by Vicky, I hold back. I wait.

"Just relax," Johnny says. "Tell him the truth and he'll understand. You're not going to miss out because of her—I won't let it happen."

Johnny waits until the rest of the guys file out before turning to me and offering me his fist.

"You got this, right?"

My nerves turn my stomach into a twisted mess, and I swallow down a lump, trying to keep my head straight.

"Right," I say, bumping Johnny's fist with my own.

He nods once before leaving, and the eerie silence of the empty dressing room hits me at the same time as the magnitude of my situation does.

This could be it. This could be my career over.

The GM could saunter in now and tell me to clear out my cubby and leave my apartment key with Hutch. And what am I left with? An extended family that I won't see every day, a hole—right in the middle of my heart—where the team, where the guys, sit. And for what?

Rochelle.

I skim over our 'off-and-on' mess, trying to understand why she's doing this. She didn't love me. And she sure as hell didn't want me either. So, what is her motive?

I pull my phone out, intending to check back on the forum, but I only get as far as unlocking the screen when the dressing room door opens and Vicky strides in, her heels clicking against the floor.

A queasy feeling washes over me.

"The GM's finishing a call," she says, coming to a stop in front of me. "But listen Mike ... for the record, I don't believe a word of the stuff online. I've tried to have the last few posts taken down but—"

She stops.

"But what? The GM does?"

Vicky shakes her head. "That's not what I'm saying. I honestly don't know what his thoughts are. He hasn't said anything."

"So, how did you know I'd need a suit?" I ask.

"Okay, I knew it was going to be soon, and I had a feeling it would be tonight. I saw an entry in his diary for a meeting at a local hotel, so I took a punt. I didn't want you to know and stress about it, even more so if it wasn't going to happen. I asked Hutch to grab your favourite suit and—" She pauses, shaking her head. "Forget about that for now ... I won't lie and tell you I'm not a little worried."

I study her expression, trying to work out how worried we're talking about. Because I have a feeling that even though Vicky knows little of the GM's opinion on all this, she's likely spoken to someone from Team GB. Between she and Jen, they know people. And they talk. I have a strong feeling that someone there has noticed my reputation. Skill isn't the only thing they consider when giving someone a spot on the national team. The off-ice stuff matters too.

"I know what you're going to say," I mumble.

Vicky sighs. "I'm not trying to be a dick, but your reputation isn't doing you any huge favours at the moment. Look at Rick Langdon—I hear he has a girlfriend. And Sean's engaged. They're both settled with pretty much next to no public drama. I mean, if you were—"

"Don't," I say. "Don't say 'in a relationship'."

A pang of something ripples through me. Sadness? Desperation? Regret?

"It's about the image. Someone who's got his shit together. Someone who's going to show up, not be out partying looking to meet a different woman every night."

There's a creak from behind Vicky and both of us look towards the dressing room door as Mr Lopez, the GM strides in.

He shoves his phone into his pocket and casually makes his way across the room as if he's got all the time in the world.

I feel sick.

"I'll make this quick, Betts," Mr Lopez says, taking a seat on the bench and gesturing for me to do the same. "I read the first post, so I don't need any detail, but what I need to know is if there's any truth to it."

I swallow, wishing my bottle of water was in reach, not shoved into the pocket of my rucksack.

"Sir, I—no. Absolutely none. For the record—"

He holds a hand up and on cue, I stop talking.

"I can't pretend that this isn't an issue. I've had conversations with the leadership team over at the Team GB office. You know how it is. They want dependable players, on and off the ice. They need someone who's committed and not getting themselves involved with unnecessary drama. It causes a distraction from the game, and it causes distraction from your personal development."

"Sir, I—"

"I know it's bull, Betts. But Team GB—they still want you to attend camp next week, but they've told me that their expectation of you is higher than the other guys. So do with that what you will. And for the love of Christ, rein it in."

I try to muster a response when the GM's phone pipes up with a call that apparently can't wait.

"I'll leave this with you, Vicky ... but remember, Betts. Focus next week. I'm keen to see your name on that roster, so do what you need to do to make it happen."

He presses his phone to his ear as he edges towards the door, disappearing into the tunnels, leaving me alone with Vicky.

I want to let out an enormous sigh of relief, but I can't. It's as if my lungs don't work.

I will myself to relax, but the GM's words float through my mind: *focus ... rein it in... distractions... drama...*

What if Rochelle is only the beginning of the online slander? What if Ellie joins the party? Not that I think she's that type of person, but my mind is whirling.

The feeling of desperation that's rising in my chest has me speaking without thinking.

"Hey, Vic—what if I told you I was, I don't know, married or something?"

Her eyes widen for a fraction of a second, then she bursts into laughter. "Marrying Paul Hutchinson in a Vegas-style club night does not count."

"No, I mean—" The dressing room door opens, and Hutch himself pops his head around the frame.

"You coming, mate?" he says, holding the door open for Vicky to slip past him.

"I—" I look up at the clock and consider if it's too late to call Ellie because the GM is right—I can't risk anymore drama. I need to apologise to her. Explain that I had no idea. "—yeah. But I don't think I'm going to travel back home tonight. I'll check with Coach, but I figured I'd pay my folks a visit whilst I'm here."

It's bullshit, but it's all I've got to save telling Hutch any more than I need to tonight.

He wrinkles his brow. "That makes zero sense. You've got to drive up here tomorrow for prelims. Can't you see them then?"

"I'll get my dad to drop me home and get my stuff," I say. "Honestly, I think my mam is a little worried so..."

"Right, well, I guess you know what you're doing," he says.

And a pang of guilt ripples through me as he takes the lie at face value.

Damn, I really am a dick.

I follow him through the tunnels, focusing on the path ahead as we make our way out the back exit to the coach. The transport is loaded, and several of the guys are mulling around outside, waiting until the very last minute to board, but I don't see Johnny.

"Anyone seen Cap?" I ask no one in particular.

"The GM wanted a word with him or something," Ryan says. "I don't think he'll be too much longer."

I nod, deciding that updating Johnny on my conversation with the GM can wait, since he's probably hearing it directly himself.

Instead of following Hutch onto the bus, I take the opportunity to find Coach Adams instead, who's standing towards the rear of the bus with Springy, the assistant coach. They have their heads together, laughing about something and since I don't want to spoil their fun, I lean against the side of the coach, waiting for them to come to a natural break in the conversation.

"Everything alright, Betts?" Coach says, shifting his attention towards me.

"I need to ask a favour, Coach," I say, standing to my full height.

His face drops into a frown. "No, Betts. I'm not letting you bring a girl home on the coach. It's for players and staff only. How many times—"

"Nah, Coach, it's not that. I just need a pass—but not for anything like that either. I need to see my folks. My mam was worried about all that negative press, and I've just had a chat with the GM ahead of next week. She'll be waiting for an update."

I allow myself the smallest of internal grins, because that's worked itself out perfectly.

Coach studies me for a second. "All good, yeah?"

"Yeah," I say. "Just need to keep my focus and since we don't have a game tomorrow..."

Coach nods. "Fine, but you check in with me before you leave for prelims. I have a few things I want to run through."

I express my appreciation and say goodbye to the guys, noting that Johnny still hasn't returned. But I don't have time to worry about that.

I step aside and pull my phone out, wondering if I should call Ellie and ask if she can meet me somewhere. But I stare at her number before deciding to call a cab instead.

ONCE UPON A TIME, Saturdays were the best day of the week. A full day of doing whatever I wanted, without a care in the world.

I could go shopping, get my nails done, lounge in my pyjamas all day watching crap TV … but that was before I grew up, got a job and bought a car.

And since things aren't going so great with my job today, it makes sense that my car would crumble too in the tune of a flat tyre.

The deflated remains of my passenger side wheel would look comical if it wasn't for the fact that this is the least amusing thing I've come across since finding that old bit of paper. And since I have no tears left in the tank, I burst into hysterical laughter for a few moments before it teeters off into an awkward silence as I consider my options.

I could call my parents, but I can hear my mother now, 'Why don't you call your breakdown service?' but that would mean having a breakdown service to call. It's just one of the things I had to carve away from my expenditure when I bought my house.

I could call Kathryn and Greg, but I can hear the exasperated huffs from my sister as she's inconvenienced, because even though she'd send Greg, it'd be my fault for ruining their evening.

Or, I could call Jessica and wait for her to drive here, which probably isn't ideal, seeing as it's creeping closer to eight o'clock.

I pop the boot of my car and lift the cover to reveal the space-saver tyre, staring at the polystyrene tray where the jack and the locking wheel nut live.

It can't be that difficult, can it?

It takes me a full hour to realise that jacking up the car is the easy part; it's loosening the wheel-nuts that proves to be the problem. I can't budge two out of five, nor can the only person who offered to help.

I'm tired, cold and it's late. And all I want to do is crawl into bed and forget about this—at least until tomorrow anyway.

I use the last of my energy to pile everything back into my boot after lowering my car, figuring I'll have to call a taxi to get home. But then I remember there's a bottle of wine in the back room of the salon; a Christmas gift from a client that I can use to drown my sorrows.

I open the shutters enough to squeeze underneath, unlocking the door and disarming the alarm at a speed of someone who's done this a lot. Then I make my way to the back room to find the wine.

My mouth feels like cotton wool; the taste of cheap wine on my breath. And there's a vibrating on my chest that persists for a few moments before I realise it's my phone. I don't even check the screen; I slide to accept the call before pressing my phone to my ear, croaking out a greeting.

"Ellie?" a voice says.

"Yeah," I say, forcing myself to swallow. "Who's this?"

"Hey, it's Bettsy," the voice says.

"Huh?"

"It's Mike Betts. This is ... Ellie Kitchener, right?"

I rub my eyes, trying to process the words that float into my ear.

"Yeah, this is she," I say.

"Can we talk?" he says.

Talk? What the—

"Sorry, who is this?"

"Are you okay?" he says.

"Yeah, fine, but—" Then there's a laugh. A laugh I recognise almost straight away; it hits me, rousing me from the hazy veil that settled. "Mike?"

"Yeah. Like I said—it's Bettsy. Sorry to call you out of the blue, but I was hoping we could talk."

I sit up, swivelling my body so I can put my feet on the floor, trying to ground myself.

I take a minute to work out where I am: the backroom of the salon, on the sofa with my coat as a blanket.

"Talk? I'm sorry, what?" I say.

"I've been thinking—the way we left things last time, I mean—"

"Look, I've had the literal day from hell—I really don't think it's a good idea," I say.

"Please? Just ten minutes—I mean, I'm back home. I had a game here tonight, so I figured it'd be a good time to talk. I'm at your salon right now so I can come and meet you somewhere," he says.

I swear to God my heart stops for a beat, then I hesitate for a moment, because the last thing I need is Mike turning up here and seeing the absolute state that is my life. Despite not wanting to care what he of all people thinks, I do. And it sucks.

"How do you know—right, your mam. Well, can't sorry. I'm busy," I say.

"Five minutes, then? You owe me that."

"I owe you nothing," I snap, letting the pitch of my voice elevate. "If anyone owes anyone anything ... it's you. You're a dick and I have nothing more to say to you."

There's a pause, then Mike's voice, now full of sarcasm, comes down the line again. "Aww—look at us, bickering like an ol—"

"Stop it, Mike."

"So, give me five minutes," he says. "Where shall I meet you?"

"You can say what you've got to say over the phone," I say.

Another pause.

"Do you know spoken communication allows for immediate clarification of misunderstandings? Trust me, this is a face-to-face thing, sweetheart."

I growl. "You're full of crap."

"You used to love it," he says. "Always said how funny I was."

He's talking like we spent twelve years together, not twelve hours. But, considering I'm running out of ways to say no and for him to actually hear me, I exhale sharply, and wriggle out from under my coat.

I make my way to the front area of the salon, where I spot Mike through the gaps in the shutter, standing on the pavement outside illumined by the streetlamps.

He's wearing a suit. A freaking suit. And he has the audacity to pull it off, too. That nauseating feeling of disgust creeps in as I will myself to tap the glass.

He turns around, phone still pressed to his ear.

"Oh, hey honey," he says, in a fake North American accent.

"Five minutes," I hiss into my phone. "It starts now."

"Aren't you going to let me in? It's fucking freezing out here."

I'm pissed at him, but I'm not completely heartless, so I unlock the door and gesture for him to duck under the shutter.

"Do you live in your salon?" he asks before cutting the call and slipping his phone away.

He steps inside cautiously, closing the door behind him.

"No. By the way, you're eating into your five minutes."

He ignores me, opting to start a game of question time instead.

"So, what're you doing here this late, then? It's not that warm, Kitch. You're going to freeze in here."

"What does it matter to you?" I ask.

Mike frowns. "Give me a break, would you?"

Honestly, his expression has me feeling sorry for him for at least a second, then I see the shiner on his cheek and remember that he's a big burly hockey player who can take it.

"I'm sorry, but I've had a terrible day and then I get woken up for a five-minute conversation I don't really want to have—I guess I'm feeling a little tetchy about it."

"Well, it's hardly the middle of the night, but the rest is fair, I guess." He sighs, shoving his hands into his pockets and glancing at his shoes briefly before looking me in the eye. "I came to apologise. And set the record straight, I guess. You left before I could explain and I've been thinking about it all week, trying to figure out what's real and what isn't and I guess I concluded I have no idea. I've seen several videos online and—I don't know. I. Don't. Know, Kitch.

"But what I do know, is I'd never lure you into doing something like that for the fun of it. I mean—why would I, huh? Why would I marry then ditch you? I know I don't always think things through, but I'm not that much of an ass."

I stare at him. Trying to take it all in.

My head is fuzzy, probably from the wine, but I guess I can see his logic: why would he do that? What would he gain from it?

Unease works its way through my bones. Because if he didn't know. And I didn't know. Then ... neither of us knew. And if neither of us knew, then both of us are in this as equals. Neither of us in this situation as a result of a conscious decision, which makes me feel a whole load worse because I have no one to blame.

No one except myself.

I swallow, trying to work out if the feeling in my chest is heartbreak or disappointment, but at least the five minutes is now up.

"Well, thanks for letting me know. Please, can you close the door on your way out?" I turn on my heel and head in the direction of the back room, but he calls my name and, as much as I want to ignore him, I don't. "What?"

"I'm sorry," he says.

I'm glad I'm facing away from him because tears I didn't realise I had left come, catching in my eyes and filling my vision with blurry wetness.

"You don't—" I choke out, swallowing hard, but he cuts over me.

"No, I do. I am sorry. If I hadn't invited you to spend the day with me, this wouldn't have happened. It's all my fault. And if you're anything like either of my sisters, you've had this idea of what your wedding was going to be like since you were ... I don't know, a kid or something."

There's a shuffle of movement before he speaks again.

"Images of how you'd be proposed to ... and what your ring would look like... and I took that away from you. I didn't even give you a proper kiss."

He exhales before he continues.

"I know most guys don't care about that sort of stuff, but I've seen it firsthand that women care. Most women, anyway. So, forgive me if I've generalised but ... anyway, I am really fucking sorry, and whatever you need to make it right, I'll do it. You've got my number now, so ... yeah."

Then the yale-lock on the shop door clicks shut as he leaves.

Chapter 8

Bettsy

I PACE THE PAVEMENT outside the salon, practically wearing a groove in the paving slabs as I try to get through to a local taxi company. I guess this is a by-product of a busy Saturday night.

I'm about to hit re-dial when the door to the salon squeaks open, shifting my attention to Ellie as she slips out onto the street wearing a coat over her fitted work tunic.

I'm not sure if it's my vow of celibacy or the fact that I'm still as attracted to her as I've always been, but I check her out. The streetlamps shine down on her and I'm drawn to the curve of her waist and—

I snap out of my daydream when she says my name. And I mean, it's rare that anyone calls me Mike or Michael day-to-day, but I sort of like the way she does.

"Yeah?" I say, shoving my phone away.

"Thanks."

"For?"

"Apologising. You're right. I had always imagined my wedding day ... and it wasn't that. I guess I was taking my anger out on you."

"Yeah, well…"

"Are you going to be okay getting home?" she asks.

"I'm trying to get a cab. I need to get back to my folks' house and see if my dad could take me to the station in the morning or something. I didn't think it through, if I'm honest. I guess … why change the habit of a lifetime?"

She gives me a tentative smile, like she's not sure how it'll land.

"I'd offer to take you, but I've had a drink, and I've got a flat. I tried to change the tyre myself, but I couldn't get the bolts undone and … never mind."

I guess this explains why she's here.

"And you didn't think to call that guy you're seeing?" My tone comes out a little more bitter than I intended. "Don't tell me he didn't come to your rescue."

Her eyes widen, then she clears her throat.

"It's still early days—I mean, I didn't want to concern him."

My heart sinks. But what gets me the most is I'm bothered. Why the hell am I bothered?

"I'm sure he'd be happy to help. Most guys take it as a win. Feeling needed and all that stuff. I would, anyway. Knight in shining armour…" I feel my cheeks heating. "Where's your car key?"

"My car key?"

"Yeah. The key for your car."

She rolls her eyes.

"You don't have to do that," she says. "I'll get Greg, my brother-in-law, to swing by."

She dips her hand into her pocket and pulls out her phone.

"Let me help. I'm here. Honestly, Kitch—I can get it swapped out in no time. You've got a space saver, right?"

"I—yeah."

"Then pass me the key, please."

She sighs then reaches into the other pocket of her coat, rummaging around before extracting a bunch of keys and handing them to me.

I stare at the mass of keyrings in my palm.

"Okay, are you a jailor, or...?"

"Shush."

"It's like ... ninety-five per cent keyring," I say, studying the bundle.

"If you're going to make fun—"

"I'm not, I'm not," I say. "Where are you parked?"

I tap the unlock button and a car across the street lights up. I check that the road is clear before crossing, Ellie following a few paces behind me, then I open the boot and get to work on jacking up the car.

Sometimes, I really wish I was the type of person who could keep his mouth shut and revel in the silence of a moment, but I can't. It feels like there's a giant stick poking me in the side, pushing me to talk ... to say something.

"So, got any exciting weekend plans?" I say, tilting my head up to where she's standing on the pavement.

She purses her lips before sighing.

"You don't need to make small talk," she says.

"Okay," I say, standing up. "How about medium talk instead?"

She furrows her brow.

"Look, Kitch—" I meet her eyes and there's something about the way she's looking at me. "I tried calling you," I say. "After my texts went un-answered. I called you and you told me not to call your number again. So, for the record, I tried."

There's a flicker of shock on her face.

"You definitely did not call. And I did not tell you not to call again," she says, indignation in her voice.

"Well, fuck knows what happened there then," I say.

I crouch down next to the passenger side wheel, waiting for her to respond, hoping she says something to make it make sense, but she doesn't.

I'm met with a wall of silence.

"And I didn't ghost you," I say.

I catch a look at her, studying her reaction, but she's staring at me. Wide eyes.

And because she still doesn't speak, I feel obligated to keep talking like the idiot I am.

"I really liked you ... you know, and I guess the joke is on me here, because I thought you liked me back. And that never happens so—"

"What do you mean by that?" she says.

I stand up and reach for the lug wrench.

"All I'm saying is, when you look like I do, you see a crush as just that—a crush. Unobtainable and someone you'll eventually get over. But imagine how buzzed I was when you said yes to wanting to spend the day with me. I thought, if you got to know me, as a person, you may overlook my exterior and—"

"Don't you dare," she says, pulling her brows together. "You don't get to tell me how I felt about you—how do you know how I felt about you?"

"Well, you didn't contact me, either."

"I didn't have my phone, remember? It was in Jessica's bag, and you were the one who took my number. You are the one who stood there and promised you'd text me."

I remember that conversation vividly. And she's right—I promised.

"And I did," I say, my voice raising a notch in volume.

"Well, I obviously you didn't."

"So maybe I put in your number wrong. You can't be angry with me for that."

She wrinkles her nose. "You knew where I lived. You didn't even bother to knock when you got home. You just went about your business ... getting with the next girl in line... Julie—"

"I don't even remember a Julie," I say, blowing out a breath. "What did you want me to do, Kitch? Knock on your door and ask you why didn't you answer my calls or texts after I was explicitly told to not call again? I was humiliated. Embarrassed that I let myself think, even for a single second, that I may stand a chance with you." My breath fogs in the cold air.

"Give it a rest, Mike. You were interested in Julie Goldsworthy, so I can only imagine how humiliated you were."

I can feel my jaw twitching as the frustration builds.

"I guess I was settling," I say. "That's the only thing I can think of. I don't mean this to sound in any way bad on Julia, but ... when you don't typically get attention, you get excited when someone is interested. And I am, again, embarrassed to admit it. I've been doing it ever since. There. I said it."

She looks at me for a moment and because I'm fucking freezing, I squat down and get to work on the bolts of the flat tyre.

"Settling?" she echoes.

"Forget it," I snap.

Silence stretches between us, tension crackling like static.

Usually, I'm the one who can't bear it—I'm the one who caves, who needs resolution. But this time, I'm weirdly relieved when she breaks first.

"Can we call a truce, please? The back-and-forth isn't helping anyone."

I don't answer. I just dig the lug wrench around the bolt and twist hard, channelling everything into the motion.

But then she says my name.

"Mike..."

A single syllable delivered in such an intense softness, I can't help but pause, keen to hear whatever she's got to say.

I shift my attention, glancing at her out of the corner of my eye—enough for her to know I'm listening.

"I need a favour," she says. "I mean—it's not a favour like that but..."

"What do you need?" I bite.

"Greg said the document I had is only part of it. It's not the full certificate and the solicitor he's lined up to help me said he needs it to proceed."

"Full certificate?" I say, standing up.

"Do you remember taking any paperwork home?"

I let out a dry laugh. "Kitch—I don't even remember getting any paperwork."

She frowns. "Well, could you at least think about it? We're stuck without it."

"I guess I could look through my old boxes," I say.

"Right, well, I'll be grateful if you could ... as soon as you can."

"I've got camp this week, so the chances are slim, but I'll get on to it as soon as it's over."

"Okay."

I crouch back down, tighten the last bolt before I stow the flat in the boot, and brush the dirt from my hands.

That's that, I guess.

"Make sure you get the tyre replaced soon. You shouldn't drive on a space saver for more than fifty miles. And don't go speeding off down the motorway—they aren't designed for speed. Best to stay under fifty. Just remember 'fifty for fifty'."

"Right, thanks."

I hand back her keys and she slips the wad back in her pocket.

"Okay. You're good to go," I say, stepping back to let her pass.

"I can't drive tonight," she says. "I've had a drink."

I look between her and the car. "Want me to drive you home?"

"You're not insured," she says.

"Yeah, I am. Team policy lets me drive anything under the fleet agreement, fully comp," I shrug. "But if you'd prefer I didn't—"

Her expression softens, then she nods.

"I just need to grab my things and lock up."

He said he was settling.

His words play on repeat in my head—not because I'm shocked, but because they ring true.

I've spent my life settling too.

Second best.

No one's first choice.

But I try not to think about that.

And that thing he said about attention—when you don't get it from the people you want it from, you take it from whoever offers. God. If that isn't a mirror held up to my own choices, I don't know what is. I want to stay mad at him, I really do, but I've never related to anyone so much.

Maybe we've both been doing the same thing all along: pretending we're fine, patching the cracks with people who were never meant to hold us together.

"You okay, Kitch?" he says.

His voice is calm, easy—like he actually cares. Like the question isn't just filler, but real.

And I don't know what to do with that. I'm not used to it.

It's unsettling. It makes me feel exposed.

"Fine," I say, eyes locked on the road ahead.

We ride in silence for the rest of the journey, save for a few directions. And when Mike finally pulls into my street, I feel the relief hit me hard—like I've just stepped out of something heavy.

"Just here?" he says.

"Yeah, wherever you can find a spot. Parking is a nightmare," I say.

Mike finds a spot big enough and parallel parks into the space with ease.

"It looks like a nice place," he says, cutting the engine.

"It was all I could afford so—"

"But it's yours," he says. "I'd love to have my own place."

"Well, I panicked, didn't think through the costs and now I'm borderline needing a new boiler, which I can't afford. I'm not sure it's worth it."

"It's—"

"You don't need to do this, Mike."

"Do what?" he says.

But I'm reaching for my keys, half-held out in his hands, clutching onto them before I climb out of the car.

"Thanks, again. I really appreciate your help," I say.

He hops out of the car and hurries around to the pavement where he studies me for a moment then opens his mouth like he's about to say something.

But he doesn't.

We stare at each other for a moment, then he nods firmly.

I lock my car, then turn away, walking the short distance to the front of my house, leaving Mike's eyes burning into my back.

It's only when I get to my front door that I realise he's still loitering on the pavement, phone in hand and screen lit up like a Christmas tree.

I unlock my door and take a breath, then I look at him one last time before I slip inside.

I'm barely two steps into the hallway when there's a knock.

When I open the door, Mike's standing there, eyes fixed intently on the toe of his shoe.

"Everything okay?" I ask.

"Yeah. Sorry—bit awkward, but I don't suppose I could take a leak, could I?"

I hold the door open for him to step inside, shifting over enough so he can pass.

"Toilet is upstairs," I say.

But Mike isn't listening. He's craning his head into my front room.

"Nice place," he says.

"It needs some work. I know it's not much..." I say, flicking on the light switch to the living room, in a depressing 'ta-da' moment.

"I love it. Loads of potential ..." He steps inside. "You know, you could even knock this wall through and—" He runs his hand along the wall dividing the living room and a small reception room.

"I wanted to keep that separate and make a treatment area. Out of hours sort of stuff ... I want to grow a little outside of my sister's business."

"Yeah, that makes sense," he says. "Mam mentioned you've got a decent set-up there, though."

I shrug.

"It's okay. I'd just like more time to..."

I snap my mouth closed, wondering why I'm telling him any of this stuff.

"The bathroom's upstairs on the right," I say.

But Mike doesn't move. He stands glued to the spot, looking around like he's surveying the place to give me a quote for decorating or something.

"Can't your boyfriend help you?" he asks, his tone teasing, but a knot forms in my chest. "You know, get it to how you want it?"

"I don't have a—I told you, it's early days."

I move through into the kitchen, flicking the light on before dropping my bag and coat onto the table in the corner. Then I turn to assess the kitchen   one I fell in love with when I viewed the house that quickly showed its faults when I moved in.

The Belfast-style sink was a selling point when I viewed the place, but now it reminds me of a dream I can't ever see coming true. And there's an enormous crack on the edge that definitely wasn't there when I viewed the house.

"I love the sink," Mike says, moving into the room. "The worktops would look so good in like … a rustic oak or something." He runs his hand along the surface.

"Well, if you want to make me an offer, this place is yours," I say.

He grins.

"Are you forgetting something, sweetheart? We're married. It's already half mine."

Sweetheart? Typically patronising from anyone else, but he pulls it off, causing an involuntary shiver to run down my spine.

"We don't know that for sure yet…" I say, but I can tell he's not listening.

"Honestly, this is a nice place. And getting things in a good shape takes time. One of my buddies on the team is renovating at the moment and—" Mike cuts himself off, then pulls at the collar of his shirt.

"Well, yeah, but I have little spare cash at the moment. And with this marriage stuff … I'm not sure how much that's going to set me back."

"What does it matter?" Mike says, leaning against the kitchen counter, clearly forgetting about his visit to the bathroom again. "I mean, eight years and we didn't know, so what does it actually matter if we don't get it done for another few years?"

"You're kidding, right?"

"No. It makes perfect sense," he says, moving towards the table.

"It does not. What if I meet the love of my life and he plans an extravagant proposal, and I have to stop him mid-taking a knee to drop the bomb that I'm already married, and I need to get divorced first?"

Mike rubs his beard. "Okay, well, yeah, I guess that could be a tad awkward. Maybe just tell anyone you're dating that you're married when it kicks off—hey have you told this boyfriend of yours? You know, given him a heads up so he doesn't get the wrong idea or whatever."

"The wrong idea?"

I raise a brow.

"Yeah. He may assume that you're still in love with me or something—but don't worry ... I won't tell if you don't." He winks and I roll my eyes.

"You're being ridiculous."

"Hey—I'm just being realistic." He glances at me. "How do you think I feel, anyway? This isn't ideal for me either. I'm abstinent. At this rate, I'll never have sex again."

I gape at him. "Excuse me?"

"Honestly, after all that shit with—forget it. I can't handle it. I'm not having sex until I'm married now—or, you know what I mean."

I stare at him in complete disbelief, but his attention has waned.

He moves around me and makes a beeline for the small drinks cabinet tucked in the corner of my kitchen.

"Wow, this is some collection you have," he says, picking up a bottle of ruby port and rolling it in his hands.

"Please don't touch," I say, moving towards him and reaching for the bottle. "That one is special."

My fingers dance over his as he hands me back the bottle and the physical contact causes me to shiver; probably because it's been a long time since I've touched anyone who wasn't a client.

"Sorry, I didn't realise—I didn't have you pinned as a drinker."

"I'm not really. It's all stuff I've sort of accumulated, and this bottle is something of a rare find, apparently. The other stuff, well, I've had one glass here and there and then ... I guess I didn't want to throw them out. I always wanted one of those globe-shaped drinks cabinets—but then I ... I don't know."

"Oh yeah? That sounds cool—shit..." He pauses. "This is special. Where did you get it from?" He points towards a bottle of Macallan ten-year-old oak whisky. "If this was sealed, it'd be worth a fortune."

I shrug. "That one you can touch." I move towards him, peering over his arm at the bottle. "I won it in a raffle a few years ago, and honestly, it wasn't even that nice."

Now it's his turn to gape at me. He picks up the bottle and turns it over, reading the label.

"You're kidding? I bet this is like ... I don't know, liquid gold? Here..."

He pops the cap off and holds the bottle to his nose, breathing deeply and sighing blissfully before stepping towards me and crowding me completely.

Naturally, I'd step back to regain my personal space, but I edge closer, more interested in the smell of his aftershave at this proximity than the bitter scent of the whisky.

"Good, don't you think?" Mike says, lowering his voice.

His eyes lock onto mine and my head spins; the fumes of the whisky mixed with the wine already swimming around my stomach.

It makes me delirious.

I shake my head. "More like gasoline. Honestly, it smells like varnish. Whisky isn't my thing."

Mike moistens his lips before peering back at the bottle.

"I wish I wasn't on a drinking ban because I'd be begging for a taste of this. Honestly, Macallan whisky is..."

He chef kisses the air, then ponders over the bottle for another moment before speaking again.

"Actually, since I'm getting a cab back to my folks' place—do you mind if I have a quick glass? I mean—one won't hurt, will it?"

Chapter 9

Bettsy

"I can't believe you don't like this," I say, holding up a glass of the Macallen.

Honestly, this is the whisky of dreams and even after the first sip, I can feel the warmth wrap around me in a way only decent single malt can.

"Are you sure you should drink that?" she asks. "Don't you have your camp thing starting on Monday?"

I swallow down another drop, taking a moment to study the liquid in the glass before responding.

"Yeah, but I won't get drunk on this. This, Kitch ... is too good to waste on getting drunk. You need to savour it ... enjoy the flavours and—"

She rolls her eyes at me. "Right, well..."

"Are you sure you don't want to try it? Maybe you just shot it down last time without giving your taste buds time to appreciate the flavours?"

I hold out my glass to her and she looks at the amber liquid for a moment before shaking her head.

"I'm good, thanks," she says, moving to the fridge-freezer and pulling open the door to the upper compartment.

"You know whisky literally means 'water of life' in Gaelic? It's designed to give people a kick up the ass—make them a little more … you know," I say.

Ellie looks away from the fridge and over towards me. "A little … you know what?"

"Lively. You seem a smidge uptight, that's all. Maybe you should … relax a little."

"Uptight? You're joking, right?" She slams the fridge shut.

"Yeah. You've been in a bad mood since you showed up at my place. Granted, you've warmed a little, but I can tell—" I pause, taking in her expression before deciding to change direction. "You know there's worse things in the world than realising a wedding experience could be real, right? Hey—maybe we can sue them or something? Every cloud and all."

Ellie looks at me with disgust.

"I'm sorry that my bad mood is not to your liking, but what you need to understand is this 'wedding' crap is just another thing to add to my ever-growing list of fuckups. I know how to have fun and relax, but I'm sorry for not having the same idea of a good time as you."

"Sweetheart, you have no idea what I class as a good time."

I throw her a wink—and if I'm not mistaken, she shivers. Though being fair, it is fucking freezing in here.

She pauses for a moment before huffing.

"Fine. Pass me that tequila," she says curtly, pointing to a bottle in the drinks cabinet.

"Hey, come on now … I didn't mean it like that."

"Pass it." She steps closer, reaching for it anyway.

A powder-fresh scent wafts off her hair and has me wondering what her skin smells like.

"Go ahead," I say, stepping aside.

But as she grabs the bottle and turns, she bumps straight into me. My hand finds her waist automatically, steadying her.

She parts her lips, maybe to say something, but then she pulls free and slides past me, heading for the cupboard above the kettle.

She pulls out a glass, pours a generous measure, and knocks it back in one go.

"Look," I start, "you don't have—"

But she's already setting the glass down, slipping her tongue out to catch a stray drop trailing her bottom lip.

Now it's my turn to shiver.

"What's wrong, Mike? Don't tell me you're too uptight for a little tequila?"

A teasing smirk plays out on her face.

I don't even like the damn stuff, but she's taunting me. The tone of her voice and the look in her eye have me setting down the Macallen, stepping forward and reaching for the tequila.

I pour a measure into the glass she used before sinking it, eyes locked on hers the entire time.

She stares at me, letting her mouth drop open a little before she blinks.

"Give me that," she says, prying the glass from my fingers.

"Be careful, Kitch. You don't want to play drinking games with me," I say.

"And why is that? Don't think I could keep up?" she says.

I let out a booming laugh.

"I think you don't understand how competitive I am. C'mon ... don't start something you can't finish," I say.

"Who says I can't finish?"

"It wouldn't be very good of me to let you sink yourself into oblivion on the premise of keeping up with me. Let's not kid ourselves—I'm double the size of you."

"You," she says, pointing her index finger into my chest, "do not know who you're dealing with."

And just like that, I turn on the flirting. There's something about knowing she's not interested that only makes me want to pursue her more. The thrill of the chase—I can't help myself.

"Ellie—come on, we both know that I'll win, or we'll end up in bed together. Drinking lowers inhibitions, intensifies emotions and—"

She scowls at me.

"I will not end up in bed with you. You may have a queue of women ready to crawl between your sheets, but I'm not one of them."

And without so much as a second thought, she takes another shot, wincing as she swallows.

"I told you ... I'm closed for business," I say.

"Right. The whole 'no sex before marriage thing'. Or is that another ploy to coerce me into bed with you? It's the ideal scenario for you, I guess."

"Just because I want to sleep with you doesn't mean I'll coerce you," I say. "I could win you over with my charm if I really wanted to ... failing that, there're always the mental images I could concoct. Right. Up. Here." I tap my temple, and she tuts.

"Stop it."

"Stop what? I'm not doing anything." I muster my dirtiest grin to get a bigger reaction out of her.

"Trying to flatter me. And whatever you're thinking. Stop that too."

"We both know you'd fall into bed with me, given the right circumstances," I say.

I'm kidding at this point. There's no way she'd *actually* sleep with me, but since I'm trying to make light of this unique situation, I figure it can't hurt to joke.

"I need another drink," she says.

"If that's what it takes..."

That wins me a scowl. And you know what? I quite like angry Ellie—all set on being pissed off.

Imagine if she wanted to tie me up and do semi-mean things to me.

Damn.

Despite the booze in my system, my dick wakes up to the thought of being restrained to the bed and having Ellie bossing over me, denying me an orgasm until I'm begging for it.

I file that in the bank for later as she brushes past me.

"Are you sure that's a good idea?" I say.

She's looking through the bottles of alcohol in her collection and stops at a fancy looking gin.

"Because you're not keeping up?" she snipes back.

Johnny's voice rings through my head ... *the partying and late nights need to be done with...*

But watching her pour herself a drink is all the encouragement I need to ignore it. I'm competitive by nature and there's no way I'm losing here.

I sink another shot while Ellie grabs a bottle of something else before pouring a measure into her glass.

"Don't you think you've had enough, anyway? Maybe you shouldn't mix..."

"I know when I've had enough. I don't need a guy telling me what to do—especially one who's led me on."

I roll my eyes. "I didn't—look, I simply want to make sure you don't regret this in the morning."

She sets her cocktail down.

"I've regretted nothing in my life," she says, her voice trembling with doubt.

I snicker, unable to stop myself. "Yeah, right? I'm pretty sure you regret the girls' trip to Germany."

"I wouldn't have regretted the girls' trip if you'd have called me afterward—even for closure. But you didn't, Mike, did you? Because you were already busy with whatever-her-name was."

Her voice quivers again as she reaches for her drink, and because I'm such a gentleman, I feel it necessary to intervene, stepping towards her.

"Okay, now let's take this away," I say, pulling the glass away from her. "I thought we'd already established I tried to call you."

"But you didn't flirt with me either," she says. "The whole day. Not a single lewd comment."

"Is that what you think?" I flash her a puzzled look but she looks away, a warm glow settling on her cheeks. "The reason I didn't flirt with you is because I didn't want an open rejection from the only girl I've ever fancied."

She laughs, but it's a sort of slurry laugh that turns into a giggle.

"You did not fancy me," she says.

"I definitely did. And for the record, I looked you up several weeks ago, wondering if we were going to be in with a possibility of cashing in on that pact. You know, if we're both single when we're thirty?"

She stares at me for a moment before swallowing.

"Because I'm a last resort?"

"No—because I was hoping you'd hold me to it, and I'd at least be in with a chance that way."

The embarrassment of laying my feelings on the line has me stress smiling. And Ellie notices in a flash, whacking me across the arm.

"What the hell was that for?" I rub my forearm.

"You were smirking at me—like this is all one big joke to you. This is my life, Mike. This is my life, and you ruined it with your crappy ideas for wedding experiences and whatever."

"I was not smirking at you," I say. "It was just a little smile." But I take a second to realise I was—and—I still am smirking, not smiling in the slightest. My face positively aches.

Her mouth drops into a frown.

"Okay, maybe I was," I say. "But you're so ... I don't know—cute. And I'm trying to be honest with you ... make you understand how much I—"

But I don't think she's listening.

She's staring at me; her lips sort of pouting outward like they want to be kissed. And boy, do I want to kiss them—kiss her.

I step forward, closing the gap between us. My hand finds her chin, and I gently tilt her head towards mine, locking eyes.

She's beautiful. *Ridiculously* beautiful.

Too beautiful for me.

But I can't help myself. I lean in—just a little ... but there's a little voice in my head.

She's got a boyfriend, Betts. Don't be that guy.

I swallow hard, drop my hand, but keep my gaze on hers.

"I'm just trying to be honest here, Kitch," I say, voice low. "I'd be lying if I said I haven't thought about you. Because I have. And I—"

A vibration cuts through the air, forcing me to halt. Her phone buzzes against the counter, and both of our eyes snap towards it.

THERE'S A SIZZLING TENSION in the air.

Was he going to kiss me? Was I going to let him?

I can't be sure, but the vibration of my phone breaks the spell and whatever that was is well and truly over as Mike and I stare at the screen of my phone, face up on the counter.

And in the split-second I take to glance back at Mike, his expression turns sour.

"Rick Langdon?" he says, his eyebrows pulling together. "Surely it can't be—that's not Patrick Langdon ... is it? What the—what's he doing texting you?"

Mike's face reddens, like the living embodiment of the 'angry face' emoji.

"I—we're just messaging socially, that's all."

His eyes widen in disgust, then his whole face seems to crumple—fury softening into something far more fragile.

"Is this who you're seeing?" he says, his voice frail and uneven.

It takes a second to register what I'm hearing. Then it hits me—he's upset. Properly upset.

Why? Why does it matter that much to him? But then I remember ... Mike and Rick were both named in the Team GB prelim squad. Are they rivals? Is it more personal than that?

"Is this who you're seeing, Kitch?" he says again, more quietly this time.

"What? No." I hesitate for a moment before continuing. "Okay, so I don't have a boyfriend. I panicked when your mam asked me and—"

"Right," he cuts in, but he doesn't look at me. He just keeps staring at the phone.

I scramble to explain, desperate to see that light in his eyes again. The same he had when he was about to—

"He's texting me because he's the best man of my sister's fiancé. That's all. He's trying to de-conflict some wedding plans."

Mike scoffs. "Like hell he is. He's a guy. He doesn't give a shit about wedding plans—he's trying to—"

"He's not trying to do anything," I interrupt.

"Rick Langdon." Mike repeats his name over and over under his breath, shaking his head. "Honestly ..."

"Why do you care who I'm texting, anyway?" I ask, though I have a feeling I already know the answer.

He downs another shot before leaning against the kitchen counter.

"Because the guy is a complete asshat with no social skills. I bet he doesn't even laugh at Christmas cracker jokes."

"What do Christmas cracker jokes have to do with anything?" I blink at him, trying to follow.

"It's my way of saying he has no sense of humour and he's not a team player. Christmas cracker jokes are terrible because everyone can agree that they are bad. Imagine there's a decent joke nestled inside, but only half the family gets it ... it'll divide the crowd and cause animosity. So, by everyone having a common enemy in the tune of a poor joke—it's a team effort."

I consider it for a moment. I can't say I've ever thought about it before, but it explains why Kathryn doesn't so much as smirk at a festive quip.

"I see," I say.

"I'm just saying. The guy is an idiot. And he owes me a few grand."

"What? How?" I say.

"The playoffs last year. Langer opted to aim a dirty hit at me and I ended up in the hospital. Concussion. My mam took it to the extreme and kept me at home all summer, which meant my job was off the cards."

He looks down at his shoes and the memory of Mike's brother, Jeremy, rises to the surface. He died from a head injury, and it was heartbreaking. A swell of emotion creeps through my chest and all I want to do is reach out and squeeze him tight.

But I don't.

"Oh, my God. That's awful," I say instead, putting a hand over my mouth.

"It wasn't ideal," Mike says. "But he knew I was a problem for him, and he targeted me specifically. Though, the jokes on him because we won, anyway. Honestly—everyone talks about death and taxes being dead certs, but there's a third thing that no one mentions." He pauses, only offering me insight when I raise my brow. "Rick Langdon having it out for me. He knows I'm better than him."

"That doesn't sound like the Rick I know," I say, though I'm not sure why. "He seems laid back and—" I'm about to say 'flirty' but Mike's scowl deters me.

"He's not laid back," he snaps. "Honestly, I reckon it's because he's probably in Matt Rodgers' inner circle or something."

Mike reaches for the bottle of Macallen and pours himself another measure.

"I don't know who that is," I say.

"Yeah, well ... I wish I didn't either. But he's another Rick—except probably worse because..." He clenches his jaw. "He's the reason someone's posting shit about me online ... well, part of the reason."

Mike stops abruptly, and I realise I've not been able to mask my expression. His eyes lock on mine as his mouth hangs open.

"You've read it, haven't you?" he says.

"Well ... yeah. But—"

"You didn't believe it, right?"

But when I take longer than three seconds to answer, Mike shakes his head.

He pulls his phone out of his pocket and unlocks the screen, tapping rapidly. Then he practically shoves it into my hands.

"Read that," he says.

It's a message thread with a contact he has saved as 'Rochelle – DO NOT ANSWER' followed by 'You have blocked this contact'.

I skim read the last few messages — all vile insults, and threats — before deciding that I've seen enough.

I hand him his phone back.

"That's what I've been dealing with," he says, slipping his phone back into his pocket. "An obsessed stalker-ish person who has nothing better to do than to ruin my life. You know they can't prove Rochelle made those posts, but there's not a doubt in my mind."

"But what's this Matt guy got to do with it?"

"It's a long story," he says, reaching for the bottle of tequila. "One I don't want to go into."

"I'm sorry, Mike."

"You don't need to be sorry. But be careful. I mean—I can't tell you who to date or whatever ... but Rick Langdon?"

"I'm not dating him," I say.

"Well ... regardless. He's still a prick," he says. "We were about to kiss, and he cock-blocks me."

I gape at him, my cheeks flaming as his mouth twists into a half-smile.

And there he is. Back to being the usual confident, self-assured self.

"We were not about to kiss," I say.

"Oh, really? Because we were having a moment."

He's right. We were sort of having a moment...

"Didn't you need the toilet like an hour ago?" I ask, trying to steer the conversation away from that particular topic.

"You're too good for him," he says, reaching for the shot glass, still ignoring his bladder.

"Excuse me?" I say defensively. "That's not for you to say."

"I'm just stating a fact, sweetheart."

And there it is again.

Sweetheart.

With his eyes fixed on mine, he downs a shot, and I swallow—the alcohol clouding my brain.

"Imagine if you got my texts?" he says, breaking away. "I reckon we'd be married for real now."

I laugh out loud. The booze is definitely running this conversation.

"What makes you think that?"

"Well, I may have a small dick, but it's not all about that, is it? I'd still have you seeing God."

He smirks again, and a wave of something ripples through me, but I shake my head.

"I'd be fixing the house up too, making sure your tyres were in a fit state ... not to mention all the flowers I'd buy you."

I gasp. "What do you mean by that?"

"About my little—"

"No. The flowers."

"You told me you're a hopeless romantic. Flowers are up there, right? I bet Langer would never buy you flowers."

I stare at him in disbelief. As if he remembers me mentioning flowers all those years ago. I don't even remember how it came up, but the fact he remembers is wild.

His lips twitch with the threat of a smile and a shimmer of something flickers in his eyes, causing a light bulb to spark on in my head.

Even though I find it hard to believe he did like me like that ... it's now written all over his face.

Chapter 10

Bettsy

THERE'S A VIBRATING IN the distance.

Buzz. Buzz. Buzz.

And Christ, it's annoying.

Buzz. Buzz. Buzz.

It's getting closer.

At least, I think it is.

Then there's a clatter of something hitting the floor, startling me out of my half-dream state, causing my heart to thud so hard in my chest I can hear my pulse in my ears.

My eyelids are stuck shut; a coarse dryness that has me rubbing my eyes to induce tears.

And my mouth is like the literal desert.

Fuck.

The vibrating starts again, across the floor this time, and I roll over, blindly reaching out to where I think the noise is coming from.

Buzz. Buzz. Buzz.

I clasp my phone in my hands, brushing the carpeted floor with my fingers in the process.

Wait … carpet? I don't have carpet in my bedroom.

Where the hell am I?

I blink, trying to clear my vision, trying to decipher my whereabouts.

Buzz. Buzz. Buzz.

I glance at the name on the screen.

Johnny.

Fuck.

Johnny's going to *kill* me.

I panic and hit decline because he's going to ask where I am … he's going to ask me a million questions that I can't answer.

I survey the room. The bed sheets are white and crisp. There's a dressing table next to the window with girl shit on—the type of stuff my sisters have. Bottles and sprays and hair bits and—the memory of last night comes flooding back to me like a tidal wave of nightmares.

The flirting. The over-sharing. The kebab I insisted on ordering.

Buzz. Buzz. Buzz.

"Oh, crap," a voice says.

Ellie.

I'm in bed with Ellie.

The echo of her giggling swims to the forefront of my mind. Giggling. Giggling…

Did we? I peep under the duvet and see that I'm naked, apart from my boxers … and I don't remember doing *that*.

"Fuck," I say.

Fuck, indeed.

'…I may as well have one for the road…'

Famous last words and typical of me. Literally no will power. Not only did I drink a third of the Macallen—which was divine, I may add—but the tequila shots and I'm pretty sure I moved over to the small collection of brandy.

The conversation echoes around in my foggy brain.

"You did not fancy me!" she said.

We'd revisited that point—several times.

"I did. And honestly, I wish I'd kissed you for real that day."

"No, you don't," she said.

"Oh, yeah?"

It was all giggles and smiles and close faces. Completely out of character from the Ellie that was sharing the space in the kitchen with me mere hours before.

And she tilted her head in such a way that had me leaning in close several times. Almost to the point where our lips were touching.

Almost.

Buzz. Buzz. Buzz.

For fuck's sake. I can't even reminisce in peace.

There's a scrambling beside me and Ellie bolts upright in bed, pulling the duvet with her as she covers her chest. I will myself to remember if I got a peek at her boobs, but I'm sure I'd recall with minimal effort if I did.

"Oh, my God," she says, her head moving at the speed of a trickle towards me.

Her eyes widen when our gazes meet.

"Morning, sweetheart." I can't stop myself from smirking, but she jerks her head away, setting her attention on the empty patch of wall directly ahead of her.

"Oh, crap," she says again.

She scrambles out of bed, muttering something under her breath—a rare swearword, I believe, leaving me laying here in my underwear, my morning wood proud and snug against the grey cotton.

Ellie's eyes drift south and stop on my bulge and the fact that I'm exposed, unprotected from her view has my dick thickening further.

"Fuck," she says, under her breath this time, but I don't miss it.

"See, I only told you it was little so you'd be pleasantly surprised."

Her jaw drops, and she shakes her head before dashing out of the room at speed, almost falling over the threshold as my phone starts ringing again.

Buzz. Buzz. Buzz.

I swear Johnny's name looks angrier than it did a moment ago, flashing on my screen with rage reserved for the captain. And because I can't face him right now, I let it ring off, enjoying the silence only for a short while before it rings again, winning my attention—although I should know better.

My sister, Kelly—or at least I think it is—until I answer and Johnny's voice booms down the line at twenty decibels louder than it needs to be.

"Thank fuck," he says, after I croak out a greeting.

"What's going on? You need me for something?" I say, trying to sound casual.

"Need you for something? You're kidding, right? Kelly's been out of her mind ... Hutch said you were at your folks' house, but your mom said you didn't show up. Then you weren't answering my calls—"

"Well, I'm fine," I lie. "Never better, actually."

"Where the hell are you?" Johnny says.

"I'm just at a friend's house—I'm heading back to my parents' place now." I sit up in bed before setting my feet on the floor, trying to ground myself.

"A friend's house? If I find out it's Rochelle, then I'll—"

Fucking Johnny—leaping to the mother of all conclusions.

"No. Not Rochelle ... it was honestly just a friend's house."

Friend? Wife? Same thing, right?

"For fuck's sake, Betts—"

"Just so you know, my battery is going to die soon so you can't waste precious moments shouting at me," I say, cutting him off.

"Well, I need to talk to you," Johnny says.

There's a clock on the wall that tells me I have absolutely no time for chit-chat.

"Mate, I need to get back to my folks' place and then get home to grab my shit. Coach wants me to stop off and see him before I leave."

"Do you need me to come and pick you up?" he asks.

I consider it, but figure if Johnny sees the state I'm in, Coach isn't the only one who's going to kick my ass, so I pass.

"Right, well, call me when you're home. I only need ten minutes."

We say our goodbyes and I hang up, knowing that I absolutely will not be calling him when I'm home.

All I need to do is call Hutch, get him to pack up my essentials and meet me at the rink with my stuff. That way I won't risk bumping into Johnny.

I begin drafting a message, but before I can add so much as a single time, Ellie appears in the doorway, still wrapped in the duvet.

"You need to leave," she says, sort of half-waddling into the room under the restriction of the duvet. "I just remembered my sister is due any minute, and you can't be here."

"I'm sorry, what?" I ask, blinking at her.

"Mike. Please. You need to go ... if she finds you here—"

"She's not your mam, Kitch. Surely you can have guys over ... in your own house?"

Ellie purses her lips. "You don't understand ... last night—it shouldn't have got to that point. I mean—the booze and..."

Damn. She looks like she's almost pleading with me.

She meets my eyes; her face blotchy and her eyes watering a little.

And because I'm a gentleman, I nod. I'm an embarrassment. Not someone anyone would actually want to be seen with—I get it.

"Can I at least get dressed first? I mean—I can't leave like this." I gesture to my dick, still proud, despite my rejection.

Ellie glances towards me briefly before looking away again.

"Well, yeah, but quickly—please, Mike. You can go out through the back garden, as she will park out front."

She scrambles around in a drawer, pulling out a t-shirt and slipping it over her head, layering it on top of the duvet, before shimmying the quilt to her waist.

Then something creeps into my consciousness.

"Wait, what does it matter if I'm here? I'm a friend, aren't I? As a minimum. Hey—maybe I want to see how your sister is. It's been a while."

I stand up and reach for my trousers, stepping into them and pulling them up over my hips.

"Is she still a controlling bitc—"

She scowls at me. And it's clear that this isn't up for debate.

"Okay, okay, I'm going," I say, pulling my shirt on.

I don't waste time with the buttons, pushing my arms into the sleeves of my jacket instead before sitting back down on the bed to pull my socks and shoes on.

By the time I'm standing again, Ellie's pulled on a pair of leggings and tidied her hair back, making her neck all exposed and stuff.

There's a brief moment when she catches my eye, parting her lips slightly before speaking.

"I ... thanks again for yesterday. With the tyre," she says. "And thanks for listening to my worldly problems."

"Yeah, no problem," I say. "Oh, I know a guy at the High Street Tyre Centre. If you call in and tell him Bettsy sent you ... he'll get you fixed with a new wheel. Sorry I can't help with the web-site stuff though."

She nods, muttering a thanks before dashing towards her bedroom door.

I follow her lead, down the narrow staircase and dipping into the living room as Ellie hangs by the front door.

"Good luck tomorrow, Mike," she says.

And I want to say something back. I want to tell her I ... but I can't find the words, so I smile and turn away.

Then I leave.

GUILT HITS ME AS soon as the back door closes, but I know Kathryn's judgement would be a million times worse.

I watch Mike disappear out of sight, standing still for a moment as I run through the events of last night, because even though it's fresh in my mind—albeit slightly fuzzy around the edges—it's still bizarre.

If someone had told me I'd end up in bed with Mike Betts two weeks after finding that cursed red wallet, I'd be asking what they'd taken because last night was the dictionary definition of 'that escalated quickly'.

But my sister's due any moment now, so I shove the thought aside and get moving, moving back to the living room.

There's a knock on the front door as I finish tidying the empties from the living room and I wonder how long I can leave her waiting on the doorstep before she knocks again.

Answer: less than two seconds.

"What the hell happened to you?" Kathryn says as I open the door.

She looks me up and down with the most judgiest of looks before she exhales sharply, reminding me I made the right choice by asking Mike to leave.

"Oh, my God. You look like shit. Are you hungover?"

I suck in a breath as I open the door wider to let her in.

"Good morning," I say.

It's morning, sure, but whether it's good or not is still up for debate given the events of last night.

She moves into the tiny hall, stepping over the threshold and looking through to the living room directly adjacent.

"You had a guy over? Don't tell me Mark finally got in touch."

She shoots me another glare, all silent disapproval as she casts her eyes around my living room.

"No, I didn't," I say, moving towards the sofa and plumping a 'Mike's ass' shaped cushion.

We'd moved into the living room when he began telling me about his warm-up routine. I don't even remember how it came up in conversation, but the topic had shifted to his long list of hockey superstitions and one of his 'non-negotiable biggies', apparently, was the exact order of his pre-game stretches.

"It's like a workout for my brain," he said. "Exercising the old muscle memory."

I didn't ask him to, but he insisted on demonstrating.

Before I could protest, he had dropped to the floor and got into a split-leg position he called a 'frog-stretch' then started humping the carpet in a way I never thought possible. Even though it's completely ridiculous in sober afterthought, I couldn't force myself to look away.

The whole thing was ridiculous. Or at least, it should have felt that way. But we were both laughing, merrily on our way to being completely wasted, which is also around the same time I let my guard down.

I let my guard down, and Mike wormed his way into my emotions, asking me questions and listening when I answered and you know what? It felt like I was talking to an old friend.

Oh, God. I bet I told him too much. I bet I—

"Well, who was here then?" she asks. "Jessica? Or—"

She pushes past me, striding into my kitchen where she continues her investigation.

That's when I notice the takeaway containers half-poking out of the bin.

Crap.

I curse under my breath, as Kathryn clocks them, her nostrils flaring as she looks between me and the evidence of a good time.

God forbid a girl has a good time, after all.

"Eleanor—you're supposed to be on a wedding diet," she says, her voice rising a few levels in horror. "What the hell are you thinking?"

She moves towards the bin and points at the offending article.

"You're not getting married for ages," I say. "One chicken kebab is hardly going to—"

She gasps. The gasp of someone who's just been told her eyebrows are too bushy.

"I'm sorry, but when are you going to take this seriously?" she says. "I mean—you've got a lot to lose, it's not going to be a quick win for you."

My eyebrows shoot up as my mouth hangs open.

"Excuse—"

"Besides ... if you're going to get this magazine deal, they'll want photos. What's it going to look like if you're battling the blubber during a photo shoot?"

I blink several times, trying to process how my own sister could talk to me like that when she steps forward a few paces and reaches for the letter I left on the counter last night, one that was delivered while I was at work.

I'd shown Mike, trying to get his view—weirdly taking his opinion seriously.

"What's this?" Kathryn says.

She doesn't wait for me to reply, she's plucking the paper from the envelope in one firm motion, skimming over the letter before I can so much as breathe a protest.

"So, you need a website, and you need to up your social media plans? I guess that makes sense. I did wonder if applying was overly ambitious of you. How are you going to do that?"

I take a moment to process what's going on before I stumble out a reply.

"I'm not sure. I—"

"Well, Greg and I can't help you," she snaps. "We're putting all our money into our half of the wedding costs. And Dad is paying the other half, so I doubt he'll have anything spare either … what are you going to do?"

"I haven't thought about it yet," I say, swallowing hard. "But I thought that seven grand which I put into the business would be handy now … or just some of it, maybe."

Kathryn stares at me like I've asked her to donate a kidney, but she's saved by the bell when there's a knock on my front door.

"That'll be the girls," she says. "Can you put the kettle on?"

Should I tell her now or later that the milk in my fridge is no longer milk but more of a new life form?

I fill the kettle before setting it back on the stand to boil, then I grab a pair of trainers and my coat.

"So, hair—I'm thinking this would be a good look." Kathryn floats into the kitchen, shoving an iPad with several wedding style updos under my nose.

Typically, wedding styles get me so excited, but right now, I couldn't care any less.

"Yeah, that looks good," I say.

She swipes the screen a few times before pointing out another style. Then she notices my outerwear.

"Where are you going?"

"Milk. We need milk," I say.

"Right, well, don't be long. We don't have time to lose—oh, and El, make sure it's skimmed."

Chapter 11

Ellie

A THIN LAYER OF sweat covers my whole body as I stop trembling. Am I dreaming? I'm not sure—at least, I don't think I am, anyway. Not anymore.

My legs are tangled in my duvet, and I feel ... hot, and ... satisfied. Like I've just—oh, my God—I didn't, did I?

I tentatively reach out to pat the stretch of bed next to me and when my fingers find nothing but the cotton fitted sheet, I exhale in relief.

I'm alone.

But that must mean...

I kick off the quilt and roll onto my back, willing myself to wake up properly. But the dream still clings to me—so vivid it plays out in front of my eyes. Mike's face, smiling back at me as I—

No.

Don't think about it.

It was a dream.

Just a dream.

But my eyelids feel heavy. So very heavy. They droop closed and his face, and his hands—rough and huge—slip back into view as he grips my hips. I'm peering down at him, my eyes roaming over his skin, toned and bruised in patches. There's a yellowy-purple mark on his right rib that I want to touch ... I want to soothe.

But I can't.

He's just out of reach even though he's beneath me, and the more I try, the further he seems to move away.

"Does your bruise hurt?" I say.

Not really sure why I'm asking such a dumb question, but he doesn't answer anyway. He laughs instead. A sound so real that when I force my eyes open, I still hear it, hung in the air like it's last night all over again.

But it's not last night. It's Sunday night and I'm alone in bed having a sex dream about Mike—except there's no way I should be having a sex dream about Mike.

But I did.

The more I try to abandon the memory, the more it sticks. Replaying, almost in slow motion: his lips on mine, his hands ... that feeling in the pit of my abdomen that sort of simulates butterflies but also doesn't. It twists, unsettles.

I don't know if it's anticipation or regret.

Maybe both.

Maybe neither.

My eyes flutter closed, and the dream resurfaces.

I'm stuck in a limbo of wanting to experience it again but also not wanting to either. And for the third time, I pry my eyes open, but instead of staring up at the ceiling, I sit up and shake my head.

My phone tells me that it's close to midnight, which means there's at least seven more hours of turmoil. Seven more hours of—wait.

My mind races, re-tracing the moments before I woke. That feeling. That sensation which had me shivering with satisfaction. I mean, it's never happened before, but that doesn't mean it's not normal ... right?

I unlock my phone and tap the icon for the search engine. Letting my fingers do all the work.

'Is it normal to have an orgasm in your sleep?'

My heart thumps harder as I wait for the results to load because if it isn't normal, then I need to stop sleeping; that's my only solution.

... an orgasm while asleep, also known as a nocturnal orgasm or sleep orgasm ... common phenomenon ... particularly during periods of sexual arousal or when not sexually active.

Well, I guess that explains it.

A conclusion that it probably wasn't anything to do with Mike and more to do with the fact that it's been a while since I've had sex or even a self-induced orgasm.

Relieved, I toss my phone down on the bed next to me, and roll over, settling myself back into position to fall asleep.

I lay for a few moments, afraid to close my eyes out of fear that I'll relive the dream all over again.

But I don't need to close my eyes to see him, stretched out on the bed while I straddle his thighs—my imagination is consumed. Except, in this vision, I'm not shying away like I typically would, nor am I insisting I keep my bra on. I'm fully naked—exposed. And there's an encouraging look on his face as he takes in every inch of me.

He's enjoying himself.

He smiles at me, and my eyes are drawn to a small scar near his lip. Did he always have this scar, is it new?

The mental image of Mike I've conjured has me sitting back up in bed and reaching for my phone—tapping his name into the search engine, curiosity getting the better of me; why it matters is a mystery.

My heart flutters when the results load and his entry on the hockey database website returns a mugshot next to a snapshot of him in his hockey gear, mid-skate.

Okay, so I wasn't imagining the scar on his lip. I got an up-close look at it last night when we were in my kitchen ... faces together and vulnerabilities exposed.

It starts on his lower lip and travels down towards his chin, disappearing under the stubble of his beard.

The more I think about it, the more I wish I'd asked him how he got it. How did he get it?

Before I realise what I'm doing, I've moved to the social media page of his hockey team, set on finding the 'before the scar' moment—curious to know if there's a point in time I can identify.

As I cycle through the photos, I take in his expression on each one in turn as I study the photo for the scar. I guess I never realised how different he looks when he's concentrating. I mean, he's usually good looking, but there's something about the way his eyes focus, like they're brighter somehow, that makes him appear more ... something.

A video loads next, and I spot the coppery-brown of Mike's hair.

There's a section of the video where he takes his helmet off and runs his fingers through his hair and I feel my own fingertips tingling with wonder. Is his hair soft or coarse? And most importantly, why do I care?

I shake the thought away, but it lingers—especially as the next clip plays and a warmth spreads through my chest.

A clip of him during a practice session—scar present and accounted for. There's a microphone cabled into his jersey or something because everything he says is audible, and I take several minutes to realise I'm smiling along with the people he's interacting with. He's goofy, but everyone seems to love it. Just like the Mike I remember from school—laughing, joking, completely in his element.

But then my eyes drift down to the comments section beneath the video, and the warmth in my chest fades.

86 comments.

And none of them are talking about the clip. They're all asking the same thing: if anyone knows why something got deleted on the forum. Comment after comment, people are speculating about what was said—but it's the one posted just twenty minutes ago that makes my stomach drop.

'Forget that ... have you seen what's on there now?'

I load up the fan forum in record time, immediately seeing what they were referring to; a new forum post.

Bettsy the playboy.

My blood thumps a little harder as I notice the username 'IlovetoPuck29'.

Subject: Bettsy the Playboy

I just wanted 2 come on here 2 WARN every1 about Michael Betts (no. 6!!!) again bc this man is such a walking red flag.

The guy thinks a home cooked meal is plain pasta and a side of ketchup ... I mean... no thx mate. And what made the whole thing worse? He's obsessed with himself. Thinks he's Gods gift to women. He spent the whole nite watching hockey highlights of himself.

What makes this even more tragic is his attachment issues. He said that he cant commit bcuz he's 'married to the game' and he's too busy focusing on his abs to put any time into having a gf. But ... get this... he took my friend out a week later 2 make me jealous and she even said he denied going out wiv me before.

STAY AWAY!!! The only player he is, is an actual player not a hockey player.

I roll my eyes. And I'm not sure if it's because of the dream or the fact that I'm delirious from exhaustion, but a swell of emotion builds inside me and before I can think through the consequences, I'm clicking the 'create an account' button intending to have my say.

Turns out, all I need is an email address, a screen name and to answer the question 'who is the current captain' which is a straightforward thing to find out thanks to our old friend, Google.

I draft a reply to the original poster, demanding concrete evidence and begging the general populous of the forum to consider the post at length for what it is—a pile of crap. And, for good measure, I add a hashtag: '#justiceforBettsy'.

I stare at my draft for several minutes, wondering if I should post it or if I should keep myself out of the drama, but the seconds tick away and the compulsion I have to get involved only grows.

I count to three.

And then I hit 'post'.

EVER HAD ONE OF those rare moments where everything goes your way? Yeah, me neither, because I'm usually a magnet for crap and drama. Though imagine my delight on Monday morning—still recovering from a booze-heavy Saturday—when I learned Langer was sick, delaying defensive sessions until Wednesday.

Honestly, I could kiss the guy. Something I never thought I'd be saying. But I only allow myself a second to dwell on that, because deep down, I'm still bubbling with rage about the fact he's texting Ellie.

Ellie.

"How are your nerves?" Danny says, as we suit up.

I push my anger aside as I switch to focus mode.

"Alright, yeah," I say. My tone has an air of confidence which it has no business having.

I'm positive I can manage whatever today throws at me, especially after Coach gave me a rundown of what to expect yesterday.

Luckily, the shower I took before stopping by the rink had washed away enough of the hangover to grant me a free pass from a lecture he would have, no doubt, given me. And when I arrived at the hotel, far later than I would have liked, I collapsed into bed and passed out until my alarm went off at six this morning, feeling considerably fresher.

But as I look at Danny, his face a pale shade of grey, I conclude that he's not feeling all that fresh.

He looks like he's about to puke into his lid as he sits down next to me. If I didn't know any better, I'd assume he'd eaten the same thing as Langer.

I search my mind for something to say to make things better.

Danny and I are the same age, and we've both been waiting for this opportunity for as long as we can remember. For a period, we both played on the U18 team, but there was a lot of competition for positions at the next level. Ultimately, we both know this is likely going to be our only chance to bag a permanent spot on the adult roster.

"We've got this. You'll be fine," I say, almost pathetically.

"Yeah. Fine. Absolutely fine," he says, keeping his head angled towards the gap between his knees.

I've known Danny long enough to know he's the opposite of fine. But I've also known him long enough to know he wouldn't want me pressing him. He's the type of guy who keeps himself to himself from a feelings perspective.

"You know, there's still time to relieve some of the stress, if you know what I mean." I wag my brows at him, trying to lighten the mood.

He scoffs.

"Still on your drought?" he asks.

"Of course," I grin.

I googled the whole 'no sex or personal time' thing and by all accounts, the body just absorbs back what it doesn't expel—but I'm feeling it. I have this strict rule against happy endings before games or practices, but I know later I'll be desperate for a release.

Before I can stop my sub-conscious, it's playing out a scenario where I'm texting Ellie, asking what she's doing.

I can see her now, scowling and rolling her eyes—which only serves to get me a little more excited.

I have to force myself to think of something else—anything else.

And the GM pings to the forefront of my mind and, thankfully, kills the excitement. Instead, I'm lumbered with the memory of the conversation I had with him, then the follow-up I had with Vicky—something that dominated my thinking space during the drive here last night.

"Hey, do you know anyone who makes websites?" I ask Danny, remembering the trail of thought I led myself down last night.

Danny cocks a brow at me.

"Websites? You're so random at times."

"Yeah, websites. You know, a set of related webpages typically used to provide information."

Danny blinks at me. "I know what a website is, you idiot, but why? Are you scheming something?"

"Nah, nothing—just wondering ... I know someone who needs one, and I just thought you may know someone," I say.

"Of course, I know someone, and so do you," he says.

I glare at him, puzzled, and he stares right back at me, as if he's waiting for the metaphorical penny to drop.

"Jenna, you dull bastard."

Jenna? Well, why the hell didn't I think of her? She's decent at it too, but—I audibly gasp, causing Danny to raise both his eyebrows.

"What?" he says.

"Jenna does websites and Vicky does social—"

"What the fuck is going on with you?" he asks.

But we get a five-minute warning, killing the conversation.

Danny stands up, reaching to grab his gloves and I reach for my own pair, slipping my hands inside and flexing my fingers.

"You'll get used to them," says Callum Greer, the Team GB starting goalie, stopping behind me.

Even though the guy plays for the worst team in the league, he's a pretty decent guy. I've known him for years. He's the same height as me, a little over six-two, but he easily has another ten kilos on me—all muscle. I make a mental note to see what he does in the gym next time the opportunity presents itself.

"How's it going, boys?" he says. "Looking forward to camp?"

"I guess you could say that, yeah," I say.

"Honestly, you've got nothing to worry about," Greer says, stretching his arms above his head. "Hey, what's going on with that gossip mill then, Betts? Any idea who it is?"

I scoff. "Well, I think so, but can't prove anything."

"Honestly, some people have nothing better to do. But at least there's someone on your side now. Have you seen the hashtag they've got going? 'Justice for Bettsy'?"

He smirks, as my jaw drops open.

"What?"

"Have you not seen?" Greer moves back to his cubby, telling me he's going to grab his phone. He wades back over moments later, his eyes fixed on his screen. "See, here it is."

He extends his phone and I pull my right hand out of my glove, taking it from him.

There's a new post from Rochelle, but it's one of the replies to that post which has my attention.

Posted by: StrugglingtoSleep1
Subject: RE: Bettsy the Playboy

Wow. Incredible journalism. Really compelling evidence. A man who eats plain pasta with ketchup? Unforgivable. Someone call the food police ... immediately!!!!

I mean, I get it. He's a hockey player, not a Michelin-star chef. But let's be honest—this whole post screams 'bitter ex with a vendetta' more than 'public service announcement'.

What is your problem? He told you he wasn't looking for a relationship and then you got mad when he didn't commit?

Make it make sense.

And you're telling me Bettsy, a guy who literally plays for a living, watches hockey highlights of himself to understand his opponent? Groundbreaking stuff. Honestly. Next, you'll be exposing him for owning multiple sticks and drinking protein shakes. The horror!!!

If Bettsy's such a 'walking red flag', then why are you still obsessing over him? Do you have nothing else do to?

I urge people to consider the integrity of this post and the poster ... where is the evidence? Because all I read was a compiled pile of crap.

#JusticeForBettsy

A grin slips over my face—I can't help it, it's brilliant ... aside from the fact there're people out there who think I like ketchup, let alone with pasta.

I read over the last paragraph several times, revelling in the moment, though a small part of me wonders who it is and why they feel compelled to jump to my defence.

I skim over the replies, but before I can read those properly, the door to the dressing room opens and Greer whips his phone away in a flash.

The coaching staff file in and the chatter dies down as every single guy looks in their direction. They stand in a line, each surveying the room in turn.

Coach Harris catches my eye. He jerks his head in the door's direction, gesturing for me to follow him. The amusement of the forum reply dies quickly, replaced with discomfort.

What does he want? Why do I need to be singled out?

I let all the possible outcomes cycle through my mind before realising he's waiting for me, and with a nudge from Danny, I force my legs to move.

Chapter 12

Bettsy

I WASN'T A TROUBLEMAKER in school, I just didn't listen.

I was more interested in making people laugh and keeping my friends entertained. They used to feed off me, join in with my jokes—that sort of thing, which used to cause an influx of laughter at the back of the classroom. Most of the time, that behaviour earned me a free trip to the headteacher's office for disturbing the peace.

I can feel it now—the bubbling anxiety in my stomach as I stood waiting to be called inside the head's bland, burgundy-walled office. I always remember wondering who in their right mind would pick that shade of wall paint. That, coupled with the freezing temperature, made for a bad time—just like now.

The same dread as I follow Coach Harris out of the dressing room and into the tunnel—and just like the thirteen-year-old me, I brace myself for a verbal beating on the basis I've done something wrong.

I'm like a compressed spring.

Is he gearing up to tell me to go home? Does he want me to give him a full rundown of the online activity? I can't be sure. I half expect him to lead me to his office or something, but he doesn't. He leans his shoulder against the wall directly outside the dressing room and sets his eyes on me, a neutral expression on his face that's unreadable.

"Betts—how are we feeling?"

He sounds casual and airy—and it feels ... I don't know ... off?

All I take from it is the clarity that this isn't just a friendly chat.

I clear my throat.

"Good, thanks, Coach. Ready for today."

He nods before straightening up, the logo on his baseball cap eye-level with me.

"I'm glad to hear it. I've had my eye on you for several seasons now. Tell me, what changed for you this year?"

I shift my weight, trying to keep my knees bent slightly so I don't tower over him too much.

"Focus, Coach. And a captain set on giving me space to guide and support our rookie D-man. It was a change that made me see things a little differently—it inspired me to do better. Lead by example."

Coach watches me, his expression unchanged, and I wonder if he's seeing through my bullshit—though it's not bullshit at all. Johnny did help. Johnny made a difference. And I'm not lying when I say Cap is the reason that I'm standing here today.

After what feels like an eternity, he nods.

"Look, let's cut to the chase here. Your stats don't lie. I know a good defenceman when I see one—and I know a great defenceman when I spot one of those too.

"My gut feeling is you're my guy. You're strong, gritty when you need to be, you're careful with the puck—and you can read the play well too. I'm impressed by your ability to shut down one-on-one situations—not to mention your shot blocking.

"But I won't keep blowing smoke up your ass. We both know this isn't all about hockey. The off-ice stuff is just as important as the work you put in out there." He gestures towards the ice. "But all this crap online? I've seen it before—a little gossip taking on a life of its own, and before we know it, it's affecting your game.

"I want your skills, but I need someone who's committed. Stable. Dependable. Not easily distracted by all that stuff. I need someone who can show me he's dedicated. I don't need a wannabe star who's only after a good time and thinking with his…"

My pulse thumps in my ears.

What can I say to that?

His expression remains unchanged, and I dig deep to figure out the correct response … I need something that will re-enforce my commitment. I need to tell him something that will give him confidence in my loyalty. I need…

"I get it," I say. "Honestly, I do—" I bite my lip, weighing my next words carefully.

The silence that hangs between us is palpable. I'm about to give him some crap about my ongoing commitment to the ice, but that's not what he wants to hear. I can feel it. It's obvious.

"I—" I swallow, and before I can stop myself, it's out. "My wife isn't overly impressed with the stuff online, either. We're trying to tune it out and focus on what matters."

My words seem to float in the air. I can almost see them, like a string of letters moving in slow-motion from my mouth to his ears.

My wife.

What the fuck did I just say?

The neutral expression he's been hanging on to since we left the dressing room threatens to change. The left side of his mouth twitches, then he sort of half-smiles before breaking out in a full-blown grin.

"Wife? I didn't know you were married, Betts." His eyes brighten as he beams at me. "Lopez said you were between relationships or something. I mean—I didn't—"

Shit.

Just hand me the shovel and I'll keep digging.

The GM was probably trying to do the right thing by keeping it vague—and now I've fucked it.

I scrape every corner of my mind to come up with something. Maybe if I burst out into laugher Coach will see the funny side of it—but apparently, I'm on a roll with the bullshit today.

"She's a private person, likes to keep herself to herself," I say. "We've not been married for long, but we're childhood sweethearts, you know? Sort of went our own ways until..." I force a grin, waving my hand dismissively, "yeah, you don't need to hear about it."

Coach's smile fades.

"So, this stuff online? A bitter ex, I take it?"

I take the bait. "Yeah, and there's no truth to it, Coach."

He studies me for a moment before his grin returns.

"What a fucking relief—honestly. I thought you were one of these partying-types but this—this has made things a load better. Maybe you should invite Mrs Betts along to the social event next month? Assuming you get to stick around."

He throws me a wink, and I die a little inside.

Mrs Betts. And we both know he's not talking about my mam.

But there's no time to worry about that right now, because there's another pressing issue I need to take care of first.

Ellie.

Ellie's going to kill me.

And the thought of telling her has me shifting all my effort into standing still, because I feel like I'm about to faint.

She's going to fucking kill me.

"Right," Coach says, pulling me away from my spiral. "Let's get started. See you on the ice."

He steps around me, pushing open the door to the dressing room. He shouts something inside and moments later, the thudding of multiple pairs of skates on the move hits my ears.

What the fuck have I done?

I stare at the floor beneath my skates, willing the ground to open and let me fall inside. But a movement from behind me snaps my attention upwards and I twist my head to spot Danny coming to a stop.

"Is everything okay?" he says, slapping me on the back.

I turn on the spot, facing him, and he visibly winces.

"Christ—you look like you've shit yourself. What did Coach say?"

I swallow down the lump rising in my throat, but it doesn't go away.

"Mate?" Danny prompts.

I shake my head, re-jigging my focus back on my friend.

"Yeah. Everything's fine," I say.

"Right. Well—"

I feel like I'm going to throw up.

"Betts, are you sure you're okay?" Danny says.

I gulp in a lungful of air.

"If I tell you something—you've got to promise me you won't tell another soul. Yeah?" I say.

"Okay. You're freaking me out. What's going on?" Danny asks, narrowing his eyes.

"I—I've fucked up. Big time."

He frowns. "It can't be that bad, can it?"

I swallow hard before telling Danny everything.

"Hey, Kitch. Have you missed me?"

Mike Betts' sing-song voice vibrates through my car speakers, causing me to gasp in panic.

Does he know? Does he somehow know about my online antics?

I decide the best thing I can do is remain passive—act like everything is how it was before he spent the night in my bed. Although I was hoping to get the chance to call him out for changing Rick's name to 'Prick' in my phone contacts, I decide against it.

"What do you want?" I ask, trying to keep my tone level.

"I'm great, thanks, I appreciate you asking—listen, don't suppose you've got my wallet, have you? I'm hoping it's in your car or something. The trousers I had on last weekend were crap and—"

"How has it taken you this long to notice you haven't had your wallet?" I ask.

"I didn't need it—I use my phone to pay for stuff, but I remembered I had a winning scratch card tucked in my wallet and ... I guess I'm feeling lucky. I want to cash it in and get a fresh one."

"I'll have to check," I say. "I'm driving at the moment."

"Oh, cool—been anywhere nice?"

I pause, tempted to open up about my social life—but I stop myself. I'm not sure where we stand, and I don't want to assume we're friends just because we've had one weird night and a few decent conversations.

"Not really," I say. "But I'll look for your wallet when I stop."

"Cheers. If you find it, could you text me and let me know? I can swing around and pick it up."

We hang up and I make it back to my place, climbing out of my car and crouching down to survey the footwell and the underside of the driver's seat. And alas, Mike's wallet has indeed wedged itself underneath. How I never noticed it before is beyond me.

I pull up his number from my last called list and drop him a text.

Ellie

Got your wallet.

He replies instantly.

Mike

Great, thanks. Shall I come get it?

I consider it for a moment before deciding it's not a good idea to have Mike over again, purely because I still have around half a bottle of Macallen left and after last time...

I tap out a reply.

Ellie

I can drop it off.

And as quick as a flash, he sends me his live location.

I climb back into the driver's seat, set the sat nav, and immediately start questioning my life choices.

The drive only takes fifteen minutes, and I spend all 900 seconds trying not to think about a half-naked Mike in my bed. I do such a terrible job, my hands are practically shaking as I pull up outside the large, detached house.

I count at least four cars on the driveway, and I wonder if I can safely make it to the front door and back with no one noticing. The plan, I quickly conclude, is formed of four simple steps: get out of the car, post the wallet through the letterbox, get back in the car and drive away, dignity intact.

But Mike has other ideas.

As soon as I reach for the handle of the drivers' door, the front door to number ten flings open and Mike jogs out like he was waiting for me.

Okay, plan 'B'...

I'll wind down my window and hold out the wallet for him to take. That way, the interaction is minimal, and he'll never guess I've been having sex dreams about him.

I watch as he approaches the car and I wait until the last second to run with the plan, winding down the window and stretching my arm out, wallet in hand.

I can't even look at him. I can't even...

"Thanks, Kitch," he says. "I owe you one."

He takes his wallet and backs away from the car. Then I breathe a sigh of relief.

I wind my window back up, desperate for the safety of my car as I keep my eyes on the road ahead.

Out of the corner of my eye, I spot him walking several paces before stopping, turning back towards my car.

Crap.

He moves closer and taps on the window.

I brace myself.

"Yeah?" I say, opening the window.

"Hey, sorry to be cheeky, but you wouldn't mind giving me a ride to the petrol station and back, would you? I want to cash in my winnings."

He pulls out the winning scratch card and waves it in the air.

"Uh, there're like four cars on your drive—"

"Yeah, but mine is cold and ... umm ... you know what? Don't worry. I could do with the fresh air. Thanks for bringing this over." He taps the front of his wallet before slipping it into the pouch of his hoodie, then he turns away, pulling his hood up over his head.

Something's not right.

I'm not overly familiar with Mike on a typical day, but he's usually self-assured and confident and during the minimal interaction I've had with him, I can see he's acting weird—and I genuinely don't think it's got anything to do with me and my smutty dreams. It's as if he's on edge or something ...

I ponder it for a moment before deciding it's not my problem—it has nothing to do with me at all.

I shift my car into gear and move to release my handbrake, but instead of pulling away and driving off into the night, I sit there, still.

Why the hell can't I drive away?

I take a breath, then push myself to release the clutch, but after a second of the car creeping forward, I stop again and re-engage the handbrake.

Drive away, Ellie. Drive away.

But I don't.

There's a tightness in my chest, and as I release the handbrake to pull off again, I creep along the pavement next to a speed-walking Mike instead.

I wind the window down, my mind telling me one thing and my body doing another in the ultimate act of betrayal.

"Get in," I say.

And he doesn't need to be asked twice. He's like a dog returning with a ball to be thrown again, jogging around the back of my car and opening the passenger door with enthusiasm.

I'm quick to move the 'to go' box I got from the restaurant earlier so he can climb in.

"Oh, this is fancy," he says, eyeing the box that's now sitting precariously on my dashboard. "Anything decent?"

"Which way?"

He shows me which direction to take while reaching for the box so he can peer inside, a noise of disapproval rumbling from his throat.

"You had a salad to go?" he says. "A fucking salad?"

"I wasn't feeling it," I say.

"I'm not surprised. No one feels a salad," he says.

"I didn't want anything heavy."

I don't go into detail about my pre-wedding-that's-not-my-wedding diet, but in all honesty, ever since Kathryn called me out, I've been overly conscious about it—and having dinner with her and her friends meant I had eyes on me the entire evening.

"Did you have a date with Langer?" he says in a prickly tone, keeping his eyes on the passing scenery.

"No. Besides, I told you ... it's social."

I can't be sure, but I'm half convinced he exhales a heavy breath. He doesn't say anything, simply points towards the Shell garage, which comes into view as I round a corner.

I pull onto the forecourt, and he hops out, leaving the box of salad on my dashboard.

I tell myself not to look. That I don't care. That I'm just waiting.

But I can't pull my eyes away. I watch him right up to the point of disappearing inside, dragging my eyes to my phone, tapping at the screen like I've suddenly remembered something urgent because there's no way he can catch me staring when he comes back.

My car door opens a few moments later, and he climbs inside, a waft of whatever scent he's wearing forcing me to hold my breath.

"Got you something," he says, dumping a pile of chocolate bars into the centre console.

"What're those for?" I ask.

"It's criminal not to buy anything for the driver when you run into a petrol station. And since I don't know what your favourite is, I got a selection."

My stomach rumbles in excitement, but I shift my attention away from the treats.

"And those?" I ask, eyeing a wad of scratch cards.

Mike grins.

"If I win a fiver or less, I reinvest. Here—have three on me. Maybe you'll get lucky."

He tears three cards off and passes them over, then digs around in his wallet for a penny, dropping it into my free hand.

"I don't even remember the last time I played a scratch card," I say, peering at the cards.

"I don't do them often—for the record. My roommate, Hutch, got me one as a celebration thing for getting selected for the preliminary roster and it was a winner."

He plucks another penny from the coin compartment of his wallet and gets to work scratching, and I do the same, brushing the silver dust off my lap as I go.

"Nothing here," he says after a silent minute. "Anything for you?"

"Two '£2's' and ... nothing," I say, handing him back the winners.

"Keep them," he says. "Maybe you'll get a bigger prize next time."

"I—"

"Keep them, Kitch. See it as a thank you for returning my wallet."

"Thanks. I appreciate it," I say.

Mike leans forward, reaching for a bar of chocolate.

"Which one do you want?"

My stomach rumbles with excitement, but I shake my head.

"I'm good, thanks."

"Really? Are you sure?"

"I'm on a wedding diet," I admit. "For my sister's wedding—"

"I fail to see what that's got to do with you. You don't need to diet, anyway."

I can feel my face growing hot, so I switch up the conversation, wondering if I can shift the topic away from me—desperate not to give anything away.

"How's this week been at camp?" I ask.

Mike scoffs, swallowing before he answers. "Fine, I guess."

"Okay, good," I say.

"Your boyfriend didn't turn up until Wednesday, but I guess you already knew that."

The way he says 'boyfriend' has me snapping my head in his direction.

"He's not my—"

"Yeah, yeah."

But he shifts uncomfortably in his seat, moving his attention to a plastic carrier bag drifting across the forecourt in the breeze as he stuffs his empty chocolate wrapper into the pocket of his hoodie.

Something definitely isn't right. And I have a feeling it's nothing to do with Rick Langdon.

"Are you sure everything's okay? With camp and—?"

"The outcome is tomorrow," he says, turning his attention to his nails this time.

"Well, that's good, right?"

"Yeah, I hope so. They typically don't make a final roster decision until after the playoffs but Coach said they're doing things a little differently this year."

"Even better then, right?"

"I guess," he shrugs. "But—"

"But?" I prompt, turning in my seat to face him.

I study his expression but it's like trying to read a badly drawn map. Impossible and confusing.

"Is this something to do with the wedding certificate? Did you find it?" My voice trembles, but he huffs, rubbing his hands over his face before tentatively turning towards me.

"Nah, it's not that—I still haven't had a chance to look yet but ... I need to ask a favour."

"A favour?"

I glare at him, racking my brain. What could he want from me? A red flag whips in the wind when he doesn't look at me. He keeps his attention fixed on the forecourt straight ahead.

"Mike?"

But then his eyes meet mine and a knot forms in my stomach.

I've never seen him like this before. Serious ... uncertain. And he looks like he's about to pass out.

"Kitch—hear me out, yeah?"

Chapter 13

"Kitch—hear me out, yeah?"

"Is everything okay?" I ask.

But the way he's acting—the nerves, the hesitation—tells me everything is far from okay.

This is something huge.

He stares straight ahead for a few more seconds, then flicks a glance at me—only to retreat toward the forecourt when our eyes meet.

"Fuck," he mutters, exhaling. He's jiggling his leg on the spot, making the car rock slightly as he shifts in his seat.

"Mike?"

"So, I ... I sort of—damn." He pauses, swallows, then says, "I need you to be my wife."

Silence fills the car. Mike freezes. The lull stretches, deafening, before I realise I've stopped breathing—a breath lodged in my throat.

I stare at him in disbelief, because there's no way I heard him correctly.

There's no way.

"What?" I squeak, my voice in a pitch I wasn't expecting. "You—what?"

He runs his palms over his thighs, focusing on the footwell of the passenger seat. "I need you to be my wife," he says. "I know you, well, I guess, officially are, but I sort of told my Coach I had a wife and—"

"This is a joke, right?" I say, cutting him off.

He leans forward, elbows resting on his legs as he finally turns to look at me.

I see it. It's written all over his face.

He's not kidding.

He's actually not kidding.

"C'mon, Kitch. All you've got to do is come to a few social events, show your face around the scene a little, hang off my arm ... that sort of stuff. Once I'm embedded into the team, we can 'split'." He air-quotes with his fingers.

"H-hang off your arm?" I say.

"You know, be seen with me, so people think it's legit."

I'm waiting for him to smirk, laugh, tell me he's kidding after all, and we can conclude he's an excellent liar.

But he doesn't. He's serious.

On what planet does he think this is a good idea?

"On what planet do you think this is a good idea?" I say.

"It makes sense, don't you think? I mean, we're probably married for real and I..."

I gape at him and he stops talking. Closing his mouth and tightening his jaw.

"Is this all a joke to you?" I say. "Is this fucked up scenario one big joke? This is my life, Mike. My. Life."

I feel humiliated. The thought of this sham marriage was bad enough, but him wanting to use it for his own gain? How would that make me look if anyone was to find out? Because there's no way I could actively be 'hanging off his arm' and have no one ask questions. Kathryn would go crazy for one.

"No, I didn't mean for it to sound like that. Of course it's not, it's just—"

"No," I say bluntly.

"No? Is that a no to my proposal or no to it making sense?" he says.

"No. It's a no. Full stop. A no. Two nos."

"Shit," he says, running a hand through his hair. "This isn't ideal."

My eyebrows shoot upward. There's no way he thought I was going to agree, was there?

"I've already sort of mentioned you to Coach," he says.

I purse my lips as I close my eyes, willing myself to breathe. Willing myself to stay calm.

"You've already 'sort of' mentioned me to your Coach?" I say, trying to make it make sense.

"I—" He bites his lip, and that scar leading down to this chin distorts; I can't help staring at it. "All this stuff online started getting some of the leadership team at my club and Team GB talking. The general manager of my club sort of hinted at me to figure it out, demonstrate that I'm a serious guy … that sort of thing, and then—" He throws his head back on the headrest, covering his face with his hands, "—it just sort of happened, I guess. The Team GB Coach was talking about being committed and stuff and I sort of blurted out something about my wife and us being childhood sweethearts … and he looked relieved."

"He looked relieved?" I say, letting my mouth hang open.

"He thought I was one of the partying types—and I think it's given him a good reason to pick me tomorrow. I think I'm in with a chance here, Kitch."

"But you are the partying type. And I've got a half empty bottle of Macallen to prove it," I counter.

"Which I enjoyed with my wife," he deadpans.

My stoney-faced glare bores into him. Then I see the sadness slip over his face.

"You're going to have to think of a way out of this, Mike. Because there's no way in hell this is happening."

"What's the big deal? All you need to do is ..."

"Hang off your arm? You mentioned that already. The big deal is ... this is my life. I'm not here for you to play with and use and—"

"Wait, is this about Langer?" Disgust creeps across his face as his expression turns sour. "Are you into him?"

"No but if it was, it'd be none of your business," I say. "This has nothing to do with Rick and everything to do with you using me. Find someone else to hang off your arm—I'm pretty sure you can pay someone these days."

"Could I not—"

"No," I snap, pre-empting his question.

"Okay, okay ... what if I get you a fancy ring to wear—one of those bridal sets? The extravagant ones," he says.

"What part of 'no' don't you understand?"

"What if I—"

"Mike. Stop it. You're not buying me anything. This is completely ridiculous. You'll have to come clean and tell your coach. Tell him you made a mistake."

Mike nibbles his thumb nail. "Nah, I don't think he'd like that."

"Well, that's not my problem."

He rubs his eyes before groaning into his hands. "This is a fucking nightmare."

"I'm sorry that you've got yourself in such a situation, but it's—"

"Yeah, yeah ... not your problem. I get it. But will you at least think about it?"

"No."

"Okay, okay," Mike says, "what if there was something in it for you?"

"Still, no."

I turn back to the steering wheel and start the engine of my car, throwing it into gear before I speed off the forecourt.

Luckily, we're not all that far from his parents' house.

My tyres screech as I come to a halt outside, and I flash Mike the angriest of looks.

"So, will you?" he says, reaching for the door handle.

"I already told you, no," I say.

"I mean think about it. Will you at least think about it?"

"Mike—"

"What if—"

"No," I snap.

And he nods once before opening the door and stepping onto the pavement.

Betsy

I HARDLY SLEPT LAST night, though not through lack of trying.

Usually, I lie down, close my eyes and count back from one hundred, drifting off somewhere after the seventies—I never remember, and I guess that's the point. Last night I reached zero. Three times. My mind reeling over the conversation I had with Ellie several hours ago.

She said no. Not maybe, not let me think about it—just flat-out, clear as day, no.

Though what was I expecting? For her to leap into my arms and declare her unwavering attraction for me?

I wish.

Eventually, I gave up and went for a walk. The walk turned into a jog, the jog turned into a 3 a.m. stop at a twenty-four-hour fast-food place, where I ate too much beige food and regretted all my life choices, including the lie I told Coach.

What the hell was I thinking? Obviously I wasn't, but that never stops me. Ever. The opportunity to see her again thanks to my missing wallet blown into smithereens.

Now not only does my head reel from my conversation with Ellie, but my stomach feels bloated and heavy from the excess of carbs.

I feel like shit in every way.

The only good thing to come from today is the off-ice activity.

A morning of sitting in the media room with the coaching staff before we find out the outcome of the roster—apparently, they don't usually announce it until the post-season, but something has driven a change in the plan which means it's even more of an issue that Ellie said no.

It buys me no time.

I had it in my head that Ellie would agree, and Coach would know nothing about my lie. But alas, now I'm hoping he tells me I haven't made the team, so I needn't worry about living up to the ruse of being married to a willing wife.

I make it down to breakfast twenty minutes earlier than usual, all thanks to Danny and his plea to meet in the usual spot for a catch up before the rest of the guys get here. Honestly, I don't know when he became such a nosey bastard, but here we are.

"Well, how did it go?" Danny says before I've had a chance to sink down into the seat opposite him.

He looks fresh, like he had an early-morning gym session and sauna, taking full advantage of the hotel facilities. His baseball cap is on the table next to his mug, already full to the brim with tea.

"Let me ask you this—how do you think it went?"

I drop into the seat opposite him and reach for the cafetière of dark roast, grateful that he at least saw the sense to order it for me.

We're sitting at a table next to the window overlooking the golf course, and typically, we'd spend ten minutes in silence, waiting for the caffeine to kick in while watching the maintenance guys outside. But today, I'm staring at Danny, trying to figure out what he's going to say next.

"She declared her undying love and wondered why you didn't ask sooner?" Danny takes a gulp of his tea before grinning like a cartoon cat.

"I'll keep it simple. She said no."

I finish making my drink before cupping the mug in both hands; I take a sip.

"Shit. What are you going to do?" he says.

"What do you think I'm going to do?" I reply.

Danny studies me for a moment before offering a suggestion.

"Find someone else?"

"No," I scoff. "I'm going to persuade her. It's the only thing I can do. I was thinking ... there must be something I can do to tip her decision the other way."

"It's a big ask, though—moving in with you and—"

I bite my lip and shift my attention to the lawn outside.

"Shit," Danny says. "You didn't tell her that part of your plan, did you?"

I watch a maintenance guy speeding over the course on a golf buggy, because I know if I make eye contact with Danny, I'll probably end up crying or something.

I'm pathetic.

"You're right. I'm never going to be able to persuade her. I need a new plan—assuming I get picked," I say, turning back towards him but keeping my eyes on the crisp white tablecloth.

Danny sets his mug down. "Honestly, if someone asked me to place a bet on who, from our team, would get themselves into this sort of situation, I'd always say you. One hundred per cent ... every single time."

"Yeah, well—" I shrug, because sadly, he's right. This is the type of thing I do. I fuck up, and instead of holding my hands up and surrendering, I insist on jumping into the hole I've dug and making it bigger. So big I can't climb out.

I take a mouthful of coffee as I draft a plan 'B' in my head.

It's simple, really. All I need is a willing female who will pretend to be my wife for the sake of a few months. Why is it so difficult?

"Hey, do you think Prez would let me borrow Jen?" I ask, letting my leg jiggle under the table a little harder.

Danny's eyes widen as I'm forced to look at him.

"You're not all there, mate. Even if he said yes, which he wouldn't—everyone knows Jen. She's been doing that iPad stuff around the league. If you rock up with Jen on your arm, people will know you're full of shit more than they already think ... or that you're a serial girlfriend—or in this case, wife—stealer."

I take another gulp of coffee, racking my brain for anything—but all that plays out in my mind is me, standing in front of Prez, asking him if I can borrow his wife.

It's all I've got. I don't want to ask Jen. I mean she's hot but she's not Ellie.

"I—"

"She's doing something with the players' association website, anyway—besides, even if Prez said yes, which, let me reiterate, he won't … Jen would still have to agree."

But Danny's mention of a website has a lightbulb illuminating in my head. Why didn't I think of this earlier?

"I have an idea," I say, in an almost comical 'eureka' moment.

Danny stares at me, a blank expression on his face.

And I open my mouth to fill him in when my phone vibrates against my leg.

I dip into my pocket, checking the screen to see none other than Vicky Koenig's name. And just like that, I've got idea number two.

I'm just about to answer the call when the rest of the guys filter into the breakfast room and I figure the chances of getting overheard are high.

I hit decline and put my phone away, sliding my chair back to make use of the buffet before we leave.

"Want anything?" I ask Danny.

He shakes his head, so I make my way to servery, joining a small queue that's forming for the hot food.

We've had breakfast in this room all week and honestly, the food is amazing. If I could get away with sneaking in here every morning, I would.

Despite my junk fest last night, I'm starving now I can smell the goodness. I'm so focused on the egg station, I don't even realise Greer has stopped behind me.

"I'm surprised Langer's even standing after last night," he says, chuckling to himself.

I turn to see Greer's attention is fixed on the entrance of the breakfast room where less than a foot away, Rick Langdon is loitering in the lobby.

He's locked in some dramatic goodbye kiss with a brunette and my heart grinds to a halt for a split second. But then I let out an almighty sigh of relief when I realise it's not Ellie.

That must be his girlfriend. His way of demonstrating he's the right choice for the team, given the speech I had from Coach.

"Him and his 'friend' kept half the hallway up last night. Didn't you hear them?" Greer shakes his head, amused. "She sounded like she was auditioning for an opera."

I force a laugh.

"Any idea who she is?" I ask, trying to keep my voice casual.

I don't really care but I'm interested to know how serious they are, I guess.

"Dunno. She's been coming and going at odd times."

Greer shrugs like it's nothing, but my jaw tightens because as Langer's friend turns to leave, she glances around the room, and I catch sight of her face, and I swear there's something familiar about her.

The line shuffles forward, and I grab a plate, passing it to Greer before I take one for myself.

Then, as if on cue, my phone vibrates again, hard and insistent in my pocket. I slip my hand inside, extract it enough so I can glance at the screen, and immediately wish I hadn't.

Vicky

Need to talk to you.

Urgently.

It's about your WIFE.

I swallow hard, reading that last message in Vicky's voice. Vicky's angry voice.

Shit.

I fumble to unlock my phone one-handed, and it slips out of my grasp, falling and bouncing a few paces along the floor but it's Greer that's bending down to retrieve it—probably trying to show off his lightning-fast goalie reflexes.

He scoops the phone into his massive hand, and I watch, as if in slow motion, his eyes flick over the screen.

"Oh, damn, Betts. I didn't realise you were married?" Greer's voice cuts through my rising panic as he hands me my phone.

I slam it face-down on the buffet counter and take a step back, nearly knocking into someone behind me. My chest tightens as my phone buzzes again, and as I reach for it and check the screen, there's an incoming call from Vicky.

"I—I need to get this," I say, grabbing my phone and ducking out of the queue, but I don't answer straight away. I can't.

Chapter 14

Bettsy

I PACE AROUND THE hotel lobby, probably pissing off the guy who's just finished buffing the floors, but I can't help it. I'm waiting, bracing myself, for the next time my phone rings.

Sure enough, I don't wait long. It vibrates in my hand and Vicky's name flashes up on the screen for the third time in less than ten minutes and I finally pluck up the courage to answer it.

Deep breath.

"Heyyyy, Vic, how's it going?" I try to keep my tone casual—jovial, if you will, but she's seething. I can practically feel her rage vibrating through my phone.

"What the hell is going on?" she says. "Because I just got off a call with Michelle and she said Coach—"

"Who the fuck is Michelle?" I ask.

Vicky huffs. "Forget it. It's not important. But do you want to tell me why the hell Coach Harris thinks you're *married*?"

Even though I knew this was coming, my throat tightens, and the nausea creeps in. I scan the lobby for the closest bin, just in case.

"Look—I can explain," I say. But I quickly realise I can't—not without telling Vicky how much of a fuck up I am. Though, let's face it, it's not *new* news, is it?

I pluck the cap off my head and perch myself on the arm of a chair in the far corner of the reception area, trying to figure out the best way to approach this. But Vicky's keen; she doesn't give me any time to think. She's on me like a forechecker on a lazy D-man: relentless and stubborn.

"Start talking, Michael," she snaps. "Because when I schedule the post—"

I tune into her choice of words.

"Wait. Post? What post?" I think for a moment, then it occurs to me that this could be *that* post. The very post I've been waiting my entire career for. "Oh, my God—did I get in?" Excitement replaces the anxiety I've been feeling. Excitement that my dream has come true ... or at least that's what I interpret. "Vic?"

She lets out a curt sigh down the line.

"Okay, fine. Yes. But act surprised. I only found out earlier and from what I understand, there're a few things that have happened outside of all your crap. They usually don't announce the roster *this* early but ... anyway, you've impressed Coach with your skills and he said new information has come to light which has cemented things for you." She pauses and I wait for my brain to catch up. "But Mike, you need to tell me what the hell is going on."

I let myself revel in the excitement for a mere matter of seconds, even standing up and punching the air with glee before the realisation that this whole wife thing is something that's going to rear its head pretty soon—even more so now Greer knows.

I settle myself down on the chair, the cushion this time, because I figure I may as well get comfortable if Vicky's going to kick my ass.

"Look—I didn't mean for it to come out like it did," I begin, then I fill her in on the rest of the details. "I didn't mean to tell him I was married, it just sort of ... slipped out. And you should have seen his face, Vic. He looked relieved. I didn't expect him to be so happy about it."

"But you don't have a wife. At least..." There's an audible gasp through the phone. "You didn't get married, did you? Tell me you didn't." Her voice shifts from its usual tone to almost a whisper, and my phone trembles against my ear.

"Well—sort of. At least we both think so ... fuck."

And I'm forced to come clean to Vicky. Telling her everything from Ellie turning up at my place, to me needing to check through my old paperwork for some sort of counterpart to the paper Ellie found.

I leave out the bit about spending the night.

"But there's a problem," I conclude. "And I need you to help me fix it. Because she's not happy to go along with it."

If Vicky was standing in front of me right now—going off how her breathing has changed—I'd have a black eye.

I pick up on her inhaling, probably ready to shout at me, so I carry on talking. A distraction technique that's typically worked well in the past.

"She's trying to kick start her business, so I figure ... if you were willing to help her with some social media stuff, and we could convince Jen to help her with a new website ..."

Vicky mutters something under her breath before adjusting her voice.

"Please tell me you're kidding."

"Why would I be kidding?" I say.

"You're blackmailing someone you might already be married to—into pretending to be your wife, just so you can save face ... in exchange for social media help?" She pauses. "That's not just reckless, Mike. That's selfish. Even for you."

My heart falls into my stomach.

Now that she's said it aloud, I hear it properly.

Blackmail.

And yeah ... I *am* a douche.

But that douche part of me has a voice. And it's screaming at me to not give up just yet.

"C'mon, Vic. This has been my dream for so long ... what would Johnny say if he knew his little sister could have helped his best bud out of a hole and—"

"Oh, no you don't," she says, cutting me off. "You don't get to do that."

"So, what do I do then?" I ask. "Unless you're volunteering to take Ellie's place and—"

That wins me the mother of all cackles from Vicky.

"You need to fix this," she says. "Come clean with Coach or—"

"Or...?"

"Actually, nothing. Come clean. And deal with the consequences like a big boy."

"I told you, it's only—"

"Stop it, Michael. Fix it. Nothing good can come of this."

And she hangs up.

But instead of the bubbling excitement I was expecting after the revelation—I feel flat. Like I've been knocked over by a Zam and run over repeatedly.

Fix it. The words ring in my mind—just like the GM's did: do what you need to do to make it happen.

I stare out into the lobby for a moment before putting my attention back on my phone, deciding to check my bank account to see if I could afford one of those mail-order brides. But considering I don't even know how much they cost, nor do I want to get caught out browsing through the internet to find out, I shove my phone away and try to come up with a new plan.

A couple exit the lift, hand in hand, merrily on the way to whatever outing they have planned. I watch as they move across the lobby, laughing and smiling. Happy in each other's company. But all I'm thinking is, *'I bet he didn't have to coerce her into hanging off his arm.'* And the guilt of asking Ellie to lie for me ripples through my bones.

What the fuck was I thinking? What the fuck was I *actually* thinking?

I guess I wasn't. That's the bottom line.

Typical, Bettsy.

I watch as the couple exit through the revolving door, the draft excluders dragging along the polished floor as the glass panels move forward. Round and round. Round and round.

They disappear out of sight and I'm about to look away when something catches my eye.

As the door spins around and the segment opening into the lobby empties, a porter steps out, carrying an enormous bouquet.

Purples, pinks, whites, greens. Fresh flowers that turn several heads as people pass.

Flowers that make me think of Ellie.

Ellie likes flowers. And I bet she'd like those flowers. Or maybe ones just like it—more purple, perhaps. I'm sure she likes purple, given the collection of towels she had in her bathroom.

Maybe I should send her flowers? I mean ... it's probably a dumb idea, but it's all I've got.

The porter sets the flowers down on the reception desk and I conclude that it's the right thing to do. I'm going to send Ellie flowers, but her bouquet needs to be bigger. I want a fuck-off bouquet that fills the door to Ellie's salon and has all her clients asking who sent them because go big or go home, right?

Don't get me wrong, I know this isn't going to fix things, but it's a start. A gesture of good meaning that may give me the chance to talk with her ... to apologise in person. I figure I can send the flowers this morning, then rock up once I'm dismissed for the day and see if she can find it in her heart to forgive me.

Without hesitating, I pull my phone out of my pocket and unlock the screen, browsing through to my contacts and hovering my thumb over my mother's name. Because if there is anyone who'd know where to get flowers from, it's her.

My heart thumps as I listen to it ring.

"Everything okay?" she asks in a semi-panicked voice. "Have you found out yet? Did you get in?"

"Morning, Mam. Um … not yet," I lie, figuring it'd be better to wait for the official news from Coach. "I've just called because I need a favour."

"Oh?"

I realise I can't tell my mam who I'm sending flowers to, so I twist the truth a little.

"One of the boys is in the doghouse. He wants to send his missus flowers in the way of an apology … local delivery … that sort of thing. Any idea where's best?"

And ten minutes later, Ellie has an expensive bouquet winging its way to her.

CONCURRENT ACTIVITY. I'VE ALWAYS woven it into my day because, let's be honest, waiting for colour to take isn't a *sit and stare* job, it's a *let it work and check back in regular intervals* job which gives me time to pin someone's hair, do a quick trim or, in my case today, update my social media with photos and news.

Except, I haven't logged on to my social media account in days because I've been spending all my free computer time on the bloody fan forum in a keyboard debate with '*IlovetoPuck29*' who has subsequently, become '*IlovetoPuck30*' because '*29*' is now banned.

She's replied to my latest post. It's taken her a whole day, but she's replied, and I can't help myself. As soon as I've finished adding foils to my client's hair, I'm running into the backroom to pull my laptop from my bag. Times like these call for a big screen—not the screen of my phone where I have to zoom in and scroll awkwardly to read properly.

From: ilovetopuck30
Subject: RE: Bettsy the Playboy
Oh, look who's got himself a fan club? Must be a lonely time at your weekly meetings. I mean who else wud bother 2 turn up? Maybe his mother, but that's because there are slim pickings on the son front.

I gasp in horror. What the—

I don't give any thought to my reply before tapping out a response.

> From: Cantsleep1
> Subject: RE: Bettsy the Playboy
> Wow, I knew you were desperate for attention, but this is scraping the bottom of the barrel. I guess it must be tough trying to land a hit when all you've got is bitterness and poor grammar.
> Honestly, have you nothing better to do? Say whatever you want about Bettsy, because I'm certain you don't matter to him. But dragging his family into it? That tells the world everything we need to know about you.
> #justiceforBettsy

My fingers hover over the keyboard of my laptop as I re-read my post. I want to call her out, let people know who she really is, but I don't. The proof is non-existent, and I've learnt acting on impulse rarely works out in the way anyone hopes.

I hit '*post*' as a shriek from the front of the salon pulls me back into the room.

Kathryn is peering out of the window, her hands cupping her face as she repeats, '*oh my God, oh my God*', over and over until I see exactly what she's referring to.

I close the lid of my laptop and stand as the door to the salon creeks open and a bouquet enters the room.

I say '*bouquet*' because I can't see the person carrying the gigantic arrangement aside from a pair of legs moving unsteadily across the tiled floor.

"Oh, my God," Kathryn says again, rushing to take the flowers from the delivery person.

She scoops them into her arms before setting them down on the front counter, pushing aside a stack of magazines to make room.

"Wow," I say, taking in the purple freesia, feeling a little envious towards Kathryn's fortune.

I've never had flowers sent to me—and I'm sure this is just one of many bunches Kathryn has had over the years from Greg. Except this one is the biggest, most extravagant arrangement I've ever seen; Greg must have really messed up this time.

"Oh, my—you're so *lucky*," my client says, turning in her chair to admire the sight.

I move towards her and check the progress of her foils to distract myself from the gushing Kathryn's about to undertake.

"Aren't I just?" my sister replies. "Honestly, he's a keeper—such a romantic."

Kathryn fusses over the flowers. I watch her move around the counter from the corner of my eye, gently rotating the presentation base as she takes in each petal in turn. Pinks, purples, whites ... honestly, they are beautiful, and I want to get a closer look, but I know Kathryn won't appreciate my breathing near them.

"I just need a signature," the woman, wearing a '*Flowers by Daisy*' apron, says, handing Kathryn a receipt book and a pen.

Kathryn scribbles a name and thrusts the book and pen back towards who I assume to be Daisy, her eyes not leaving the bouquet for a second.

"Oh, they really are the best I've had," Kathryn says, and Daisy, with a sharp nod, turns and exits, the salon door thudding behind her as she leaves.

"What's the occasion?" my client asks.

"Oh ... probably 'just because', he's that type of guy—" But Kathryn's face freezes in a comedic horror—like she's just witnessed Greg in a lip-lock with Daisy.

"What's wrong?" I ask. "Is everything okay?"

She tilts her head towards me, leaving her eyes locked on the flowers right up until the last second. She stares at me. Blinks several times, then draws my attention to a small white envelope peeking out of the foliage.

"They—they're for you," she says, her voice frail.

"For me?" I ask, my eyebrows shooting upwards.

"For Ellie?" my client says, clasping her hands together. "Oh, how wonderful."

Kathryn plucks the card from a small wire card holder.

I see it. My name, written in curly letters on the front of the envelope.

Kathryn is itching to peel back the flap; there's a hungry look in her eyes. I stride forward and whip it from her fingers, faster than either of us was expecting.

"Who are they from?" she says. "Who sent them?"

But I'm edging away, trying to come up with an excuse to open the gift card in private because I have an idea I know exactly who these are from.

Kathryn sticks to my side and I know I'm out of luck. I'm going to have to open it right here. Right now.

I brace myself. Peeling back the flap of the envelope and tugging the card upwards. Waiting for Kathryn to say something.

Ellie,

I suck, and I'm sorry. I hope you can forgive me. If I've not ruined things entirely, I'd love to start over and take you out for dinner.

M x

There's no doubt in my mind who these are from and my heart flutters involuntarily as I fight back a smile.

I stare at the card, and Kathryn doesn't hesitate. She pulls it from my hand and moves it closer to her face.

"Mark? Mark is apologising after all this time? Honestly. You should be grateful he didn't text you when he said he would. The guy is an idiot."

I pluck the card from her and slip it back into the envelope, thankful for the conclusion Kathryn arrived at.

I never did hear from Mark, nor have I thought about him since the stuff with Mike reared its head. But here I am, grateful that 'M' can stand for both Mike and Mark, and relieved I won't have to explain the drama between me and Mike to Kathryn.

Not yet, anyway.

"I need to get on," I say, stuffing the card into a pocket on my stylist belt. The tips of my fingers lingering on the paper for a second before I pull my hand away.

"You're actually going to accept his apology?" she says.

"I'm with a client, Kathryn," I whisper under my breath.

"Well, you can't leave those there," she says bitterly.

Funny, because I'm convinced they'd be in prime place if they were her flowers.

I march over to the counter and lift the bouquet, getting a delicious waft of sweetness as I carry them over to the windowsill and set them down, allowing myself the smallest of giddy grins as I do.

"There. Out of the way," I say sharply, resetting my expression before I face my sister.

"Well, tell him it's not professional to send things like that to your place of work," she says indignantly.

But I'm not really listening. I'm thinking about Mike. And a smile pulls at my lips.

But then I remember his desperation. The bridal set ... are these flowers his attempt to worm his way in and convince me to agree to his ridiculous scheme?

I make my way back to my client, standing behind her chair and looking at her smiling back at me in the mirror.

"Well?" she says. "Who's this lucky man?"

I shake my head dismissively.

"Let's check how we're getting on," I say, swallowing down the emotion that's creeping its way upward. I can't quite decide what it is. Uncertainty? Excitement?

I peel back a foil, feeling my sister's eyes burning into me from her place at the counter.

"We'll leave it a few more minutes," I say, folding the foil back over.

And as I turn, I lock eyes with Kathryn. A flicker of something on her face.

She's jealous.

Chapter 15

THE MEDIA ROOM. A place for reflecting, conversation and, usually, camaraderie. But today, it also happens to be the place where Coach seals my fate. It all comes down to the decision of a leadership team who have, likely, been watching me play for years.

Danny sits on my left, scrolling through his social media, and Greer on my right, sipping the same cup of coffee he's been nursing for the past half hour—not that he has anything to worry about. He's starting. He knows this and everyone else does too.

"This forum is still rife with gossip," Danny says, slipping his phone into his pocket.

"I've stopped looking," I say. "Honestly, I've had bigger things to worry about."

My leg jiggles of its own accord and I nibble my thumb nail, my eyes fixed on the door, waiting for Coach to make his appearance.

"Well, I'm just saying," Danny says. Leaning closer, he whispers, "do you think this'll be good news?"

I didn't tell him Vicky sort of gave the game away earlier today, probably because I don't believe it myself. I guess I'm convinced that until I get the official notice from Coach Harris, it's not happening. He could have changed his mind right after Vicky found out.

"I guess we need to wait it out," I say, flashing a look at Langer.

He's sitting on the opposite side of the room next to one of his home team buddies, and every so often, I feel compelled to tear my attention away from the door to go and flick him on the nose—enough to make his eyes water but not enough to get me kicked off the team.

He's made this week harder than it needed to be. Snide remarks and insults forcing me to be on my best behaviour, knowing that one tiny little fuck up on my part would be enough to have my name plate ripped from my cubby faster than I can say 'puck'.

Danny nudges me in the ribs and nods towards the door. A shadow of someone outside.

Everyone stops talking instantly and we all watch as the handle dips and the door swings open, Coach Harris leading his coaching staff inside.

"Right then, boys," he says, coming to a stop at the media cabinet at the front of the room. He sets down the laptop he had tucked under his arm and fiddles with a bunch of cables, extracting an HDMI and plugging it in.

Torture.

This is torture.

I thought my blue balls were painful enough, but waiting for windows to finish updating features is horrendous—even more so when everyone seems to be looking either at me or at Langer.

"While this does its thing," Coach says, nodding at the screen, "I want to take the time to thank you all for this week. You've given it your best and I'm hugely impressed with the talent that British ice hockey offers. Now, I want everyone to know that our ongoing roster is always flexible. So getting a spot, even if you're returning, is not guaranteed long term. I expect you to practice like you've never won and play like you've never lost—I think that's how the saying goes, anyway."

The log-on prompt steals Coach's attention for several seconds as he types in his password, and up comes a slide deck with the title 'Upcoming Roster', set on a Team GB corporate template.

I'm starting to feel pretty smug right about now, as Coach lists off several qualities he's been looking for that I know describes me perfectly. But when he flicks the slides to the next screen, my heart drops out of my ass.

What the—

"You'll notice here I've got my first line forwards the same as last season, we're planning on mixing the lines a little between second, third and fourth—with the introduction of Danny Owens—" there's a whoop and cheer from several guys as Danny grins awkwardly, "—but it's our defensive lines that have the biggest change."

I swallow, willing my dry throat to give me some grace as I watch Coach move from left to right, his arm extending as he points towards my name at first, then—

"First pair stays the same, but our second pair is Betts and Langdon."

I'm fucking paired with Langer.

There's no way.

A heavy knot of dread tightens in my stomach, like I'm about to pass out. This was a scenario I never thought possible.

"I know this wasn't what we were expecting, but I've had to make a few changes," Coach says, moving directly towards the screen and pointing at a list of names on the far right titled 'LTIR'.

Honestly, I've been so wrapped up in my own mess, I haven't even considered the long-term injured reserves list.

"Unfortunately, Hill is out for an extended period, but we were lucky to have had two strong D-men on trial this week. It was a simple choice to make and even though we're pairing you guys," Coach looks between Langer and me, "we can see how things go."

There're mumbles of congratulations around the room, but Coach isn't done.

"Just another point to note—there are some really talented players on our LTIR—should they become fit to skate, we will re-evaluate. Your spot could quickly become their spot if your performance drops. That goes for everyone in this room."

There's a mutual agreement of nods before Coach continues.

"Netminders then ... Greer, Sutherland, and Callaghan."

But it's the part next that has my palms sweating. Coach flicks over to the next slide where we're presented with a list of dates: training, media days ... but worst of all, that social event he was referring to.

"Mark your calendars, boys. I'll get it sent out via email so there are no excuses, but here's the agenda."

I scan the slide, trying to work out how long I've got until I have to come clean or fake my own death.

Four weeks.

"Right, enough of that, I think you've all earnt yourselves the afternoon off. Relax, take it easy and enjoy your league games this weekend. I appreciate some of you have travelling to do so until next time—"

I tune out, dropping my head into my hands, only for Danny to nudge me merrily.

"We've done it, mate. Do you want to be the one to tell Cap? Or should I? Oh—or maybe we can call him together."

"Yeah, maybe," I say through gritted teeth as people around me file out.

"What's wrong? Aren't you happy?" Danny says.

"Of course I am, but—"

I flick my eyes towards the schedule, still on the big screen.

"Ah, shit, yeah. The whole Mrs thing," he says, dropping his voice. "Well, I guess that's something to figure out."

He's not wrong.

What the hell am I going to do?

"He asked you to do what?"

Every fifth Friday, my friend Jessica makes the two-hour round trip to visit me at the salon, always my last appointment of the day and the reason is purely selfish: she won't let anyone else wax her lady parts.

Jess is the best sort of friend. Low maintenance—we can go weeks without actively talking, but we just pick up where we left off. It's drama free and ideal for both of us.

"I know—I couldn't believe it either," I say.

I've just finished her treatment and I've been steadily filling her in since she got here and saw the bouquet from the street, still dominating the window of the salon.

I've told her all about the mystery document, the visit I paid Greg, the trip I made to Mike's apartment and the stuff online—minus the part about me starting a '#justiceforBettsy' campaign and him spending the night. I've just finished telling her the bit about Mike asking me if I can pretend to be his wife.

"And you said no?" she says, pulling on an old pair of leggings out of a small holdall she brought with her.

"Of course I did," I say.

Jess straightens up and shakes them out before stepping into them.

"But why? I don't understand."

"You don't understand why I would turn down the offer of pretending to be married to someone?"

"It's not pretending though if you may actually be married," she says.

I scowl. "That's not what this is about. He's using me for his image."

She scoffs. "Take that as a compliment. Where is your sense of fun? I'm just saying—you wouldn't even think about it? Hell, I'll do it!"

"You're married," I say.

"Well, yeah…" but Jess looks down at her pedicure as if it's the most interesting thing in the world and when she lingers for longer than ten seconds, I know something's up.

"Jess? What's going on?" I ask.

She sighs, then tentatively raises her head to meet my eyes.

"I'm separated, but it's … whatever."

She says it in such a nonchalant tone, I wonder if I heard correctly.

"Excuse me?"

"Yeah, Phil and I are getting a divorce … but it's no big deal. It's clear that some things aren't meant to be."

"What happened?" I slump down on the tub chair in the corner of the treatment room while Jess works on the leggings.

"He's a lazy ass who wants a mother, not a wife. I'm just annoyed I didn't work it out until after we were married."

"And that's it?" I ask. "You're done?"

"Yes. He tried begging. And he even cooked me a lasagne—from scratch. But I think I must have mentally checked out a long time ago because it made me feel sorry for him more than anything else. Too little, too late."

I feel like a rock has been dropped in the pit of my stomach. From the outside looking in, Jess and Phil were the epitome of a couple, happy and in love, much like my sister and Greg. They were everything I was hoping for myself, because I'm a romantic at heart and I'm stuck on the idea that someday, someone will come and sweep me away. Just like Phil did to Jess—or so I thought.

"Are you—"

"I won't change my mind. And now it's awkward as hell because we're still having to live together. He won't move out and I have nowhere to go, so … until we can plan a way forward and sell up or something, we're stuck there. The only good thing is that there's a spare room, so we don't have to share a bed—oh, and we don't have children to consider."

Jess pulls on a hoodie and stuffs her work clothes into her bag while I stare at her, completely flabbergasted.

"But—"

Jess waves her hand, dismissing that part of the conversation.

"Forget about me and Phil. I'm still keen to know why you said no."

"But you—I mean, are you okay?" I say.

"El, please—I don't want to talk about it," she snaps and the look she gives me tells me she won't change her mind.

"Right, sorry," I say.

"Well—like I said, I'm still keen to know why you said no."

And just like that, she forces the direction of the conversation back to me.

"Why would I say yes?"

"Why wouldn't you?" She throws her bag over her shoulder and straightens up. "I'm sorry to be blunt, but you're living in Kathryn's shadow. Practically running her salon ... where is she now, El?"

"She's out looking at wedding venues," I shrug, actually grateful for her leaving early today.

"Yeah? But why is it up to you to stay here until eight? On a Friday night?"

"I've got clients," I say.

"Your clients? Or ones Kathryn palmed off on to you? I'm going to say it, but you're a glorified skivvy. What happened to the Ellie who wanted to run her own show? What happened to living your own life? I mean, imagine you say yes, and Mike introduces you to one of his friends and you meet someone who blows you away."

"I'm not sure that's how it would work. I think I'd be needing to pretend to be with him, so it wouldn't look good if I was trying to get with his friends."

"Okay, fine … but I mean, once it's all over. Or—" She pauses, a creepy smile forming on her face. "What if you realise that you and Mike are meant to be together after all and this is one big love story I can live vicariously through you?"

The idea brings a chill to my spine. "I'm not sure—"

"Or … I like this, hear me out… or maybe you can play him at his own game. Freak him out a little. Lay it on. Yanno, so when you attend these functions together … you could show up looking your best, flirt like hell with him, make him wish like he was really married to you, mess with him a little? Because if he's anything like he used to be, he wouldn't be expecting that, and I don't think he'd know how to react. It'd be hilarious."

"Or maybe I just say no and leave it at that."

"Or maybe you live a little?"

Jess slips her coat on.

"I don't know. It's all a bit … much, I think. We don't even know if we are married. I'm waiting for him to check through his paperwork. Besides, I think deep down I'm still upset about him not reaching out when he came back from Germany. It's like I didn't even matter to him, but now, when it's convenient for him, he's interested."

"But he said he called you and he was told never to ring this number again?"

"Yeah, but he must have had the wrong number or something," I shrug. "Still, he knew where I lived—"

"Or Kathryn answered and told him to do one. It's the sort of thing she'd do. God forbid you meet someone and can't tend to her every waking call," Jess says in a tone laced with sarcasm.

I gape at her. "Wh—do you think she'd do something like that?"

"I definitely think she's capable. I mean, she'd have had to of had access to your phone and deleted messages or whatever. Then she probably blocked his number or something—look, I don't know but it's possible. Wasn't she madly in love with

Jeremy Betts at one point? Maybe she figured *'If I can't have Jeremy then Ellie can't have Mike'.*"

I feel wrapped in my naivety. Because there was a point, way back, when my charger went missing, and I'd had to leave my phone in Kathryn's room while I used hers. I mean ... what Jess is saying is possible, but she wouldn't, would she?

"Now, are we going for dinner? Because I'm starving," Jess says.

We head down the stairs to the main salon area, where I automatically head for the front door to take the lock off. A habit I got into when working in the upstairs treatment room, when it's just me. But as I reach for the lock, a figure darkens the doorway and my heart stops as I come face to glass to face with Mike Betts.

"Oh, my God," Jess says. "Speak of the devil ... he's aged well."

I flash her a look of despair before turning back to the door, locking eyes with Mike, standing on the other side, grinning at me.

I take a breath and steady my hands as I twist the lock.

"You got my flowers, then," he says, nodding to the window display.

I focus in on his scar—and his lips before I realise I'm staring.

"I—yes, thank you, but it won't work," I say.

"What? No. I don't intend them as a bribe. Just an apology," he says. "I was a dick. Simple. And I'm sorry."

"Well, thanks but—"

"Wow—it's been a long time," Jess says. "I feel inclined to say I hope you're keeping yourself out of trouble, but from what I hear, you've been doing the opposite," she says, coming to a stop behind me.

"Well, well. It *has* been a long time," Mike says, narrowing his eyes. He takes a second of contemplation before he realises who my friend is. "How are you keeping, Jess? I can only assume Kitch has been filling you in."

"Well, I'm about to be divorced before I've hit thirty, but I guess you can't have it all."

"Oh, shit. Sorry to hear that. But at least we know where to come to for advice, right, Kitch?"

Mike flashes me a wink.

"See what I mean, Jess? This is all one big joke to him," I say.

Jess grins. "Honestly, El, you need to lighten up. If you are married … you may as well ride the storm and have a little fun." She looks at Mike. "For the record, I told her she needs to help you out. I mean—you'll show her a good time, right? Treat her like the queen she is and all that?"

Mike, already grinning, widens his mouth. "Oh, you've been re-considering then, Kitch?"

"No," I say, sternly. "Actually, I was asking Jess if she'd volunteer to be your fake-wife," I lie.

"Why bargain for a fake one when you're the real deal?" He does this thing with his eyebrows, causing my cheeks to flush red, betraying me.

"I was just telling Ellie that she should live a little. Do something outside of her comfort zone. Get out of Kathryn's shadow."

"You did not—"

"Shush, El. But we're just off out to dinner, so I have," Jess looks at her watch, "at least three hours to convince her. I'm sure she'll be in touch."

I stare at Jess, waiting for her to break out into a smile, telling me she's kidding, but she doesn't. She's shifted her attention to her phone instead.

"Ah, fuck," Jess says under her breath as she taps at the screen furiously. "Why is he such a knob?"

"Is everything okay?" I ask.

She lets out a mammoth sized sigh. "Actually, I'm sorry, El, I probably need to dash. Phil's gone and flooded the kitchen. Apparently, there's a sock stuck in the washing machine pump and there's water everywhere." She holds her phone up to flash a photo of her kitchen floor.

"Oh, my—looks like a nightmare. Do you want me to come with you?" I ask.

"Oh, no. Don't worry. I'll just have to sacrifice my nice towels if Phil hasn't already done so. Honestly, the sooner he moves out, the better." She slips her phone away and pulls out her car keys. "Are you going to be okay?"

"I—yeah. Yeah, all fine. I think," I turn to look at Mike.

"I'll text you," she says, slipping through the doorway and out onto the street.

And just like that, it's only me and Mike.

Chapter 16

Ellie

"That sounds like a headache for Jess," Mike says, after blowing out a low whistle. He takes it upon himself to waltz right into the salon, closing the door behind him. "Hope she gets things—hey, are these all your certificates?"

He stops at the front counter, studying the row of frames mounted to the wall behind.

"Some of them are mine, some are Kathryn's," I say, starting the close-down routine, reaching for the pull cord of the blinds.

"Oh, wow. You've done a lot," he says. "Looks like there's not much you can't do."

"You sound surprised," I say. "I've been busy. And get this, I'm still not doing what I want to be doing."

"What's that?"

"Bridal—" I stop myself, wondering why I'm opening up to someone who felt it appropriate to use me ... to make me feel disposable. I finish drawing the blinds closed before turning towards him. "Mike, why are you here? I know you came to apologise, and I appreciate it. But why are you here? You could have texted or called or whatever."

"I—" He leans back on the counter. "I, I wanted to say sorry in person, and I'm not naive enough to think that a fancy bouquet is going to fix things but, I wanted to—I don't know, Kitch." He doesn't even look at me. He keeps his eyes fixed on a point in front of his fancy looking trainers. "I'm shit with this sort of stuff, and you know I don't think things through."

"So that's a reason to say 'thanks for the flowers, I forgive you?'"

"No, of course not, but that's why I'm here. I want to make things right because I shouldn't have asked you to lie for me. And I should have considered how it'd make you feel. But of course, I didn't." His cheeks flame red as he peeks a look at me. "I didn't want to not try, I guess. I didn't want to let history repeat itself."

"Slightly different, Mike, but okay."

"How is it?" he says

"Because this time, you made me feel cheap—like you messed up and thought *'Oh, I know who can get me out of this hole ... I'll ask Ellie. She's got nothing else better to do.'*" My voice transforms into a shaky mess as I finish speaking.

"Nah, this is what I'm saying, Kitch. I don't think things through, do I? I didn't actively think about how it'd come across. I didn't consider how it'd make you feel, but honestly, it wasn't like that."

Folding my arms across my chest, I purse my lips, finally meeting his eyes.

"I really like you," he says.

And there's that look again—the same look I saw him wear in my kitchen.

Oh, God. This isn't good; there's a smile trying to fight its way to my lips.

"I'm sorry that I made you feel anything other than ... wanted, I guess." He straightens up and moves forward a step. "But I do want you." He rubs his hands over his face. "... ah, fuck. See? I mean, I want to spend time with you, get to know you more, I want to do that too but—I'll shut up now." He snaps his mouth shut and watches me, apparently waiting for a response.

"I—I don't know what to say," I stutter.

"Can we start over?" he says. "Pretend like none of this—well, actually, I know I still need to look for that wedding paperwork, but can we start again? Because I know it's crazy to think this way but, do you think that maybe, just maybe, this all came about because we were meant to reconnect?"

"I don't know, Mike."

He exhales, shoving his hands into the pockets of his sweatpants. Team GB sweatpants. And I know I shouldn't care—or at least that's what I'm trying to convince myself, but I do. I feel...

"I should have tried harder before. When I got back from Germany ... I should have—"

"Did you get in?" I say, cutting him off. "Team GB. Did you get in?" I eye the logo on his hat this time, completely taken aback that I didn't notice before.

"Uh, yeah. I guess—I mean, the roster is changing a lot, so nobody has a guaranteed long-term position, but yeah. For now, I'm in."

I can't help myself. The moment pulls me in before I can think better of it. My feet move before my brain catches up, and suddenly, my arms lock around his neck.

Only yesterday, I didn't really understand the significance of this achievement, but the forum has been an eye-opener. A lesson in British ice hockey, if you will. Mike's a homegrown, a player developed in Britain, turned professional in Britain and now he's on the national team. The boy next door—playing for *Team GB*.

And here I am, my arms around his neck and my head half-resting on his shoulder, where I get a big ol' whiff of *him*. His aftershave, his skin—fresh and musky—causing a tingle to run all the way through me.

I realise my mistake, but before I can pull away, he's settled his arms around my waist and he squeezes me, ever so slightly, but enough to close the tiny space between us.

Warmth. There's warmth. A warmth that shifts from my chest and radiates outward as my pulse quickens. His body, strong and solid, engulfs me in a way I've never experienced before. And then I feel his breath in my ear as he whispers, "thanks, Kitch."

My own breath catches in my throat.

"I—I need to get on," I say. "I've got to close up and—" A moment passes before I pull away and Mike's arms drop to his side.

I busy myself with a stack of magazines, tidying them with more determination than ever.

"Uh, yeah, no problem. Can I help with anything, or?"

I can't look at him. My cheeks feel hot and my head, light and fuzzy like it's been pumped full of cotton wool.

"Uh, no. Thanks. I can manage."

"Kitch—"

He's standing behind me now. I can feel him watching me as I straighten up. But I'm digging for the courage to turn and face him again—because I think he'll see the same thing he's shown me. I like him just as much as he likes me. Perhaps more—if the sex dreams are anything to go by.

"Kitch," he says again, closing the gap between us, my back almost flush against his chest. A rough finger dances over my neck as he brushes my hair aside. Then I smell him again. Musky and—oh, my goodness... "Can we start again?"

Half of my brain is screaming 'yes', probably the same part that wants me to turn around and acquaint myself with that scar on his chin—but the other half is reminding me of how he made me feel. How I felt—

"I promise to do better," he says.

I swallow, looking past the magazines to the flowers on the windowsill. And you know what? I think I believe him. I think he will.

I tilt my head to reply. "I'll think about it. But that doesn't mean I'm going to—"

"I know," he says.

And I believe that, too.

Bettsy

RYAN PRESTON'S HOUSE RENOVATIONS have become a team effort. I'm sitting in his brand-new kitchen with his wife, Jen, and Danny, half a week later drinking tea and eating custard creams while we wait for a delivery of something Prez wants help to unload. Honestly, the guy's rich enough that he could pay people to do this sort of shit for him, but here we are, roped into helping and for the compensation of a biscuit—not even a chocolate covered one.

"Are you making another brew, Jen?" Danny asks, helping himself to another biscuit.

"Yeah, but I'm still wanting to hear how Bettsy has found it so far. I want all the details," she says, picking up the kettle and taking it over to the sink.

Jen and Danny have been discussing the Team GB stuff, but I've been preoccupied trying to figure out how I can make things good with Ellie. We've been texting, at least. But it's ... I don't know, guarded. Like she's put up a wall to protect herself from my emotional ignorance.

"I—yeah," I say. "It's been fine."

Jen sets the kettle on the stand and flicks it to boil.

"You don't sound convinced," she says. "Is this about the Johnny thing?"

I snap my eyes to hers. "What Johnny thing?"

"About you and him playing together again, you know, for the Challenge Cup final. It's a change, so I wasn't sure if it would affect your hockey head with your superstitions and all."

"Nah, it's nothing like that," I say, draining my tea.

"Well, you're quiet," she says. "And excuse the generalisation but it's not like you at all."

"I'm fine," I say, setting my mug down.

Jen rests her arms on the kitchen island and raises an eyebrow.

"Do you guys want to tell me what's going on?" she asks, looking between me and Danny.

Automatically, I check Danny's expression. He and Jen have been friends since they were kids and now, I'm wondering if he's told her. Perhaps this is one of those scenarios where Jen knows but doesn't want me to know that she knows and—

"He's just preoccupied with the forum stuff, right mate?" Danny says, nudging my arm.

I tense my jaw.

"Oh, yeah. I guess that makes sense. Honestly, we're on *'ilovetopuck33'* now. I'm trying my hardest to keep up but the IP address is inconsistent. I think Vicky and the GM have been talking about getting it shut down, but I can only guess a non-affiliated forum will spring up in that case." She pauses, and the kettle finishes boiling. "Hey, have you seen your hashtag? '#justiceforBettsy' is taking a life of its own," she says, her tone perkier, but I know what she's doing.

"I've seen bits," I say, dropping my eyes to my empty mug.

"Yeah? Aren't you a little curious as to who it is?" she says.

"I am," Danny says. "I'd love to know. I mean ... it's probably someone we know, right?"

"Hm," I say.

But Jen is intuitive as hell.

"Right. Enough is enough," she says. "This is ridiculous. What is going on?"

I can feel Danny's eyes on me, burning my skin.

"Is everything okay?" she asks, her voice a tone of genuine worry.

Ah, shit.

A wave of nausea washes over me as my stomach clenches.

I glance towards the bi-fold doors, spotting Ryan and Liam at the far end of the garden, prepping space in the garden for whatever the hell is getting delivered, and I cast a look towards

Jen, wondering if I should tell her. It may be useful to get a woman's view, actually.

I flick my eyes back to Jen. "If I tell you, please, can you keep it to yourself? That includes Prez because he'll tell Liam and then Johnny will find out and—"

"Okay, calm down," she says. "I promise. It'll stay between us. Unless it's something I need to inform the police about because—"

"Nah, it's nothing dodgy. Christ—what do you think of me?"

"You're right. I'm sorry," she says.

"Well, I'm a fuckup, so I guess it's a logical conclusion to arrive at," I say. "But anyway..." I brace myself; closing my eyes tightly and taking several deep breaths. "I may have got married when I was eighteen and then..." I look up to see Jen's jaw practically on the counter. "...all this forum stuff kicked off and..."

"Wait. Wait. Wait. Am I hearing this right?" Jen's attention shifts between me and Danny. "What the—"

"Well, Vicky sort of implied that my chances of a GB career would be greater if I was drama free and if I had my shit together, so—"

"No—go back. Rewind," she says.

But I keep talking.

"Well, I sort of told Coach Harris I—"

But Jen slaps a hand over her mouth, her eyebrows practically becoming one with her hairline, showing me the penny's dropped.

"Honestly, you can't make this shit up," says Danny. "Oh, you need to tell Jen the bit about her turning up at your place looking for you."

I cringe, but I figure I've come this far, so I may as well give all the sordid details over, relaying the story from the start.

"...so yeah, Coach thinks I'm married, so I asked Ellie if she'd ... sort of, fill in for a little, attend a few events with me and whatever, but she said no. She said she felt used and—" I exhale sharply, rubbing my hands over my face.

Jen stares at me, her hand dropping from her now half-open mouth.

"Coach thinks you're married ... but you are actually married...except you're not really married?" She says, enunciating each word as if she's teaching a child to read.

"May be married," I correct. "I need to search for some kind of certificate—like the full wedding one or something, but I haven't had a chance yet."

My face reddens; I can feel the glow of shame. I've been telling myself I haven't had a chance, but the truth is, I don't want to face the reality of this. Not yet anyway.

It's Danny's turn to gape at me. "Surely you'd remember if you were given a wedding certificate or not?"

"Well," I shrug, "I don't know. I got given stuff, not sure what half of it was—I think I assumed it was tourism crap or something, you know, like when they try to sell you timeshares or something."

But Jen's not listening to this part, she's still mouthing the word 'marriage' in slow motion as she processes the word over and over.

She shakes her head before speaking again.

"Honestly, if someone told me there was a guy on the team who may have got married but couldn't be one hundred per cent sure ... I'd guess it was you, but..."

"See, I said the same, Jen. It's just typical Bettsy," Danny says.

And there it is—the reminder that this sort of behaviour is practically expected of me.

"Anyway," I say sharply. "She's pissed off and I need to make it right because ... well, the thing is," I bite my lip. "I really like her."

"Oh, my God," Jen says.

"But that aside, Vicky found out, didn't she? And now she's told me I need to come clean." I look down at my hands. "How's it going to look if I rock up to Coach's office next Tuesday and tell him I'm a liar?"

"You could just tell him that you're separating," Danny suggests.

"I honestly can't even think about that right now. My priority is making things right with Ellie." I look at Jen, mustering my biggest 'puppy-dog' expression. "What can I do, Jen? How can I fix things?" I absentmindedly pick at the plastic of the custard cream wrapper, trying to avoid looking at either Danny or Jen. "I really like her."

"I don't think I can help you with that," she says. "I think it needs to come from you, Betts. From the heart."

And said heart sinks. Sinks and falls right out of my ass.

"I sent her an enormous bouquet," I say, as Jen takes our mugs and returns to the kettle. "Maybe I need to ... arrange for a barbershop quartet to show up at her salon and—"

"Absolutely not," Jen says, shaking her head.

"Absolutely not what?" Prez's voice floats through the bi-fold doors as he and Liam step into the kitchen.

I groan with the pending doom of having to reveal all to the twins—because this will travel around the dressing room faster than the common cold.

Jen sets a mug down in front of me, offering me a pitiful look. "Bettsy wanted to order pizza, but it will not do his training schedule any favours."

Phew.

"Well, if you have any other ideas what we could have instead—please let me know," I say, hoping Jen can read between the lines.

Prez moves towards his wife and wraps his arms around her waist, casually, like he's done it every single day for his entire life.

I watch on with envy; thinking about the moment I held Ellie in my arms. Those few seconds that have replayed over and over in my head.

"Well, you don't want to spoil your dreams over a pizza. Nothing tastes as good as fit feels, Betts, you know that," Prez says.

"Yeah," I mutter.

"But that Team GB stuff is only one thing. We should all be focusing on the Cup Final. You and Cap ... back together again. The dream D-pair."

He's right. That's this coming Wednesday. After all this effort, this is what we face. A single game and the potential for some silverware.

But I'm distracted. As Ryan, Liam, and Danny—even Jen—launch into a conversation about the Cup. Typically, I would be equally invested, but I can only think about Ellie.

Chapter 17

Ellie

I'm TRYING TO MUSTER the courage to tell Kathryn that I want to focus on bridal hair. I mean, it's not like she doesn't know that's my aspiration, what with the magazine and stuff, but I need her to understand that it's time for me to take it more seriously. It's time for me to take a step back from nails and spray tans.

And it's all thanks to Mike. He may be impulsive, but he's full of heart. He's ambitious. Driven. And I've probably been watching too many of his hockey clips this weekend because I took a leaf from his book and spontaneously booked myself onto a workshop with last-minute availability.

Seeing him achieve his dreams, standing in the salon wearing the tracksuit he's worked his whole life for ignited something inside me. It made me realise I need to take control of my circumstances. Jess was right—and Mike, too, in his own way. Watching him chase what he wanted made me realise I've been hiding behind Kathryn's plans for too long.

I watch Kathryn move towards the blinds—waiting until she's turned away from me before I speak.

"I've booked myself onto a bridal workshop tomorrow," I say. "I think it's time I put more focus on hair than nails."

I brace myself for her reaction.

She freezes, then turns around slowly after a long pause, meeting my eyes.

"Bridal? I thought you did that for fun more than anything."

I bite back the frustration rising inside me. "Well, I enjoy it, and it's what I want to concentrate on," I say. "I figure doing a new workshop will strengthen my skills. It's been a while since I've done any formal training."

She doesn't respond straight away. Instead, she moves towards the counter and busies herself with the reception computer, aggressively clicking the mouse.

"I see you've cleared your day," she says after a painful stretch of silence.

"Yeah. Everything's sorted," I say.

"Right, well, who's going to open the salon tomorrow? I've got an appointment first thing."

"You're first client isn't until eleven. You can open when you get here," I say.

I know what game she's playing. She's trying to guilt me into giving in, cancelling the workshop and pandering to her every need. But today, I'm compelled to stand my ground, even if it means being subjected to Kathryn's sour mood.

She glares at me for what feels like an eternity, the tension crackling in the air as I wait for an outburst, but she mutters, "I guess I'll have to," barely looking at me.

The conversation dies there, and I feel relieved; pleased I stood my ground. And for the rest of the day, she hardly acknowledges me as we move around the salon, working alongside each other with absolutely no chit-chat.

Not that it's a bad thing because I've got too much thinking to do.

Mike.

Mike and his infectious personality. His carefree attitude and passion. And the moment he held me in his arms and made me feel ... I don't know—present. Like hugging me was something special.

There's something about him that pulls me in and makes me feel like I'm eighteen again and everything is fresh and exciting and simple.

Simple.

And the more I think about him, the more simple things become.

Why am I resisting the obvious pull between us?

Because I think he likes me as much as I like him ... and that terrifies me. It terrifies me because I don't really know him at all. I mean, I know who he is, what he does ... but I don't know him. I don't know what he's interested in outside of hockey aside from whisky and bad jokes. But I do know I enjoy being around him. I enjoy how he makes me feel. I enjoy listening to him talk—and the way he articulates himself? As if he doesn't care about speaking his mind. That's something I could only dream of doing.

But I'm still terrified.

Terrified of making the same mistake as before. Trusting him, only to be let down. Waiting for him to call ...

I stop in my tracks, playing Jess' words in my head as I look towards Kathryn, who busies herself with her client, making idle conversation about the weather.

She wouldn't, would she?

But she would.

Deep down, I know she would.

Maybe I should come out and ask her, or maybe I should let it go.

But half an hour later, I can't let it go. And it's at the forefront of my mind when Kathryn's new client arrives.

At the sink, washing my client's hair, I catch the conversation my sister's having; there's talk about my flowers, still on display in the window, much to Kathryn's irritation.

"They're Ellie's," she says, dismissively.

And when her client looks at me, expectantly waiting for me to elaborate, a surge of courage surfaces and I realise now is the time. After all, I've already annoyed Kathryn today, so what's another thing to add to the list?

"Yeah, funny story," I say, keeping my eyes on my hands.

I swallow, taking a moment to decide if this is something I really want to do. But what have I got to lose? Several more hours of the silent treatment from my sister, no doubt. No biggie.

I look at Kathryn. "Remember how you thought they were from Mark?" She tilts her head to show me she's listening. "Turns out, they were from Michael Betts."

I wait for something—anything ... then I see it. A flicker of contempt in her eyes.

"Michael Betts?" she says, her tone cold.

"Yeah. We re-connected recently. Long story short, he was keen to make things right because apparently ... all those years ago, when he returned from Germany, he tried to call, but I didn't get his messages."

I watch Kathryn stiffen.

"Apparently, he called." I keep my voice casual. "And someone told him to 'never call this number again'."

And I look up from the sink just in time to lock eyes with her.

She stares at me for a moment, and I know, I just know, it was her. She's guilty. Call it intuition, call it a feeling ... I don't know, but there's a sensation in my gut that's telling me all I need to know.

"I need to grab something from the back room," she says. "Won't be a moment." She plasters on a false smile as she walks away, then her lips form a straight line as she passes me, keeping her focus ahead of her.

I guess I wasn't sure what I was expecting, but I know I'll never get a confession from her. She'll admit no wrongdoing.

But maybe that's okay. Maybe I don't need her apology. Maybe I just need to stop waiting for one—and start being who I want to be.

Bettsy

Ellie

Where shall I meet you?

Bettsy

By the big clock. I'll be the one with the red carnation.

Ellie

Are you being serious?

Bettsy

Yeah, the clock is huge. You can't miss it.

Ellie

I know where the clock is, dumbass :P I'm just trying to work out if you really are standing there with a flower pinned to your chest.

Bettsy

Too much?

Ellie

Maybe.

Train is pulling in now.

And just like that, I'm nervous as hell. My stomach is in a tight knot as I step back from the main concourse, settling myself into the entrance of a coffee shop.

I've got a decent view of the exit barriers, so I should see her when she comes. All she needs to do is head to the big clock—that's all she needs to do.

18:31

There's an announcement over the loudspeaker broadcasting the arrival of Ellie's train, and my pulse picks up speed. What if this isn't a good idea? What if—

18:32

It's like I'm a teenager again. Loitering in the corridor of the science block, waiting for her to pass on her way to class—trying my hardest to pretend I'm not stealing a glance. I explicitly remember thinking she was too good for me. And as I watch the barriers, waiting ... I'm wondering the same thing. Am I enough? Can I make things up to her? Because I don't think I'll get another chance. This is it.

18:33

My heart is beating so fast, it feels like it stops.

I see her.

She's coming.

I notice her smile first, highlighted by a flash of deep red lipstick. Next, I pick up on her hair; vintage curls pinned to the side in a 40s style look that she pulls off with ease.

Damn, she's beautiful.

I fight the temptation to run forward and scoop her into my arms as she passes through the barrier—purely because that's not part of my plan. I need to wait. I need for her to be standing near the clock.

But she doesn't. She's looking around and then she roots around in her handbag. Retrieving her phone, she taps the screen before pressing it to her ear.

Shit.

I tug my phone out of my pocket and watch it ring for a moment before answering.

"Have you stood me up?" she asks, her voice cracking in a way that pulls at my heart.

She's looking around. Turning on the spot, studying the surrounding traffic of people.

"No, no—please, can you just stand by the big clock?"

"But—what's going on, Mike?" she says.

"Please, Kitch. Can you trust me with this one?" I ask.

She sighs down the line, then I watch her move towards the clock.

"I'm here."

"I—you look incredible, by the way," I say.

I hang up before slipping my phone into my pocket, trying to steady my breathing, trying to settle my racing heart.

I watch her for a moment longer, wondering if this is a completely ridiculous idea.

She's looking around again; peering around the concourse and I figure that I've literally got nothing to lose. She agreed to meet me here today. This is it. This is my chance to start fresh.

I relax my shoulders, then step out of the coffee place, striding towards the big clock, trying to act busy—unfazed by the world around me. Then I pull out my prop. A newspaper I've had tucked into my jacket pocket. I unfold it and pretend to read, flicking my eyes towards Ellie, standing with her back to me, to check I'm on course.

One step closer. Another step closer. And bump. Gentle enough to get her attention.

She straightens up and turns to face me. "Sorry—"

"Oh, my. I'm so sorry. I—" We lock eyes, and her brows knit together. "—God. I'm sorry," I say again. "I—wow."

Okay, she looked good from afar, but up close, she turns my brain to mush. I stare at her, trying to urge myself forward with the plan, but I'm gaping at her like a fish.

"Mike? What the hell are you doing?" she says.

"You're beautiful," I stutter. Then I shake my head, forcing myself into gear. "Uh—have we met before? Because I swear, I'd remember if we did."

She rolls her eyes, but a grin creeps across her lips. Lips all ... full and inviting.

"I—" She pauses. Then her expression relaxes, like she's twigged on to what I'm trying to do. "I'm—I'm not sure," she says. "But I like your flower."

"I'm Michael," I say, going down the formal route and holding out my hand.

"Eleanor," she replies, taking my palm. "I think you should be more careful, Michael. Reading whilst walking is dangerous ... apparently." She eyes the newspaper.

"I am so sorry," I say, keeping my eyes locked on hers. "Could I buy you a drink in way of an apology?"

"I'm not sure," she says, looking around. "I'm supposed to be meeting someone."

My stomach drops. "Right."

She looks at me, cocks her head to the side. "Yeah, he's pretty special, actually. A tad impulsive, but gives excellent hugs ... and he's tenacious. Inspiring. He's given me the kick I needed to push myself. He's the reason I'm standing here with a fancy hairdo. Wedding style practice. I've been to a workshop today because he gave me the motivation."

Well, fuck. My stomach feels light—like I'm about to take off.

I swallow, testing my voice. "Sounds like you may be into him," I say shakily.

She nods. "I ... I think I am, but see, he thinks we should start fresh, but I think we've got a good foundation—despite the hiccups."

"So what could he do better, going forward? Apart from doing a little more thinking. I mean, he's trying to do better. He's trying to—"

But I'm halted mid-sentence when she kisses me. A peck on the lips but my body sparks alight, and I feel *alive*.

She pulls away. "Let's go for a drink, Mike."

Chapter 18

Ellie

I can't believe I did that. I can't believe I mustered the courage to kiss him and now I'm flustered and embarrassed and—

"Let's go for a drink, Mike," I blurt, turning away to hide my glowing face; hot and flushed.

I grab his hand to lead him away, but I come to an abrupt stop. My hand trapped in an anchored embrace.

"Kitch?" he says.

Oh, my goodness. I'm going to have to turn and look at him. I'm going to have to look him in the eye while he asks me what the hell I just did, and he'll force me to come clean—tell him how I feel.

But I can't. Because I'm already out of bravery today. I've depleted the well and all that's left is the silt at the bottom.

"Hm?" I murmur, opting to go passive.

But he tugs on my arm, and I know I can't leave it any longer. I have to look at him; I have to turn around and ... I lock eyes with him and the concourse full of people, busy and frantic, floats away until there's only us.

Oh, God.

He takes a step forward and tugs my hand, pulling me towards him, then he releases his grip, letting my arm drop to my side.

"Kitch—you've got to give me more than that," he says, a teasing tone in his voice.

"I—" Whatever I was going to say catches in my throat when his left hand cups my cheek. Heat. Sizzling contact as his skin touches mine. Then he dips his head, slow and sure, like he's giving me a chance to step away. But I don't. My body does that thing again ... where it decides before my brain catches up.

And before I know it, I'm moving in and closing the gap.

"Betts!"

There's someone shouting his name. But instead of backing away, his lips are on mine and the world around me fades again.

Oh, God.

I feel drunk. Like my head is fuzzy and there's a current flowing through my veins. And the feeling increases tenfold when he parts his lips and mine follow in sync. Eager. Desperate, even. And my hands take on a life of their own, gripping his suit jacket—clinging onto him like I'll collapse if I don't.

His tongue brushes mine and I've lost it. I've folded into him and anyone could be watching—someone *is* watching.

"Betts!"

Mike pauses, cupping my chin with his hand as he pulls away, resting his forehead on mine for a beat—his eyes closed for a fraction of a second longer before he peels them open, locking eyes on mine. He smiles, intertwining my hand in his, before he turns towards the voice.

"Coach," he says. "Sorry, I didn't—"

"Nah, I don't suppose you did. And I guess I wouldn't typically interrupt a public display like that. I wondered if I was mistaken at first, because I wasn't expecting to see you here."

"I guess I could say the same thing about you, Coach."

"Just passing through," Coach says. Then his eyes linger on me for a second, like he's waiting for Mike to introduce us ... why isn't he introducing us?

Then it hits me. Coach. Mike's Coach ... and for the second time today, I act on impulse, letting my instinct take over. I hold my hand out and step forward to introduce myself.

"Hi, I'm Ellie—Mike's wife. It's so nice to meet you."

He grins at me and Mike swivels his head in my direction, mouth open in a perfect 'o', a hint of my lipstick smeared on his lips.

"Well, I must admit, I'm glad to see you've settled down," Coach says, flashing a grin towards Mike. "I never thought he'd have it in him."

Okay, now I'm confused. I stare blankly at Mike.

"Uh—yeah," he says, turning back towards Coach. "Ellie, this is Coach Sinclair. He used to coach me at junior level. I mean—how long's it been, Coach?"

Oh, *God*.

I purse my lips, trying to suppress the horror. Because this is unbearable. Only I could blurt something out like that to someone who doesn't actually give a crap.

"Oh, it's got to be over ten years. I mean, what are you now? Twenty-six?"

"Yeah," Mike nods.

But I'm dying of mortification. Fixed on the moment I introduced myself as Mike's wife. I mean...

"Ellie?"

"I'm sorry, what?" I say, blinking away the memory.

"I hear congratulations are in order," Coach says. "I was just asking how you're feeling about Betts here getting a Team GB spot. I mean—I can't take any of the credit, but I sure as hell did all I could before I moved on." He takes a breath. "I still can't believe that replacement of mine didn't think you were good enough for—"

"Well, yeah. I think it's worked out okay. I mean, I've got a terrific team, and I feel at home where I am."

"I'm glad to hear it—listen, my connection is due any minute, but I saw you and couldn't pass up the opportunity to commend you. And wish you luck for tomorrow. You were one of my favourites, and I want to see you do well. Get your name on that cup."

There's a flurry of goodbyes and he turns away, striding towards the platforms.

This is it. This is where I die of embarrassment. Here on the concourse.

But I don't give Mike anytime to ask questions. I throw a question at him, hoping to cause a distraction.

"What's tomorrow?" I ask.

"Challenge Cup Final," he says, raising an eyebrow. "But oh no you don't." He turns back towards me. "You don't get to throw out the wife card and pretend like you didn't."

There's a smile the size of the sun on his face and all I want to do is kiss him again, but I bite my lip.

"You called him Coach so I—"

"Yeah, sorry about it. Old habits die hard. It's like ingrained. And he was a really good Coach, too—but c'mon, Kitch ... you said..."

I look down at the polished concrete.

"I guess, I did."

"Right," he says.

I'm fixed on the shiny floor for a moment longer before I lift my head, meeting his eyes.

"I guess ... I mean... I thought—" I swallow, trying to understand, but I can't fully place it. Why did I blurt it out? Why did it feel natural and easy? Like it was on the tip of my tongue the whole time ... waiting for the right moment. Then it comes to me in the most obvious of reflections. "I thought, why not? Why not? I can't think of a reason why not anymore."

Mike nods. A slow movement of his head, like he's thinking.

"Right," he says again.

"I mean ... why not, right?"

He stares at me for a beat longer before rubbing his hand over his stubble.

"Well, you don't have to decide today. I mean—Coach Sinclair probably won't see anyone to mention anything."

"Mike—"

"Honestly, I'm sorry I put you on the spot like that. I didn't even think—I guess that's typical of me, right? I saw him and—"

"Of course you'd call him Coach. It makes sense. I mean, it's a respectful thing to do, right?" I settle a hand on his forearm.

"Yeah, but ... I just don't want to lock you into something. That's not fair. I get that now."

Maybe he's right.

"Okay, how about this—we get a drink? Back to Plan 'A', yeah?"

"Of course," he says, holding out his hand.

I slip my palm into his and we make our way towards the exit, joining the stream of people moving towards the street.

"So, why the clock?" I ask Mike as we head outside.

"Imagine when our kids ask us how we met. We can tell them about the clock and how romantic it was because when you think about it—it all comes down to time. Right place, right time."

I roll my eyes with a smile. "But we didn't actually meet for the first time under that clock. We met in Maths. Year seven, Mrs Jones' room."

Mike adjusts himself to look at me, eyebrows pulled together. "Nah, it wasn't then," he says. "It was before Maths. It was in registration. I remember thinking you were the most beautiful girl in the world."

A grin cements itself on my face.

"Regardless, it wasn't—wait ... our kids?"

He chuckles. A deep rumble that warms my whole body.

"Don't you want kids?" he asks, tilting his head to the side.

"This is ... deep," I say, unsure of myself.

"It's just a general question," he says. "Sorry I was—"

"I'm—I'm not sure. I guess I haven't really thought about it," I say. "I hate the idea of having a favourite child if I were to have more than one. Because I think every parent has a favourite, even if they don't admit it."

"Well, you're not wrong," he says. "I'm definitely my mam's favourite. My dad ... not so much."

"What make's you say that?"

"Just a feeling I get, I guess," he shrugs, but his eyes stick to mine, bright and full of wonder. "But there's no way you aren't your folks' favourite. I mean ... you or Kathryn." He frees his hand and aligns it with the other, suspending them in the air, palms upward. He moves them up and down, sizing us up—apparently.

The Ellie hand wins.

"Well, favourite or not ... I'm definitely not Kathryn's favourite sister. Something happened yesterday and I, uh..."

He takes my hand again, planting a kiss on the back.

"Wanna tell me about it? I mean, you don't have to, but I'm here if you want to vent or whatever. I'll warn you though ... I'll probably offer suggestions on how you should fix it."

I let out a deflated laugh. "I think you've already done the fixing. Even though it wasn't really your *thing* to fix."

And as we walk, hand in hand, down the street, I tell Mike all about Kathryn and the phone call he made when we were eighteen.

Bettsy

"WHAT DO YOU MEAN, it was her?" I say, as Ellie concludes her story.

I was busy revelling in the fact that Kathryn initially assumed ownership of Ellie's flowers but this ... I halt on the pavement, and Ellie, a couple of paces ahead of me, stumbles to a stop when our hands disconnect.

"I—"

But I don't think. I spin around, intending to stalk back towards the railway station, even going as far as taking several steps along the pavement before Ellie slips in front of me, blocking my progress.

"Mike, what are you doing?" she says, her voice level.

"Going to have a word with your sister," I snap.

"No, you're not. We're going for our drink," she says, tugging on my arm. "Or at least I am. I'm celebrating. And I think there are better things for you to be doing than having a verbal altercation with my sister. She loves drama. Don't give her what she wants, Mike. Please."

"I'm sorry but—"

"Mike, come on," she says, softening the grip on my arm. "Do you really want to spend the evening on a train?"

I exhale, letting the air leave my lungs in hope it'll take some of the frustration with it, but the heaviness sits firm in my chest.

Fucking Kathryn. Honestly.

I clench my jaw, wondering if...

"Mike," she says again, soft and warm, and I take little more convincing, apparently, because I'm nodding in agreement and swivelling around to follow her.

I guess she's right. What good would it do? Like Ellie's already alluded to, Kathryn wouldn't admit it, anyway, and I'd only end up losing my temper and giving someone somewhere more hot gossip to write up on the fan forum. It's the last thing I need, considering I've only just made the Team GB roster.

"So, where do you fancy going?" she asks airily.

"What are we celebrating? Anything in particular?" I ask.

"I had a good day," she says, pausing for a moment. "At the bridal workshop. I'm feeling positive. It feels good to think about what comes next for me and to do something I want to be doing. And it's good for my professional network. I just need to figure out what I'm doing about my marketing, I guess. But that's a problem for tomorrow. Is here okay?"

She stops outside a cosy-looking pub, and I instinctively reach for the door to pull it open.

"Well, I may know some people, if that helps? I can have a word and see if they'd be up for helping."

"You know a web designer?" she says, stepping over the threshold. We're immediately hit with the faint smell of hops and charcoal.

"Yeah. My mate Ryan, from the team. His wife does all the stuff for the club. I'm sure she'd be happy to help—I mean, I have been providing free manual labour for their home renovation. It's the least they can do."

"Oh, right. Well, I don't want to impose or anything. But if she is looking for work and she could give me a quote ... I need to figure out what my budget is, but yeah, it's a start, right?"

We weave through the tables and head towards the bar, where I pull out my wallet.

"What're you having?" I ask.

"I guess a white wine, please. Since I'm getting the train back."

I wait for the bartender to make her way over to us and order a large glass for her and a diet Coke for me, letting a frown slip over my face as I do so.

"Oh, I'll get a soft drink too, if you are," Ellie says, leaning onto the bar to check the fridge.

"Nah, it's fine. Don't let me impede your celebration. Believe me ... I'd rather something stronger, but with the game tomorrow I—"

Ellie turns towards me, mirroring my frown. "Oh, my gosh. I'm sorry. I've been too busy complaining to even ask about it."

"There's not much to tell," I say. "It's the cup final. If we win, we win the shiny cup. If we lose, we don't win the shiny cup."

I tap to pay for the drinks and we find a seat, opting to settle ourselves into a table near the window.

"But it's a big deal," she says, sitting down.

"Well, yeah. We've worked hard to get here. It's all down to sixty-minutes, but it's nothing we haven't done before."

I set my drink down and slip into the seat opposite, but I know straight away something's up.

"Is everything okay?" I ask, watching Ellie fixate on her glass.

"Yeah, of course." She pulls her eyes away from her drink and offers me a smile. But I'm not convinced. It lacks the warmth and brightness it typically holds, like she's forcing it.

"Okay—I don't believe you."

She fiddles with a lock of hair. "Have you won this sort of thing before?"

"Well, yeah but—"

"See, I feel like I should have known," she says, pulling at her lip with her teeth.

I study her for a moment, trying to work out how I can lighten the tension of the situation.

"Well, I mean, if you were as obsessed with me as you claim to be, then..." I grin, trying to catch her eye, but she's making it difficult. Like she's feeling off. "Kitch, come on ... talk to me."

"I guess I'm just ... I don't know. Never mind," she forces the smile again, though harder this time, and I think I've worked it out. She's disappointed. Or at least, I guess she is, though I can't be sure why.

Maybe it's because she feels like this is the sort of stuff she should know? Or perhaps it's because this highlights how much we don't know about each other? I mean, there's so much about her I don't know either.

I sit on the observation for a moment longer, watching her sip her drink and fixate on the beer mat it rests on, now damp with condensation. Then it occurs to me: I should ask her to come to my game. I mean ... we've moved forward tonight, right? The kiss ... fuck me, the kiss that's lingering on my lips in a way I never expected. And the declaration to Coach Sinclair ... I should ask her, shouldn't I?

I swallow down the anxiety of being rejected, then I brace myself, taking a sip of my drink, revelling in the coolness to calm my nerves.

"I, uh ... don't suppose you'd want to come and watch the game tomorrow, would you?" I ask.

She looks up, locking eyes with me as I wait. Hopeful.

"Tomorrow?" she says.

"Well, yeah. Tomorrow evening."

"I—" She traces a droplet of condensation down the side of her glass. "I—I don't know anything about hockey."

"So? It's literally just five skaters—three forwards, two defence—and a goalie. All fighting over a rubber disc. I mean, there's more to it than that, from my perspective ... it's not about the puck so much but more of the other players... or D. It's a game of trust and strategy and—" I tail off, realising I'm on transmit before clearing my throat. "I'll get you a ticket next to Kelly. She can give you some guidance. Though she knows too much, if you ask me. And it's even fucking worse now she's seeing Johnny—our captain. The two of them together are like—" Ellie's gaze drops to the table again and panic hits me.

This is too much. I've bombarded her with information, and now I've asked too much of her. And why, oh why, did I suggest she sit with my sister? That'll open the door up to a load of questions and ... I panic, almost stumbling over my words as I try to backtrack.

"I mean, you don't have to sit by Kel," I say. "I can get you another seat somewhere else, or you could just come another time. It's not a big deal."

"Where is it?" she says. "Home?"

I nod. "Yeah, since we were the highest seeds."

"I see." She's quiet for a moment and I'm trying my hardest to think of something else to say, but she looks up again, her big brown eyes melting into mine. "I can see if I can, I mean—"

Oh, shit. She's hesitating. She doesn't want to come.

"Honestly, don't worry. It's fine. I get it. You've got clients and then there's travel…" I force a smile, trying to act indifferent.

"I would really like to see you play, Mike," she says, stretching out a hand to rest on my own. "Can I let you know tomorrow? I'll see what I can figure out." She pulls out her phone and starts flicking through the screens. "I've got some afternoon appointments, that's all. Maybe Kathryn can cover them for me."

My heart, already thumping loudly, picks up speed as I nod. "Sure."

Chapter 19

I KNEW THIS MORNING was suspiciously perfect. That's what they say, right? If something's too good to be true, then it probably is.

I woke up ahead of my alarm. I checked the forum to find *'ilovetopuck'* banned again. I even texted Mike to agree on a plan for this evening, pushing myself well and truly out of my comfort zone. I was riding on the high of last night. The drinks turned into food, which turned into a late-night conversation at a quiet bar before we boarded trains going in opposite directions.

Not to mention the goodnight kiss.

I could still feel it lingering on my lips as I did my makeup. I could still feel his hands running through my hair as I did my blow dry.

I was sated.

Was being the operative word, because the moment I pulled up at the salon, my good mood came crashing down like a stylist trolly with a dodgy wheel.

Five seconds. That's all it took.

And now I'm still sitting in my car, across the street, staring.

The first thing I noticed was the scaffolding, tubes of vertical and horizontal supports crowding the front of the salon. The second was Greg in a suit, loitering next to the open door, talking to a guy in a hi-vis vest. The third was the sign, black with gold lettering, a fancy font of loops and curls, but there's no mistaking the three words shimmering in the morning sun.

House of Kathryn.

She's re-branded.

Kathryn has re-branded.

I run my eyes over the gold lettering—bold, pompous, a testament to Kathryn's self-importance, no doubt. And I wait to feel something ... anger? Hurt? Betrayal? But there's nothing. The happiness I woke up with drains out of me, leaving only numbness.

I sit still for another second, wondering if I should drive off. Wondering if she'd even notice. But she'd love that. She'd love for me to act like this wasn't happening.

I'm out of my car and marching towards the salon in a flash, grateful I'm wearing flats. As I get closer, Greg turns and clocks me, cutting the conversation he's having with the construction worker.

"Ah, good, Ellie's here," he says, as I come to a stop. "Ellie." He beckons for me to move closer, like he's giving me permission. "This is Jordon. He's just about to dismantle the scaffolding, then you can open properly."

I plaster on a sickly sweet smile as I greet Jordon, then I round on Greg.

"What's going on?" I say.

"What do you mean?" he asks, following my gaze to the new signage. "Oh yeah, Kathryn had me pull some strings to get this up today. Apparently, it couldn't wait." He shrugs.

"Where is Kathryn?"

"Ah, she won't be long," he says. "She said she'll be back in time for Chantelle's arrival."

Chantelle? Chantelle? Do I know a Chantelle? I think for a moment, searching the corners of my mind for any recollection, but there's nothing familiar about the name Chantelle, nor the pending arrival of anyone. Maybe she's a new client of Kathryn's, though I don't know why Greg would be interested enough to learn her name.

"Um, Chantelle?" I ask, folding my arms as I turn towards him.

"Yeah, the new stylist," he says, absentmindedly signing something Jordon thrusts under his nose.

I gape at him. "The new stylist?"

Greg narrows his eyes. "Y-yeah. Why do you look so surprised?"

"I wasn't aware we were recruiting a new stylist," I say.

"Really? Kathryn said you'd both spoken about offering wedding services, so it made sense to hire someone who specialises in bridal." Greg pulls his phone out of his pocket. "Sorry, El. I need to get this—oh, actually," he says. "... we need to catch up about the 'you know what'." He taps the side of his nose before slipping away, phone pressed to his ear.

A heavy hollowness settles in my chest. Chantelle. Bridal. House of Kathryn. What the—

The click of heels against the pavement slabs behind me draws my attention away from Jordon the scaffolder, and I turn to see my sister strutting towards the salon, with a brunette who looks like she's just stepped out of a modern-day production of *Hairspray*.

"Morning," Kathryn says as she closes in. "Glad to see you made an effort today." She casts me an 'up and down' look, not even trying to hide her assessment of my appearance.

She breezes past me, practically dragging who I can only assume to be Chantelle through the salon door. Like a lost sheep, desperate to find my way home, I trot after her—impatient for an explanation.

"When did you decide to re-brand?" I say.

"Oh, it's been on the horizon for a while," she says. "Genius, don't you think? I mean ... it really captures the image I'm trying to portray. Besides, this is about growth. My growth, really." She lets out a false laugh. "I'm taking control of my business."

Her business.

I'm lost for words, really, I am. Because even though it is technically Kathryn's salon, we'd agreed it was a joint venture. After all, I've put money into this place too.

Kathryn, smug and triumphant, turns to her new companion.

"Anyway—Ellie, this is Chantelle. Chantelle, this is my little sister, Ellie." She flicks her hair as she turns back towards me. "She's going to be starting here today. Would you mind grabbing her coat and putting the kettle on?"

Chantelle, on cue, slips out of her coat and holds it out to me, but I don't take it. I stand rooted to the spot, committing my attention to my sister.

I lazily point towards the back of the salon before saying, "the coat hooks are there."

Chantelle backs away and I shuffle closer to Kathryn.

"Do we need a new stylist?" I ask.

"Yes," Kathryn says. "It'll give you a chance to focus on the business side of things, El. Get the accounts in order. I mean, I know you do a pretty good job at that, anyway, but you won't have any more distractions now."

"The accounts?" I say, my voice breaking.

"Yes. The accounts. I'm doing you a favour here, El. You said you'd rather not do treatments so—"

"I said I'd rather not do nails and spray tans," I snap. "That's not what I spent years perfecting. I didn't even want to do those things ... ever. You—" I jab my index finger towards her "—you were the one who as good as forced me to do extra training."

Kathryn glares at me. "God, you're so ungrateful. After all I've done for you." She pauses before relaxing her shoulders. "Look, take this as an opportunity to learn from Chantelle. She can show you the ropes of what it takes to be a real stylist. You know, get into the wedding game. Maybe then you can try to get a deal with the magazine."

Oh, my God. She actually thinks she's the one doing me the favour. I wish I hadn't stopped Mike last night. I wish I'd let him put Kathryn in her place.

"Is this because of Mike?" I say.

Kathryn looks like she has smelt something considerably unpleasant.

"Mike?" she says, with an air of someone feigning ignorance.

"You know exactly who and what I'm talking about," I say. "The flowers—" I look towards the window, grateful that I had the sense to take them home before I attended the bridal workshop. "—ever since those flowers..."

"I don't know what you're talking about," she says. But I see it on her face, in her eyes. There's something she's not telling me. And it's so infuriating, I could shake her. "Are you going to stand around or—"

"Jeremy Betts," I say, more to myself than to Kathryn.

"Sorry?"

"Jeremy Betts," I say, louder this time, looking her right in the eye.

"I—I'm not here to talk about Mike's dead brother," she says with a sharpness in her tone.

I widen my eyes. "Kath—"

"Can you just get on with opening the salon?" she says. "Maybe if you spent more time working and less time playing 'Little Miss Detective' then—"

"I'm sorry, what?" I say. "Working? Working? Are you sure you don't mean pandering to your every will?"

"You're being ridiculous," Kathryn says.

And that's it. That's all it takes for something inside me to snap like a cheap comb.

After all the compromises I've made, all the times I've let Kathryn have her way—I'm done.

"Am I? Because I don't think I am. I think ... you're scared that I'll make something of myself. I think you're scared I'll find my own way and I'll make my own decisions and mistakes. And you won't have control of me any longer."

Kathryn's eyes flash, and she turns, reaching for a decorative vase full of glass pebbles sitting on the counter. Before I can register what's happening, in one firm swoop she half-spins and the vase sails through the air, clattering to the floor after it rebounds against the mirror opposite my stylists' chair.

Thousands of pieces of glass and mirror rain down and all I can do is stare at the wreckage. My jaw on the floor.

For a long moment, no one moves. Not me. Not Kathryn. All I can hear is her laboured breathing, heavy and urgent, until there's a shuffling to my right, and I drag my attention away from the mess to see Chantelle, in an almost comical shock.

Then Kathryn moves. Her expression shifts to horror, then panic as she realises the magnitude of her actions. She looks at me, then back towards the mess.

"That's your fault," she says.

I open my mouth to speak, protest even—but nothing comes. I can only stand flabbergasted, willing myself to say something.

But Kathryn, being Kathryn, does what she always does when she doesn't get her own way. She runs. Without another word, she turns and grabs her bag and bolts for the exit, leaving Chantelle and me in complete disbelief.

Bettsy

"YOU KNOW WHAT I found out last night?" I say to the guys as we're readying up for the game. "The whole concept of hiring a hitman is bullshit. See, the media industry has glamorised the whole 'assassin for hire' thing, but in reality, they don't exist in the way people think they do."

Johnny stares at me. Hutch and Danny roll their eyes. Ryan and Liam laugh.

"A hitman?" Hutch says. "What the hell are you doing looking for hitmen?"

"I'm not," I say. "I was listening to a podcast, and I got curious. Wanted to learn more."

"What was the podcast? Dumb things to Google to get yourself arrested?"

I roll my eyes. "Har-har. Nah, there's a site on the dark web claiming to knock people off for, like, a few thousand dollars," I say. "But it's a hoax. No hitmen. Just some asshat rolling in money from people dumb enough to pay up."

"People don't actually pay for that sort of stuff though, do they?" Danny says.

"Yes. That's the scary part," I say. "They do. And it turns out, someone hacked the site and had access to all the requests. Hundreds of them. Then he spent months trying to track the targets down, and when he did, he'd call them and tell them what he found to warn them."

"But I thought you said the hitmen weren't real?" Danny says.

"They aren't, but there's still someone who put the hit out, isn't there? No doubt they'll realise their request isn't getting fulfilled and opt to do something about it themselves. Honestly, it's wild. People just don't give a shit, do they?"

Johnny stands up and pulls on his jersey. "Are you okay, bud? I'm not sure the dark web is the place for you."

"I just find it interesting," I shrug.

But he's right. It's probably not the place for me.

It started with an informative podcast when I couldn't sleep last night; I was still buzzing from the evening I spent with Ellie.

The next thing I knew, I'd discovered that for two hundred pounds, you can pay someone to hack a social media account, and for another few hundred, you can pay to have someone harassed online. And did I think about paying up? It crossed my mind, I can't lie.

For a second, I thought about hiring someone to operate the 'justiceforBettsy' stuff full time or perhaps, figure out who's behind it. Surprisingly, it's made a positive impact on my public image; another finding of my late-night jaunt online. In addition, getting Rochelle harassed on the side would be an opportunity to give her a taste of her own medicine. I briefly considered doing some reputational damage to Kathryn too, but then I slept and woke up feeling less malevolent.

Honestly, I should never trust the ideas I have between the hours of one and four in the morning.

"You haven't paid anyone to ... you know, kill someone off, have you?" Johnny says, in a quiet voice.

"No, of course not," I say. "Just heard it on a podcast and thought I'd share."

I'm not kidding, but since it's becoming even more enticing, I figure it's better to share. That way, the dark web can't tempt me because everyone in the dressing room knows too much.

"Or are you seeing a gap in the market?" Hutch grins. "Because it sounds like there's money to be made."

"Well, I guess I could—"

"Enough," Johnny says. "Can we focus, guys? Can we get our head in the game and think about the outcome of tonight? Because we've worked our asses off all season and the last thing I want is for someone to decide tonight is the night to start a side-hustle." He pauses, looking around the room. "That can wait for the off-season—though no 'killer-for-hire' schemes, please."

That shuts me up, anyway. Because Johnny's right, I need to focus.

My head is elsewhere, and it's got nothing to do with hitmen. It's Ellie. All about Ellie.

The shit I just rambled was a crap attempt to distract myself because I haven't heard from her since this morning and I'm worried. And as far as I'm aware, she's not been in touch with my sister, Kelly, either.

The plan was for her to sit with Kel on the basis that Ellie is in town for work. Just an old friend watching an old friend's hockey game. Simple. Except, Kelly hasn't confirmed if she's here or not and I don't want to sound keen by texting her to ask, either.

I pull my phone out to check my messages when Coach Adams comes in, followed by Springy. They loiter near the door to the dressing room as they call us to listen in. I fire off a quick text to Ellie before tossing my phone into my cubby.

"How are we feeling?" Coach says, looking around the room and it's at this moment the gravity of the situation hits me.

This isn't just a silver cup. This is a demonstration of success. Hard work. Focus. And the unease in my stomach turns up a notch—reminding me I'm human.

"Remember boys, we don't need to do anything special tonight. We just need to remain focused—keep thinking about the next goal. Stay disciplined ... don't let them get you too excited. You've done this before, and you can do it again. Over to you, Koenig," Coach says.

All heads swivel in Johnny's direction.

"Well, boys, as Coach said—there's nothing special here. Another game, another opportunity to prove ourselves. But we don't have time for silly mistakes. Think about the next move, think about the next play. Look after each other. Communicate…"

My phone vibrates. I catch it on the edge of my hearing, and that's all it takes for me to zone out. The intrigue. The curiosity. Has Ellie texted me back? Is she here? Is she about to watch me lose focus—or worse, throw up on the blueline?

The chorus of cheers brings me back into the room, where I snap my attention back to Johnny, who's beaming around the room at the guys. He takes in the scene before turning away from the crowd, suddenly invested in his tape bag, sitting on the shelf of his cubby.

Ah, shit.

"We've got this, Cap," I say, forcing myself to smile. Forcing myself to set my own anxiety aside. "You know that, right? We know what we're doing. We'll be on fire out there."

He's still for a moment before he turns towards me, a half-assed attempt at a smile creeping over his face. "Yeah, bud. You're right."

Coach claps his hands to regain the attention of the room.

"Right," he says, holding out a piece of paper to Johnny. "Starters."

Johnny grabs the paper and unfolds it, skimming over the content before he exhales sharply.

"Let's hear the energy," he says. "We've got Jonesy and Yatesy starting us on 'D'." A roar of applause fills the room. "Preston one and two on wing, and Jani taking the centre spot. Between the pipes—" He pauses for effect, "Ffordey." The boys go wild, and of course, I join in, acting like I'm not fazed in the slightest. Acting like I'm not about to throw up.

My phone vibrates again. And I turn to grab it, desperate to check it before we leave, but Danny's quicker, smacking me on the back and steering me towards the door.

"Ready, mate?" he says.

"Yeah, you know me. Born ready," I say, forcing a grin, and Danny buys it.

I wait right up until the moment he steps ahead of me before mumbling some bullshit about needing to grab my other mouthguard, and because the guys are forming a line in the tunnel ready for the announcement, I know I don't have long.

I just need to know if it was her.

Chapter 20

Bettsy

I LIVE FOR MOMENTS like this; they're part of the reason I was so keen to pursue hockey professionally. The crowd, all chanting in unison. The prospect of winning a cup. The way my lungs burn from the effort.

But my favourite thing?

The perfect first stride when the ice is smooth—untouched. For a second, everything fades away. No noise. No lights. No chaos.

That moment of clarity. Where everything is as it should be. Just me and the ice.

Except today it's different. It doesn't feel the same. I'm unsettled. Anxious. And it's got nothing to do with this being the cup final.

"Ready?" Johnny asks.

I nod, trying to convince myself I'm focused, confident and fired up. As I take my place on the blueline for my first shift of the final period, I channel all my energy on one thing: defence. Forty-five seconds of high-intensity concentration and defence.

"Smart plays only," Johnny says before taking his position on the left. I find my spot on the right, waiting for Liam to lean in to take the face-off.

There's a pause. Then the ref blows his whistle. Then the puck drops.

The moment it hits the ice, Lee gains control and flicks it towards me with no hesitation. I accept the pass and play it back, keeping the puck close to the blade of my stick as I move in reverse. I'm letting the guys find their places, assessing the opposition. I wait for their positions to stabilise before I decide on my next move: a pass to Jani, waiting in the neutral zone.

It ricochets off the shin pad of one of their defencemen as Jani attempts a forward pass to Prez, right into the stick of an opposition winger, who takes control, moving in my direction.

"On me," I call, and Johnny and I quickly adjust, falling back to cover the attack.

I fight to keep focus. Desperate to keep my head in the game.

The next few moments are a blur of motion. The opposing forward, trying to gain an edge, dangles the puck, trying to lure me in. But I stay patient, my body tense, knees bent. As he attempts a quick pass, I extend my stick to intercept, but he skates around me, sending the puck wide. The shot comes off his stick fast and slams into my shin guard with a jarring thud, knocking me off balance.

Okay, I may be a little distracted. There's a tiny part of me thinking about that text message.

But I get back to my feet, wincing in pain, using that to concentrate on the game. I follow the direction of the puck, but there's a rush, and I have no choice but to charge, knocking a forward into the boards with a satisfying rumble.

The volume of the crowd intensifies.

"Good block, bud, but let's clear those rebounds faster," Johnny says as we skate back to the bench half a minute later. "Remember, they're looking for mistakes. Keep your focus and we've got this."

He's right. My focus is not what it should be. And I can't afford to carry on this way. We're tied 2-2 with around eighteen minutes left. It's crucial I live in the moment.

Johnny and I take our places on the bench, leaning forward to watch the play progress, watching the movements of the opposition's defence. But I'm struggling to invest.

Concentrate, Bettsy. Concentrate.

"He's heavy on the forecheck today," I say to Johnny, pointing towards their number four. But I only say it to keep on topic and to stop my mind from wandering.

"Ah shit," Johnny says, leaning further forward. "This is our chance."

We watch the sequence of play, keeping our attention on the ice as our attack moves up the ice, forcing their defence into action.

Clink.

The crowd makes a unanimous groan as the puck rebounds.

"Good pressure, though," he says. "And now it's up to us to keep it going."

He nods his head towards the returning pair of defenceman, swinging his legs over the shelf as he waits for Jonesy to coast to the bench, and I do the same, hovering for a second longer until Yatesy is clear.

I hit the ice, joining the play on the transition to the offensive zone.

"Cover the slot," Johnny shouts back at me as he breaches the blue line.

And I do. Focus and concentration.

I throw my body against my mark as I survey the play, trying to work out his next move. All it takes is a rogue pass in my direction and I shift my weight, leaning forward and diverting the puck, sending it through the air back towards Johnny, who whacks it around the boards to a waiting Prez.

"Good job," he says, as we fall back, positioning ourselves on the point.

Lee sends it out of play, and we're forced to take a face-off in the neutral zone.

Focus, Betts. Focus.

"If Lee gets it, I'll quick up," Johnny says before he circles into position. "Follow my lead."

And of course, Lee flicks it back towards Johnny, who executes as planned, sending a sharp pass towards Prez to initiate a rush. I watch Prez move forward for a split second before I clock their right defenceman, watching his reaction.

He pinches aggressively, trying to disrupt Prez. But Prez is fast—too fast for him. Prez pokes it past him. The footrace for possession is on, and I know I need to stay back—wait for the turnover I can feel coming.

Focus, Betts. Focus.

It's Johnny who gets my attention next. He's calling for support, and I have to push forward to protect against a counterattack.

But that's when Prez takes a heavy check into the boards, losing the battle as he crashes to the ice. My eyes widen as I watch him, waiting for him to move, relieved as he clambers to his skates as the puck is snatched away, an opposing forward gaining possession. He breaks away, flying at speed towards the neutral zone.

This is on me. This is my play.

I barely have a second to react. I burst to life, keeping up pace with him as I aim to cut him off. I use my body to block his movement, creating a barrier. I hold him off just long enough for Johnny to get there, taking position close enough to Ffordey.

Mr Offensive fires it, and Johnny's shin becomes the point of deflection, sending it into the air and out of play.

That's our sign to change up. I glide back to the bench with Johnny on my heel.

"Nice play, bud," he says. "Honestly, it surprises me you had to wait so long for a Team GB slot."

I look up at the clock, checking how long I need to keep things cool before replying to Johnny.

"Well, yeah, I'm grateful, don't get me wrong, but it's not all sunshine and roses."

Our backup nettie holds the bench door open and we hustle, taking our seats as the play resets. I reach for a towel, running it over my visor before tossing it aside and grabbing a water bottle, keen to keep myself busy.

"Langdon? I thought you said practices were fine?" he says. "He's not been giving you shit, has he?"

"Well, they've been bearable. He's hardly said a word, if I'm honest. And that's probably what's putting me on edge. He doesn't seem his usual shitty self. It's like waiting for a ticking time-bomb to detonate."

Johnny shrugs. "He's probably feeling the pressure."

We lean forward, looking out on the ice as the face-off is taken, watching in eager anticipation as Danny wins the battle and sends it back to the third line defenceman on his left.

"Maybe. But I don't care enough to think about it. I guess I'll see how things go."

The truth is, I can't think about it. My mental capacity is teetering on the edge. I'm using all my energy to focus on the game, not what the Team GB schedule looks like, nor what—

"This is it..." Johnny says, snapping me back to the game. I blink, expecting to see something triumphant, but instead, I realise that this is very much not it.

The puck flies in slow motion, connecting with the crossbar and rebounding off with a clink and it lands at the feet of an opposing forward. He takes a beat to react, looking between the puck and the empty stretch of ice in front of him, then he bursts at speed, breaking away.

Right up the ice towards a lonely-looking Ffordey.

GOD, I HOPE HE answers.

With a shaky hand, I press the buzzer for Mike's apartment, trying to steady my breathing.

Please pick up. Please pick up.

"Yeah?" The line crackles to life as a voice cuts through the speaker, causing my heart to bounce in my chest.

It's him. Thank God, it's him.

"It's me," I say, swallowing down a fresh wave of tears. "Kitch."

I stare at the intercom, waiting for him to say something, but there's a static *buzz* as the lobby door unlatches seconds before the connection drops.

The lobby is empty, all bar a plastic-looking plant next to the lift. I edge closer, hiking my bag higher on my shoulder, and jab the call button several times.

Seventh floor.

Sixth floor.

Fifth floor.

Fourth floor.

A door swings open behind me and I spin to see Mike, jogging from the stairwell, trainers unlaced, a cap pulled low over his eyes.

"Oh, my God," he says. "Are you okay? Did she—" He rushes towards me as the lift pings to a stop behind me. "You're alright, yeah?"

And that's all it takes—someone asking how *I* am for me to burst into tears. Full-on, heaving sobs, like I've been holding them in for years. Big, bulbous tears streak down my cheeks, hot and relentless.

My shoulder lightens as Mike lifts the strap of my bag away. Then, in one smooth motion, he scoops me up like I weigh nothing. His fresh, woody scent fills my nose, momentarily dulling the ache of betrayal inside me.

"I'm sorry, Mike. I'm sorry I missed your game," I say, blinking away the tears. "I got to the rink and there was no one there and—"

"The rink?" he says. "Your text said you might not make it and—"

"I had the webcast and my phone died and when I got off the train I just got a cab to the rink and the driver was asking me all these questions and then I missed—"

I gasp. Waiting for the air to hit my lungs.

"You're okay, sweetheart," he says, his voice soft and buttery as he holds me tighter.

Sweetheart.

"But I missed your game," I say into his chest. "I tried to get there in time for the end but I missed it ... and I asked someone and they said you—"

But I can't bring myself to say it. *Lost.*

"Ah, don't worry about it. I play lots of games," he says. "Honestly, I was really worried about you. I mean, Kathryn—"

I pull away sharply and peer up at him.

"Oh, my God—it was my fault, wasn't it? I knocked your concentration. I'm the reason you—"

He plants a kiss on my lips, stopping the words in my throat. "It wasn't your fault. I mean, if I'm going to point fingers it was our third line D but ... it's a team game. We couldn't pull it back. Shit happens."

He shrugs, like it was just a casual friendly that they'll play again next week, but I see it. The flicker of disappointment behind his half-smile.

"But—"

"Kitch," he says. "Don't worry. Honestly, it's fine. In fact—it's probably better you didn't see that game. I mean, imagine having *that* as your first memory of seeing me play."

He lets a smirk creep across his face.

"Shall we go up?" he asks, wiping a rolling tear from my cheek with a coarse thumb.

I peel myself away from him, nodding and moving to reach for my bag, but he picks it up and bundles us into the lift, hitting the button for the fifth floor.

"So, she knows, huh?" he says, keeping his attention on the illuminated '5' on the control panel.

"She does," I say, trying to remember how much detail I went into on my text message.

I told him about the salon, the change of name, the new employee, and I told him that Greg turned up half an hour after Kathryn's disappearance with 'bad news'—the bad news being that she read his emails. The ones he sent his 'friend' about my predicament.

Kathryn knows Mike and I are married—or suspects we are, anyway.

"I think you should probably tell your mam," I say. "She had an appointment last week and mentioned she was going to look at having a coffee and a catch-up with my mam and if Kathryn knows ... it's only a matter of time. It's probably better coming from you."

Mike exhales sharply. "Right."

The lift comes to a stop, and he tugs at my hand, pulling me into the hallway and leading me towards a door propped open by a hockey bag.

He leads me inside, stopping to take his shoes off in the cluttered entrance hall.

Hockey stuff, shoes, a coat rack full of clothes. There's stuff everywhere. But it doesn't feel overwhelming. It feels *cosy*.

"Uh, sorry about the mess," he says, kicking the door closed behind us. "Hutch is having a clear out and—"

"Don't worry."

"Come on through," he says.

He guides me to the living area, almost in darkness, bar a lamp in the corner. He nudges me towards the sofa where I drop down, letting the cushions envelop me.

Mike disappears, returning a moment later with a glass of water and a roll of toilet paper, bunching off several sheets and thrusting them into my palm.

"I'd make you a brew, but we're out of milk," he says.

"It's fine, thanks."

And I just sit there and cry. Mourning the loss of my tattered relationship with my sister. Because there's no going back from this. There's no way she can make this right.

"My sister's such a bitch," I say, dabbing my eyes with the tissue. "And do you know what's worse? My mam knew the whole time. My mam knew Kathryn was re-branding. That came out too. When I rang her earlier, she told me it's Kathryn's business and I need to support her. I need to support her. I mean—when has she ever supported me in return?"

The reality of the situation hits me hard in the chest. Everything I've done for her in the past and this is how she repays the favour?

A fresh wave of tears flow and Mike's enormous arms engulf me. He smooths my hair and pulls me onto his lap. Cocooning me in a warmth I didn't realise I needed.

"Shhh, it'll be okay," he whispers.

"I don't know if it will. And now I've lumbered all this crap on you and—"

"It's fine," he says softly.

"And now I can't face going home, Mike. I mean ... Kathryn would likely call in and tell me I'm over-reacting. She'd lecture me and give me a rundown of the way things are going to work and there'd be an expectation for me to wear a smile and get on with it. And I can't go to my mam and dad's because they're on 'Team Kathryn'—well, Mam is, and Dad goes along with anything to keep the peace."

"It's okay," he says, but I'm barely listening. I'm still reasoning, probably for my own sanity more than anything.

"And Jess is having issues with Phil and—"

"C'mon, it's okay. I'm glad you came here." He pauses. "I've got you."

I swallow down a sob.

"You can stay here," he says. "You're my wife, remember? What's mine is yours and all that." His tone is jovial, like he's trying to make this shitty situation a little less so, but his words spark something in me.

I dab my eyes dry and focus in on him, his eyes meeting mine with a shine of *something* in the dim light of the room.

But there's something not-so-funny about this. There's something about the way he's looking at me. Like this isn't just a joke anymore.

"Mike?" I say, pressing a hand to his cheek.

"Yeah?"

It's probably the pent-up emotion I've been harbouring all day—that, and the fact I haven't had sex in a very long time, but I'm looking at his lips and I want him to kiss me again.

I can feel the space between us closing, but he doesn't make a move. He's just looking at me with lust-filled eyes and longing.

This feels different. Charged. A pull I can't ignore.

He leans in, his lips brushing mine, and it's like a fire has ignited in my stomach. He pulls me in, relaxing around me. Then his hand is cupping my cheek, his coarse fingers making me shiver—it feels *good*. Like I want more. Like I want his hands to roam, to see if they feel like *that* everywhere.

I shouldn't … I really shouldn't. Shouldn't I?

Maybe I'm overthinking this. But then I completely surprise myself; I lean back onto the sofa and pull him down on top of me.

Chapter 21

HE LOSES HIS SHIRT first. I tug at the hem, encouraging it over his head, and his hat comes off with it, both tumbling to the floor with an air of unimportance. Then our lips meet again. A deep kiss that works its way to every single cell in my body; I feel like a coiled spring, desperate to unravel.

"Are you sure this is what you want?" he says, pulling his lips from mine.

I nod. "Yes."

Yes. This is exactly what I want. It's like this is exactly what I've always wanted.

"Are you—"

I knit my hands around his neck and pull him back down, hot and heavy breaths mingling as we kiss. I loosen my grip, moving my hands down the plain of his back, feeling his muscles—solid and tight—under my fingers.

"Mike—"

"I'll be right back."

Then he's gone. Leaving me cold and confused. Almost desperate, even. I sit up and peer around, only to see him emerging from a door a moment later, a fleece blanket slung over his arm.

"Are you sure, Kitch? I mean—"

He swallows, watching my fingers dance over the buttons of my blouse and then he's on top of me again, roaming hands and lips before he kisses me again. Slow and deliberate, sending a warmth all the way from my lips to my pussy.

God, this is infuriating.

"Mike—" I breathe, practically into his mouth.

"Hmm?"

"Mike, please..."

His hand slides down the outside of my thigh, leaving a trail of warmth. And there's the tingle. And the way my skin ignites and the desperation I'm feeling for him to go lower. For him to touch me.

"What do you need, sweetheart?" he growls, shifting his position to plant lazy kisses against my neck. Right on a spot I didn't know I had.

"I want you to—" A pressure on my nipple through the fabric of my bra steals the words from me.

"Is this what you need?" he says, right into my ear, reading my mind. "Do you need me to touch you?"

I shiver as his fingers—oh my God, his fingers—trace down my stomach, coming to a stop on the waistband of my trousers.

The anticipation. His breath in my ear before his lips trail over my skin. All he needs to do is flick open the clasp and slide his hand down and—

"Oh, God," I gasp.

It's like he's reading my mind. In a single motion, his hand is inside my trousers—over my underwear—almost tickling my skin as his hand stops on my pussy. Cupping me before stroking, once, twice, then he comes into contact with my clit. All through the thin fabric.

"Because you know—" he whispers, peppering kisses on my neck. "—as your husband, it's my job to take care of you. All of you."

A breathy groan escapes me, and I have no idea what to say because I am quaking. All I can do is nod and mumble something in agreement. Because yes. Yes, this is what I want.

"Mike—"

"I'll warn you, sweetheart. It's been a while since I've touched myself and you've got me really fucking hot."

Oh, God. Why does that turn me on too? Knowing that I've got him excited. And he can no doubt feel how wet I am if I can feel how wet I am.

Before I can stop myself, I'm running my hands over his chest, hard pecs, and coarse hair that has me melting beneath him.

Masculine. That's what it is. That's what he is. Masculine and arousing, and then he adjusts himself so I can feel *him* against my leg. Hard. Imposing. Definitely not how he described it to me—but I already knew that. I saw the outline.

And now I want to touch it. I want to touch him.

I move my hands over his abs next, then I reach his naval, brushing my fingers over his skin, the heat from his breath tickling my cheek before he kisses me again, tenderly trailing kisses from my lips down to my throat.

I hold my breath, nervous, but I lower my hands, sliding them underneath the waistband of his sweatpants.

He's commando.

"Oh, God," I say, then I grip him in my fist.

He grumbles, low and throaty, and it sends a wave of excitement through my bones. I move my hand in lazy strokes up and down his shaft. Thick. Heavy. Hard in my hands.

Perfect.

A word I never thought I'd be using to describe a penis, let alone the one attached to Michael Betts, but here I am, revelling in every single inch of him. Desperate for more.

"Fuck, that's good," he says.

And my brain adds to the equation, because now all I can think about is him being inside me as I pump my hand a little faster.

He sucks in a breath and tugs my hands away.

"Let me—get you there first," he says. And his face is in my neck, kissing and nibbling and I know, it won't take him long at all. I'm like a rocket, ready to launch.

The rest of our clothes disappear in haste. Frantic pulling and tugging until we're both naked. Lying on his sofa with the blanket wrapped around us. But I don't care. I haven't even asked if his roommate is likely to come home. In fact, he could be watching us—creepy, yeah, but I'm so immersed, I don't—

"Oh, God," I say. A hot breath hits my left nipple, then a second later the pressure of his tongue, flicking and teasing, has me clamping my fingers into his hair.

He snickers. "Bettsy's fine, if you're wanting to give me a nickname," he says, "but I guess God will do—"

I'm chuckling. Completely lost in the moment, grateful that this is anything other than awkward and Mike is being so very much *Mike*.

"Hmm," I mumble, willing my brain to come up with something else, but my focus has disappeared. Because his tongue flicks over my right nipple this time, as his hand slides down my body. Inch by inch. Lower and lower.

Then he touches me. Exactly where I need to be touched, forcing a moan to escape me. He sucks down hard on my nipple right before he slips a finger inside me.

And that's all it takes. A finger inside and his thumb circling my clit, probably only a handful of times, to get me close. Like I'm standing on the edge of a cliff, desperate not to fall over. Not without him coming along with me.

"I'm close," I say, and without hesitation, he pulls is mouth and hand away. Then he's moving, reaching for something from the coffee table. A condom. Suddenly my legs are in the air, resting on his shoulders. Strong and solid.

"Are you sure?" he says. "Because I very much doubt, you'll only want this once—I mean, once you've—"

"Shut it, Mike and—"

There he is, lining himself up, then a second later, he's pushing inside of me. Slowly, just the tip at first, but he adjusts himself a little and pulls me in closer, planting a row of kisses on my calf before exhaling, and then he's still. Breathing deeply as we fully connect.

"Fuck, you feel good," he says, but I can't find any words. My body and brain have sort of disconnected because everything I have is focused on the feeling—the fullness. The sensation.

He pulls out slightly before thrusting back in, taking my breath away in the process. I'm gasping, moaning, and Mike's breath becomes laboured and heavy. He moves in slow and deliberate strokes that have my whole body shaking with anticipation, because I want more.

He parts my legs and leans down, kissing me and building a gentle rhythm with his hips.

"Can you come like this?"

"Hmmm—"

He shifts his angle, and I feel it. The gentle grind of his body against mine. And I'm nodding into his mouth. Because I'm close. And when he picks up the pace, whispering that he's close, I say three little words I never thought I'd say.

"Fuck me, Mike."

And he does. Long strokes. Fast and hard. And his lips find mine as he kisses me, soft and tender: the complete opposite to the effort he's putting in elsewhere.

And that's all it takes for both of us to come. Lips locked together. Bodies damp and hot. His moans, erotic and intense, making me forget where I am, what I'm doing here. I'm completely lost in the moment because this orgasm feels different, like it's everywhere. Every single cell in my body feels it.

He breaks away from my lips, dipping his head into my neck, nuzzling my skin.

"That was—wait, you came, right?"

I nod, a smile creeping over my lips just as there's a thundering bang on the door.

Thump, thump, thump.

Then a voice, calling through the boundary and Mike exhales.

"Ah fuck," he says.

Thump, thump, thump.

"I know you're in there, Betts. Open the door before I piss myself."

Bettsy

"WHAT THE HELL IS going on?" Hutch says, bursting through the door as soon as I release the deadbolt. "You never—" He stops in his tracks and looks around the entrance hall, eyes landing on the bags.

Ellie's bags.

"You've got a girl here?" he says. "I thought you were abstaining? No sex before marriage and all that crap." He moves into our apartment and tosses his keys onto the worktop before turning back towards me.

I don't even know what to say to him. Because, like always, I succumbed to temptation and all it took was a kiss. A single kiss that had my insides burning with want—no, need. I was like a man possessed, and I guess that's what no sex does to you. That and the fact that I've been lusting over her since I was a teenager.

She was worth every single second of the wait.

And now Hutch is robbing me of that blissful post-sex closeness where you just be.

I step towards my bedroom, depositing the bags inside my room before shutting the door. Then I brace myself as I face Hutch.

"Relax," I say. "It's just a friend. She was upset and I gave her a cuddle. We didn't do anything."

I'm lying to save face, but the truth is, I don't know if Ellie meant for things to escalate in the way they did. I don't know how she's feeling. Perhaps she'll take her shower and decide we need to pretend it never happened. And since I know I won't be able to face the rejection, I decide not to bring it up. Ever. It's probably better living in this sweet state of ignorance.

"Did you have sex on our sofa?" Hutch's jaw hits the floor as he spots the comforter.

My cheeks burn hot.

"No," I say. "I told you ... we just cuddled."

I suppose lying also saves Ellie the embarrassment. Because she'll come out here at some point and I know what Hutch is like—he can't leave anything to rest.

"Why don't I believe you?" he grins, revelling in my circumstance.

"Mate."

"Oh, well, sorry." He holds his hands up. "Next thing you're going to tell me is that it was Rochelle you were comforting." I wince at the sound of her name and Hutch shakes his head. "It wasn't ... was it?"

"No. God, no." I fold my arms, looking down at the floor, letting an extended silence fall between us. There's only the sound of running water in the distance.

But it's Hutch who eventually breaks the quiet. He steps closer and drops his voice to a tone of concern.

"What's going on, Betts?"

I look up, meeting his eyes, and I realise it's time to come clean. It's time to tell him everything. The story so far, if you will, and considering Ellie's going to be staying here for a few days, I don't think it's something I'll be able to carry on hiding.

I step past him into the kitchen and open the store cupboard, reaching for the first bottle I can find, then I grab two glasses from the draining board and flip them over, pouring a measure of whisky into each.

"Bettsy?" Hutch says, looking between me and the glasses, eyes quick, shoulders tense.

"I think you need a drink when you hear this," I say. "And I need a drink because—well, this is my life, after all."

Hutch studies me for a moment longer. Then, to my relief, he nods and takes a seat on the other side of the counter, perching on a bar stool and reaching for one of the glasses.

"I take it this isn't about the game?" he asks.

I shake my head, taking a drink, trying to compose my thoughts. Then there's nothing left to do but tell him.

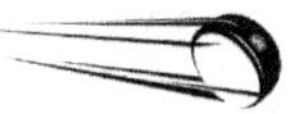

"Who knows?" Hutch says, knocking back another mouthful of whisky. "Out of our lot. Who knows?"

I swallow. My throat is already dry from the talking and the burn from the whisky, but I answer him anyway, telling him how Danny came to find out.

"And I think I'm going to have to tell everyone else soon, though I don't know how to play it." I run my hands through my hair, looking up at the ceiling. "I've fucked up. Massively. I've fucked up, mate."

"Well, yeah. Because people talk. I'm genuinely surprised that you haven't had a call from Coach Harris yet."

The sickness I felt earlier comes back. Because Hutch is right. People talk and it's a small world in British Hockey. Everyone knows everyone, or at least someone else who knows that someone. It's tiny and word spreads pretty quick.

"But let me get this straight. He thinks you're married. But you may actually be married ... but Ellie doesn't want to go along with being married?"

I open my mouth to reply when I catch Ellie on the edge of my vision. She's standing on the threshold of the kitchen wearing an oversized jumper—a relaxed look. A look that has me wanting to snuggle up on the sofa with her and watch crappy TV.

She looks perfect.

She meets my eye and smiles.

"Ellie *does* want to go along with being married," she says.

And there's a squeeze in my chest; it's unmistakable. It's everything.

Hutch's attention shifts from me to Ellie, and he gapes.

"Sorry, I didn't mean to intrude," she says.

But Hutch simply bursts out laughing and I flash him the mother of all death stares.

"I'm sorry, but there's no way she is your wife," he says.

"I—"

"What the hell is that supposed to mean?" I snap.

"I'm just saying she's too pretty for you. C'mon, Betts, you said so yourself—you're like a—"

"Shut it," I say. "God, you're such a dick at times."

But he ignores me, swivelling on the barstool so he's facing Ellie entirely, a grin on his face the size of the moon.

"I'm Paul Hutchinson," he says. "The guys call me Hutch. Nice to meet you."

"Hey," Ellie says, looking between Hutch and me, "It's nice to meet you too."

"So," Hutch says, leaning back so his elbows rest on the counter. "How much is he paying you?"

I'm quick off the mark, grabbing a tea-towel and whipping him across the biceps of his left arm.

"Shut up," I say. "That's enough."

"Okay, okay," Hutch says. "But in all seriousness, I don't see how this is going to work, realistically." He turns back to me. "People have seen you out and about—they'll know this isn't real." He wags his eyebrows, and I know exactly what he's saying. People have seen me with other women. Rochelle, being the main offender.

But Ellie surprises me. She moves in closer before she says, "Who says it isn't real?"

Hutch's expression drops as he stares at her.

"I've been thinking about it, actually," Ellie says, and I cast a look in her direction, hopeful that she's going to give me a lifeline out of the hole I've dug myself. "I think we tell people we're childhood sweethearts who lost our way for a while but found each other again. Now we're committed to giving it a go since we both realise we want the same things in life." My eyes widen; that's a decent idea.

"I guess it's a good thing you got picked over Rick, as he'll probably wonder why I didn't mention you to him," Ellie says.

I almost hear Hutch's jaw hit the floor.

"Wait—Rick. As in Rick Langdon? Your new pairing? What's he got to do with this?"

I swallow, ignoring his question as I keep my eyes on Ellie, watching her hands run through her damp hair.

I want to run my hands through her hair.

"New pairing?" She says, looking at me. "You didn't mention that."

"Yeah, I'm not overly excited about it—hey, Hutch, how long do you think I'll have to suffer before Coach shifts us around?"

He shakes his head. "That's the least of your worries. God, you're in a fucking mess, Betts."

"I know," I growl, reaching for the bottle of whisky before stopping myself.

"I'm not sure your plan is going to work," Hutch says. "Because who gets married that quickly? Though ... I think people will buy it. Because if there's any one of us who'd get married on a whim, it'd be you. Hands down. People would definitely believe that. Maybe not Johnny, but at least you have Kelly on your side there—shit, does your sister know?"

God, this keeps getting worse. Because of course I'll have to tell my sister. And I know she'll probably force me to tell my mam—assuming she doesn't already know. Although, I am supposed to be telling her anyway and—fuck. This is a complete nightmare.

"I told you the score," I say to Hutch. "Kelly doesn't know." I bury my head in my hands before looking back towards Ellie. "Kitch, this is—"

"Don't worry," she says, cutting me off. "We just need to work out a timeline. Besides, what we're doing shouldn't be anyone else's business. All you need to say is that our relationship is private, and you want to keep it that way."

Okay, well, that makes sense. She's smart, and that's exactly what I need in this situation. Someone with their head on straight.

"Or…" Hutch butts in, "now hear me out … you could tell Coach you lied and forfeit your spot." His voice is playful, but I know there's a small speck of realism in there. "Maybe he'll take pity on you, with all that stuff online. Just like that 'justice for Bettsy' person."

"He's absolutely not giving up his spot," Ellie says.

"Well, maybe—"

"Stop it. Please, Hutch," I say and his eyes meet mine, the desperation I'm feeling hitting him square in the chest as he nods.

"Okay, I won't say anything. You know that. And neither will Danny. So just keep it that way. Everyone else, well, they can think it's legit."

But I know there's no way in hell I can lie to Johnny. And it's his reaction that I'm worried about the most.

Chapter 22

Ellie

WELL, THIS IS DIFFERENT. The buzz of excitement I was never expecting. It warms my skin. It warms my heart. It … it's happening.

Was it the sex I didn't realise I needed? Sex with Mike, I didn't realise I needed. Or was it the freedom to choose my own path? Making it my decision to go along with Mike's narrative.

Whatever it is, it feels oddly satisfying. Like this is the way I was heading all along and, for some reason, fate forced me to take the scenic route, just to make sure I'd appreciate the destination.

And as I sit on the sofa with Mike—the same sofa we had sex on, an hour ago—I realise my life will never be the same.

And I'm okay with that, because Mike is here and there's no pressure. No expectation of anything now. We're simply two people who have an unwavering connection that has somehow pulled us back together after years apart, watching an old episode of a TV game show like we've been doing it for years. Though I'm convinced he's seen this one before because he answers every single question in fluid certainty, and he's only been wrong once. Once.

"How many times have you seen this episode?" I ask.

"I haven't," he says, his eyes flicking towards me for a second before he looks back at the screen.

"Really?"

"Damselfly," he says, answering the next question before the multiple-choice answers pop up.

"Huh," I say. "How did you know that?"

"Damselflies have more flexible wings than dragonflies," he says, matter-of-fact. "That's why they fold them in when they land." He points at the screen, considering the other options. "And it's definitely not a horsefly or a mayfly—unless either of those suddenly learned grace."

I stare at him. Blinking several times before asking, "and how did you know that?"

"Saw it on a documentary," he shrugs.

I reach for my phone and tap 'damselfly' into the search engine, looking through the image results.

"I can't say I've ever seen a damselfly before."

"Well, they're abundant near freshwater so maybe we need to go damsel-watching." He grins at me, a smile that sends a wave of flutters to my stomach.

"I—that's interesting."

"I know a lot of crap," he says. "Did you know before they mate, males use their secondary genitalia to sort of scoop out the semen of a rival male from the female to give their sperm the best chance? Wild, right?"

I let my jaw drop open before I snap it shut, raising my eyebrows. "Really?"

He chuckles. "Yeah."

"What other crazy facts do you know?" I ask.

"Oh, sweetheart ... you don't want to ask me that."

"Why not?" I scoot closer to jab him playfully in the ribs.

"I can talk crap all day, honestly. I don't think anyone really listens to me anymore."

"I do," I say. "I enjoy listening to you. It's a damn sight more interesting than where you're going on holiday this year, which is all the conversation I usually get."

He tears his eyes away from the TV, peering at me with an expression I can't place. And because I'm beyond curious, I try to coax it out of him.

"What?" I ask.

He stills. Not letting his attention wane from mine as he shakes his head, his lips twitching with the unmistakable sign of a half-smile.

"Nothing. Nothing at all."

"No, go on. I want to know," I say.

He sighs, letting his head rest on the back of the sofa for a moment before running his hands over his face.

"It just blows my mind that you're interested, that's all."

"In damselflies?"

"Nah, well, yeah, but me, I guess. Hutch is right. You're a fucking ten and I'm—"

I whack him across the arm.

"Stop it," I say. "I'm not listening to it. Every time you try to put yourself down, I'll be disciplining you."

"Don't threaten me with a good time," he says.

"What's that supposed to mean?" I say, creasing my brow.

He has that look again. The half-laugh and cheeky expression as he shakes his head. "Forget it."

"Stop doing that, too," I say. "If we're going to be married and acting like it in front of people, you can't shut me out and leave me guessing. We're supposed to be getting to know each other, like more than just the basic stuff of—"

He kisses me then. Pulling me towards him in a fluid motion that makes it hot and all-consuming.

My brain turns to cotton wool again.

"It's my dirty mind," he says, breaking away. "If you really want to know."

"Oh? Was the sex not enough?"

He chuckles in that deep rumble that vibrates through me.

"It was more than enough. It was better than I imagined."

"Y-you were imagining it?" My voice comes out in a whisper, the reminder of my dreams, popping into my head.

"Damn right I have. And I know there's no way you've not imagined the same. I mean…"

"You're such a dick," I say, trying to hide the smile cemented on my face.

But I can't. I feel my face growing hot, so I scramble to change the conversation, saying the first thing I can think of.

"So, how do you think the guys will take the news?"

Mike pauses for a moment and I give him time to think, opting to stroke his forearm with my index finger while I wait.

He clears his throat before he speaks.

"I guess I'm nervous, to be honest. The judgement. The speculation, maybe. I know the guys are decent but…" he sighs. "I don't know. I think I want to talk to Johnny first. He's the one I trust the most and if I can get him on my side, then the rest of the team will be fine." He reaches for my hand and laces his fingers with mine. "You are sure, right? I mean, it's not too late to back out. I can square it with Hutch. He'll understand."

"I'm not backing out," I say. "Besides, this is for my benefit as much as yours. Considering my sister knows now. Imagine her revelling in the fact that my marriage has failed … well, if you know what I mean."

"How much does she know?" he asks.

"Apparently, she read the emails Greg sent to a friend working in family law. So, she probably knows there's paperwork I don't have."

"I'll make an effort this week," he says. "To look for it, I mean. Because regardless of how things go with us, we need to know, right?"

I nod. He's right. Of course he is.

But his words settle on me. His choice of words. Us. Are we an 'us'? I don't know. In fact, I don't even know what it's like to be 'us' with anyone. All I've had is micro-relationships. The ones where you text for weeks before having a first date. Then a second date. Then a third. Then the sex starts and the texting fizzles out and before you know it, you're being ghosted.

"Hey, Kitch," he says, after a moment of silence. "Do you mind if I drop in on Johnny? I think he'll still be awake. He always struggles to sleep after a big loss. It'll make things easier in the morning."

And there it is. That sickness I felt earlier when I got to the rink to find I was too late. To find I'd missed his game.

He was downplaying it. And my problems preoccupied me too much to notice.

Bettsy

I GUESS I WAS secretly hoping Johnny would take an early night, because when he answers after a three solid knocks, my heart drops into my stomach.

He studies me, eyes narrow, before he greets me.

"Hey, Cap. Do you mind if I come in for a sec?" I shove my hands into my pockets and will myself to maintain eye contact.

This is it. Time to come clean and tell the only person whose opinion really matters to me, perhaps apart from my mam.

"What's going on, bud?" he asks, checking the time on his wristwatch. "Is everything okay?"

He beckons me inside and I slip my trainers off, setting them to the side before following him to the living room.

It's quiet, and I spot a book open on the coffee table, cover face up, like he was reading, and the guilt of ruining his night creeps in.

"Where's Kel?" I ask.

"Sleeping," he says.

"Right, yeah."

"Well, what's going on?" he says. "Is this something to do with the game?"

"Nah."

"Langer?"

I grit my teeth, flopping down on the sofa and reaching for a cushion— hugging it to my chest.

"No, but that's something else I need to figure out," I say. "I'm not sure what Coach was thinking, but I don't think we're a good match."

Johnny sits on the arm of the adjacent chair, leaning forward to look at me. "I actually beg to differ. But since that's not what you're here to talk about and we have an early practice—let's not keep either of us from our beds. Is this about the forum?"

I shake my head.

"This is really difficult for me," I begin. "But I need you to know I didn't think things through, as per usual, I guess, and now I'm in a bit of a mess."

"Ah. So this is about your fake wife," he says.

Ah, shit.

I swallow down a lump, braving a glance in his direction.

"Danny told you?" I ask, sheepishly. "Why didn't you say anything?"

"No, my sister did. She told me about the stuff with Coach and whatever, and I figured you'd tell me when you were ready," Johnny says.

"Vicky," I scoff. "Of course."

"Yeah, I think she's expecting you to tell Coach the truth, though," he says.

I groan into my hands. And then I fill Johnny in. I tell him everything—almost everything.

From the trip Ellie made when she was eighteen to when she showed up earlier today, cutting out the sex bit, because I don't want Johnny thinking of me how I already think of myself.

"Well, shit," Johnny says once I come to a close. "So, you really are married? Does your sister know?"

"Well, we think so. I need to look for some paperwork or something. But no, Kelly doesn't know and you're not going to tell her," I say.

Johnny raises his eyebrows. "That's rich coming from you."

I sigh, resigned to the fact that I'm going to have to tell her myself sooner rather than later.

"I need to tell her. I'll call her tomorrow," I say.

Johnny nods. "So, what happens now?"

"I tell the guys and then Ellie comes along to a couple of Team GB functions. Simple."

"Yeah, but people will start asking questions if she's only socialising at those events. What about our stuff? We've got that testimonial night coming up, not to mention the end of season celebration. All that's happening before the Team GB stuff kicks off properly—aside from the welcome event. The GM will notice if there's no consistency and people talk. You can't have this double life in the hockey world. You know that's not how it works."

And of course he's right. My shit show advances from a onetime performance to a national tour. And what's worse? I'm going to have to change the goalposts for Ellie, and I'm not sure how she's going to take it.

We agreed earlier that she'd support the Team GB stuff—whatever I needed on that part. But my league team? I'm not sure if that's too 'relationshippy' and I'm not sure what she wants—how much she wants.

I exhale, letting out a groan as I do.

"This is it," I tell Johnny. "This is how I'm going to die. Death from lack of forward thinking... the stress of it all."

"Well, where does Ellie live?" Johnny asks. "Is she local?"

"She has a place back home, but this whole drama kicked off with her sister and their beauty salon and—"

"Oh, don't tell Vicky she's a beautician," Johnny laughs. "She'll never leave her alone."

"Hairdresser," I say.

Johnny nods.

We spend the next half an hour mulling over my woes, trying to figure out how this can actually work, but I'm no further forward from the plan Ellie and I already have apart from the fact that I have to convince her to come to several more things than she was originally expecting.

"Well, I guess I'll sleep on it," I say, standing.

Johnny rises too, patting me on the shoulder and giving me the most pitiful expression.

"Betts—do me a favour, will you? Don't get emotionally invested. Because if this is just something for her to pass the time, the last thing you want to do is catch feelings."

"Feelings? Nah, don't worry about that," I say.

But I fear it's already too late.

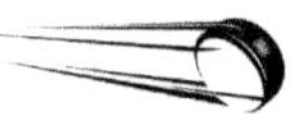

I GET BACK TO my apartment and settle myself on the sofa for the night, not wanting to wake Ellie up or assume because we slept together, she'd be comfortable sharing a bed.

I pull my phone out and navigate to the team group chat, hovering my fingers over the keyboard as I pick my words because there's no way in hell I'm telling the guys in person, face to face—eyes on me as they judge; a text will do to break the news.

I take a breath, navigate away and scroll socials for a bit before finding the confidence buried within me. The confidence I need so desperately.

Bettsy

Just wanted to let you all know I got married.

I stare at the words, then tap delete, clearing the text.

Bettsy

Guys ... good news. I'm married!

I delete that too.

Then I try for a third time.

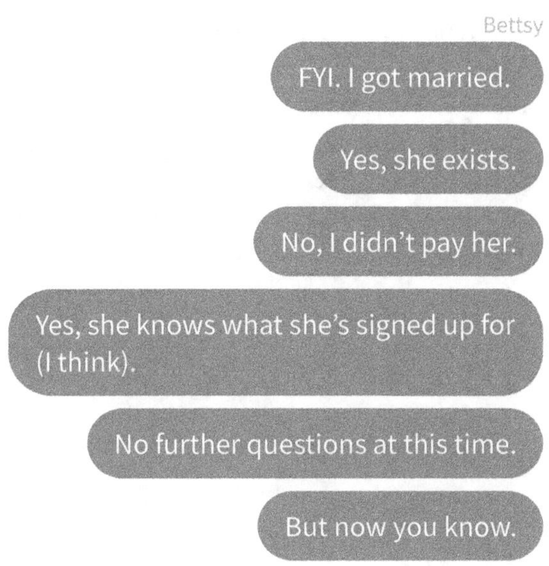

I realise there's no simple way of putting it. And with any luck, no one will read it until the morning, and I can save the ridicule until tomorrow—

Ah shit.

There's an influx of replies; my phone buzzing in the palm of my hand as the messages stream in. But I don't read any. There's a noise from the hallway that draws my attention away.

I crane my head to see Ellie standing at the threshold of the living room.

She says nothing. She simply pads over to the sofa and pulls back the fleece blanket. Then she squeezes herself onto the cushions next to me, pulling my arm around her.

And it's everything. Everything I didn't realise I needed.

Validation. Wanting.

Ellie.

"I'm really sorry I missed your game, Mike. And I know you said you didn't want that to be the memory of my first game, but I'm really proud of you. Win or lose. I'm really proud."

And all I can do is kiss her head and squeeze her, pulling her in as close as possible. Because no one outside of my family has ever said that.

Especially not Rochelle.

But hearing it from Ellie is something really fucking special to me. So much so, I don't realise I'm crying. A single tear trickling down my cheek as I feel a different kind of something for the first time ever.

Chapter 23

Bettsy

I'VE BEEN SO WRAPPED up in my Ellie-filled world that I forgot today is the day Johnny formally regains his captaincy. And I forgot Liam's stag do is tonight. A ridiculous day to pick if you ask me, but with the season quickly wrapping up and playoffs looming, there're few practice-free days, tomorrow being one of them.

But one social nightmare at a time, I tell myself as I root through my pockets for my swipe card, because all I need to do is get through the pre-practice dressing room grilling which I'm confident is coming.

I'm purposefully late, which was a good idea when I woke this morning, but a terrible one when I open the double doors and come face-to-face with Vicky.

She's standing in the tunnel in a trouser suit to match our primary team colour, a clipboard clutched to her chest, but it's clear she's been waiting for me. Her eyes shift to meet mine and her expression remains tight. Like she's ready for a fight.

I let the door close behind me and slip my access card away, forcing a smile as I come to a stop.

"Hey, Vic. How's my favourite—"

"Nice of you to show up," she says, resting a hand on her hip as she cuts over me.

"I had ... car trouble," I say, flashing her a gappy grin.

"Right." She narrows her eyes before straightening up. "Michael—"

"Look, I know what you're going to say and..."

"Do you?" She raises a brow.

"I—I don't know, do I?" I say, wincing.

She sighs. "So, you're doing this, then? Going along with it?"

I tilt my head to the side, and she rolls her eyes.

Apparently, playing dumb isn't going to work.

"Johnny told me," she says.

Oh, how the tables have turned.

"Well, yeah ... before you ask, I didn't bribe her or—"

"I wasn't going to ask that. I just wanted to make sure you know what you're doing. Because Roch—"

"Vic, come on, will you?" I stop her mid-sentence.

I'm not in the mood for this. I don't want to hear Vicky's opinion of Rochelle and how badly she treated me. And I don't want to—wait.

I study her expression. Trying to work out the meaning behind the look she's giving me, but I can't place it. Not at first, anyway. Because it's not something I've ever associated with Vicky. Her eyes are wide and her mouth down-turned at the sides—trembling slightly as she glares at me.

Then it clicks: pity. That's what I'm seeing. She's pitying me.

"I just don't want her taking advantage of you, Mike. I know how you are with women and—"

"Excuse me?" I snap. "Just because I've made a few poor decisions doesn't mean I'm not capable of making a good one every now and again."

Vicky's mouth opens, but nothing comes out for several seconds.

"You're right. I'm sorry," she says. "Johnny told me you're actually married. I mean ... married, married."

She stumbles over the words, blinking like she can't quite believe she's saying them. Then she settles on a sentence that knocks the wind out of me.

"Don't you think it's a little convenient that she showed up in time for you to be named on the Team GB roster?"

I gape at her. Properly gape.

But Vicky doesn't stop.

"I don't want her to take advantage of you," she says.

"She's not," I say. "She's not like that at all. She actually sees me—not just the jersey. In fact, she's never even been to a game." I blow out a breath. "I appreciate your concern, but it's not needed. Now, if you'll excuse me, I need to suit up."

I stride past her, long steps towards the dressing room where the low buzz of chatter filters out.

The nerves I felt on the other side of the double doors are gone—burnt up and replaced by rage. My temper's sizzling, sharp and hot.

The double doors open in the distance, and I stop short of the dressing room, turning to see Vicky hurrying away.

One. Two. Three breaths. So deep I can feel the pressure in my chest—like my lungs are close to bursting.

Then I exhale, pushing out the tension and ill feeling I have, because there's no way in hell I can walk into this dressing room half-wounded.

What's wrong, Bettsy? She's dumped you already?

The guys will have a field day.

So, I do what I do best. I push on the door and force a grin, strutting into the dressing room with my head high.

Then I wait for the influx of questions. The demands for information. The inquest.

But nothing comes. There's stunned silence as everyone looks in my direction, but no one says a single word.

The guys are sitting in their cubbies, in various stages of undress. As I close in on mine, dropping my bag down and shrugging off my jacket, I'm met with a wall of nothing.

No questions.

No side-chat.

Nothing.

And this is the most worrying thing I've ever faced.

Simply put, these guys are never quiet. And I've never in my entire life entered a dressing room to render everyone speechless.

It's only when I sit down and look around the room do I realise no one is looking at me anymore; it's unsettling.

I tilt my head to peek at Johnny, busying himself with his shin pads. I cast a glance at Hutch, who's trying to find the end on a roll of tape. I pan across to Danny, lacing his left skate with so much concentration I can practically hear his brain ticking over.

Every single guy in the room is busy.

"Right. What the hell is going on?" I ask the room. "Because there's no way in hell—"

And that's when everyone dives on me. Like they were waiting for the puck to drop—gloves flying, tape rolls launched. A full dressing room pile on that says any more than words could. It's like we're kids again.

Everyone's cheering and yelling, and I'm sprawled out on the floor, underneath a load of bodies.

"Right, that's enough," Johnny says. And one by one, the load lightens.

But that's when the questions pour in.

"When?"

"What?"

"How?"

"Who?"

"Guys, guys, guys," Johnny says, and he tugs my arm, pulling me from the ground.

"For Christ's sake," I say. "Give a guy a chance to breathe."

Someone ruffles my hair, and I make a grab for my cap, displaced on the dressing room floor.

"So, what's the story?" Liam says, raising a brow.

"Don't pretend you don't already know," I say, narrowing my eyes as I sink my cap down onto my head.

He smirks.

"No, but what is the story?" Ryan this time. And I offer him the same look.

He holds his hands up.

"Honestly, I don't—wait, does Jen know?" He turns and glares at Danny, who shrugs.

"Okay, okay," I say. "Bottom line is ... she's real, like I said. And we're just seeing how things go. I mean, we're old friends and we reconnected recently, and it turns out—" I swallow, looking down at the carpet tiles. "—we've been married since we were eighteen." Jaws drop, and more questions surface. I do my best to fill them in.

"That's all you need to know," I say eventually. "And she's really fucking nice, so when you meet her, you'll be nice back. Got it?"

"CAN I HELP YOU?"

I snap my head up from my phone to see a woman—long brown hair, and team logo stitched on the breast of her coat—walking towards me. She's carrying a box, which she sets down on the floor as she beams at me.

The taxi dropped me off ten minutes ago and I've been loitering awkwardly ever since, convinced that Mike will eventually appear from the double doors six feet away.

All I need is a quick chat, face-to-face, before I get the train home.

"I'm, uh, waiting for someone," I say, slipping my phone away and returning the smile awkwardly.

She cocks her head to the side, a smile forming on her lips.

"Who are you waiting for?" she says.

I delay my response, wondering if me showing up at Mike's rink will cause trouble for him. What if there's a strict 'no visitors allowed' policy and here I am, lurking like a super fan?

But she's waiting for me to reply.

"Mike Betts," I say. "Uh, Bettsy."

I'm not sure what I was expecting, but I didn't expect her face to light up in the way it does. Her smile widens, and she steps forward a pace, almost squealing with delight as she speaks.

"You're Ellie, right?"

Oh, crap. She knows who I am.

"Um, yeah," I say.

She stoops to pick the box up.

"It's nice to meet you," she says. "I've heard so much about you—and I'm—oh, sorry." She holds out a hand, balancing the box on her hip with considerable effort. "I'm Jen. Do you want to come inside and catch the end of practice?"

I stare at her, wondering if she's kidding—waiting for her to laugh. But her expression remains warm and neutral, and I take a second to realise she's serious. She's deadly serious.

"P-practice?" I say.

"Yeah," she says. "They're almost done but—"

"Practice ... like the team practice?"

"Yeah," she says, a chuckle following. "The guys are great. And I'm sure they'll be excited to meet you."

And the anxiety that's been simmering just below the surface kicks up a notch—teetering on the edge of a full-blown panic attack.

There's no way I can go in there and see practice. How many players are on a team? Ten? Fifteen? Twenty? I mean, meeting Hutch last night was nerve-wracking enough and there was just one of him. Imagine a whole...

"Come on, I'm sure he'd love to see you." She gestures towards the double doors and moves towards them, swiping a keycard on a panel on the wall before pulling the door open and holding it ajar. "Are you coming?"

I flick my eyes between Jen and the door, then I look back at the pavement. An escape. A way out.

But then Mike's grin surfaces in my mind and my stomach clenches.

Mike. Surely the moment of discomfort is worth it for Mike? Besides, I'm going to have to meet his teammates at some point and there's a warmth about Jen that's oddly familiar—welcoming in a way that quiets the nerves buzzing through me.

And before I know it, my legs are moving.

"I—I guess," I say, and I follow her lead.

She leads me down an open corridor, past several rooms and notice boards, only stopping when we reach the players benches' where she sets the box down at the far end before turning back towards me.

"Sorry, I should have warned you about the smell—I'm sure you'll get used to it."

I'd love to say I hadn't noticed, but there's a lingering stench in the air. Sweat and cold and—I turn towards the direction of the voices.

"I think they're almost done, but—I see Bettsy there." Jen points towards a cluster of guys on the ice.

I don't spot him at first, but I see the group Jen's referring to. Three guys on the blue line, waiting their turn. One of them says something and the others laugh, and that's when Mike adjusts himself slightly, so I catch sight of him.

And that familiar feeling fills my stomach. The feeling I used to associate with severe dislike, but now, I couldn't imagine it being anything other than the complete opposite.

My stomach twists—like it's turning upside down and around—and my pulse thunders in my ears.

I lock my attention on Mike, and without warning, he bursts into action, skating hard and fast across the ice towards the opposite blue line, skidding to a halt before doubling back.

"Are you okay?" Jen says. "You look a little pale. Is it the cold? Do you need—"

"Uh, yeah, sorry. I'm fine, really. I think I had a little too much coffee," I say.

"Here, come and take a seat," she says, stepping over the bench and settling down.

I do the same, perching right on the edge of my seat, ready to spring up at a moment's notice. Jen, on the other hand, is clearly a natural in this environment. She's calm, unfazed, and positively in place. And she chats to me like she's known me all my life. It's comforting.

"Have you met any of the other guys yet?"

"Just Hutch," I say.

Jen nods. "That's Danny there, and that's Johnny—the captain. And that's ... my husband, Ryan. Gosh, I still can't get used to saying that."

"Have you been married long?" I ask.

"Long enough for me to be used to it by now. We had a quick wedding, and see Liam there," she points. "That's Ryan's twin brother. He's due to get married in four weeks' time and Vicky—his fiancée is hoping we can have a joint party or something."

"Oh, wow. That sounds incredible," I say, beaming at her.

"Yeah, well—oh," she claps her hands together and turns to face me "I hear you're a hairdresser. You must come and do trials for Vicky and me. Honestly, I'm crap with things like that. And Vicky had a falling out with her stylist over God knows what—"

"Kitch," Mike's voice booms through the air, causing Jen and I turn towards the ice. "Kitch—what are you doing here?" He skates over to the bench, beaming as he glides. He comes to a stop, leaning over and plucking a water bottle from the space below. "Is everything okay?"

I hesitate, looking between Mike and Jen for a second before she stands and shimmies down to the end of the bench, busying herself by rooting through the box she brought.

"I—I didn't want to leave without saying goodbye," I say. "I was going to wait outside for you but—"

"Wait. You're going?" he says, pulling off his helmet.

"Well, yeah. I know I was going to stay for a little while, but I did a lot of thinking this morning and I figured I can't hide from my situation forever. I need to talk with Kathryn—make sure she knows I'm not going back and—" I lower my voice. "—and I need to ask her for my money back if I'm going to go at it alone."

Mike's eyebrows knit together. "Money? What money?"

I open my mouth to answer, only to halt on my in-breath, because what seems to be the entire roster swarms in behind him, all casting curious and slightly too interested glances my way.

This is what I was afraid of.

"See, I told you," Hutch says.

"Yeah, you're right," another voice says. "She's too hot for you, Betts."

My face flames red.

"Hey, move along boys, move along." A blond guy—Johnny, I think—freshly de-helmeted, swings open the access door to the ice.

He ushers the guys off, one by one. They step off in turn, each of them casting me a glance as they go; creepy smiles on all their faces.

"Don't mind them," he says. "They don't get out much."

"Oh."

"I'm Johnny," he says. "Nice to meet you. I would shake your hand but ... yeah, anyway."

"Great to meet you," I say. "I've heard a lot about you."

"Yeah? I guess you know Kel, right?" he says.

"Yeah. It's been a while, but I'm looking forward to catching up with her."

Johnny looks towards Mike. "Yeah, Betts. We'll have to set something up."

I nod, trying to be enthusiastic but deep down I know that if Kelly knows, then Judith will know. And if Judith knows, she'll also realise that I've been lying to her.

"Bettsy tells me you're going with him to the Team GB event next week? Looking forward to it?"

"Sure, yeah, it'll be fun," I say.

He nods. "Well, I need to get going but, yeah. Nice to meet you."

Johnny moves away, his skates thudding on the rubber flooring as he goes.

And then there's just Mike on the ice and a couple of the coaching staff in the far corner of the rink, heads together, deep in conversation.

"I'll be in the training room if you need me to show you out," Jen says, passing me on the bench.

Mike steps off the ice and moves in close.

"You're okay, right?" he asks. "Do you need me to come with you?"

"No, I'll be fine," I say, not sure if I will be, but forcing myself to go along with it, anyway. "But I didn't want to leave without seeing you. I wanted to say thank you. For being there for me last night. I really appreciate it."

"Yeah, no problem," he says.

I look down at the floor, focusing on the small pools of water from the pairs of skates as they left the ice.

"But I'll see you soon, yeah?" Mike says.

"Of course." I pause, listening to my heart pound steadily in my chest.

Before I realise what I'm doing, I'm pushing myself onto my tip-toes, not flinching at the sweaty smell coming from him—because I'm far from repulsed. In fact, there's a heat that swarms my body and when my lips touch his, warmth spreads through me, deep and all-consuming. A clammy hand comes to rest on my cheek, igniting the fire further.

And when I pull away, his expression tells me I've surprised us both.

"I, uh—" He stumbles on his words, coming to a halt instead of continuing.

"I really like you," I say.

And he kisses me again.

Chapter 24

Bettsy

I'M EXHAUSTED. ALL I want to do is crawl into bed and sleep for days—weeks even. But I can't. There's too much going on and the desperation to hear from Ellie is intense.

Ever since she left the rink this morning, I've been checking my phone on the off-chance that I've missed a text or a call or something.

Has she spoken with Kathryn yet? What did she say? Did she get her money back? Because I swear to God, I'll drive there tonight and have a word with her sister myself, if I have to.

But realistically, I can't do that. Not if I want to keep my balls because Liam's stag-do is a non-negotiable, even when it comes to errant sisters.

"Do you want another beer?" Hutch says from the sofa.

He's lounging, nursing a beer while I iron both of our shirts; I'm leaning awkwardly over a far-too-low ironing board with a flowery cover—courtesy of my mother.

"Does a penalty box have walls?" I say before pressing my lips together as I hunch lower to attack a particularly stubborn crease.

Moments later, Hutch hands me a beer and I hand him his shirt, reaching for my own when there's a knock at the door and since I'm busy, I don't protest when Hutch disappears to answer it.

"It's your sister," he calls.

I wasn't expecting Kelly.

I set the iron on its end and move away from the board as she comes into view. She's wearing her work uniform, her name badge fastened to a fleece, which she takes off and drapes across the back of the sofa.

"Kel," I say. "Everything okay?"

"Yeah, Johnny said you wanted to see me?"

Fucking Johnny. This is his way of saying *tell her before I do'* and considering she looks indifferent; I figure he hasn't uttered a word.

Part of me wonders if I can get away with playing dumb until Hutch saunters back into the room, clad in his freshly ironed shirt.

"How's life, Kel? Fancy Bettsy's news, huh?"

She pulls her brows together and gapes at me. "News? What news?"

"I—"

"I'm going to check in on Ffordey," Hutch says, making a swift exit stage left, letting the apartment door slam behind him.

"What's going on?" Kelly says. "Are you okay? Did something happen?"

I move back to the ironing board, straightening my shirt against the edge and getting to work on the sleeves.

"Mike?" she prompts. "You're scaring me."

I wince, then set the iron back on its heel, before I shift my focus to my sister.

"Do you want a drink or something?" I ask.

"I've got work." She pauses, tilting her head to the side. "Do you ... think I need a drink?"

I shake my head. Because if there's *anyone* who will understand, it's Kelly.

"Remember Ellie?" I say, breezily. "Who lived next door?"

"Yeah ... what about her?" She pauses, blinking a few times. "Wait—did she get in touch about that silly pact you made? The marriage one?"

I titter. Because now Kelly's said it out loud, I realise how silly this all is.

"Nah, but she did reach out." I pick the iron back up and run it over the back of my shirt. "Turns out..." I cast Kelly a look, keeping my eyes settled on hers as she waits. Patient as ever. "Yeah, so ... turns out we might've got married when we were eighteen."

I expect questions. Gasps. Exclamations of horror. But she doesn't blink. Doesn't move. It's like she's buffering.

I look back down at my shirt, adjusting it while I wait.

Still buffering.

I finish ironing the shirt before I decide to prompt her.

"Kel? Are you going to say something?"

"You ... you got married?"

"Well, we think so—" I fill in her in the on the details while I pull off my tee and slip my arms into my shirt.

The Germany trip. The ferry ride. The wedding experience...

I come to a natural pause, waiting for her to respond.

She blinks. Starts. Then purses her lips.

"Okay," she says, eventually. "Couple of things."

"Shoot."

"Number one," she holds a finger up. "How do you *not* remember getting married?"

"I remember the *experience*," I say. "But we both thought it was just that. An experience. And then Ellie saw a video online and—"

"Two," she says, holding up a second finger, cutting me off. "I thought she was engaged—oh, my God, is that why she reached out? Because she's due to get married and—"

"No. I said she reached out because she saw a video online. And she's not engaged."

But Kelly's clearly not paying my words much attention. She paces instead and because I'm lost for things to say, I watch her.

Back and forth. Back and forth.

Eventually, there's a knock on the door and Kelly turns on the spot and strides towards it, pulling it open to find Johnny on the other side.

She says nothing to him. She simply resumes her pacing, letting him close the door as he lets himself inside.

"I take it you told her then?" he says, slipping onto one of the bar stools.

I offer him a *'what do you think'* look.

"Right," he mutters, and because I don't know what else to do, I move to the fridge to grab Johnny a beer.

We both watch Kelly pace. Like she's doing a sponsored walk or something. And I'm close to intervening for the sake of my floor when she comes to an abrupt stop. Pivoting on the spot to face me.

"What now, Mike?" she says. "Do Mam and Dad know?"

I open my mouth to speak, but she's not done.

"Are you getting an annulment? Is it even real? Have you spoken to a solicitor? Because I assume she doesn't want to stay married if she's engaged."

Johnny's eyebrows shoot up.

"She's not engaged," I say. "I found the wrong profile before."

Johnny sets his beer down. "Before? What do you mean, before?"

I blow out a breath before telling him about the pact and my Facebook stalking experience.

"Well, that's a relief," Kelly says. "But you can get an annulment, right? You can square this all away."

But my non-answer is answer enough.

Kelly gapes at me.

"You've..." She swallows. "You've slept with her," she says. "Oh, my God." She covers her mouth with her hands, her eyebrows practically hitting the ceiling.

"In my defence, you can still get an annulment if you've consummated ... on the grounds that the marriage was entered into without consent. And since neither Ellie nor I knew..."

"You've done your research," Johnny says. "I assume this is to make things easier when you're done doing what you're doing?"

"But if you've slept with her..." Kelly says, still focused on her reveal. "You're ... not involved, are you? I mean, not realising you were married is ... well... wow. But actually, getting close and—"

But I'm fixed on what Johnny said.

"What's that supposed to mean?" I snap, putting my attention on Johnny.

"Well, it's just a convenience thing, right? Once the season is over and the Team GB stuff dies down, you can go back to your lives."

There's a clench in my chest. What if I don't want to *go back* to my old life?

I look down at the floor.

"I knew it," Johnny says, getting to his feet. "You're catching feelings. Are you sure she's not going to lead you along?"

Am I catching feelings? Well, I can't deny it, that's for sure. There's something—an ache, perhaps—hung in my chest, but maybe it's the anxiety of worrying if I'm enough.

My sister looks between us, head turning like she's umpiring a tennis match.

"She's not like that," I say, turning to Kelly. "Kel, tell him she's not like that."

"Well, no," she says. "I don't think she *is* like that. But her sister's a nasty piece of work, and—"

"You were nice as pie to her earlier ... even asked about setting up a double date," I say.

"But Vicky—"

"Oh, of course. I should have known. The pity party."

"What happened with Vicky, Mike? Johnny, what happened with Vicky?" Kelly moves closer to Johnny, but his attention is on me.

"We just don't want you to get hurt. We don't want you to invest in something that isn't long term. We just want to see you happy," he says. "Remember when—"

"Please don't bring any of my exes into this," I say. "Because this is different."

"You said that about—"

I flash Kelly a glare and she halts mid-sentence.

"I am happy. Why can't you see that?" I look between my best friend and my sister, almost on the cusp of desperation. Begging for them to understand. "And what's more? I could have kicked off when you told me you'd been *sneaking* around with my little sister, but no. I didn't. I let you make your own decisions and if those decisions turn into a mistake, then you know what? It'd kill me but I'd be there. For both of you. Because you're my family. And I guess it was my mistake thinking the same of you."

I drain the rest of my beer and work the buttons on my shirt. Then I stomp over to the ironing board and pull the plug out of the wall.

"You're right," Johnny says. "Of course, you're right. We just don't want to see you getting hurt, but if you think this is something ... then we'll support you, right, Kel?"

I turn back to face them just as Kelly launches herself towards me, attacking me with the most *huggiest* of hugs.

"We love you, Mike. You know that. And yeah, we don't want you to get hurt, but ... we're here for you," she says.

Kelly steps back and smooths my collar, fussing over me like she's the big sister.

"Thanks," I say, batting her away. "Now are we going, Cap? Because there's no way Liam's getting away with not being strapped naked to a lamppost."

Johnny stands, and I reach for my phone, frowning before slipping it into my pocket.

I'D BE LYING IF I said I wasn't a little envious of Kathryn's house. She and Greg bought it a few years ago and within months, she had it exactly how she wanted it. No half-painted walls, no worn carpet, no chipped sink—but that's where the envy stops. There's no character, no warmth, no feeling. In fact, it doesn't even feel like a home most of the time, just an empty shell made to look pretty.

Which is funny because that's how I'd describe my sister.

I pull up outside and cut the engine, stepping out onto the kerb before I can convince myself it's a bad idea; because, despite running over my lines in the car, I know for a fact that as soon as I come face-to-face with Kathryn I will deviate from the plan.

There's a small path leading to their front door, a freshly painted bottle green gate at the threshold which I push open, making my way towards the house.

Deep breaths, Ellie. You can do this.

But the truth is, I hate confrontation. I've never been good at it. I come across feeble, like a soggy biscuit dunked for too long in a hot brew and on the cusp of breaking.

I pause for a moment, considering my options of either knocking or running away, when the door opens a crack and Greg, still in a grey work suit, tie loosened, pokes his head out.

He holds my gaze for a second, then he says, "Ellie, is everything okay?"

I raise my eyebrows, folding my arms over my chest. The audacity of this guy. What is he expecting me to say? *'Oh, hi, Greg. Kathryn screwed me over, but everything's peachy. Thanks for asking.'*

"No, everything is not okay," I say. "I need to speak with my sister. Now."

He turns to look away, checking something behind him, but he keeps his body in the gap between the door and its frame, blocking my view into the house.

A moment later, he faces me again, a frown pulling at his lips.

"Kathryn's got a headache. Maybe you should come back another day."

Headache, my bum.

"It won't take a minute," I say, smiling sweetly.

But Greg has his response ready.

"She's not up to it, El, honest."

I sigh, studying the door, wondering if I can barge it open, but Greg must catch on because he squeezes onto the doorstep and pulls it shut behind him.

"Look. I'm sorry about the email thing," he says. "But—"

"I just want my money back," I say. "That's all. I don't want any drama. I don't want to cause a fuss in front of your neighbours." I cast a glance over my shoulder, already feeling the burning glare of Mrs 'Across-the-Street' peering at us through her net curtains. "All I want is my money back."

"Your money back?" Greg pinches the bridge of his nose. "I'm sorry what?"

"My money," I say again. "The money I lent Kathryn to start her business. Seven grand. I wa—" I stop myself. "I need it back."

Greg's face twists into a contorted smile, then he laughs. A belly chuckle I associate with mockery.

"Seven ... seven grand?"

"Yes," I say, my expression sombre.

His laugh dies, and his expression turns sour.

"Seven grand to start—"

"Yes. Like I said, I lent her seven grand to start the business. My share of Grandad's money," I say. "And I could really—"

"No," he says, shaking his head. "I put the money in the salon. All of it."

"Well, you couldn't have paid for it all," I say. "I definitely lent her money, and I've got proof." I rummage in my bag for my phone, but the unmistakable sound of a door slamming pulls my attention back.

He's gone. He's actually gone.

I try the handle, but it's locked; I'm met with its firm resistance, not willing to budge.

"Greg?" I shout. "Greg?"

I use the palm of my hand to pound on the frosted glass of the door.

Bang, bang, bang.

I try the knocker next. Frantically forcing it up and down, desperate to make myself heard. Not like he could have forgotten I'm out here.

But there's nothing. No shadows through the glass, no muffled conversation. Nothing.

I idle on the doorstep for a moment before fumbling for my phone, hoping to call, text, something... but the screen stays dark, and I remember—I was meant to charge it on the drive here.

Throwing it back into my bag, I knock again. Hammering my fist this time.

Bang, bang, bang.

But still nothing.

And when I tread across the perfectly manicured lawn to peer through the window, I find the curtains drawn shut.

I feel defeated. Defeated and exhausted. But I hold out for another few minutes before backing away, retreating to the comfort of my car where I lock my doors and lean back in my seat.

What now? I guess I could wait out here. Keep tabs on her front door ... because she'll have to leave, eventually. But I'm getting hungry and after all the travelling I've done today, I'm keen to crawl into bed and sink into a deep sleep—after I text Mike, of course.

I dig through the centre console, looking for the cable to charge my phone, when my fingers brush across the paper of the winning scratch cards from the petrol station trip with Mike. A moment that actually feels like forever ago.

They were winners, right?

I plug the cable into my phone before picking up the cards, scanning the detail. What did Mike say? Anything under a fiver … reinvest?

With the hope of speaking to Kathryn swept away like a pile of hair clippings, I start the engine, toss the cards into my bag, and pull away from her street, heading in the direction of the big supermarket on the edge of town.

I'm in and out in less than fifteen minutes, grabbing something to make for dinner, a bottle of wine and four replacement scratchcards. Typically, I'd be keen to drive home and get into my pyjamas, but I can't wait. I dig in my purse for a penny and read the rules, coin poised ready.

Match three to win.

Okay, that's straightforward enough, and if I lose, then I have lost nothing. But if I win … maybe I won't need to ask Kathryn for anything back. Maybe I can go there tomorrow on the premise of gloating instead.

I chuckle to myself. The realisation that I have more faith in a bit of card than I do my own sister.

I get started, rubbing away the surface as I whisper a silent prayer to whatever God is listening.

Card one is a loser.

Card two is a loser.

Card three is a winner. Two whole pounds.

But card four is even better.

"Huh," I say to myself, turning the card over in my hand. That can't be right, can it?

I grab my phone, wait for it to power on and pull up the camera app, snapping a picture of the card before sending it on to Mike, tapping out a caption.

Would you reinvest this? Or take it as the ultimate win?

I flick through several messages from clients as I wait for him to reply, but I'm halted mid-read when my phone rings in my hand. Mike's name flashing up on the screen.

A video call.

My nerves kick up a notch, though I'm not sure why. I saw him this morning and—God. I realise I was just as nervous then too.

I take a breath and hit accept, beaming back at Mike as his face fills the screen.

"Sweetheart," he says, a buzz in his voice like he's been drinking. "Remember when I told you a fiver is the limit? That was for good reason. I once bought fifty scratch cards with my fifty quid winnings, and I won a grand total of thirty quid. Which naturally, I reinvested and won even less so ... bottom line: take the fifty."

"Fifty scratchcards?" I say, my jaw dropping.

"Yeah, but now I think about, perhaps I should have done twenty-five two-pound cards ... or ten fiver cards or—"

He cuts off, turning to speak to someone on his left before grinning back at the screen.

"Lee isn't even here yet. Would you believe it?"

"Really?"

"Yeah, apparently, he's meeting us in a bit, but anyway—what happened with your sister? Did she sort out the money?"

I close my eyes, inhaling slowly, then looking back at Mike.

"No. She wouldn't see me. I saw Greg, though, told him I didn't want drama. All I wanted was my money back and, given his reaction, I don't think he knew about it. Which makes me even more annoyed because I want to know what the hell she did with my money."

"What?" Mike says. "He didn't know?"

"He had no idea."

"So, what now?" he says. "Do you need me to pay her a visit?"

I roll my eyes. "You're not an extortionist."

"But I can be, for you." He winks, sending a ripple of something through my body. "Honestly, though, it's no trouble. I'm back in a few days ... need to tell Mam what's going on, since I told Kelly and—"

I gasp. Cutting Mike off.

"What did she say?"

"Yeah, all good." He looks away again, then nods firmly. "I've been summoned, Kitch. But I'll see you when I'm home, yeah?"

"Sure."

"Promise? Because ... well, I—I miss you."

"Are you sure it's not the beer talking?" I ask, cocking my head to the side.

"Nah, I do." His lip tug into a smile and my heart squeezes.

"Miss you, too. But have fun, yeah?"

Then he does this ridiculous show of kissing the camera.

I probably would have been cringing if it were anyone else.

But it's Mike.

And Mike isn't just anyone else anymore.

Chapter 25

Bettsy

How DID I FORGET the silent treatment is a hell of a lot worse than the glare of disappointment? Honestly, I don't know how long she's planning on dragging this out for, but I'm pretty sure she's got several days in her—more if she's feeling particularly stubborn.

But Mam being Mam won't let anyone go hungry—not even me, the son she's stuck with. The fuck-up. The child who doesn't think things through. No. She sets down a sandwich on the table with a heavy thud and pulls out a chair. Silent message: sit down and eat. And since I'm not in the mood to fuel her fire and piss her off even more, I do as I'm told.

She stalks back to the kettle, lifting it off the stand and pouring boiling water into three mugs. One for me. One for her. And one for—

"I'm home."

Ah, shit.

Dad calls from the front door, announcing his arrival, slamming it closed behind him before dropping his keys into the bowl on the sideboard. His routine plays out in my head.

He'll use the bathroom, then there'll be a moment of silence as he takes his shoes off, followed by his belt.

Mam finishes making the tea, then turns to me, her mouth in a straight line as she watches me—scoffing down the sandwich—as we wait for my dad.

Though, I'm not sure what I'm waiting for because my dad's soft as shit. He's told none of us kids off once—Mam is the authoritarian. She can rule with a single look.

"You can tell him," she says.

And I face no choice but to nod, swallowing my pride along with a chunk of bread. Because even though Dad is laid back and generally carefree, I'm not overly excited about breaking the news to him.

The silence stretches out before the kitchen door finally opens. Dad enters, stopping next to Mam and planting a kiss on her cheek before reaching for his mug.

"Everyone okay?" he says.

But Mam's silence tells him what he needs to know—everything is far from okay in her world.

"Didn't realise you were visiting today, Mike?"

He takes a sip of his tea.

"Yeah, I've got the social thing with Team GB tomorrow, so I figured—"

"Go on. Tell him," Mam says sharply, cutting me off.

"Tell me what?" Dad says, looking between us.

"Why don't you ask *your* son?"

I wince. This is how I know things are bad. I'm not 'her son' in this moment, or the collective 'our son', I'm *his* son. Dad's son. Dad's responsibility.

He realises this too. The last time I recall her throwing that out into the world was when I broke a £200 stick the day after I got it. Weeks of begging, that took me. Weeks of trying to justify my needing it, for it to be gone a day later. Snapped in half after a failed one-timer. Needless to say, I didn't have one that fancy again—not until I started playing pro.

"What's going on?" Dad says, looking right at me.

I swallow hard and brace myself to talk—even getting as far as opening my mouth, but Mam cuts across me again, turning to my dad and sticking a hand on her hip.

"He's only gone and told his new Coach he's married, Tony. Married. Apparently—Coach Harris from the Team GB squad implied being settled in a relationship would be better for Michael's image, you know, grounded and all that—so bright spark here casually dropped the mention of a wife into the conversation and now—"

"Married?" Dad says, contorting his face as if he's trying to work out what the word means. "You're joking?"

And if I'm not mistaken, I think there's a hint of a smile.

He looks around the room and I shrug, not sure what else I can offer.

"I wish I was joking," Mam says. "And now he's convinced some poor girl to go along with it."

Dad laughs. His deep chuckle fills the room, only to halt at the sight of my mother's unamused face.

"What? Who?" he says, straightening up.

I open my mouth to answer when the doorbell rings and Mam looks at me, absolute rage in her eyes.

"Oh, my god," she says. "I've got a home appointment, so Tony, I'll leave you to deal with this."

She dips out of the kitchen, leaving Dad and me alone.

"Outside. Now," he says, pointing towards the patio doors.

My pulse picks up as I get to my feet, wondering if the disappointment will come from Dad instead. I force myself to move forward. Left foot, right foot, a steady movement right out into the garden, clutching my brew like it's going to save me.

Dad pulls up a weathered patio chair and points at it, "Sit," then grabs one for him, sinking down onto it before hissing, "talk."

"It's actually a funny story," I say, choosing to add a bit of humour to the mix, but his face remains solemn—clearly deciding this isn't as funny as he first thought.

See, when I told Mam, I omitted the part about Ellie and I potentially being married for real. I also missed out on the mention of who was playing along, but for some reason, I choose to tell Dad the entire story. Starting at the very beginning.

I tell him about the eighteen-year-old me, and the naivety it came with, then I tell him about the fact that I tried to get in touch with her once I got home—then I skip forward to her turning up at my apartment and the events that followed quickly after.

He sucks in a breath. "Christ's sake, Mike."

"I know," I say. "I didn't plan for it to happen, obviously."

Then he asks me the question I've been dreading.

"Who is she?"

I pick at my cuticles. My dad's not dumb. He'll know that there's no way a girl like Ellie would actively choose to be with a guy like me. Rough around the edges, covered in bruises and scars and missing several teeth.

Maybe that's why Vicky acted the way she did.

I gear myself to answer. Gathering all the courage I have. "It's—"

But something catches my eye, and I let my attention slip to the kitchen window, where I notice movement inside. Two people. One being my mother and the other, taller, hair a warm chestnut. The reflection of the garden blurs against the glass, making it hard to see—and it doesn't help that my dad is glaring at me, waiting for a reply.

He prompts me again. "So, who?"

"Ellie?" I gasp.

For a second, I think it's my mind playing tricks on me, but nope. There she is, standing in the kitchen with my mother.

Ah, fuck. My stomach lurches. My heart pounds—like I'm a single defenceman on an odd-man rush.

Dad follows my eyes, and he says something—except I don't hear him because there's a pull in my chest at the exact moment I realise Ellie is crying.

I set the mug on the floor before standing, and stride over to the door, pulling it open and stepping inside, where I catch the end of her sentence.

"...I'm so sorry, Mrs Betts. I didn't mean to let you down or anything, but hopefully we can line up home appointments from now on."

Ellie looks at me, her eyes widening.

"What's going on?" I ask.

"Can you give us some privacy, please, Michael?" Mam says.

Ellie sniffs loudly before wiping a plump tear from her cheek. "Kitch?"

"It's nothing," she says.

I don't even think about what I'm doing until I'm doing it—I step towards her and pull her into my arms.

"What's going on?" I ask, keeping my voice low and level.

"I was about to ask the same question," Mam says. "What—Michael you can't—"

Ellie pulls away slightly, sniffing loudly before dabbing her face with a tissue.

"It's nothing. I'm fine honestly—your mam's appointment didn't get fulfilled and—"

"Oh, don't worry about that," Mam says. "Come and sit down, love."

She steers Ellie to an empty chair at the table before turning and making her way to the kettle.

I kneel in front of Ellie, trying to catch her eye.

"Did something happen with Kathryn?"

"No." She swallows, rummaging in her bag for a packet of tissues, pulling a fresh one from the wrapper. "I hate letting people down and your mam's appointment—"

"Honestly?"

"Honestly, Mike."

She dabs her eyes, then pulls on her best fake smile.

I rack my brain for something—anything because if Kathryn has done anything ... but Dad is apparently more switched on than he leads anyone to believe. He's been watching the scene unfold from the doorway to the garden, and he steps towards me, tapping me on the shoulder, forcing me to look up at him.

"Want to tell us what's going on?"

Ellie

IMAGINE THE FEELING THAT consumes me the moment I open the door to find Mike in a tuxedo.

A tuxedo.

I thought a suit was something, but him in a tuxedo is something else.

His jacket is moulded to his frame like a glove, showing me every single thing I remember from our moment on his sofa. And a heat fires inside me as I wonder how I ever thought of Mike as anything other than everything he is.

Hilarious. Endearing. Masculine and gorgeous and—his smile. Oh, his smile is something else. And he smiles—no beams—at me from the threshold.

"Hey, sweetheart. Looking good. How are you feeling?" he says, straightening up to his full height.

His hair, freshly cut, has me desperate to run my hands through it—and he's trimmed his beard. I liked it before, but the clean angles make him look ... refined, which on top of the suit and his manly scent of whatever it is, has me lost for words.

Damn him.

I'm still in a robe, hair pinned up and a full face of makeup, still thinking I had plenty of time to finish getting ready.

"I—you're early," I say.

"Yeah, sorry—I can wait for you out here if you'd prefer," he says.

"No, no, come in," I say, moving aside.

He walks into the living room and sits down on the sofa like he's been here hundreds of times before.

"How's your mam?" I ask, hovering by the doorway.

I know exactly how his mam is, though. She rang me this morning to apologise for her son's erratic behaviour.

But I ask Mike on the basis that she was upset with him, and I know the reason he didn't come over last night was because he was begging for forgiveness.

"She's okay," he says. "Sorry you had to be there for that. I mean, I guess it was my fault. I only told her half a story and—" He blows out a breath, resting his head on the back of the sofa. "It took me ages to pry it from her, but she said I disappointed her. She didn't get to see me—her only living son—get married, so yeah, that's the guilt I'm living with for the rest of my life."

I bite my lip. "I'm sorry, Mike."

"Yeah, well ... any news on Kathryn? Has she sent you a cheque yet?"

"No, but she has read my messages. I'm not sure if that's worse. And I spoke to my mother today, and she said she hasn't heard from Kathryn either, so 'try not to worry'." I use my fingers for air-quotes, but Mike's not looking. He's gazing up at the ceiling, apparently deep in thought.

"Do you know how much you'll need?" he says, tentatively looking in my direction. "For the website and socials?"

"Not yet."

He nods, but he still doesn't look at me.

"If you need money ... I can help, I mean, if you want, I don't want you to think I'm thinking you can't manage or—"

"What's going on?" I say, pacing to the sofa.

I don't sit next to him, instead I get to my knees and settle myself in between his legs, prodding him in the chest.

He meets my gaze, and his breath catches for a second before he says, "oh, fucking hell."

"What?"

"You're sitting there and—"

I scramble to my feet. Though the idea of kneeling between his legs has a negative effect on my ability to stand up straight.

"I can't commit to doing that while I've got a fresh face of make-up. Not when I don't have time to fix it."

Mike tilts his head to look at me again. "My dirty thoughts are killing me. You're killing me."

"They'll be time for that later," I say. "Once you tell me what's wrong."

He runs his hands over his face, groans, then stands up.

Is he shaking? Oh my God, I know guys enjoy a blowjob, but—

He dips his hand into his pocket and pulls out a small black velvet box. The sort of box rings come in.

I gasp—I can't help myself. I gasp, looking between the box and Mike, who looks like he's about to pass out.

"Kitch—" he says. "I know you said ... but ... fuck." His head dips to his hands before he looks at me again. "I figured if we show up and we're not looking ... you know, fully dressed, then people may get suspicious."

I stare at his hands, visibly shaking under my watch, as he pries open the box. My heart picks up speed, already heightened after the tuxedo entry, now beating franticly in my chest.

"What—"

"I went to a jeweller today, and it's weird because I don't have a fucking clue about rings or anything, but when I saw these, I just ... thought of you." He turns the box around to face me. "It's sort of like one of those wedding rings that fits around the engagement ring and, ugh ... I hope you like it enough to wear, I mean—"

My eyes brim with tears. In the box sits an Asscher-cut diamond. And it's ... breathtaking.

"It's on a platinum band and the clarity's something like 'VS1' or something—I'm not sure what that means, but apparently, it's nearly perfect. Like, you'd need a loupe to spot any flaws ... one of those magnifying glasses jewellers use."

"Oh, my God."

"Do you like it?"

I'm trying to think of anything to say that will convey how I feel about it—because this is the most beautiful set of rings I've ever seen.

"I—I—" I swallow. "I love them, Mike. But I can't accept them."

His half-crooked smile falls into a frown. "Why not?"

"I'm not even asking how much they cost you, but it's too much—I mean, this isn't—I just—"

Frustration fills my chest. I can't find the words. I can't find any words to explain how I'm feeling right now.

Mike takes a step towards me.

"Hey, have you ever heard the term, 'if he wanted to, he would'? Because I wanted to get these for you, so I did. Honestly, Kitch, all the other rings in the cabinet looked like crap compared to these. I saw the set, and I knew these were meant for you."

I stare at him, letting my mouth hang open in complete disbelief. All I ever wanted was to be seen, to be something to someone—and in comes Mike, showing me that he does see me and he probably saw me all those years back too. I mean ... these rings. These rings are familiar.

"I need to finish getting ready," I say, "I need to finish my hair and touch up my makeup and—"

"Yeah, no problem," he says, clearing his throat.

Then I spot the silver band he's wearing on his left hand.

He catches me looking, then sets the ring box down on the coffee table, holding his hand out.

"I just figured it'd make sense if ... you know."

I push down the emotion that's building, excusing myself and rushing upstairs on the premise of getting ready, but instead, I dig through the bottom of my wardrobe, pulling out my memory box, the sight of the rings reminding me of something I think I have.

I rummage through various items. Old notes, old postcards, ticket stubs, receipts.

Then I find it. Tucked in the very bottom of the box.

How did I forget this existed?

A Polaroid photo of me and Mike on our wedding day—or whatever you want to call it. Our teenage selves not quite understanding the pivotal point that moment would play on our future. We weren't posing as newlyweds but as a couple of friends who weren't actually friends, making the best of an adventure.

I stare at the photo, taking in the smiles we both wear, and with it comes the memory of the events that followed shortly after. The phone calls I never got. The texts I never received. And then there's the bridal set downstairs—so similar to the one I had shown him as we gazed through the window of a jeweller, hours before the 'wedding experience'.

I really fucking hate my sister.

I look at myself in the mirror, half-ready and heart literally aching from the whirlpool of emotions, trying to stop the tears as I pull the rollers out of my hair. Instead of running a brush through the length, I reach for a hair tie and pull it back, setting it into a ponytail before pulling on a pair of leggings and a baggy jumper.

Then I descend the stairs to tell Mike there's something I need to do.

Chapter 26

AFTER CONVINCING MIKE I'LL be as quick as I can and I definitely don't need his help, I head to my sister's house, cranking up the volume on a 'Power Ballads' playlist to help build up courage. I don't proclaim to be a decent singer, but there's something about the protective bubble of my car which makes me feel invincible, even more so when the crescendo builds and I pull off a high note.

She won't answer any of my questions. She won't admit she sabotaged my chances with Mike all those years ago. She won't come clean about the money she owes me. So, why do I think she's going to be any different tonight?

She'd probably do something crazy, though. The mirror in the salon would be just the start for her. Maybe I should take a leaf out of Kathryn's book. Because if she can play games, so can I.

I shake my head, upping the volume on the stereo, trying to distract myself, but it's no use. Because she wouldn't think twice. In fact, she doesn't think at all. Not really, anyway. Not when it comes to anyone else.

I come to a stop at the crossroads. Typically, I'd continue straight on, but something's pulling at me to turn left. Maybe it's the courage acting. Maybe it's the fact that I've had enough.

As the lights flick from red to amber to green, I signal left, speeding off towards the salon, wondering if this really is a good idea.

Five minutes later, I conclude it's absolutely not a good idea, and by the time I pull up outside the salon, I've decided it's the worst idea I've ever had, but I'm going to do it anyway.

I owe this to myself. And to Mike.

The emptiness of the salon is obvious as soon as I get out of the car. I go around to the boot and pull out the stash of reusable shopping bags I never remember until I'm at the till, tucking them under my arm as I head towards the doors.

Deep breath.

At least there's no one around to see me—not that they'd suspect something unless Kathryn has updated the neighbourhood watch—but I slip the shutter key into the lock and rotate it fifteen degrees. The shutters spring to life, jutting upwards as they clear the bottom of the door. Then they breach the half-way mark and I cut them there, ducking underneath and rooting through my keyring for the front door key.

Bingo.

She's not changed the locks ... but I know for a fact she'll do that once she's noticed I've been here.

She must have got Greg to remove the mirror, along with the fragments of glass and the broken vase, because the floor is clear, which makes things easier for me. Less pussyfooting.

I shake out several bags, setting them on the floor, then I start grabbing things. All my things, anyway.

My scissors, hot tools, combs, and brushes. My stylist belt, prep products, dye samples—basically anything I bought or invested in. I decide to leave the trolley—because frankly, getting that replaced is relatively easy and carrying it out may draw too much attention to myself and I'm not sure it'll fit in my car. But I finish stuffing the bags as best as I can, turning back to the window to check the coast is clear before ducking outside and cramming them into my boot.

But I don't feel satisfied.

I stand on the pavement for a few seconds, worrying my lip before I head back inside, straight for the counter where I fire up the computer.

How pissed would she be if I deleted her entire bookings record?

It's petty but—

I shake my head and back away from the desk, the glow of the computer screen fading as I move over to the nail station instead. The rows of gel polish are lined up like soldiers. Kathryn's army of colours, ready for battle.

A thought flickers through my mind.

I can't ... can I?

But I'm impulsive. Not capable of thinking rationally, apparently.

Just like Kathryn.

I pick up one of the bottles from the middle row—*'Pillar-box Red'*. The colour of danger—untwisting the cap. I set it back down, lid open, air rushing inside.

Exposed.

Then I move along the row, *'Leonardo's Model'*, a glittery shade of purple is next. Followed by *'Pigment of my Imagination'*, and *'You Had Me at Halo'*—summer favourites, now slowly spoiling under the glare of my payback.

Five shades in, I pause. This is pathetic, right? Petty and childish and—maybe a few more won't hurt. I'm not exactly ruining her relationship with Greg, right? It's not like I'm smashing the bottles, is it? I'm not storming in here, breaking mirrors and causing chaos.

No. I'm just doing a little sabotage—like she did with my mirror.

I'm just ... letting air in.

Giving these bottles space to breathe so they can feel as free as I do.

She'll be wondering why her stock is gloopy next week. She'll probably call the rep and complain, accuse them of sending her a bad batch; something she'd have got me to do before.

But this can be her time to waste.

Not mine.

Not again.

I know two wrongs don't make a right, but surely this only scrapes the surface of wicked given Kathryn's extensive list of wrongdoing.

'Love is in the bare' is the next victim. Followed by *'Baby, take a vow'*, then *'Lavendare to find courage'*, which makes me laugh out loud before I change my mind and fasten the lid, slipping it into my pocket instead.

Battle paint.

Armour.

The last colour I let free is *'Fifteen minutes of flame'*, then I step back, gradually retreating to the counter where I change the password to the terminal instead.

I slip out, locking the door behind me and pulling the shutters back down, then I slide behind the steering wheel of my car.

A half-hour later, I'm back in the comfort of my home, staring into the mirror of my dressing table, fixing my makeup and finishing my hair, wondering if I've made a huge mistake, but several minutes later, I'm calling Jess, wondering if she can convince me otherwise.

I prop my phone up on the dressing table as it rings out.

"I need your advice," I say as she answers. "Though it's something I've already sort of done, so I basically need you to tell me I did the right thing."

"You did the right thing," she says on cue.

I fill her in on the story of 'House of Kathryn' and Kathryn herself, avoiding every attempt I've made to contact her.

"Basically, I got to the point where I wanted to get my stuff back," I say. "So I went to the salon, and I let myself in. I grabbed my things, literally throwing them into the bags ... but I couldn't call it quits, Jess. I did something."

She raises an eyebrow. "Is this going to sicken me or turn me into a cheerleader?"

I bite my lip. "I changed her password for the bookings computer," I blurt out. "And I took the lids off several gel polishes."

Jess bursts out laughing. "Oh, my God, Ellie. I love this."

"But it's petty, right?"

"Yes, but not petty enough, if you ask me. I'd have redirected the phone lines to a premium rate number or something."

"No, that's not good for the clients," I say.

"True. So, what now?"

"Well, now, I wait. Because if she didn't want to talk to me before, she probably will want to talk to me now."

I stand up and make my way to the wardrobe, opening the door and reaching for my gown.

"Wait," Jess says sharply. "Come back to the phone. Now."

"What?" I say. "I'm sort of on a time crunch."

"Sit back down," she says. "Show me your hand."

I clench my jaw but slip back into the seat.

"Start talking," she says.

And I have no choice but to tell her everything.

Bettsy

"IF IT MAKES YOU feel any better, Langer's missus hasn't turned up either," Danny says, leaning into me and lowering his voice.

"She'll be here," I say, but even I don't believe it.

The more I check my phone, the more I'm worrying she's stood me up.

Maybe she's come to her senses. Looked in the mirror and saw her worth. Maybe—

I flick my gaze towards the bottom end of the table where Langer and his league team buddies chat and joke, completely oblivious to the crippling heartache happening at this end of the table. Selfishly, I'm grateful Danny's here without a plus one—it makes me look a little less pathetic.

"Poor woman probably wanted a break," Danny says.

"A break from what?"

"All the shit you talk," he grins.

"Har-har," I say, taking a swig of beer from a fresh bottle.

It's my third of the evening, the two before this being short-lived, a failed attempt to push down the anxiety.

"But seriously—is everything okay?" Danny says.

He keeps his voice quiet, and I force a nod, putting my attention on the paper label stuck to the bottle, picking at the edge of the logo adhered to the glass.

What if this is it? What if the something she needed to do involves an ex she's never mentioned? Maybe she realised...

"Mate?"

I snap out of my spiral. Angling my head towards Danny as I force a smile.

"Uh, yeah, all good," I say.

He doesn't buy it. I know he doesn't.

I wait until he's pulled into another conversation before sneaking a peek at my phone, curious to see if I've missed a call.

There's nothing.

She should be here by now, but I've not received so much as a text from her. Nothing. Radio silence.

"Maybe I should check in on her? Call her, perhaps?" I say, nudging Danny in the arm.

"What? Oh ... well, it's your funeral. Women don't like it when you nag them," Danny says. "And they don't like being told that they're taking too long to get ready—learn from my mistakes."

I push my seat back and stand anyway, moving towards the far end of the bar area, avoiding Greer and Frenchy.

Once I'm out of earshot, I pull up her number and hit dial.

Voicemail.

It doesn't even ring.

And automatically, I try again.

Voicemail.

I exhale, pinching the bridge of my nose as I slip my phone away and head back to my seat, putting all my effort into being passive.

Luckily, I've done this enough times to pull it off. Though, this time, it feels less like a rejection and more like a punch in the stomach.

"All good?" Danny says.

"Oh, actually..." I say, pulling an excuse out of my ass. "She's got a headache. I think it's the weather," I say. "Barometric pressure, temperature, humidity ... you know."

Danny blinks before taking a sip of his own drink. "Right."

Lucky for me, that's when Greer and Frenchy return to their seats, setting down a tray of drinks. Bottles of beer, shot glasses, and a magnum of champagne. It's enough to draw Danny.

I finish my beer and grab another one while contemplating whether I should call her again.

Whoops and cheers fill the air around me as the drinks flow. I half-zone out of the conversation going on around me, replaying the events of the evening instead, trying to figure out where I went wrong.

Maybe it was the rings—rings I was sure she'd love, but maybe it was too much. Maybe I spooked her and ruined all my chances.

"How about you Betts?" someone says, as I snap my head up to see Greer looking at me, waiting for a response. "Come on, everyone's got something."

"I'm sorry what?" I say.

"Your secret pre-game superstition?" he says, taking a swig of his beer. "You know, something you do, but don't tell anyone else about. Time to come clean."

I force a laugh. "I don't have anything."

"Yeah, right," Greer snickers. "Everyone's got one."

I'd usually be all over this sort of thing, but I'm not in the mood. I'm tense and anxious, desperate to know if Ellie is okay … if we're okay.

There's jeering around me, encouragement, so I make something up about only using a fresh roll of tape before I excuse myself, telling the guys I need to take a leak.

I head towards the lobby in the direction of the men's room and when I round the corner, my eyes land on a figure in the far corner.

My heart stops in my chest.

What the—I can't believe she's here.

I freeze on the spot, my stomach practically falling out of my ass when I spot her, leaning against a window wearing a tight red dress.

I look around, surveying the immediate area, grateful that I'm alone and no one is here to witness the shit show that's about to unfold.

"Bettsy," she calls. "I was hoping to catch you. Have you missed me?" The shrillness of her voice has me shivering with disgust, memories of the shit she dragged me through flooding to the surface.

The fake pregnancy. The lies about Rodgers and their broken relationship. I mean, she told me she was single for Christ's sake, and I fell for it. Desperate for the attention—the fake admiration.

I'm such a fucking loser.

She's walking towards me, pushing her boobs out, trying to distract me, no doubt. And I'll be damned if I let her this time. I focus my attention on the floor—telling myself not to look her directly in the eyes; don't look the devil directly in the eyes.

"Oh, come on—you're still not speaking to me?" she says, reaching out a hand and setting it on my forearm.

I pull away, taking a step back. "What do you want, Roch?"

"I just want to speak to you. I heard you guys were here tonight, so I thought I'd stop by and—I want you to know how sorry I am."

I swallow down the bile rising in my throat and glance up, risking a look. "What are you sorry for?"

She bats her eyelashes. "Excuse me?"

"I said, what are you sorry for? You said you wanted me to know how sorry you were, and I'm keen to understand the details."

She rolls her eyes. "If I knew you were going to be like this, I needn't have bothered."

I gape at her. She's delusional—more so than I led myself to believe before.

"Why are you being like this?" she says.

I scoff. Complete disbelief that she'd even ask such a question.

"I was the best thing to happen to you. We both know that you won't do better than me, so why are you trying to hide from your feelings?" she says.

My temper rises from zero to one hundred before simmering back down after several deep breaths because the last thing I need is this getting out of hand.

I stare at the floor, trying to come up with anything to say to her that may make me feel better. A bitter retort, perhaps.

I've got nothing.

Nothing except a tiny voice in the back of my head whispering to me, *she's right, and Ellie's not here because she realised she can do better.*

She steps forward and puts a hand on my chest. A hand that doesn't feel quite right. It feels heavy and tainted. It makes me think about Ellie's hand, and how she touched me. How different she felt. And how she kissed me at the rink, with no care about who could see. No hiding in the shadows, meetings behind closed doors. And the feeling in my chest intensifies and I realise I've done exactly what Johnny warned me not to do—let myself get attached. Attached to someone who isn't here. Someone who—

I shake my head, desperate to push her out of my mind because what good is this? Pining after someone who's already checked out.

"You need to go," I say, stepping aside and moving towards the exit.

"Bettsy, don't do this," she says. "Hear me out and I promise I'll stop the forum stuff. I mean, it's getting old now, anyway."

"Oh well, at least you admit that," I say.

"Come on," she says. "Let's get a drink. Have a chat. Figure things out."

I should say no. I should tell her to fuck off and leave me alone, but I can't. Not because I want her, but the deep-rooted human desire to feel loved fights its way to the surface. Ellie doesn't want me, but Rochelle can pretend enough to pass for someone who does.

Maybe she's right. Maybe she is the best option for me. And maybe that's enough.

Chapter 27

Ellie

EVERYONE TURNS TO LOOK at me when I walk in. I wish I was exaggerating, but every single person turns in my direction and all I can do is smile, hoping Mike will appear from the crowd and save me.

But he doesn't come.

I scan the faces, none of them familiar except for one. Rick. Sitting with a cluster of guys, drinking beer and laughing at something on the screen of someone's phone.

He looks up at me, double taking before recognition dawns. His eyebrows pull together and he mouths something, something I can't decipher. The guy on his left nudges his arm, and he looks away as I continue to scan the room.

Guys in suits, women in evening dresses, the heavy smell of expensive cologne, but nothing that I recognise. There's no flash of auburn. No Mike.

Then I hear footsteps behind me. A dull thud as they grow closer—but they don't sound like Mike, either.

I spin around anyway, greeted by a guy around an inch taller than me. He's dressed in—you guessed it—a suit. Dark hair swept to the side, and he's wearing glasses; thick black frames that remind me of Clark Kent.

"I'm—I'm looking for Mike Betts," I say. "Is he here?"

His eyes widen and his expression changes. Shock? I can't quite tell because he tries not to make it obvious, but it's there. Something I can't quite put my finger on.

"Uh, Ellie, right?" he says. "Nice to see you again. I'm Danny."

I take several seconds to realise I must have met him before, at Mike's practice session, probably, but an interruption cuts our conversation short.

"Sorry, can I help you?" Another suited man, albeit a few inches shorter than Danny, comes to a stop behind us, angling himself towards me.

"I'm looking for—"

"This is Bettsy's missus," Danny says.

The second man nods firmly and offers out his hand. "Nice to meet you. I'm Brett Harris, Team GB Head Coach."

"Ellie," I say, returning the shake. "Thanks for having me."

"Nice of you to come and support Betts—where is he?" He stretches himself up, peering around the room like a meerkat.

"I think he's just stepped out," Danny says. "Shouldn't be long."

"Right, well, make sure that you get yourself something to eat," Brett says. "There's a buffet table at the back there and there're several waiting staff dotted around if you have any special dietary requirements. Owens, get the lady a drink, will you?"

A cheer from the back of the room grabs Coach's attention and he excuses himself.

"Did you want a drink? Sorry, I should have asked." A smile tugs at his lips. "How's your headache?"

"Head—oh, yeah, better thanks. Strong painkillers. So, no booze for me."

He nods. "Got it."

We head towards the bar, but I'm busy surveying the room as Danny orders for me, handing me a diet Coke a few moments later.

"Well, I don't know where his is. He disappeared to use the bathroom around twenty minutes ago and when he didn't come back, I went to look for him but..." he shrugs before continuing. "No idea."

"I should probably call him," I say, abandoning my drink and pulling my phone out.

"I've already tried that but—" He pauses, and an uneasy feeling settles in my stomach.

"But what?"

"Nothing," he says sharply.

"No ... you were going to say something, but you... what's going on?"

But Danny doesn't reply. His eyes flick over my shoulder and I twist on the spot to see Rick striding towards us, stopping a few feet away.

I inwardly groan.

"Ellie—what're you doing here?" he says. "Is everything okay with Kathryn and Greg and—"

I shrug. "No idea—"

"Mate, you haven't seen Bettsy, have you?" Danny asks Rick.

He snickers. "Bettsy? Why would I care where he is?"

"Ellie's looking for him. Just wondered if—" Danny says.

Rick narrows his eyes as he turns towards me. "And why do you care where he is?"

"You know they are married, right?" Danny says.

Rick's jaw hangs open. He blinks several times, looking between Danny and I like this is some kind of 'in joke' between us, but since neither of us are laughing ... he gets the message.

"You and Bettsy?" he says.

Before I can stop myself, I say, "Yeah. Childhood sweethearts. We reconnected recently and—"

"What the—"

"Oh, that reminds me actually—while I've got you. I'm not going to be Kathryn's maid of honour anymore, so there's no need to include me in any of the big day plans."

Rick's sour expression takes a sharp turn toward confusion.

"Really?" he says.

"Yeah," I reply, cool and clipped. "But you can run that past Greg if you need to."

I turn to Danny with a polite smile I barely manage to hold. "Excuse me—I just need the ladies."

I don't wait for a reply.

My heart pounds as I step away from the bar and cross the lobby, already unlocking my phone.

I scroll straight to Mike's name and press call, lifting the phone to my ear as the empty foyer swallows my footsteps.

Brr-Brr.

Brr-Brr.

Brr-Brr.

I'm about to give up when the tone stops and the voice of someone trickles down the line.

"Hello?"

Except, it's not Mike. It's a woman.

Bettsy

One last look at her and I realise that no matter how shit things are, I'd rather cut off my dick and feed it to the pigeons than let Rochelle anywhere near me again.

I turn and head for the hotel exit, and the fresh air hits me, clearing my mind and reminding me I've done the right thing.

She doesn't get the message.

I stride away, as fast as I can. Two streets later she's still following me, randomly calling out insults as she walks.

Apparently, blocking her number wasn't a nice thing to do. Nor was ignoring her at Liam's stag do. Not that I really saw her—she tried to get into the VIP area in the club we ended up in, but Johnny cut off any chance of her worming her way inside.

Long live the captain.

As she trails behind me, through the empty side-streets, there's no Johnny. It's just me.

Just me and my resolve and what I need is for her to fuck off and leave me alone.

Maybe I can call Danny, get him to come and meet me and—where the fuck is my phone?

I dip my hand into my left pocket, but it's not there. Nor is it in my right. Nor inside the jacket—which, I realise, is where I should have put it.

I come to an abrupt stop. Turning and facing the direction I came from to see Rochelle still trailing along behind me but with a phone that looks familiarly like my own, clutched in her hands.

When the hell did she take my phone? How could I not have noticed?

"She hung up on me," Rochelle says, looking down at the screen in disgust.

"What the hell are you playing at?" I say. "Why do you have my phone?" I stride forward and she moves away, holding my phone a little out of reach so I'm forced to close in.

"Talk. To. Me," she fires. "If you want your phone back. Talk to me first."

And I'm reminded of the turmoil, the demands, the controlling attitude.

But I'm done.

Done with her shit.

"Give me my phone back. Here, this is me, talking to you," I snap.

"Oh, lighten up, Bettsy. I'm only having a laugh," Rochelle says.

I make a quick dash, catching her off guard as I rip my phone from her hands. She wobbles on a strappy heel but keeps her balance.

"I just wanted to see who's keeping you so busy. I'm sorry, but there's no way you'd turn me down unless there was someone else—" She freezes mid-sentence. Her eyes looking down at my hand. "—what are you wearing?" she says. "On your finger. Why are you wearing a wedding ring?"

I don't want to entertain her with an answer. I turn around and hurry away, checking over my messages, grateful I keep my phone locked because there's no way she wouldn't rifle through my messages.

Speaking of which ... there are several unread in the group chat.

Then calls from Danny, Johnny, Vicky, and Ellie.

Ellie.

Ellie called me.

Has she changed her mind? Has she—

"Bettsy," Rochelle screams, the sound of her heels clicking against the pavement as she hurries in my direction. "Don't you walk away from me."

"Fuck off," I snap. "Honestly. Leave me alone or I'll—"

"Or you'll what?" she says.

And we both know I've got nothing. I can't hit her—no, I won't hit her. No matter how vexed she gets me. And I don't have anything on her to return the social slander favour...

"God, you're pathetic," she says. "Wearing a wedding ring ... are you that desperate, Bettsy?"

"Fuck. Off," I say again, slow words ... each enunciated.

I'm not interested in Rochelle. Not now—not anymore. I pick up pace, hitting re-dial and pressing my phone to my ear as it rings out.

Brr-brr.

Brr-brr.

Brr-brr.

It rings and rings, eventually cutting off.

Fuck.

I've blown it.

I've—

"Bettsy," Rochelle calls.

And it hits me. This is all her fault.

"You," I say, turning and pointing a finger at Rochelle. "This is your fault." It's clicks together—Ellie must have been the one to hang up on Rochelle.

She stares at me, a blank expression on her overly made-up face. "What—"

"Why can't you leave me the fuck alone? Why can't you just fuck off?"

"Is that really what you want?" she says.

I laugh. "Of course, that's what I fucking want. You've been harassing me for months. All the crap you've written on the forums and—"

My phone vibrates in my hand, and I fumble to answer it, almost sending it three feet into the air but steadying my grip before spotting the name on the screen.

Danny.

"Yeah?"

"Where the hell are you, Betts? Ellie showed up and now Vicky's here for photos and—"

"Is she still there?" I say, cutting him off. I swallow hard, pushing down the bile that's rising as I wait for him to reply.

"Vicky? Yeah, she's—"

"No," I say.

He blows out a breath down the line. "Nah, mate. She's gone."

I stare ahead, not hearing anything else he's telling me, trying to work out what the hell I do next.

What do I do? How the fuck do I fix this?

I end the call and slip my phone into my pocket, not giving Rochelle any of the attention she's craving as I walk past her, towards the direction of the railway station. They'll have cabs. I can jump in a taxi and go straight to Ellie's ... try to straighten this out.

But Rochelle has other ideas.

"Bettsy?" she calls after me. "You know I left Matt for you, right? You know I gave up everything I had with him for you and this is how you thank me? You're pathetic. And you know what?" There's a pause, like she's waiting for me to answer before she adds, "you're not even that good in bed."

I snort. Because I've never cared less about what anyone thinks of me. I keep walking, long strides to out-step her in my desperation to get away.

But she's sort of running along on the pavement after me, heels clipping the concrete as she moves.

"Bettsy? Will you stop?"

I feel a hand on my arm, then it's gone, then there's a pull on the sleeve of my jacket. But her hand slips away as she loses her grip. And as I turn, things sort of happen in slow motion.

She stumbles forward, toppling over herself as her face hits the ground—the heel of her shoe caught in a crack of the pavement.

I freeze.

She's face down, splayed across the pavement, ragged breaths—then she lifts her head up, pulling herself onto her hands and knees.

Then she screams.

It's a scream that goes right to my bones.

There's blood everywhere.

Her face, her hair, her neck—everywhere.

I wait for the horror to hit me ... for me to feel something... for me to panic and hurry to her aid, but I don't.

All I can do is stand here.

Chapter 28

Ellie

THERE'S A BANGING ON my door.

Hard and furious.

Urgent.

It's like someone's trying to break in.

At first, I think it's part of my dream; clear and realistic—just like the sleep-sex, except I can feel the banging vibrating through the walls of my tiny house.

I blink several times, trying to force myself to wake fully, urging the brain-fog to clear when I catch the sound again.

Then I hear his voice. Rasped and ragged. Like he's gasping for air.

I bolt upright in bed, my heart pounding so hard I can hear my pulse. I throw the covers off my legs before scrambling for my dressing gown.

Bang-bang-bang.

I leap towards the window and open the curtains, trying to peer down to the street below, but I can't see. I need more leverage.

Bang-bang-bang.

The sash window opens with relative ease—which is odd considering it seems to be jammed every other time I need to open it—and I poke my head out.

It's him, his hand balled into a fist as he pounds on my front door, clearly not giving any consideration to the neighbours—though I don't know what time it is.

"Mike? What the hell are you doing?" I yell.

He takes a few moments to realise I'm shouting from an upstairs window. He backs away from the door before craning his neck upwards.

"Kitch—I need to talk to you," he says. "Can you let me in?"

I want to tell him to leave me alone. I want to tell him to go back to her. But I can't. There's something about the way his voice shakes. Something about the urgency and desperation.

He's distressed.

He's in need.

He steps back further towards the road, his body illuminated against the streetlights in an eerie glow. An odd shine on his shirt has me squinting, trying to make out what's covering his chest. Dark patches of colour, contrasting against the white.

Wet and shiny.

I swallow down a wave of nausea.

I think I know what it is—or what it looks like, at least.

"I'll be right down," I say, sliding the window closed and rushing down the stairs.

He stumbles in as I open the door, and the full impact of the blood hits me, knocking the air from my lungs.

Splotches of rusty brown cover his shirt, and a faint, metallic smell lingers in the air, filling my mouth as I gasp for air.

"Blood," I say, gaping at him. "Oh my—Mike, are you bleeding?"

He stares at me for a moment before looking down at his chest. "Me? No, I'm ... fine. It's not my blood, don't worry."

His tone is airy, but his eyes are heavy, drooping closed—like he's exhausted.

"Then whose blood is it?" I say, my voice elevating in both pitch and speed.

"Rochelle's."

"Rochelle's?" I clamp a hand over my mouth as I try to slow my thoughts, picking out the details to make them make sense. Blood, Rochelle, a ruined tuxedo. But I can only conclude one thing. I'm trembling, forcing my legs to keep me upright. "Did you kill Rochelle?"

Mike's face drains of colour—turning as white as his shirt was at the start of the evening. He shakes his head.

"Oh, no, no, no. Of course, I haven't. She turned up earlier ... tried to get me to leave with her, took my phone ... I was trying to get away from her and she fell—landed face down on the pavement and ... I couldn't leave her there. I couldn't get a taxi to take her to A&E because of the blood ... Vicky had to bundle her in the back of her car ... I—I tried calling you. I wanted to explain, I—"

I'm overcome with relief. Not because of Rochelle, but because of Mike. And I know there's no way he'd lie to me. I just feel it. I just know it.

"Slow down," I say. "Come on, slow down. Take a breath."

"She's going to press charges—I know she will," he says, eyes watering with tears. "She won't tell anyone she fell. She'll probably come up with some crap about me pushing her or something."

I pull him into the living room where he collapses onto the sofa and buries his head in his hands as he wails; shoulders shaking with near-silent sobs.

I've genuinely never seen a man cry before—which sounds odd thinking about it, but my dad never has, nor has Greg, not when I've been there. And I've never had a proper boyfriend for long enough to have his emotions on display. Not like this. Not like the tears of desperation that Mike is shedding.

I drop to my knees in front of him, rubbing my hand over his thigh, trying to offer any comfort I can.

He takes a laboured breath. "My career will be ruined. They'll kick me off both teams and that'll be that. No hockey. Like—what would I even do? How would I—" He sniffs deeply as his head rises, then he pauses. His breath slowing.

"You're wearing your rings," he whispers, looking at my left hand.

"Uh, yeah, I am."

He nods, slow and steady, his gaze focuses on my hand.

"They're a perfect fit," I say.

It feels like a dumb thing to say, but he takes hold of my hand, cradles it in his, his own ring brushing against mine.

Together.

"It's because you've got a perfect hand," he says.

I can feel myself flushing, warm heat rising through me, but then I get a lung-full of bloody-sweat.

"Let me run you a bath, make you a cup of tea—then get you to bed. I think you need to rest. We can talk properly in the morning."

"I'm sorry," he says. "I really am. I didn't mean to drag you into any of this."

"Shh," I soothe, giving his thigh another rub. "Let's get you the tea."

I stand up and make my way to the kitchen, getting as far as a doorframe when he calls my name.

"Kitch?"

"Yeah?"

"Can you put two sugars in?"

Bettsy

I CAN FEEL SOMEONE watching me. I've got my eyes closed, but I can sense it. A prickling awareness which would usually have me feeling uneasy, but this feels different somehow. Like there's a warmth over me, almost intoxicating—thrilling, maybe.

But the events of last night trickle back into my working memory, fragmented and disjointed as they piece together like a puzzle.

An icy shiver runs down my spine as panic sets in; my eyes snap open, half expecting to see a bloody Rochelle lying next to me, but I exhale in relief when Ellie's eyes meet mine. A chocolate-brown warmth that causes my stomach to tighten with excitement.

Déjà vu? No. I'm not hungover this time. I don't have a headache, and from what I can tell, I definitely don't have any boxers on.

We stare at each other for an extended time, and I try to remember if she's mad at me, upset at waking her up, but then I remember her running me a bath and making me a brew.

I'm about to speak, wish her a good morning, when she beats me to it.

"I should have reached out to you," she says.

Okay, that wasn't what I was expecting.

"What?" I say.

"When you got back from Germany. Instead of waiting around for you ... I should have reached out," she says.

Am I dreaming? I can't be sure because this is all weird. Really fucking weird.

"I'm sorry I lashed out at you before, because I've been thinking about it, and it wasn't all down to you." She pauses, biting her lip for a second before continuing. "I know you started seeing Julie but—"

"I don't even remember her," I say.

"Julie?"

"Yeah. I don't even remember what she looks like. In fact, I only remembered her when you mentioned her, but—you know, I never forgot you, Kitch."

"Oh."

I reach out and touch her face, just to check that she's real, reassured when my fingers meet skin, soft and warm and all I can think of doing is pulling her into my arms.

"Do you want a cuddle?" I say.

She stares at me, unmoving, probably deciding the best way to turn me down.

It's not like it hasn't happened before, the rejection, that is. I'm built ready for it. A thick skin and a sense of humour equipped to make it into a joke if necessary.

To get myself a step ahead, I mentally sift through my options, wondering if there's a cuddly toy nearby I can present in jest, but she surprises me a moment later by shuffling in, nuzzling into my chest like she's done it a million times before. She makes it feel so natural and effortless, but my body, primed to face rejection, takes a beat longer than it should to respond by embracing her, wrapping my arms around her.

She smells fresh, a hint of flowers or something that has me fully reassured that I'm not wearing any boxers; I can feel my dick between us, and if I can feel it—she can definitely feel it.

I wait for her to roll away, loosening my arms in anticipation, but she doesn't. She snuggles in closer.

Our breathing evens out so we're in-sync, a by-product of us being in the same space. And when I think of how many women I've shared my space with, I've never felt so me. Like I'm not trying to think of the right thing to say to impress, or if she's in bed with me for me or for the image that comes with bedding a hockey player. Something I hardly cared about before, but suddenly, it feels like the most important thing in the world—to be me.

I feel her breath against my skin, then she speaks again, barely audible against my chest.

"I've been having these dreams," she says.

"Dreams? What sort of dreams?" I say.

"Just ... dreams."

She shifts and suddenly she's looking up at me, and what the hell possesses me, I don't know, but I'm pulling her chin up and dipping my head to meet her, capturing her lips with mine.

For fuck's sake, why did I wait so long to kiss her? We could have been ten minutes in by now. But I don't let myself get too excited. I keep it slow, steady, familiarising myself with her lips—soft and full, delicate, and sweet. But the best thing? I don't have to think about it. I wait for the noise to start, for my brain to scream at me, tell me I'm doing it wrong, tell me she's not really into it. But it doesn't come. It's like it knows this is different. I'm not second-guessing if I'm doing it right or if she's enjoying it—because she's kissing me back like it's the most natural thing in the world.

But then she pulls away.

"This scar," she says, tracing her fingers over my lower lip and down my chin. "How did you get this scar?"

"High stick to the face. It's when I lost this tooth..." I point towards the gap. But something occurs to me, something that I've never thought about until now. "How come you've never asked me about my teeth? I mean, usually it's—"

A smile tugs at her lips. "I guess it's just part of you, Mike. Like ... it's just *Mike*. And everything about you is..."

She leans in to kiss me again, and I groan into her mouth. *God, this girl.*

"What do you need, Mike?" she says—no, whispers. It's a whisper that pulls me in. Like there's only me and her in the entire world.

"You." I swallow. A cliché answer, sure, but it's true. And it makes every single time I've been close with someone feel like a practice—all leading up to the main event. Because the meaning of life and my universe isn't '42', it's Eleanor Kitchener.

"Can I—" I say, pulling away to give my words a chance.

"Can you...?"

"I want to see you," I say.

"I'm right here."

I roll onto my back, pulling her with me, manoeuvring her to straddle my thighs, dick laying on my stomach between us, begging for attention.

But all my attention is on Ellie.

"That's not what I mean," I say. "Can I see you? All of you?"

She meets my eyes for a moment before looking away, cheeks flushing pink.

My hands automatically move to her thighs, rubbing along the outside, stopping shy of the hem of her nightshirt. I do this a few times, edging the fabric away little by little. Not too much, but enough so she knows I'm waiting for her permission.

"Okay," she says, reaching down and tugging at the shirt.

It's over her head in a flash, cast aside on the bedroom floor.

An empty-net to score on. A hot shower after a long game. The playoff cup with my name etched onto the plaque—all things that used to compete for the top spot of my adoration.

Until now.

Now, they're officially relegated to I don't give a crap status. Ellie is the top of the list, forever and always—playoff cup being a close second.

I let out a groan, not able to stop my hands from roaming. The curve of her hips, the softness of her stomach, and her breasts: full and heavy in my hands, nipples a dark-pink that I tug lustfully.

"Fuck, you're perfect."

"I'm—"

I cut her off, needing my mouth on hers again—not able to waste another second.

I pull her down to take her mouth; our kisses becoming deep—frantic.

"Tell me about your dream," I say, breaking the kiss.

"It's—nothing," she says.

"I want to hear about it. Was I naked?"

"I—a few times."

"Oh, fuck," I say, threading my hand through her hair, gripping her head as I look into her eyes.

"The other times, you had the suit on."

"Oh, yeah? Because I have lots of suits—one for each day of the week."

She chuckles.

"Dream Mike was quite bossy," she says, and with that, I grip her hips and roll her onto her back, falling onto my side so I can see—so I can touch her.

"Was he? I mean, I can be bossy if you want me to—in fact, I—"

"Mike," she playfully scolds, planting a kiss on my lips. "Don't overthink it."

She's right. I'm doing that thing—trying to be who I think she wants me to be, trying to appease her. But I want to know. I want to understand what she likes, what she doesn't like, what gets her hot, what triggers the breaks. And then I realise there's literally so much about her I don't know. What's her favourite colour? I want to say purple because I get that feeling. The towel she gave me last night was a Cadbury purple, matching the bathmat, so that's a pointer, right?

I push my thoughts aside as I kiss her back, nibbling on her lip.

"Why don't you take these off and let me see all of you?" I run my hands over the crotch of her underwear, revelling in the fact she shivers underneath me.

I kiss her neck, breathing in the sweetness of her skin, while she wriggles her underwear down. I have to steady myself ... count to ten, tell myself that it's not time yet as my dick throbs between us.

Honestly, if she touches me again, I'm done for. The last time I came was the time we had sex.

I shift my weight, gearing myself up to move after kissing her again. Lips, throat, neck, collarbone...

"Where are you going?" she says, her breath catching as I move away.

"I'm going to make my wife come on my tongue—maybe my fingers too, depending on what you like. Unless you'd prefer I didn't?"

She lets out a low hum as I kiss her thighs, excited by how much I'm going to enjoy them wrapped around my head. I honestly enjoy going down on a woman—always have, and probably always will, but for some reason, this time I feel nervous. There's a tingling in my stomach—butterflies of anxiety dance around because there's a question floating on the edge of my mind: what if I can't make her cum like this?

Except, I don't get much time to dwell on that because I glimpse her pussy, practically glistening and I'm pushing her legs apart before I can doubt my ability further.

Her clit, hard and so damn inviting, has my mouth watering and my dick painfully hard. I plant one last kiss on the very inside of her thigh before setting my tongue on her pussy, licking tentatively at her clit to see how she responds.

"Oh, my—"

Her hands bolt to grip my hair, which only encourages me further, working my tongue in a rhythm before I get my fingers involved.

"Is the pressure good?" I ask. "Do you need some—" I slip my middle finger into her pussy, feeling her clench around me. Tight. Hot. And really fucking wet. And if I wasn't so invested in how good she tastes, I'd be begging to fuck her.

"Mike—"

I position my lips to suck on her clit, slowly working my finger in and out as I do.

"Mike—"

I swear to God I feel her clit throbbing against my tongue as her hands grip my hair firmly. Then she cries out, clamping her thighs around my head and honestly—I've died and gone to heaven and I groan as I come right there. On the sheets.

Oh, fuck.

It was the sounds, the way she was shaking...

"Oh, my—"

"Okay?" I ask.

"I—"

She's breathing heavy, laboured gasps as she catches her breath. And I plant a last kiss on her thigh before going back to her clit.

"I'm supposed to be taking care of you," she breathes.

"You are. You did. This is what I needed."

"Mike—I..."

"Yeah?"

Chapter 29

Ellie

I HAD CONVINCED MYSELF I was a 'one and done' girl, but apparently, I can orgasm twice in close succession, and I think I'm bordering on a third time when I hear the moans coming from Mike as I tease him with my tongue.

All he needed was several minutes to reset.

I did that to him.

So it only makes sense I return the favour.

I'm not a blowjob expert or anything. In fact, I can probably count on one hand how many I've given in the past. They always seemed too intimate, *too* personal, but nothing could stop me from shifting Mike into position against the headboard.

I like the control it gives me. Knowing I'm the reason he's making those noises, gripping my hair, guiding me with his hands. And there's a way he's looking down at me, eyelids heavy, pleasure carved all over his face that gives me so much satisfaction.

I think *I* may come from the sight alone.

"You're ... fuck."

"Hmm?"

It's not taken me long to find the sensitive spot, right under the tip of his dick, and if I flick my tongue over it as I bob down, he groans in such a way that makes me want to stop what I'm doing and sink down on top of him.

"Whatever you're doing ... there... that. Fuck. You're going to make me ... stop."

I pull away. A hard task, considering I was enjoying it so much.

"Did I do something wrong?"

"No, no—you definitely didn't. I ... I don't want to come again yet."

I scoot closer to him, straddling his thighs, trailing my hands up and down over his chest. Oh, how is his chest so ... I don't even have the words. His muscles, hard and defined under my hands, feel unreal. But the more I touch him, the more his dick twitches in the space between us.

"Why not?" I ask.

"I want to ... I don't know, make it last. I like the idea of not finishing until you tell me I can." His cheeks flush pink.

I can't help myself. I lean in, kissing his ear, his neck, his cheek, his jaw, finally landing on his mouth, pulling at his bottom lip with my teeth.

Damn, I'm really horny. What is he doing to me?

"Fuck," he breathes. "Fuck."

His hands grip my hips, and he shifts me back an inch.

I reach down and grip his dick in my hands, squeezing gently before letting go.

This is something else I'm not familiar with. Pushing boundaries. Seeing how far he can go, but if that's what he wants, then I don't see why I can't appease him. Tease him.

I lean back, positioning myself so my legs are either side of his torso and I open my thighs, bringing my hand to my pussy and running my fingers over myself.

"Oh, fuck," he says, watching me. "I think this is going to be difficult."

But I don't let that stop me. I dip my finger into my pussy and circle my clit with the tip, shuddering in pleasure as I do.

"Can I…"

"Touch yourself," I say.

And he does. Small pumps, stopping just shy of the tip, and I lock eyes with him; the self-conscious Ellie, well and truly absent in the moment.

"You're killing me, Kitch." His voice is almost a growl, pained and husky as he pulls his hand away.

"How long do you think you can go?" I ask.

"Why don't you come here and find out?"

I'm about to move when he pulls me towards him, settling his dick in between us. All it'd take would be for me to move forward a fraction, adjusting my angle, and he'd be inside of me. The reminder of how he felt inside me when we were on his sofa makes me desperate for more.

He pulls my head down, finding my lips with his. Light pecks before he deepens the kiss, a slow tease with his tongue before he pulls away.

"Do you have any condoms, Kitch?"

I lean across him, fumbling in my bedside table, before handing him the packet.

Far too many seconds later, he's ready, shifting our bodies down the bed so he's lying on his back and I'm positioning myself so I can sink down onto him, my heart picking up speed as he fills me, inch by inch.

"Tell me I can't come yet," he says, looking up at me, eyes narrowing in concentration. "I'm going to need to hear you say it."

I wriggle my hips. "You can't come yet," I say. "Not until I do, anyway."

"That's the best deal I've ever heard," he says, reaching for my breasts, cupping them in his hands, rolling my nipples between his thumb and forefinger.

God, that feels good. The roughness of his skin drives me wild, forcing me to lean forward in desperation to find that angle—the perfect grind of his pubic bone against my clit.

"Use me," he says. "Come for me."

I do use him, building a rhythm that has me fighting for breath, my orgasm building at speed.

"I'm close," I say.

"Can I—"

"Yes."

And it's like he's got a secret route, right into my soul. He holds my hips, thrusting into me, as I come apart.

I slump down onto his chest. His heart thudding in my ear—the steady rhythm of Mike.

He scoops me into his arms, nuzzling into my neck, peppering kisses along my damp skin.

"Can we just stay here all day?" he asks. "I mean, I don't have any clothes so..."

I chuckle.

"I can pop out and get you something to wear. Supermarket fashion. Besides, I have next to no food in and I can't imagine you'll cope without sustenance."

"I appreciate it, thanks."

I pull myself away from his chest, looking down at him, amber eyes bright.

"Mike?"

"Yeah."

And I kiss him. Deep and profound, hoping he can feel what I'm saying, understand what he means to me.

I pull away and we stare into each other's eyes, the moment completely surreal but also not so, at the same time.

Then he nods.

Bettsy

"Good news?" I turn towards Ellie, my hands still in the washing-up bowl. Since she cooked, it makes sense that I do the washing up while she made a few phone calls.

She walks over to the table in the corner of the kitchen, setting her computer down first, followed by her phone.

"Yep. So, Megan has a chair she's happy for me to rent. And she said I can start whenever I'm ready; I told her about my sister, and I think she felt a bit sorry for me."

"Or she knows how great you are and what sort of clients you'll attract to her place," I say.

I pull my hands from the water and dry them on a tea-towel before turning to face Ellie.

"Or she's just helping out an old friend. It's been ages since I've seen her. I'm terrible at keeping in touch with people," she says.

"Same. If I didn't see the guys every day, I don't think I'd stand much chance, either. And it's not for lack of wanting, just … things take over. Days slip by."

"Yeah, I know what you mean." She pauses then reaches for her phone. "And I'm just waiting for confirmation from Jenna, about her hair trial."

"Oh yeah? That'll be good."

"She mentioned something about this weekend. And the possibility of coming to your playoff game or something."

She flashes a look in my direction, her eyes twinkling in a way that has me rushing towards her, scooping her into my arms, taking in a blend of perfume and her freshly washed hair.

"Mike—stop." She laughs, and I feel it everywhere.

"But I'm excited. It's playoffs, baby! Playoffs!"

"I don't know what that means," she says as I set her down.

"Oh, sweetheart—you have a lot to learn." I run a hand over my beard. "This doesn't get properly cut. Just know that. Not until we're done."

"Is this a tournament or something?" she asks.

Damn, honestly. Ellie's naivety surrounding hockey is refreshing. I get to build up the excitement, get her as revved up as I am. Give her a view from my lens.

"It's the ultimate tournament. No room for mistakes. No room for anything that's not the best hockey we've ever played. We're not just playing for the joy of winning..." I pause for effect. "... we're playing for the cup."

Ellie blinks at me. "I thought you played for one of those before? The—"

"No, no, no. This is different. It's an emotional attachment. It's all or nothing. It's gritty, it's—everything I love about hockey." I can feel my heart racing in my chest—the very talk of playoffs sending me into a frenzy. "It's why we work hard all year. It's why we play through injuries and—"

She gasps. "You don't play through injuries, do you?"

"Sometimes," I shrug. "Look, you'll get it once you're there. The atmosphere is electric. It's just ... playoff hockey."

Ellie smiles, reaching for her phone.

"Well, speaking of playoffs ... Jen has added me to a group chat and there's talk about playoff jackets?" She wrinkles her nose in confusion.

"Lemmie see." I take the phone and scan the screen. "Oh, the 'WAG' group. Lucky you. I ought to tell you, even though my sister should officially be the boss—being the captain's girlfriend—Vicky calls the shots."

The reminder of my feud with Vicky springs back into the forefront of my mind.

"What are the jackets for, though?"

"Well, all the wives and girlfriends usually get matching jackets or something. Team logo. Their guys' name on the back. It's a playoff thing," I say.

"Oh, right."

Ellie's eyes are down on her phone as she scrolls through the chat, messages flying in every few seconds.

"Do you ... uh, do you think you'll wear a jacket?"

It's a loaded question and I'm desperate to hear her reply, though she's still wearing the rings I gave her. They could well be a leftover prop from last night—but the jackets? Those are a public display of affection. Those tell everyone the story.

"Wait—actually, don't worry." I chicken out. She's still here, still wearing the rings, and I'm not ready to test how fragile this all is.

"Mike—"

"Kitch, actually, I've been meaning to talk to you about something," I say, concluding that this needs to happen now because if she's going to call it a day, then she needs to do it now, before the playoffs.

"Is everything okay?" she says, catching my eyes.

I dip my head.

"I—I just want to know where we go from here, I guess. Because the event was last night and ... I still need to look for the certificate and, if I'm honest, I've been putting it off because I'm afraid to find out the truth." I exhale, running a hand through my hair. "I'm ... I really like you. And I want you to tell me now if this is ... it, I guess. Because I can't bear it."

I think about the look she gave me. Post sex, sexy eyes looking at me. I think I know what she was saying, but that little voice in the back of my head is—

"Mike," she says. "Come here."

I step forward.

"Hug me, please."

And I do. Wrapping my arms around her and breathing her in.

"I'm going to wear the jacket. And whatever the certificate says, when you pull your finger out and find it, we'll deal with it. Okay?"

She peeks up at me and I see that look again. The warmth in her eyes that makes me want to score *all the* goals for her—defensive defenceman or not.

And she just made me the happiest guy on earth—at least for the evening.

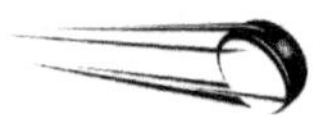

IT ALL COMES CRASHING down several hours later after we've drank tea, watched a game show, and revealed our favourite jokes. We're in bed and I'm in the best place in the world. Right between Ellie's legs, making her come over and over again.

The vibrating starts. Confusing me at first, but when it stops and starts again, I realise it's my phone, shaking against the wood of the bedside table.

But I'm not in the mood to talk to anyone right now. I'm busy.

Ellie giggles, trying to push my head away, mumbling something about feeling sensitive, so I back off as my phone vibrates again.

Third time's a charm.

Ellie grabs it and hands it to me, and I glance at the screen to see Hutch's name.

Icy dread fills my stomach.

"Yeah?" I say, still halfway down the bed.

"You going to be home soon, mate?" he says flatly.

"I was going to head back tomorrow for practice," I say.

"Well, it's probably a good idea that you get home tonight. Like, as soon as you can."

"I'm a little busy—"

"The police are here, mate."

The words land like a puck to the groin. My mouth opens, but nothing comes out.

Ellie sits up beside me, eyes wide.

And just like that, the best night of my life is over.

Chapter 30

Bettsy

I ALWAYS PICTURED MY career ending because of an injury—a snapped ligament, eye injury, shattered bone. Something dramatic. Something I could point to. Something I could *blame*.

I'd be one of those washed-up has-beens, sitting in the stands yelling about the youth and how they should play—the bitterness of my forced retirement getting the better of me.

But this? This is beyond anything I could have imagined for myself. Whispers, headlines, media scandal, a bitter ex ... though, that being said... it's my fault. All this is my fault. It's not how I want to go out, it's not how I imagined my career ending, but it's my fault.

And by the look on Hutch's face, he's thinking exactly the same thing as me: you did this to yourself, Betts.

"They didn't stick around long," Hutch says. "But they left this."

He hands me a piece of paper: flimsy, see-through almost, black ink scribbled in such a way that has me squinting to read the writing.

"Voluntary interview?" I say. "What do they mean, I need to attend a voluntary interview?"

"They sort of implied it would be in your best interest to do it sooner rather than later," he says. "You know, go down to the station."

I groan, the sickness I've been feeling the entire journey home increasing tenfold.

"And they didn't give you any more detail?"

"No—well..." He shoves his hands into his pockets. "...the copper sort of slipped up, really. He said your name came up in an ongoing investigation, but I'm not sure he was meant to tell me that."

"My name came up? What the hell does that mean?"

I'm trying to work out how Rochelle would have played this. How she would have layered on my guilt while giving her version of events; the epic sob-story.

"I dunno, mate. Maybe just go and see what they want."

I reach into my pocket for my phone, perching myself on the arm of the sofa as I unlock the screen. It's almost eleven, but I send a quick text to Ellie, telling her I'm home and not to worry, then I call Johnny, desperate for him to tell me what to do.

He answers within a few rings, and once I check Kelly isn't listening, keen on saving her the worry too, I explain the situation, forcing my voice to stay level.

"I'll meet you in the stairwell," he says. "I'll drive you and we can get this thing squared away. Don't worry."

Honestly, telling me not to worry is laughable. But I force myself to keep breathing. Deep and controlled.

I keep it up while telling Hutch that I'll see him later. And while I make my way to meet Johnny. And during the car ride.

In fact, I keep my hockey-head on the entire time. Focusing on the here and now. Not concerning myself with the end result.

Right up until Johnny pulls up outside the station.

"You ready?" he says.

And that's all it takes for a panic attack to set in. My chest tight, my breathing ragged, my whole body shaking.

"Not really," I admit, gasping for air. "She's going to end me. She's going to ruin my career." I turn towards Johnny, practically pleading with him. "You know I didn't do anything, right? I didn't push her or shove her or—all I did was help her into Vicky's car then—"

I put my head in my hands. My gut clenches. The air in the car feels thick, like I'm breathing through treacle. I can still hear her crying—fake as it was—as Vicky slammed the car door.

"Calm down, buddy. Take a moment." He cuts the engine. "Look at me."

"Cap ... I—"

"Bettsy. Look at me."

He grabs my face and turns it towards his, locking eyes with mine.

"Right. Forget about the police. Forget about Rochelle ... this is just another shift, right? We're a goal down. Defence, Betts. Stand tall. Watch your marks. Show them who's stronger." He breathes in deep, puffing his chest out and I copy—instinct, mostly. "And out.... in ... and out. Deep breaths. Steady breaths." His voice softens. "I'm going to be there with you ... it's just another shift, yeah? We'll go inside and get this figured out. Okay? I've got you."

I nod, following Johnny as he steps out of the car, and we ascend the steps.

THEY KEEP US WAITING for over an hour. I know this because there's a loud, obnoxious clock fixed to the wall behind the flimsy plastic chairs which we've been told to sit in. Ticking away. Minute by minute.

All I can focus on is that ticking and the smell of stale sweat mixed with tobacco. It makes me feel like I'm about to pass out.

Johnny tries to distract me, though. Playoff hockey is not a light topic where he's concerned, so we fill the time, discussing plays, working out approaches, the tick-tick-tick in the background ... right up until a constable sticks his head around a door and calls my name.

No time for distractions now.

I get to my feet and swallow down the threat of vomit; the bile burning my throat.

"I'll be here, bud," Johnny says.

Left foot, right foot, left foot, right foot. All I've got to do is tell them the truth. Tell them—

"Michael Betts?" The copper says my name again as I stop in front of him, enunciating each syllable like he's learning to read.

I nod. "Yeah."

He looks at me, knitting his brows together, then leans back into the room, the muffled sound of distant conversation on the edge of my hearing.

Then he's back.

"Michael Betts?" He says it slower this time, like he's trying to catch me out.

"Yes," I say.

"Right. Does the name 'Billy Hobbs' mean anything to you?"

I stare blankly at the officer.

"Hobbsy?" I say.

God, *that's* a name I haven't heard in a long time. Not since my junior days.

The cop turns around again, retreating into the room this time, the door closing with a thud behind him.

I turn back towards Johnny.

"What's going on?" he mouths.

But all I can do is shrug.

The door opens again, pulling my attention back, my heart banging wildly in my chest.

"Sorry, I—" He rummages through a pile of papers. "—I think ... you weren't anywhere near Kings Road tonight, were you?"

I gawk at him. "No, I—"

"Right, thanks. You're free to go."

"What the—what's Hobbsy got to do with this?" I ask.

The officer clenches his jaw.

"Your name came up in an investigation, but you definitely don't match the description or the CCTV footage. If I'm honest, we weren't banking on it being you, but—look, thanks for your time. Take care."

And the door slams shut.

I stand frozen to the spot, completely dumfounded. All that worry ... all the stress and ... for that?

"Bud? Everything okay?" Johnny sets a hand on my shoulder.

"I—" I turn towards him, my jaw tight. "Fucking Hobbsy," I say.

"Hobbsy? Who's that?" Johnny says.

"I played junior hockey with him and he—I—"

"What happened?" Johnny says.

"Well, they didn't tell me, but ... sounds like they were looking for someone in connection with him. He probably gave them my name for whatever reason. Honestly—"

"So, nothing to do with Rochelle?"

I shake my head. "No."

Johnny blows out a breath. "Well, that's great news."

We turn and walk back to his car, an odd anti-climactic stress sitting heavy on my shoulders. Because despite this being a false alarm, there's still every chance *she* could cause me a problem in the near future.

As soon as I'm in his car, I'm on my phone, searching the internet for information, trying to find out if there's a window of opportunity for her. Trying to figure out how long I'll be worrying about this.

I say goodbye to Johnny in the stairwell, pulling him into a quick hug and thanking him for having my back.

I drag myself upstairs, every limb heavy, my spirit shrivelled. The weight of the false alarm still clinging to me like that stale tobacco smoke—sharp and sour—even though I'm in the clear. For now.

I open the door to my apartment, expecting an inquisition from Hutch, but he's nowhere to be seen. Instead, I'm greeted by the faint smell of...

It can't be, can it?

But it is. It's her. She's here.

Ellie.

Curled up on my sofa in my hoodie, sleeves hiding her hands. She looks up from her phone and offers me the gentlest smile.

And I exhale—like I've been holding my breath since the second I left her.

"I hope you don't mind," she says, plucking at the hem of the hoodie. "I was cold."

But I've never minded anything less.

Ellie

"How long can you stay for?" Mike says.

We're in bed, the morning after the night before, his forehead resting on mine. He's still inside me, the heaviness of his body, relaxing into mine in a post-orgasm fog that keeps me clinging onto him.

"I'll probably need to go back tonight. I can start at Megan's tomorrow," I mumble.

"Can't you stay another night?" His mouth finds my neck, dotting kisses along the sensitive ridge that has me squirming under him.

"I wish I could, but I'm losing income. I can't afford to miss any more appointments, and I've got regulars waiting for me to fit them in. I hate letting people down."

"I know."

"Mike..."

"Sorry, I—" He rocks his hips, and oh ... my, God. I was half-expecting him to soften, but he's hard still, making me buck against him, needy and desperate for more.

"Mike..." I say again, a breathy exhale this time.

But he rolls off me, leaving me with an emptiness—and not just from his physical absence.

"I'm worried," he says, adjusting himself under the covers; probably removing the condom.

"About?"

"Us, I guess. I mean, your life's there ... mine's here ... and I know it's not far-far, but it still feels—" He shakes his head. "Actually, we can try our best, yeah? See each other when we can." He rolls onto his side to face me. "Sorry, I know I'm being all needy and shit."

"You're not. I get it. You need to be here and I ... well, I guess, I can be wherever the work is. In theory."

Bang. Bang. Bang.

Mike pulls the covers away and climbs out of bed. Except, instead of getting dressed, he reaches for a pillow and covers his crotch before he opens the door, blocking the view so whoever's on the other side can't see me.

"Jen's here for Ellie," Hutch says, not even bothering to question his roommate's state of dress.

"She'll be right out," Mike says, pushing the door shut and turning back to me. "Were you expecting Jen?"

I shake my head. "No, I mean, I told the girls I was here since they were asking how you were, but that's it."

"Huh. I guess news travels fast."

I climb out of bed and freshen up in the bathroom, quick to pull on some clothes before I leave Mike to get himself ready. Slipping out of his bedroom and into the kitchen area, I spot Jen sitting at the counter chatting with Hutch. She's got a laptop open in front of her, a mug of something steaming beside her.

"Ellie, how are you?" She slips off the stool and pulls me into a hug like we've been friends for years.

"Good, thanks, you?"

"Yeah, I'm great. Look ... I hope you don't mind about the group-chat thing, but I thought you may be keen to join in. Please tell me if I've over-stepped the mark."

"No, no, not at all. I appreciate you including me."

"What group chat?" Hutch asks. "Is this a girls only thing or—"

"You're not being added," Jen says, cutting him off.

Hutch rolls his eyes.

"Anyway," Jen turns towards me. "I know this may be a little forward and ... well, you can say no or tell me if you hate it, but—I wanted to show you something."

"Oh?"

She waves me over to the counter, sitting back down before tapping the seat next to her.

"Look ... I know you were thinking about a website and since you're helping me out with my wedding hair, I thought I'd just have a play with a few things." She twists her laptop towards me, and she scrolls through a website; lilac and a blush of pink with snippets of white fill the screen. "I can change anything you're not keen on but—"

The colours feel natural and so very un-Kathryn like. But it's the logo at the top of the page that gets my attention the most when Jen scrolls back to the top: Styled by Ellie: Bridal & Beyond.

"I've just put that in as a placeholder," she says, her eyes flicking towards mine as my jaw drops because it's perfect. Perfect and it feels so me.

I take a moment to scan over the screen, completely in awe that Jen went out of her way to make this.

"Oh, my God," I say. "It's beautiful."

"Really? I mean, I thought you could keep it simple. I think you need a section for 'Prices', 'Services' and 'Contact Information'. That's it," Jen says.

I stare at the screen, completely mesmerised—still in complete shock, if I'm honest.

Then a pair of arms wrap around me, the fresh smell of Mike as his head rests on my shoulder.

"Wow, Jen. This is great," he says. "Isn't it great, Kitch?"

"Well, yes. I absolutely love it."

But then an anxious knot settles in my stomach. Because something like this looks expensive. And something this expensive is out of my price range considering I'm currently trailing behind when it comes to paid work.

"What's wrong?" Mike says. "Is it the colours? Jen can change that sort of thing, right, Jen?"

Jen offers me an encouraging nod.

"No, I love the colours, but—how much will this cost?" I ask.

"Less than a bridal hair styling would. And it'll be easy to maintain. I can set you up with a mechanism to upload new photos and reviews."

"But—"

"Ellie, don't worry. I enjoy doing this sort of thing. And I liked the challenge since I've never made a website for anything that isn't sport or e-commerce before," she says, reaching for her mug and taking a sip.

"But—"

"Please," Jen says, setting her mug down.

I worry my lip, because this is probably the nicest thing anyone's ever done for me.

I throw my arms around her before I can stop myself, tears already prickling behind my eyes.

"Thank you. But, please let me do your hair in return. No charge. It's the least I can do," I say.

Jen squeezes me back before pulling away. "Okay, deal. But you need to let me have some photos. We need to get real snaps and—"

"Ah, that's the thing," I say. "I'm terrible at remembering to take photos. I mean, I definitely have some, but nothing remotely new."

"Well, it's good timing that you'll be doing trials soon," Jen says. "Do you have any I can use to get us going?"

I rummage for my phone and unlock the screen, pulling up my gallery and flicking through the photos I have saved. I only have a few decent ones I'd consider web-site worthy though, but Jen picks out several and taps in her email address for me to send them over.

"I need to figure out my social media, I guess. Get some decent photos and—"

"I'll ask Vicky," Jen says. "She owes Mike a favour."

"Does she?" Mike asks, pulling away.

I turn to catch the look on his face, brows knitted together.

Hutch sniggers.

"Yes, she does," Jen says, gritting her teeth.

Jen and Mike's voices fade into the background as I zone out, gravitating towards one of the most thoughtful gifts I've ever received: my new logo. And the name I didn't know I needed until now.

It's everything I wanted it to be—absolutely nothing to do with Kathryn.

Chapter 31

Bettsy

Vicky's waiting for me when I swipe through the back entrance of the rink, and if I didn't know any better, her glum expression tells me she's about to deliver bad news.

Shit.

It's been over a week since my visit to the police station and I'm still on edge—waiting for something that may never happen. My sleep's been crap, and my game's been lacking focus, and now Vicky—standing here, staring at me in the way she is—has the alarm bells ringing.

Did Rochelle rock up and give her a false version of events? Is this the end of my career? Is she here to march me up to the GM's office, watch him tear up my contract and order me to clear out my cubby? That'd leave me with no hope or prospects for any sort of career in hockey.

I stop in front of her, bracing myself for the summons, waiting for her to rip one half of my heart out. My mouth's dry. My palm sweaty against the strap of my gear bag ... everything in me braced for impact.

"Michael, I..."

I keep my eyes on the ground, forcing myself to take deep breaths.

"Make it quick, Vic," I say, swallowing down the fear as best I can.

I grip my bag tighter, my knuckles probably white, telling myself not to cry—telling myself it's only a game.

"Michael," Vicky says again.

But it's not just a game. It's—almost—everything I've ever wanted. It's the best job in the entire world.

"Mike, I—I just wanted to catch you before practice. To apologise."

It takes a second for the words to hit me.

Apologise? Apolo—

I straighten up, glancing in her direction—keen to check if she's about to burst out laughing or something.

Her expression flicks to a meek smile, one of desperation.

She means it.

She's not joking.

There's only sincerity in her eyes.

"I was wrong about Ellie and ... I'm sorry. She's great—in fact, I think she's better than great. We've been chatting about the wedding hair and ... I think she's great for you. And I hope you can forgive me."

There's a swell of pride in my chest, knowing that someone else sees how fucking perfect Ellie is—how perfect she is to me, anyway.

"Right," I say.

"Mike—"

"I just wish you'd met her before you made such an assessment," I say.

"I know and I'm sorry. I am."

"And I wish you'd kept your opinion to yourself because Johnny—"

"I know," she says. "I know. I'm sorry. I can't help myself. I'm working on it. I promise you."

See, one of the things about me is, as much as I want to hold a grudge, I can't. I'm genuinely surprised I've lasted this long.

I linger for a moment, letting Vicky sweat with the knowledge I may turn her apology down because she'd hate that. I know it and she knows it. But after another beat, I drop my bag on the floor and hold my arms out.

She steps forward and squeezes me into an embrace before pulling away.

"I know I'm shitty but ... I was trying to look out for you and—"

"Yeah, I get it. But still. You owe me a favour though," I say, pointing a finger at her. "In way of an apology."

"Is this about the socials because I'm already on it. She's coming down on the weekend for the game and we're meeting beforehand to run through things. Friday ... hair, Saturday, before the game ... social media."

That's when I'm reminded that Ellie will be here. Watching me play for the first time.

The butterflies arrive in full force. My stomach dancing with an energy that makes me feel beyond nervous. I'd go as far as to say I'm more nervous than I've ever been about anything—except maybe my visit to the police station.

Vicky's phone buzzes in her pocket, and she fishes it out, glancing at the screen.

"You don't have long," she says. "Suit up and I'll see you later."

She pats me on the shoulder before hurrying away, leaving me a clear path to the dressing room.

I take several steps forward, stopping a few feet away from the entrance, where I take my phone out of my bag. Ellie could be free now—depending on what time her next client is due—and since I figure she won't answer if she is busy, I hit dial before pressing my phone to my ear.

"Vicky's just reminded me you're coming to the game this weekend," I say.

"Oh yeah? How could you forget?"

I chuckle. "I guess I'm over-thinking. She was waiting for me when I got to the rink and I thought the worst ... like she was... actually, never mind."

"Mike—" Ellie says, "try not to think about her. Focus on what's important ... this coming weekend. And seeing me."

"Yeah, I can't wait ... when do you think you'll get here?"

"I'll be there for ten and the girls will be over around eleven."

I groan. "All of them?"

"Yes, all of them. But until then..." she says. "... I need you to do me a favour. Try to relax."

"Yeah, of course I will," I say, forcing myself to smile.

"Promise me you'll try."

Damn. Even over the phone, she can read me like a book.

It's not like I haven't been trying. I mean, aside from the usual stuff that keeps me occupied—the gym, hockey, renovating Ryan's house for free ... I've tagged along to Johnny's morning swim and I went as far as baking banana bread...

Nothing worked, though. None of it switched my mind off. I'd argue that these things made free-thinking even more achievable. But I consider Ellie's suggestion, wondering if there's something else I could try, something that would fully immerse me.

"I probably need to find a new hobby," I say. "Maybe I should join video game night with Liam and Danny, listen to audiobooks about the civil war or spend my time figuring out who's behind the 'justice for Bettsy' hashtag ... because since the forum posts have died down, so has my own personal cheerleader. Danny says there's not been a peep—"

"Why would you want to do that?" she says.

"I'm just curious ... that's all," I say. "I mean ... there's someone out there on my side—apart from you, of course... and my immediate family and guys. Someone random. Someone I've probably never met before. If I can figure out who it is, maybe I can thank them for keeping me going through the tough times."

"Mike—"

"Fine, maybe I should join a mariachi band, then?"

"You're joking?"

"No? If Kelly can play the cello, I can learn the trumpet—the genes are there."

She chuckles down the line. "Okay, park the trumpeteering. What would you normally do in your spare time? Why can't you do that?"

"I'm saving myself for you," I say, trying to suppress a grin.

I can hear the frown in Ellie's voice. "You're insatiable."

"Forgive me, but sweetheart, I'm dying here. I miss you. Hey, what are you doing later today? I could drive to your place, and you can help me relax," I say. "Help me take my mind off things."

"Come on ... by the time you get here, it'll be time to turn back, and I mean, we're—" Ellie inhales sharply. "—oh, crap."

"Is everything okay?" I say.

"My sister has just pulled up outside."

"Wait—how did she find out where you're working?" I say.

"I don't know, but she doesn't look happy."

I don't remember Kathryn all that well, but I don't recall ever seeing her happy, not unless she was bossing someone around.

"What do you think she wants?"

There's a beat of silence before Ellie replies. "I think it's about my visit to her salon."

"Visit? What visit?"

"The night of the event ... I—"

"Did you do something?"

There're voices in the background, and the unmistakable sound of a door slamming before I pick up a shirty greeting from Kathryn.

"I've got to go. I'll talk to you later."

She hangs up, and I'm left staring at my phone for a few seconds before putting it away only for it to ring again and, assuming it's Ellie, I answer it with my most playful voice, hoping that she's changed her mind about visiting tonight.

"Is that a yes to the sex, then or—"

"Michael."

But it's not Ellie. It's my mother.

KATHRYN LOOKS TANNED. THE kind of tanned that screams carrot oil and questionable SPF choices. Like she's been baking somewhere hot, trying to bronze herself into a new personality.

I guess that explains why it's taken her so long to confront me, though the last thing I want right now is an altercation with my sister, even if I am seeking a distraction.

All morning, I've done nothing but stress over how to tell Mike about the hashtag, because the longer I leave it, the worse it's going to be—especially now he's mentioned how keen he is to uncover who's behind it.

But I can't dwell on that right now. Kathryn marches up to me, waving a bottle of nail gel in the air, not giving one iota of consideration to the full salon of clients—mine due at any moment.

"I need to speak with you," she snaps.

"Me?" I say, looking around in mock surprise before settling my gaze back on my sister.

"This." She waves the tiny bottle. "This is a twenty-five-pound bottle, and it's ruined."

"That doesn't sound right," I say.

I pluck the bottle from her hands, turning it over before loosening the lid. The thick, sticky substance clings to the brush as I swipe it against the bottle, a grin barely suppressed.

"Maybe it was a dodgy batch?" I offer, all wide-eyed. "Have you called the rep to complain?"

Her mouth thins to a tight, angry line. "I know it was you," she says. "I know it was. And I know you changed the password to the bookings computer and stole my clients."

"How can I steal your clients when you don't do hair?" I say. "Look, I came and got my things, yes. But this?" I flash her a glare, forcing myself to lie. "I'm trying to get myself up and running, I don't have time to—"

The vein in her forehead pops as she stiffens her jaw.

"Bull. Shit," she says. "I know it was you. You were the only person with keys and ... do you realise what you've done? You've ruined all my spring colours and—I can't even..."

"Maybe you should look after your things better," I say, thrusting the bottle into her chest.

Her nostrils flare as she stuffs it into her bag. And for a second, I think I've won. I think she's going to leave. She even takes two paces back before she stops.

"Maybe you should stop being such a jealous little cow."

Everyone in the salon turns to gape at her. Everyone. Even my client standing next to the half-open door.

What I should do is turn and walk away—leave Kathryn to stew, but I can't. She wants me to bite back, and I do—the years of pent-up anger leading me to this.

"Jealous?" I snap. "Of what?"

"Me," she says—but it comes out in an *isn't it obvious* sort of voice that has me reeling.

"You?" I say. "Why would I be jealous of you?"

"I have Greg ... Greg has a great job. He can provide for me. My house—the car I drive ... my business. The list is endless, Ellie."

I burst out laughing, acutely aware that people are looking, but I can't stop myself. I'm like a bull, fixed on the mesmerising red that my sister's emitting.

"Greg?" I scoff. "Why the hell would I be jealous of *Greg*? He's got the personality of a soggy newspaper."

She rolls her eyes, stepping towards me.

"We both know hockey players don't make a lot of money, Ellie. I can only guess you jumped into whatever the hell you're doing with—" Her mouth twists into an expression of disgust. "—Michael Betts, because you can't stand to see me married first. It's desperate, and it's pathetic."

I was wondering how long it'd take her to bring Mike into the argument.

I throw my head back in amusement. "Oh, I get it," I say. "This isn't about me or Greg at all. In fact, it's nothing to do with Mike, either."

Kathryn glares at me. Eyes in a fiery rage, like she knows the hand I'm about to play.

"Don't," she snarls.

I purse my lips.

Kathryn takes another step towards me. "Don't. You. Dare."

"Jeremy," I say. "This is everything to do with Jeremy, isn't it?"

I expect her to say something—no, scream something. I expect her to spew out all the reasons why I'm never to breathe his name again, but she doesn't.

Her eyes fix on mine, her breathing ragged, her eyes wide and—

Before I realise what's happening, she launches herself at me, talons for nails digging into my scalp as she grabs my hair, pulling at the roots.

The air leaves my lungs as I'm knocked backwards, falling to the floor in a scramble of arms and legs, Kathryn on top of me, screaming into my ear.

I can't make out what she's saying. I'm too busy fighting back, trying to unclasp her fingers from my hair—burning at the scalp.

Then Megan's face comes into view, alongside Grace, the apprentice stylist, both hooking arms around Kathryn to restrain her.

"Don't you dare say his name to me again. Don't you dare." She fights against Megan. "He never loved me—the same as Mike will never love you. They're both the same. Fuckboys with no hearts. And now look at you—"

"That's enough," Megan says.

"Don't you—"

"I think you should leave. And I'd be grateful if you didn't come back," Megan tells Kathryn, shoving her awkwardly towards the open door of the salon—my client stepping aside to let her pass.

But I'm standing here. Humiliated. Crying silent tears.

"I'm so sorry," I say to no one in particular. "I'm so sorry you had to see that."

Then Megan's back by my side, her arm wrapping around me as she squeezes my shoulder. I'm expecting her to boot me out, right behind my sister, but she doesn't. She lowers her voice to a tone of softness and understanding.

"Why don't you take a few minutes? And I'll fix your hair once I'm done with my client."

The air leaves my lungs in a whoosh that has my knees wobbling beneath me.

Oh, God. My hair. What the hell has she done to my hair?

I bolt over to the mirror, forcing myself to look at my reflection—to see the damage. There's a clump of hair missing. A whole patch of it, pulled out from the roots, or so it looks. And all I can do is stand here and cry. Though it's not over the loss of my hair—but the loss of my sister. Because there's no way I'll speak to her ever again.

Chapter 32

Ellie

I GET TO MIKE'S apartment just before ten, buzzing the intercom and making my way up to the fifth floor via the lift.

I've got three bags. One for my stylist stuff, one for my clothes and one for all the bits I couldn't fit anywhere else because I've never been to a hockey game before—not like this anyway—so I have no idea what to wear. The girls told me not to dress for the cold, which—given the fact that we have jackets and we're definitely not allowed to take them off—means no layering.

Kelly

It's the body heat. That's what kills you. Everyone crammed in a small space.

Jen

It's the beer as well as the body heat.

For me, it's the rage. I spend half the game shouting at idiots. Warms me right up.

I'm not sure if I should wear the jacket yet, but I am anyway. The truth is, I've been dying to show it off ever since Jen shipped it to me, though I'm nervous about Mike's reaction. And although I'd told myself I'd bring up the hashtag as soon as I saw him, that thought vanishes the second he comes into view. The lift doors spring open and I spot him, leaning against the door to his apartment. The size of his grin tells me it was a good idea.

In a cinematic moment, I hurry forward, dropping my bags and flinging myself at him.

This is exactly what I imagined coming home to feel like: perfect and inviting, but more importantly, a safe-hair zone.

"How was the journey?" he asks.

"Fine, yeah."

We make our way inside with my bags, only making it as far as the hallway before they're abandoned, and his lips find mine, the familiar warmth of Mike engulfing me.

"That fucking jacket—" he says.

That's all it takes to ignite the fire. The searing hot kiss and the way his hands are everywhere. My hips, my waist, my back ... slipping the jacket from my shoulders so it exposes a fair amount of skin.

"Are we alone?" I whisper, tilting my head to the side, letting him access that sensitive patch of skin that has my entire body tingling.

There's a vibration of laughter, mixed with a groan of something ... as he answers, "yes."

That's all the encouragement I need.

I tug at the waist of his sweatpants and slip my hand inside, rubbing him over his boxers, desperate to tease him.

"Can I fuck you here?" he asks, planting a kiss on my lips, firm and deep. "Can I push you up against this wall and show you how much I've missed you, Mrs Betts?"

Oh, my ... I nod my head, our mouths meeting again.

I dip my hands in under his boxers, squeezing his length before building up a steady rhythm with my fist; the noises he makes driving me wild.

One of his hands cups my cheek, locking my mouth onto his, and the other, hikes my leg up—fully clothed, but the angle makes me cry out, gasping as my hand shifts to allow the bulge in his sweats to press into me.

He could do absolutely anything to me right now. Honestly, this guy...

"I need you, Kitch," he whispers, pulling away from our kiss, pressing his forehead against mine.

And because I need him just as much, I'm wriggling free to lose my shoes, hitch my top up, and push down my leggings and underwear. I fumble with one leg, cursing the clingy fabric, but then he's got a grip on my thigh and nothing else matters. In one firm motion, he's inside me, that familiar ache of him, deep as I adjust, making me quiver.

The first time we're feeling each other completely. No barrier. Nothing between me and him.

His hips rock as he thrusts. Slow and steady. I reach a hand between us, circling my clit with trembling fingers as he moves, the desperation to come while he drives into me pushing me over the edge as I moan a warning of my orgasm.

I'm coming.

It hits me hard and fast—blinding and hot as I cry out against his mouth as he continues to move inside me.

"I'm close," he says.

And that's when this all-consuming need to taste him takes over. It's like I can't think of anything else.

I nudge him away and the look on his face changes to painful desperation, right up until I drop to my knees, and I look up at him, my tongue darting out to flick the tip of his dick.

"Fuck."

I slide my mouth around his shaft, pushing deep.

He unravels instantly. The wild groans of his pleasure as he grips my hair, not exactly hard but firm enough, so I wince as I swallow him down.

He's wrapped up in his orgasm, but then his expression changes as he looks down at me, his eyes flicking to the top of my head.

Ah, crap.

"What—oh, fuck, are you okay?" he says. "Did I—"

He stops. Freezing on the spot for a second before he pulls out, then his hand gently smooths my hair—next to the patch of scalp that Megan did her best to cover by adjusting my parting.

I did not want to tell Mike about this ... I mean, I've told him everything else, but this? I wanted this to be something I never had to speak about ever again.

His voice shakes. "What the—what the fuck is this, Kitch? What's going on?"

"It's nothing," I say, getting to my feet. I hurry to dress myself, painfully aware that I'm half naked now since the post-sex fog has cleared.

"Like hell it is ... it looks like someone—" His face slackens. A horrible realisation settling behind his eyes. "Kitch ... did Kathryn do this to you?"

"Mike, please—"

"Is this about the money?" He crouches down to tug his own clothes back into place. "Because I'll—"

"Mike. Please." I lay a hand on his chest, trying to find his eyes. "Please."

But I see it. The fiery look, the way his jaw tightens.

"This is enough," he says. "I know she's your sister but—"

"I'm not going to see her again," I say. "She humiliated me in front of a salon full of clients ... but I was angry and I did something stupid—"

"What did you do?" he asks. "Is this about the night..."

My cheeks flush with shame as I inhale.

I nod. "I loosened a few lids on some nail polishes." I cringe. "I know it's petty, but—"

"That's what you did?" He says through clenched teeth. "That's what you did, and she ripped your hair out in return?" He shakes his head. "Nah ... this isn't on. This isn't—"

"Mike, we're just going to forget about it," I say.

"This is one step too far."

"What are you going to do? You can't go there and pull her hair in return."

"No, but I can pay Greg a visit."

"Mike," I say, stepping towards him, closing the space between us and putting my hands on his face, forcing him to look at me. "It's over now. That's it. I'm not entertaining the idea of seeing her ever again. Please, can we leave it?"

"Kitch, I—"

"Please? For me?" I whisper, digging deep—mustering everything I have to plead with him, my eyes locked on his as I force my desperation to the surface.

And after several minutes, he finally nods. Sharp. Reluctant. But it's enough.

Bettsy

THE BEST THING ABOUT allocated tickets is knowing exactly where to look to see who's using your seats. Even though I can't say I've never had a girl in the stands before, this time, it feels *different*. And I sort of get where Liam Preston was coming from when he told me he sort of shows off a bit in front of Vicky; like he can't help himself...

I definitely want to show off.

As we skate out for warm-ups, I do an extra lap of our defensive end so I can check she's here and when I spot her, sitting next to my sister, wearing the Betts jacket, my pulse picks up a little speed.

"She's here then?" Danny asks, falling in to skate next to me.

"Yeah, she's with Kelly," I say.

I try not to look, because there's a time and place, and right now, I need to run through my warm-up routine or bad things will happen. At least, that's what I tell myself.

I fire one puck towards the empty net, circling around to repeat the shot a second and a third time before stopping on the blueline, dropping to the ice and positioning my stick out in front of me so I can stretch my groin.

I've set my routine in stone: lower body, upper body, then fire at the net a few more times. I thrive on the predictability of a very unpredictable game.

"Don't suppose you've asked about the golfing trip yet, have you?" Danny says.

I stare blankly at him. "Golfing trip?"

"Yeah. After the playoffs and before we go to Romania with Team GB ... assuming we get formally selected. Come on, mate. It's the same thing every year." He rolls his eyes.

Honestly, the last thing on my mind has been golfing. Between ex's, marriages, Team GB stuff, and Ellie, I've had little time to think about excursions.

"Well, I've been busy ... but why would I need to ask about it?"

"You have a *wife* now," he says, emphasising the word 'wife' with an air of envy in his tone. "You'll need to get permission."

I stop dead, mid-stretch, like a cat busy cleaning themselves, leg in the air, only to hear a mouse twenty feet away.

"Permission?" I say, tightening my jaw. "I don't think I need permission ... do I? We don't even live together."

Danny shrugs. "Well, you don't see Johnny going anywhere without asking Kelly, do you? And they don't officially live together either."

"Nah, he tells her out of courtesy, there's a difference."

"Whatever you say. But maybe it doesn't matter now, anyway. Are you guys ... serious or?"

That's the question I've been dreading, and it clearly shows on my face. Danny gets to his skates and glides away, perfectly content with the knowledge he's put me on edge.

Do I need to ask for permission? Surely not ... but I wouldn't want to upset her or whatever. The only thing I've really got to go off is whatever Rochelle and I were because that was a head-fuck, and I had to ask permission to take a piss.

I spot Vicky at the bench, lingering behind her camera set up on a tripod, peering at the screen of her phone.

Maybe a female perspective would be useful.

Without hesitating, I skate towards her and come to a stop at the boards, leaning over to grab a water bottle as a ruse.

"How's it going, Vic?" I ask, noticing her frown.

"Yeah, fine." She keeps her eyes on her phone, brows knit together.

"Busy? Or..."

"I'm just looking at Ellie's sister's social media—you know, just to see ..." She flashes her phone in my direction, and I laugh.

"That's not her sister," I say.

"Uh, yes, it is."

I look at the photo again. "Nah, it can't be."

Vicky narrows her eyes as she looks up at me. "Yes, it is. Kathryn Kitchener ... owner of House of Kathryn. Ellie and I had an entire conversation about this very profile today. Ellie's in this photo with her and—"

I tuck my right glove under my arm and grab Vicky's phone right out of her hands.

The image filling Vicky's screen is someone I recognise, sure, but only because this was the woman connected to Rick Langdon's face in the lobby of the hotel weeks ago.

"Wait—this is her sister?" I can't stop the nervous laugh that escapes from my throat.

"How do you not know that?" she says. "And get your sweaty hands off." She swipes her phone back and I lean in, keen to see more.

"I haven't seen her sister in ... years." I bite my lip, briefly wondering if I should tell Vicky before deciding there's no way I can keep this to myself. "Vic—if you knew something about someone doing something or someone they shouldn't be doing ... would you tell someone about the something?"

Vicky's jaw hits the shelf as she stares at me.

"Excuse me? I got lost on the first 'some'... whatever," she says, waving her hand. "What the hell are you talking about?"

I blow out a breath. "You remember Langer, right?"

"Yeah, he plays for—"

"Don't say it." I hold my hand up, forcing Vicky to halt. "When I was doing the GB training camp, I saw Langer one morning, making out with someone in the lobby. And I'm ninety-nine per cent sure that was her."

"Who? Kathryn?" Vicky says, pulling her eyebrows together.

"Yeah. Kathryn—who's supposed to be engaged to some guy called Greg ... who happens to be Langers best mate." I pause before adding, "Langer is Greg's best man."

"Stop," Vicky says. "Oh, my God." Her hands fly to her mouth, phone still clutched tightly in her palm.

"So, do you think I should tell Kitch?"

I say it, but I don't need Vicky to tell me the answer; I know I should tell her.

The reflection of the timer in the glass, ticking down on the jumbotron tells me I've eaten into too much of my warm-up time and the anxiety of not finishing my routine sits heavy in my stomach, causing me to abandon the real reason for my intrusion on Vicky's time.

But as I skate away, I allow myself a glance in Ellie's direction, wondering how the hell I'm supposed to tell her about her sister.

Chapter 33

Ellie

HE'S BARELY SAID MORE than a few sentences all morning, and absolutely nothing since we got into my car. He normally glances over at me while driving, but he hasn't looked my way at all. All he does is stare at the road ahead, his hands clenched tight on the steering wheel at ten and two.

I turn my head to look at him again, trying to assess the expression on his face—is he pissed off? Upset? Anxious? I mean, they won both games on the weekend, so I don't think it's that. Could it be something to do with Team GB? Or is this something completely unrelated to hockey? Is it me? Did I do—or not do—something?

Oh, my God ... did he work out that it's *me* behind the hashtag?

"Mike? Is everything okay?" I ask.

He nods. Keeping his attention on the road ahead.

Okay, time for plan 'B'.

"Kelly's been teaching me about hockey," I say, trying my 'casual conversation' approach. "I still don't think I have a firm grasp on the delayed penalty thing, though."

I pick a topic I know he'll have an opinion on, but he says nothing. His jaw remains tight—clenched in an emotion I finally pick out as nervous.

What's he nervous about?

"She explained the referee can delay any penalty, technically, by letting play continue until the opposing team loses possession."

Still nothing. Not even a comedic gasp of shock that I've remembered and relayed a hockey fact.

"She said that due to the fast pace of the game and how quickly the opposing team usually gains possession or clears the puck, delayed penalties are rare in the grand scheme of things. Refs whistle most penalties because the opposing team usually 'touches up' soon after the call."

Nada.

"Don't you think 'touching up' is a weird concept? Because you can't actually touch the puck, right? I mean, not unless it's flying through the air and you catch it to throw it back down..."

... nothing.

"But what I find most interesting is that you get sent to the box for like an adult time-out and ..." He keeps his focus forward—still grasping the wheel tightly... still ignoring me. This is very much not Mike. Something is wrong and I need to know what it is so I can help.

"Mike? Are you listening to me?" I say.

"Yeah, of course."

But he still refuses to look at me.

"Right, I'm done," I say. "Do you want to tell me what the hell is going on? You've never been this quiet before—I usually can't get a word in edgeways."

He exhales. "Do you want a brew or anything? There are services coming up."

"No, I don't want a brew. I want you to tell me what's going on."

He flicks down the indicator switch with his ring finger. A single swipe down before his hand reverts to 'ten'. Then he checks his mirror, a brief glance in my direction, but only because he has to.

He pulls off the motorway, meandering on the single-track road to the parking area where he finds a spot at the farthest point from the entrance, cutting the engine.

"Kitch," he says, rubbing his hands over his face. "I—"

"Is everything okay?" I ask. This feels like a moment relived. Except that time we were on the forecourt of a petrol station, and I was in the driving seat. "You're not going to ask me to go along with another wild idea of yours, are you?"

He shakes his head. "No."

"Then—"

"If you knew something about someone doing something or someone they shouldn't be doing ... would you tell someone about the something?"

Mike shifts in his seat.

"If I knew something about someone doing something or someone they shouldn't be doing..." I repeat. "Do you know something about someone, Mike?"

He groans. It's the type of frustrated, deflated groan that makes me want to comfort him.

I reach out for his hand, clasping it in my own.

"Yeah," he says, looking down at our intertwined fingers. "Yeah, I do ... and—I..." He looks at me. The first time in what feels like forever. There's a fear in his eyes—like what he's about to tell me is going to change things and he's not sure how I'll react.

"Mike?"

"I think you know by now I—uh, I love you, right? Like I really love you. And I know we've not been together together for long, but I feel it in here..." He uses his free hand to rub his chest, right where the branding of his team logo sits on his hoodie. "...like I feel it and..."

"I know," I say. I unclip my seatbelt and lean over the centre console to wrap my arms around him. "I love you, too."

"You do?" he says.

"Of course, I do. I mean..." I break off, leaning back to look at him because there's more to this; his expression is still just as stoney ... still just as tense.

"Sweetheart ... I don't want to hurt you or anything," he says. "And I know things aren't good with you and Kathryn at the moment, but if you make up and then—"

"Mike? What's going on?"

"Your sister's been cheating on Greg," he says. "I'm sorry. I just didn't know how to tell you and it's been fucking eating away at me and—"

"What?" I say. "How—I, what?"

"I thought you should know because it's not right, is it? I mean, I know this Greg guy sounds like a complete ass, but no one deserves that. No one."

"You're not making any sense," I say. "Kathryn's cheating? With who?"

"Rick Langdon. I saw them at the hotel together. You know, the one we were staying at for the Team GB stuff ... and I thought I recognised her, but I haven't seen your sister in such a long time I—"

"Right," I say. "Well, I guess it makes sense. I mean, it's just something she'd do, right? Sleep with her fiancé's best man."

I let the words float in the air as I wait for *something* ... *anything* to make sense. I wait to feel—to feel angry, upset, deceived, but instead of those things ... I burst out laughing. A hard laugh that comes right from my stomach, causing my eyes to water.

Because the whole thing is just ... Kathryn. Snide and vindictive. And completely Kathryn.

"Kitch—"

I'm in hysterics, cackling in a way that has me gasping for air while Mike watches on in confused-horror. Like he wants to join in but doesn't at the same time.

"Kitch?"

"You know why this is so funny?" I ask once I've composed myself. "Because it isn't funny at all, really."

"Do you think we should tell Greg?" Mike asks. "Because I've been cheated on before and—"

"No," I say.

"No?"

"No. Because he won't believe us. He's so invested in whatever him and Kathryn have, he won't believe us—well, he won't believe me, anyway. He'll assume I'm trying to sabotage their wedding."

Mike nods. "I guess that makes sense. Ruined nail polish and a wedding? What's next for Eleanor Kitchener?"

"Eleanor Betts," I say.

Mike stares at me, a flicker of something in his eyes before he breaks out into a smile, though only for a second before his face falls.

"What?" I say.

"This is—"

"Is it too much? I mean, I don't have to use it, I—"

"No, no, it's not that." He reaches for my other hand, pulling me closer to him and planting a kiss on my lips. Heat ripples through me. "I really like it ... like, I really fucking like it. But, my mam called..."

"Yeah?"

"She's been up in the attic, and she found my old paperwork and boxes and stuff."

I lean back to look at him. "Oh, my God. Do you know if—"

"No, no. And neither does she. She said she's brought them down and put them in the spare room, ready for when I can visit and look. I take it as a kick up the ass. No more hanging back."

"Right." I look down at our hands. Our rings.

"Hey," he breaks his right hand free, placing his index finger under my chin and lifting my head, meeting my eyes. "We said that we'll deal with whatever it is, yeah? And it doesn't have to change anything, right?"

"Yeah, of course."

"Now let's get a brew."

Bettsy

As much as I want to let it rest, I can't. Greg may not believe Ellie, but he's got no reason not to believe me. I mean, if anything, it's my neck on the line because I'm the one who has to sit on the bench next to Langer knowing I ratted him out.

Greg's office is on the high-street, only a few doors down from a derelict looking 'House of Kathryn' and a short taxi ride from Ellie's house, which I took as soon as she left for work; I dug Greg's business card from my wallet and made it over here before I could talk myself out of it.

I have one day here before I need to head back home for a practice filled week and the last thing I wanted to do was to spend it in a stuffy solicitors' office, but here I am.

"Can I help you?"

I've barely closed the door behind me when the blonde behind the front desk directs her attention towards me. She flicks her eyes up and down, lingering on my hockey jumper before she surveys my hat.

I whip it off my head, setting it down on the counter and leaning in to reply.

"I'm here to see Greg Jamison," I say, forcing my formal 'phone voice'. "I don't have an appointment, but I need to talk to him briefly."

"He's in a meeting," she says.

"Well, I'm sure he can squeeze in a quick tête-à-tête with me once he's done," I say with a smile. "I can wait."

I don't give her a chance to turn me away. I grab my cap and move over to the hard-looking tub chairs next to the window.

Sitting in the grey one, I reach for a magazine from a pile on the glass table to my left.

Railway Timetable Digest—jeez.

I thumb through the pages, more out of curiosity than anything, because there's no way there's a whole magazine dedicated to timetables. But ten minutes later, I'm intrigued, my brow furrowed as I try to work out if a thirty-five-hour train ride from Moscow to Nice would be worth it. Spoiler: probably not, but I'd do it anyway just to say I had.

A throat clears in the distance and I pry my eyes away from the Japan segment to see a mousey-haired guy in a cheap suit glaring at me.

"Can I help you?" he says.

I toss the magazine aside and get to my feet, striding over to who I can only assume is Greg.

"Michael Betts," I say, holding out my hand. "Nice to meet you."

He cocks a brow, dipping his head to stare at my out-stretched hand.

"Not a hand-shaker? I get it, don't worry. Anyway—"

"Is this about the marriage stuff? Because I told Ellie she'd need to enlist the help of a family lawyer on a formal basis. It's not my bag," he says.

"Actually, it's not," I say. "It's about marriage stuff, sure, but—" I look around, spotting the blonde pretending not to eavesdrop. "—is there somewhere we could go for a quick chat?"

He exhales in an over-dramatic fashion. "I'm a little busy right now."

"Trust me ... you're going to want to have this conversation in private."

He studies me for a moment, eyes narrow. Then he nods. A single nod and a flick of his head towards a small office to his left.

"Did you know Japan's bullet trains are so punctual their average delay is under a minute?" I say as I follow him inside.

"Excuse me?"

"Never mind—look ... there's no easy way for me to say this, but bro-code dictates I tell you what I know... but since we're not actually 'bros' in that sense, I'm not going to sugar-coat it." I pause, waiting for him to give me permission to continue, I guess, but he stares blankly at me. "Right, well ... your wife-to-be Kathryn is screwing your best man. Rick Langdon, just to be clear."

He glares at me, unblinking, then he scoffs, a half-laugh that's awkward and dry.

But I keep my expression stable, showing him that this is definitely not a joke.

"I'm sorry but what?" he says.

"I—"

"You come in here, tell me this and expect me to—who the fuck are you?" he says, his forehead glowing red.

"I'm ... Michael Betts, but my friends call me Bettsy."

Apparently, that was not the answer he was looking for.

"I know who you are ... but... what the fuck is your problem? Ellie's ruined Kathryn's business, so you think you can come in here and ruin my—"

"You're kidding right? Kathryn mauled Ellie's scalp. She ripped her hair out, for Christ's sake. If anyone's got a problem ... it sure as hell isn't me."

"What the fuck?"

"Oh, another secret she's keeping from you, then? Looks like she's a conniving b—"

Greg's features tense. "Shut your mouth," he says.

"Mate, look," I hold my hands up in surrender. "I honestly don't give a shit about you, nor Langer, nor Kathryn, for that matter. But I do care about Ellie ... a lot. And I'll tell you something for free, if Kathryn touches a single hair on Ellie's head again, I won't be responsible for my actions."

Greg scowls, muttering something under his breath before he turns away.

"Now I've done a nice thing here today. It may not seem like it now, but one day you'll thank me for it. I've told you what I know ... now you can do whatever you want with that information. Oh, and while I've got you ... if you could write me a cheque for that seven grand Kathryn owes Ellie, that'd be great."

Greg turns back towards me. "I don't know what Ellie's told you, but Kathryn doesn't owe her any money. I funded the start-up."

"You funded the salon? So why the fuck does Ellie think she funded it? I mean ... Kathryn isn't the sort of person who'd lie about something like that, is she, Greg? Getting two lots of seven grand and—"

"I—" His face drops as realisation dawns on him. "Shut the fuck up."

I've hit a nerve. I can tell. But I can't back down.

"Hey, all I want is the money back. That's it."

But he's not listening. He's retreating to his desk, pulling open draws and rummaging through paperwork. Piles and piles of it.

"Oh ... fuck," he says, flattening out a stack of papers—credit card bills by the look of it. "She told me her card was stolen but—"

I don't have a clue what's going on. No idea at all, but what I'm guessing is whatever Kathryn told Greg she did with his money isn't actually what she did with his money.

I step closer, my nosiness getting the better of me, but all I can see is line upon line of transactions.

Hotels. Hotels. And more hotels.

"Yeah, that was the hotel we stayed at for the Team—"

Greg looks up at me, his eyes red and blotchy with the threat of tears.

Damn, I'm feeling sorry for the guy. He looks like his heart has been ripped out and all I can do is stand here and watch his demise.

But it is probably better that I told him, right? I mean, if it was me ... I'd want to know.

"Right. Well, yeah ... look Greg, I'm sorry I had to be the one to have told you, but no one deserves to be treated like this. No one. I'm sorry that it happened to you."

I turn to leave, taking a step towards the door when Greg stops me. His hand resting on my shoulder.

"Mike?"

"Yeah?"

"I ... thanks, I guess. I mean. You're right. You don't owe me anything."

He turns away and hurries towards a filing cabinet in the corner of the room, pulling open the second drawer and flicking through the tab dividers.

"This is yours," he says, turning back towards me, handing me a brown envelope. "It's your wedding certificate."

"My—"

"I guess I thought it would be funny to see how this played out. Fun to watch Ellie panic ... send her on a chase for something that didn't exist, but—I'm sorry."

Well, fuck me.

"You really are a prick, you know that, right?"

But he says nothing to that. He can't. He knows I'm right.

"And I'll see what I can do about the money. I don't have a lot of spare cash ... I mean... but I'll see what I can do."

We stare at each other for a moment, tense air between us. Then I slide the envelope into the pocket of my hoodie and get the hell out of there.

Chapter 34

JOHNNY'S BEEN READING OVER the document for a long-two minutes, and I've been pacing in the space between the living room and the kitchen while I wait for the verdict.

No matter how many times I look at it, I can't work it out.

"Hmm," he says.

"Hmm?" I ask. "What does that mean? What do you think?"

I stop pacing and look at him, desperate for his assessment.

"Well," he says. "I guess we should take this to a lawyer. Get them to check it over."

Damn. I was afraid of that.

"Do you think it's real?" I ask. "Because I get a weird feeling about Greg and if he lied to Ellie once before then—"

"I can't be sure, but then again, I've never seen a wedding certificate before."

"But you must have a vague idea?" I ask. "Come on, Cap. Give me something."

I walk over to the sofa and flop down, pulling a cushion from under my head and pulling it down over my face so I can scream into the fabric.

"I can't say for certain, but it looks legit. And that looks like your signature."

I clocked it too. The memory didn't hit me at once. It came slow, foggy at first—then sharp enough to slap me in the face.

I toss the cushion aside and turn to face Johnny.

"I don't think I can tell her until I know for sure. I think it'll cause more worry, and she seems to be in a good place now—with work and all that. The last thing I want to do is ruin things."

"I get that," Johnny says, slipping the paper back into the envelope and handing it over. "So—"

"So, do you know any decent family solicitors?" I ask.

"What do you think?"

"Right. Maybe I can ask the guys?" I pull out my phone and navigate to our group chat.

"Nah, you don't want to do that," Johnny says. "They'll jump on it. Assume the worse. You won't hear the end of it."

"Good point." I slip my phone away, only to pull it back out again a second later.

I could call my mam, she'd know someone. But she'd go full nosey mode, especially since she hauled all that paperwork down from the attic—which I'm still meant to rummage through. Telling her it was pointless wouldn't go down well.

But there must be someone I know ... someone... I run through the names of the guys I know, from our team first, then Team GB.

The light bulb switches on.

"Got it," I say. "Greer's old man is a solicitor. I can ask him if he can recommend someone at his firm—someone discreet."

I pull up his number and hit dial, and luckily, he answers after a few rings.

"Bettsy, mate. I was just going to text you," he says. "Wondered if you'd heard about Langer."

"Langer?" I sit up straight, casting a look towards Johnny, who's watching my conversation. "What about him?"

"He's done for the remainder of the season. And signed himself off the Team GB roster. Personal reasons," he says.

A pang of something hits my chest as I process Greers' words. Relief? Maybe ... because he's one less problem to worry about, but this isn't about me. The Langer I know wouldn't back down for shit.

"No injury?" I ask.

"Nah. Not that we know of, anyway."

Fuck.

I dip my head in my hands, swallowing down the emotion that's pushing hard to the surface. Langer out ... it's got to be because of Greg finding out, right? Maybe Greg showed up at his place and it all kicked off. Maybe ... fuck me... maybe Langer is on his way here now to break my legs for ruining his sordid affair.

"When did this happen?" I say, lifting my head up.

I meet Johnny's eyes and offer him my most fearful look.

"Yesterday. We found out this morning. But I guess I was keen to know if you knew anything about it because it directly affects you and what happens with the lines and that."

"Nah," I say, wondering if I should tell Greer about Langer. My head is telling me to blurt it all out in a Bettsy-type fashion, but my heart is telling me not to talk shit. My throat is dry, but I force myself to speak. "Nah, not heard anything, mate."

"Well, I guess we'll see how it pans out ... but anyway, mate, all good with you?"

I switch ears.

"Yeah, I just wondered if your old man is still a solicitor?"

"Yeah, he is. Why'd you ask? You're not getting a divorce already, are you?"

I swallow down a laugh. "Good one ... nah, one of the boys has a problem, and he wanted to run it by someone. Family law stuff. Just wondered if there was anyone at your dad's firm you could recommend? You know, someone with discretion."

"Uh, yeah, of course. I'll text you over a number."

"Cheers."

"No problem. I'd wish you good luck for the weekend, but no offence, I want to see you lose."

"Same. Later."

I hang up and glare at Johnny.

He raises an eyebrow, showing me he's listening, but I can't talk straight away. I stand up and make my way over to his kitchen, grabbing a glass from the cupboard and turning the tap on to let the water run cold.

"Everything alright, bud?" Johnny says.

But as I fill the glass, watching the water flood in, my mind races.

I feel sick.

This is all my fault, right? If I'd kept my mouth shut...

I turn off the tap and take a swig of water, holding it in my mouth for a second before swallowing it down. Then I do it again.

Christ, months ago ... my biggest problem was getting roasted on the forum, the beacon of hope being a 'justiceforBettsy' hashtag. And now it's this? The unpredictable Langer, potentially out for revenge ... what's next? '#justiceforLanger'?

"Bud?"

"You don't think Langer would ... do anything stupid, do you?" I ask.

"What type of stupid? Like drunken antics or..."

I fill Johnny in on the conversation with Greer.

"I guess I'm thinking more like a crime of passion ... why else would he duck out this close to the end of the season? I mean, they just won the league title for crying out loud—the guy should be buzzing," I say.

"Well yeah, but you don't know how he feels about this Kathryn girl. He could be halfway around the world right now ... they could be running away to start a life together," Johnny says.

"Or he was happy living in the mess he'd created and he's on his way here to break my legs…"

Johnny stands up.

"I'm sure it's fine. You did the right thing. Whatever happens next isn't your fault. I mean, how are you supposed to control his actions? If he's been sleeping with his best friend's fiancée, more fool him."

I know Johnny's right. But it's not about what I did—it's about what Langer does next.

I don't give it a second thought when that text from Greer comes through, and I'm forced to make another phone call.

GREG IS WAITING FOR me when I leave the salon on Wednesday afternoon. At first, I mistake him for an ill-dressed traffic warden, eager to hand me an unwarranted parking ticket. But as I get closer, I recognise the receding hairline—not that I've got anything against thinning hair on a man, but Greg wears his denial in the tune of a hairstyle.

I've got no idea what he wants, but I doubt it's anything I'll want to hear. He's leaning against my car in such a way, it'll be impossible to hop into the driver's seat and speed off unnoticed.

For a second, I consider abandoning my car and taking the bus home instead. But then he spots me, lifts a hand in an awkward wave and—brilliant—I'm left with no choice but to talk to him.

"Have you got a minute?" he asks.

Instead of answering him, I make my way to the rear of the car, popping open the boot and slinging my bags inside. I linger, searching for a reason to avoid giving him even a minute, but come up with nothing.

Nothing.

Damn it all.

"Ellie?" Greg straightens up and makes his way over to me, standing on the pavement right next to the rear driver's side.

Definitely no chance of a getaway now.

"What do you want?" I ask.

"I—I wanted to give you this."

He holds out a cheque, the creamy off-white paper practically glowing against the dimming evening light.

"A cheque?" I say.

"Yeah." He thrusts it towards me, his hand shaking as I take it from him.

I run my eyes over the writing, trying to work out what the hell is going on here ... aside from the fact people rarely use cheques these days, he doesn't owe me any money. Kathryn does.

Pay Eleanor Kitchener four thousand pounds only. Signed *G Jamison.*

"Four grand?" I say, wrinkling my nose.

"Yeah. I mean ... I know it's not the full seven, but it's the best I can do right now."

"The best—why are you giving me a cheque for four grand? It's not you who owes me. It's Kathryn."

Greg rubs the back of his neck. "Kathryn doesn't have much in the way of spare cash at the moment. I'm paying you back—well, as much as I can—on her behalf."

"On her behalf?" I ask, my voice shaking.

I glance down at the cheque again before looking back at him.

Surely this is a joke.

"Yes. See, I've recently learnt that..." Greg shuffles on the spot, burying his hands into the pockets of his jeans. "I've recently learnt that Kathryn has had some commitment issues, so we need to take some time away. We're trying to rebuild. To move forward. We can't have people digging things up or dragging us backwards—whether that's you or Bettsy."

The coin drops into the slot.

Of course ... this whole situation has Mike's name written all over it.

"Ah."

"He came to see me on Monday. Came to tell me about Kathryn and ... well, I guess I'm not ready to say his name out loud just yet."

My brain begins to piece it all together.

"So ... you know about Kathryn and Rick?" I ask, more to hear it confirmed than anything else.

But the way Greg winces answers that question for me. No words required.

"You know and you're staying with her?" I say.

"I've spoken to Kathryn, and she assures me he coerced her into a sexual relationship. It was purely physical and—"

Poor, naive Greg.

I catch his eye and see it: pain and sorrow.

"Coercing her? What the hell does that mean?"

But Greg ignores my question, reverting to the topic of the cheque I've got clutched in my hand instead.

"Look, the main thing is, I'm paying you back," he says.

"But—but that doesn't explain where it went in the first place?" I say. "If you funded the start-up..."

Greg sighs as he looks towards the pavement.

"It doesn't matter," he says. "You're getting your money back, aren't you?"

"That's beside the point," I say.

But when he doesn't look at me, I understand. And honestly, I'm wondering how I overlooked it for so long.

"So that's where my money went? Funding an affair? Brilliant. Absolutely brilliant. Glad to know Kathryn—"

She wasn't out on appointments or checking in on clients too sick to come in or looking at venues. She was playing house with Rick—with my seven grand burning a hole in her pocket.

And poor Greg is financing the aftermath.

"Please, Ellie, stop," Greg says, cutting me off. "Cash the cheque and I'll try to get the rest to you ... after the wedding."

"After the wedding?" I say, my voice several notches louder than it was a second ago.

"El—"

"You're still marrying her after *that*? After how she treated you?"

Greg looks crestfallen, like his world's already ended and all he has left are the fragments to cling to.

"I love her, Ellie," he says, his voice grave.

"But you don't love yourself?" I ask.

Greg looks at me, his eyes meeting mine for a second before he looks away.

"I'm not perfect, Ellie. Far from, really. We all make mistakes, and I forgive Kathryn."

"Well, you're a bigger idiot than I thought," I say.

Greg doesn't respond to that, but he looks at me again. Holding my gaze for longer than necessary.

"I'm sorry, by the way," he says, after an extended period of silence—only the passing traffic to break the quiet.

I blink, unsure whether to scoff or brace for more bullshit. "For?"

"Lying to you about the certificate."

"What?" I say.

"Best speak to Bettsy," he says. "Anyway, I wish you and him all the happiness in the world. I'd be grateful if you could return the favour."

I want to ask him what he means. I want to demand answers … but before I can even open my mouth to reply, he turns and hurries along the pavement. Disappearing around the corner.

And it's goodbye, Greg.

Chapter 35

Bettsy

T-MINUS THREE DAYS. THAT'S all we've got until the playoff finals.

Everyone's still pretty chill—probably because the reality hasn't sunk in yet—but Johnny's already in mother hen mode. He's flapping around his apartment, clucking over us like we're chicks in a coop, making sure we're fed, watered, and mentally ready for war.

We're all sitting in his living room, crammed in tightly as we watch a replay of last week's quarter final, trying to understand our mistakes, our weaknesses and, most importantly, how we can tighten our game.

"See this here," Prez says, pointing to the slot on Johnny's flatscreen. "This is where we need to speed up our backcheck."

"And this," Johnny says, pointing to the trapezoid on the paused frame, "is where we need to watch our positioning."

I know Johnny's talking specifically to our third line D, but I nod along and mumble in agreement as his eyes sweep across the room.

Lead by example. That's what he's expecting for this weekend. And since I'm a rare entity, sitting on the first pairing with Johnny, this is something I'm keen to deliver.

See, Brits rarely get the ice time they're so desperate for when the talent pool is full of seasoned imported players. I know my place is something I need to keep grafting for. Hard work and hustle. Head down. Eyes sharp and—

My phone vibrates against my leg and once I make sure Johnny is busy with the TV, I slip my hand in and pull my phone out of my pocket—not all the way, just enough so I can check the screen.

Ellie.

I tap the screen to open her message, flicking my attention back to Johnny and Prez to check the coast is clear.

Ellie

Can you talk?

I reach for the cushion wedged between me and Danny, trying to make out I'm getting myself comfortable so I can pull my phone out properly. I angle myself so I can shield the screen.

Bettsy

Just in a video review with the team.
You okay?

Ellie

Just need to talk to you.

Ah, shit.

What does that even mean? Is it the same as 'we need to talk'? Because that never leads to a positive conversation.

My gut twists and I wonder if I'm about to see my last meal for a second time.

Did I say something? Did I not say something? Shit—did I forget her birthday? No, no ... that's in June. So, what—

"—but Bettsy will tell you that," Johnny says, with a half-grin. "Ask him how many blocked shots he's racked up this month."

Heads swivel in my direction.

"I—uh, quite a few," I say, tearing my eyes away from my phone.

There's a ripple of hushed amusement.

Johnny frowns, then raises a brow, offering me a 'I knew you weren't listening' look, but the panic rises in my chest, making it difficult for me to care.

Need to talk to you.

I check my phone again, wondering if she's followed up but there's nothing.

I tap out a reply.

Bettsy

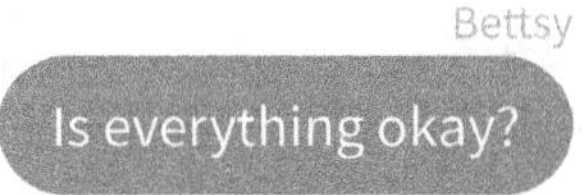

I watch the three little bouncing dots as she types. My heart somersaulting in my chest.

Then things go from bad to worse when her reply comes through.

Ellie

Just call me when you can, please.

This is it. Our game of happy families is over. Done. Finito.

It's always the case, right? If something's too good to be true, then it probably is. And this type of stuff always happens to me.

A dull, heavy ache fills my chest and as my thoughts spiral, the conversation around me turns to travel, and the plans for the evening before the finals kick off.

Someone mentions visiting a health club. Hot tub, sauna, full on tranquil environment. Someone else mentions a few hands of poker. Typically, I'd be suggesting both, but I can't think of either of those things right now; there's no way I can drag my fate out any longer.

I need to call her.

"I'm going to use the bathroom," I say to the room, prying myself away from Johnny's sofa.

Danny says something in reply, but I don't register it. Instead, I hurry towards the front door of Johnny's apartment, ducking out into the hallway.

I take a breath, then press my phone to my ear, the dial tone pulsing like a countdown, mocking me.

"Hello?"

"Hey, is, uh … everything okay, Kitch?" I say.

My voice comes out shaky—an octave too high, too uncertain.

I grip my phone tighter, pacing the narrow stretch of carpet outside Johnny's place, waiting for her to answer. Praying she lets me down gently.

"Is there anything you want to tell me, Mike?"

Ah, shit.

My heart stutters. She knows something.

I freeze, suddenly unsure which secret she's found. The certificate? The visit to Greg? Both?

Unless she's testing me.

I feel that familiar burn of panic in my chest, and without thinking, I fall into old habits.

Default to joker. Default to safe. If I pretend everything's fine, maybe my world won't come crashing down.

"Is there anything you want to tell me?" I aim for light and playful, buying myself time.

She sighs, then a heavy silence sits on the line.

"Actually ... yeah. There is," she says.

My mouth drops open as I try to process her words.

Wait ... what?

"It's been on my mind for a while and I've sort of been hoping that it'll go away, but you keep mentioning it and—"

"Kitch, what's going on?" I ask, resuming my pacing.

"You know the whole *'hashtag justice for Bettsy'* thing?" She pauses. "Well, it was me. I started it."

I stop dead. Halting mid-step, my phone pressed against my ear like I'm frozen in time.

Well, shit the actual bed.

"Mike?" she says.

Her voice echoes through the line, and I take a full second to reboot.

Then I burst out laughing.

"Good one, Kitch."

"I'm serious," she says.

"But—but that stuff kicked off before you and I—"

"I know," she says.

"But you were—"

"I know."

"So, you—"

"I couldn't stand sitting back and watching everyone latch on to the crap Rochelle was saying. It wasn't right."

I try to piece it all together because this—

"Wow."

That's all I can manage.

She was out there defending me in secret. Quietly. Fiercely.

My chest aches, but differently now. Like there's a big Ellie-shaped hug wrapped around me from the outside in.

"Mike? Say something, please? You're not angry ... are you?"

But as I try to comprehend my feelings, I realise I've never been less angry about anything ... ever.

"I love you," I say.

"I love you too," she replies.

"No, you don't understand," I say. "Like, I really love you."

"Mike—"

"I do."

I let out a shaky breath—and it's only then I realise I'm crying. A hot tear sliding down my cheek.

She's quiet for a moment before she clears her throat.

"I know you do," she says. "Which is why I know you're going to tell me what's going on. It's your turn to start talking."

Ellie

One single buzz on the double doors at the back of the rink. That's all it takes for the door to swing open and for Mike to tug me inside so fast I nearly lose my balance.

It's been four whole days since I've seen Mike. I sink into him, letting his arms wrap around me as I breathe him in.

"I've missed you," he says.

"I've missed you," I say.

It's all so very cliché, but also not at the same time. Because I have missed him.

"We're okay, yeah?" he says, pulling back to look at me.

"Of course."

"And as soon as I know, you'll know. Okay?"

"Okay," I say.

"And did you cash the cheque?" he asks.

"I'm still deciding," I say.

"Well, I understand. Whatever you decide, it'll be the right decision."

I snuggle back into him and nod into his chest.

"What time are you meeting Vicky?" he asks.

"In around ten minutes. Why?"

"Can you spare me five?" he says. "Come with me."

Before I have a chance to react, he slips his rough palm in mine, then he pulls me to follow him.

"Where are you taking me?" I ask.

He doesn't reply. He's busy hurrying along the tunnel in a direction I've never been before—not that I've been anywhere other than the direction of the ice.

We come to a stop in front of a room labelled *'Equipment Storage Room'*, Mike fishing a key out of his pocket and unlocking the door with a 'click' before he pulls me inside.

God, it stinks in here. The smell of stale sweat and something I can't quite put my finger on.

"Mike? What's going on?" I ask.

He closes the door behind me and pushes a heavy-looking box across its width, blocking the exit.

Then his lips are on mine.

The four days since we've seen each other, all crammed into this moment. Four days' worth of kisses to make up for.

Four days of longing.

Four days of wanting.

Four days of wishing we were closer.

When he said he wanted to see me before the playoff finals started, I underestimated his intentions. But as he parts his lips and I invite him to deepen the kiss, I get the message.

His hands roam, skimming over my hips as he toys with the waistband of my jeans before he slips his hands, ever so slightly upwards, under my t-shirt. Skin-on-skin almost blistering hot.

"I've missed you. I don't like this long-distance thing," he says, leaving my lips wanting as he kisses his way to my throat. "Move in with me? I know it's a lot to ask but—move here. Please. We'll figure it out."

And a question so big ... so life changing shouldn't have me reacting the way I do. I jerk away slightly, forcing him to look at me and my body reacts before my mind catches up.

I nod. "We'll figure it out," I say, gripping the back of his neck to steer his lips towards my mouth again.

And with that, his fingers fumble with the button of my jeans.

We've had 'quickies' before. Stolen moments of time before he needs to leave or before I have to meet a client—but this, in a stuffy room at the back of the rink ... it seems dirtier somehow.

My breath catches in my throat when the pad of his middle finger brushes my clit, then he presses himself into me, tearing his mouth away so he can whisper into my ear.

"Are you ready for me, sweetheart?"

He knows I am. I know I am. But I'm frantically nodding, not wanting anything else right now—eagerly pushing into him.

He shimmies my jeans down and his fingers move down, right towards my pussy.

"I knew it," he says, clearly feeling how wet I am. "Did you dream about me last night? Did you wake up aching for me?"

His confidence has been growing every time we do this. It's in his voice, in the way his mouth moves over my skin—down, down, toward my collarbone—until I'm trembling, clutching at him, silently begging for more.

I spread my legs a little wider, giving him everything.

With a thumb circling my clit, he slips a finger inside me, and I moan, clutching onto the fabric of his hoodie.

I know what he's doing before he's doing it. Building me up … pushing me right towards the edge before pulling his hand away.

"Turn around," he says.

But I don't. I can't.

I drop to my knees instead, tugging at the waistband of his sweatpants, gripping his boxers too as I tug downward, freeing him.

It juts out, hard and as impatient as I know he is.

I look up at him, locking eyes as I take him in my mouth.

One. Two. Three.

That's all I manage before he's pulling me to my feet and spinning me around to face the door, keeping my eyes on his as I look over my shoulder.

Then everything else melts away as we connect.

It's just me and Mike.

His breath on my neck, his hands on my hips, rough and reverent.

I need more. I need him to—

"Oh, my god," I gasp.

"Tell me if you don't like it," he says, his thumb pushing into me—somewhere new.

But it's—

Everything feels—

It's too much, but it's not enough at the same time.

He presses a little harder and I brace myself against the door, one hand slipping between my legs as he moves behind me, steady and strong and relentless.

Because every cell in my body is right there. On the edge.

It takes me seconds to come apart. It's almost instant and unstoppable. All the while, the steady rhythm of Mike—thrusting into me, carries me over.

Then the pained, delicious sounds of him—coming right along with me, fill my ears.

He kisses my neck, then my jaw, then my cheek.

"I think you've got about a minute to spare," he says.

Chapter 36

I KNOW I SHOULD leave things alone, but I can't. I physically can't, and as soon as Ellie texts me back with his number, I'm poised and ready—my thumb hovering over the call button.

Honestly, this is the last thing I thought I'd be doing. But it's been on my mind ever since my conversation with Greer.

I've been where he is … or close, anyway. Letting everything come second to an unrequited love who doesn't really give a shit about you or your career.

Thing is, I didn't understand the why back then. But I do now. It was Ellie.

Everything. All the heartache, sleepless nights, the sting of rejection … it was because of her.

Because I wasn't meant to be with anyone else.

And maybe the universe was just showing me the lows, so I'd know exactly how lucky I am to feel this high.

Now, I need to pay it forward.

I should be playing poker with the guys, but instead, I'm locked in the bathroom with my phone pressed against my ear—desperately listening to it ring out.

Ring. Ring.
Ring. Ring.
Ring. Ring.
"Hello?"

I swallow and lean against the vanity unit, willing myself to speak.

"Hey, it's uh ... Bettsy."

The line goes quiet. Several seconds pass. Long enough for me to wonder if I've made a mistake.

"Bettsy?" he says. "What the hell do you want?"

"I don't really know," I say. "But I do know I'd not be able to live with myself if I didn't try."

He lets out a dry laugh. "So, this is just an ego boost for you? Perfect."

"Nah, it's not like that," I say. "I just wanted to say—" I take a deep breath, trying to find the right words. "I just wanted to say I'm sorry things worked out the way they did."

"Yeah, right. I bet you've been laughing at my expense."

"Not at all. Really, I haven't. In fact, I've been trying to figure out what I can say to get you to change your mind about the team—which is funny because if someone had asked me a few months ago I would have told them it was a dream come true. We don't have to be friends, but we should appreciate we share the same love. And you and I both know the hard work and the sleepless nights and the bruises and the—"

"What's your point, Bettsy?" he says.

"My point is ... it's not worth giving up for the sake of a woman with no backbone. Believe me, I've come close myself and honestly, it's not worth it. Now, more than ever, you need the guys, and you know ... that deep-rooted feeling of belonging."

The line goes silent for a long beat. And I wait. I wait, wondering if I've wasted my breath—wondering if I'm a fool for trying.

"Look, I see what you're trying to do here and—"

"Do you?" I ask, cutting him off. "Because believe me, if there's anyone I'd love to see not icing tomorrow ... it's you. But ... I know you need to be there. For you. For all the years you've put in. You'll only regret it if you don't."

Another stretch of silence. And I can feel the tension through the line, like he's about to punch a wall or something.

But then he speaks again.

"Well, thanks for the pep-talk but I think I'll pass."

I was afraid he'd say that.

I have no choice but to pull out the taunts; try to coax a reaction from him.

"Really? You don't want one more stab at kicking my ass?

"Betts—"

I snigger to myself, then reset my expression. "I'm just saying. Jokes aside ... this is your life."

"You're right. And it's my decision," he says.

"Well, okay. If you're sure. I guess you really are an asshat."

He huffs. Then I get an odd feeling he's smiling—wherever he is.

"Ring Coach, Langer. Tell him you changed your mind. If he's got his head screwed on, he'll be expecting your call."

The silence draws out, and I wonder if he's hung up on me. I'm about to pull my phone away from my ear to check the screen when he speaks. A single word that fills me with both dread and relief.

"Alright."

"Why can't I see him yet?" Kelly's best friend, Tom, stands on his tiptoes as he peers down at the ice. "Shouldn't he be out by now?"

He's been asking the same question for the past ten minutes, but as if by magic, there's a rumble of cheers as our guys step out onto the ice for warm-ups ahead of the semi-final game.

Tom, raising his beer high in the air, is the loudest of us all. He waves and applauds, all while wearing the same 'Koenig' labelled jacket as Kelly, even down to the matching '56' etched underneath.

Next to Tom, Kelly rolls her eyes, though she claps along.

"There's Mike," she says, nudging my arm and I turn to see a flash of auburn as he settles his helmet down onto his head; my heart thudding like crazy at the sight of my number six.

"But where's Johnny? Do you see him yet?" Tom asks, bouncing on the spot. "Why is he always last?"

"He's the captain," Kelly says. "It's like a thing."

"It's offensive, that's what it is," Tom says.

But I can hardly hear their conversation play out. I'm watching Mike take his usual half-laps of the ice.

He shoots one puck towards the empty net, circling around to repeat the shot a second and then a third time before stopping on the blueline. Dropping to the ice he positions his stick out in front of him so he can do that ridiculous-looking 'frog pose' stretch he demonstrated on my living room carpet.

It shouldn't send a tingle of excitement through me, but it does. And the same feeling makes me think about that moment in the rink—that shady room that I now associate with one of the best orgasms I've ever had.

And it's as if he knows I'm watching. He gets to his skates, turns and locks eyes with me for a brief moment before he winks.

My knees wobble.

Oh, God.

"So, what I was saying before Tom rudely interrupted..." Kelly says, bringing me back into the conversation. "Oh yeah, you haven't told my mam yet?"

I was telling her and Jen about the deal with Greg. The cheque, the wedding certificate, the bonding experience he had with Mike in his office before the excitement of warm-ups took over ... oh, and the fact that Mike and I are moving in together.

The focus of the latest part of the conversation, understandably, had been surrounding the legitimacy of the certificate and the fact we're waiting to hear from the solicitor Mike enrolled to help.

And we should hear back at any moment.

"I think we'll tell your mam and dad once we know for certain," I say. "But she called to ask me to remind Mike to pop in and check through the paperwork she got down from the attic before she does it herself. It's probably for the best that we tell them as soon as we know."

I meet Kelly's gaze.

"Yeah, she'd do that—actually, I wouldn't put it past her if she's already done it and she knows full well there's absolutely nothing for Mike to find."

"Well—"

"You know she'll be okay with the outcome though right?"

Kelly rests a hand on my shoulder, and I nod, trying not to let my true feelings show.

I'm dreading the answer. Because the more I think about it, the more I'm convinced it's fake—I mean, I was so sure it was real before, but now ... it's all too good to be true. And the truth is, I've been feeling ... I don't know, sort of happy to have an extended family unit on my side. Because I feel the warmth and love of Mike's parents and his sisters from the limited interactions I've had with them.

It's like I fit right in.

"Mam has got over the shock now ... and she really likes you. She thinks you're good for him. Level-headed and whatnot, and you know ... whatever the outcome, we're glad it brought you two together."

Kelly gently squeezes my forearm as she beams at me but I don't have chance to reply because Jen is nudging me to get my attention.

"El, did you see this?" she says. "The forum's blowing up. Shame we are about to shut it down."

Kelly leans over to look at Jen's phone, held out for both of us to see.

I'm half-expecting to see more slander... more opinions... more gossip. But it's the complete opposite.

It's an apology. An apology from—

"Oh my God ... is that—?"

"Yeah," Jen says grimly. "'ilovetopuck60'. Rochelle. Someone finally linked the account to her by the look of it because she crossed-posted on another forum. Everyone's piling in now—calling her out properly."

She scrolls, and my eyes catch on the replies. Line after line of fury, disbelief, and righteous anger.

'You almost wrecked a man's life for what? Breakup pity points?'

'Hope you're proud, Rochelle. This was psychological abuse.'

'What were you trying to achieve?'

And my personal favourite...

'Pathetic.'

Jen whistles low. "Look at this one— *'You built an entire smear campaign and called it grief … and brought his brother into it? Unforgivable.'"*

And to think—people actually believed her at times.

"She's trying to backpedal now," Jen adds. "Look—she's posted again. 'We all make mistakes. I was hurting.'"

"Oh, give over," Kelly mutters. "You don't get to hide behind heartbreak when you deliberately lie."

"Yeah, and people are using your hashtag," Jen says, scrolling down. "There's a whole different vibe on this forum tonight."

Jen's right. All I can see is line after line of '#justiceforBettsy'.

"About bloody time," Tom yells above the noise, but he's not talking about Rochelle, he's signalling towards Johnny Koenig, who finally steps out onto the ice. If I didn't know any better … I'd think he and Johnny were a thing, not Johnny and Kelly.

And as if on cue, Johnny turns towards us and offers Tom a wave.

But behind the team captain, I spot Mike, moving towards the line at centre ice, and then I spot someone moving towards him with intent; like they are purposefully meeting there for a quick chat.

Is that normal? Do they do that? Fraternising with the enemy during a semi-final game…

But then I clock who it is. My breath catches. The player stops on the red line and turns at an angle and I notice the name on his jersey.

Langdon.

"Oh, my God," I say.

Rick.

He's here.

I gape at Mike—though he can't see me, so instead, I turn to Jen, nudging her arm.

"Rick is here," I say.

She looks up from her phone, and a second later, her face mirrors mine.

"I thought Vicky said he quit?" she says.

"Well, yeah. I did too."

I glance back at the ice—at the way Rick nods, and the way Mike claps him on the shoulder before skating away.

And I know.

That's why Mike asked me for his number. He didn't want to 'show him what he was missing'—he wanted to 'show him what he's missing'.

And that's just one of the many reasons I love him.

Chapter 37

I'M RACING THROUGH THE concourse, desperate to find her as quick as I can. There are people everywhere, bodies blocking my way, forcing me to skid to a stop on several occasions ... and that's until someone notices me.

"Hey, hey—it's Betts..."

"Bettsy, can we have a photo?"

"Bettsy! Hey, can we grab a photo?"

"Congratulations on the win, Bettsy ... how are you feeling about the final?"

I let the fans take a few pictures, posing in such a way so I can make a quick exit ... right where I've spotted the jackets. The cluster of matching jackets and the number '6' on the back of Ellie's.

It's noisy as hell, the chatter, and energy from the spectators, forcing me to shout out her name.

And when she turns and locks eyes with me, I rush forward and scoop her up into my arms.

"Oh, my God. You were brilliant," she says. "You were right ... playoff hockey is..."

"Special, right?"

She leans into me, and I kiss her, hot and heavy as always ... because there's no other kiss I can go for.

"What are you doing here? I thought we were meeting you outside the back entrance?"

"I needed to see you," I say, setting her down.

I pull my phone out of my pocket and fumble with a shaky hand to unlock the screen.

"Oh, my god," she says. "Is this...?"

"Yeah. Just had the email. Well—two emails."

"Two?"

"Yeah. The first one to say I'm going to Romania."

She blinks several times.

"Romania? Does that mean you're in in?"

"Yep. Officially on the roster."

She squeals. Like actually squeals and throws herself towards me, leaping into my arms.

"And the second email?"

"Yep. From the solicitor. Apologising for taking a while to get back to me ... blah blah blah."

She playfully smacks me on the arm. "And...?"

"Well, what do you think?"

Epilogue

Bettsy

I HAVE FOUR NEW bruises. One on my calf, another on my ribcage, another on my upper arm, and the fourth's not technically a bruise—just a lingering ache somewhere lower, a reminder of a very long week without Ellie.

I knew I'd miss her. I just didn't expect it to hit this hard. Seeing her off at the airport was almost soul-destroying. Having her there to watch one of my Team GB games was great—but it wasn't enough. It's never enough.

But now she's here. Without her travel companion, Jess, this time, so I finally get her all to myself—for a little while, anyway.

"We definitely don't have time to go home?" I ask, peering at her from the passenger seat.

She picked me up from the airport an hour ago and the second I spotted her in arrivals I abandoned my luggage and flung myself at her. And all I've wanted to do since is—

"No, your mam is desperate to see you," she says. "And Johnny's there ... and your sisters. I think it's a bit of a welcome home party."

"Yeah, but they can wait..." I say, reaching over to run my hand up her thigh.

"Mike—"

"What? Is it so wrong of me to want to come home and spend a little alone time with my wife?"

Ellie extends her arm out and places her hand, palm up, on my leg instead.

"A handy?" I ask. "I mean ... it may be a little dangerous, but I'm willing to let you—"

"No, silly. Hold my hand," she says. "I've missed you."

And I do, because having her hand in mine sends a warmth from the tips of my fingers through every cell in my body.

I'm home.

"We can have our time later, I promise. Just ... everyone is really proud of you, Mike. They want to celebrate."

I nod. I understand. I mean, it's not ideal ... but I understand.

"It's not every week you win the playoffs and a promotion to the top flight of the World Championship. Maybe you should be less successful," Ellie says with a mock frown.

"Well, yeah, but I can't really help it..."

"Besides," she says. "We need to tell your parents we're moving in together."

Ellie squeezes my hand, and I spin my head in her direction, watching her grin intensify.

"You've figured things out? With work and your place?"

"Yeah, I mean, it'll take a bit of time to get in a good place with work, and I've committed to being back here for a day a week—I mean, it's a good trade-off." She glances in my direction before settling her attention back on the road. "Vicky said she knows someone who can help grow my reputation, anyway. It's worth a try."

"And Jessica's agreed to rent your house?"

"Yep. Well, it turned into more of a beg, to be honest. Her begging me. She's come to an agreement with Phil ... she wants to move in as soon as possible."

God, I'm smiling so hard my face hurts.

"Did she call Greer yet?" I ask.

Ellie shakes her head. "She won't even talk about it. Ever since we got home, she's been ... weird. I don't know, but she's desperate to move out so..."

I blow out a breath. "Well, I guess we'll never find out. But it'll be good for her to start fresh. And what did your parents say?" I ask.

It's a leading question—one I'm not sure she'll want to answer, but she sighs and glances in my direction before she replies.

"They—well, my mam, said she's happy that I'm happy."

"That's it?" I say. "That's all she had to say?"

"What else were you expecting?" she asks, looking towards be briefly.

"I dunno—maybe ... something? I guess I was hoping your mam and dad would ... care a bit more?"

"I'm surprised you're surprised," she says.

"Yeah but—"

"I think they're just worried about Kathryn. And that's fine. She needs more support—and I think it's obvious that it's been this way for a long time."

I cringe at the mention of Kathryn's name. But only because I feel a little sorry for Langer. Not because he was the 'other guy', but more because he believed Kathryn. We caught up properly in Romania, and he told me all about their plans—the ones he made with Kathryn and her promise to leave Greg. More fool him, really—but I guess you can't help who you fall in love with. They just went about it all the wrong way.

I'm just really fucking glad I got lucky with it.

Eventually.

I reach into the pocket of my hoodie, pulling the Polaroid out—the one Ellie gave me before I flew to Romania with Team GB—the one I've carried with me ever since.

I glance at it, wondering what the eighteen-year-old Bettsy would say about this moment—how he'd feel, knowing he got everything he ever wanted?

"I guess we can start looking for a place then, Kitch," I say, slipping the picture back into my pocket.

"Yeah. You're stuck with me now," she says.

"I've always been stuck with you," I say, turning to look at Ellie. "It just took us forever to figure it out."

Acknowledgements

Writing this book wouldn't have been possible without the help and support of some very wonderful people...

A huge thank you to Jess, Karen, Jo, and Nat, my alpha readers, the girls who dealt with me spamming messages and sending chapters with little notice, then disappearing for weeks.

Another big thanks to my beta readers, the girls above who read it all again ... and, of course, Emily, Casey, Becki, Beth, and Amy.

A special shout out to my husband for letting me write well into the evening.

And finally, you, the reader. Because without a reader, a story is just words on a page.

About

Alys J. Clarke is the pen name of a British Author, who loves all things hockey.
She lives in Wales with her husband and children and writes part-time.
www.alysjclarke.co.uk

By Alys J. Clarke

The Import Slot (2023)
The Tape Job (2024)
The Alternate Captain (2024)
The Home Grown (2025)

By Alys J. Clarke

The Import Slot (2023)
The Tape Job (2024)
The Alternate Captain (2024)
The Home Grown (2025)

www.ingramcontent.com/pod-product-compliance
Lightning Source LLC
Chambersburg PA
CBHW050957180726
48291CB00006B/1867